PRAISE FOR AMANDA PROWSE

'A tragic story of loss and love.'

Lorraine Kelly, *The Sun*

'Captivating, heartbreaking and superbly written.'

Closer

'A deeply emotional, unputdownable read.'

Red

'Uplifting and positive, but you may still need a box of tissues.'

Cosmopolitan

'You'll fall in love with this.'

Cosmopolitan

'Warning: you will need tissues.'

The Sun on Sunday

'Handles her explosive subject with delicate care.'

Daily Mail

'Deeply moving and eye-opening.'

Heat

'A perfect marriage morphs into harrowing territory . . . a real tear-jerker.'

Sunday Mirror

'Powerful ar   h.'

Heat

the art of hiding

OTHER BOOKS BY AMANDA PROWSE

The Idea of You

Poppy Day

What Have I Done?

Clover's Child

A Little Love

Christmas for One

Will You Remember Me?

A Mother's Story

Perfect Daughter

Three-and-a-Half Heartbeats (exclusive to Amazon Kindle)

The Second Chance Café (originally published as *The Christmas Café*)

Another Love

My Husband's Wife

I Won't Be Home for Christmas

The Food of Love

OTHER NOVELLAS BY AMANDA PROWSE

The Game

Something Quite Beautiful

A Christmas Wish

Ten Pound Ticket

Imogen's Baby

Miss Potterton's Birthday Tea

the art of hiding

AMANDA PROWSE

LAKE UNION
PUBLISHING

Text copyright © 2017 by Amanda Prowse
All rights reserved.

Published by Lake Union Publishing, Seattle

www.apub.com

Amazon, the Amazon logo, and Lake Union Publishing are trademarks of Amazon.com, Inc., or its affiliates.

ISBN-13: 9781611099553
ISBN-10: 1611099552

Cover design by Debbie Clement

Cover photography by Amazon Imaging

Printed in the United States of America

For my son Ben, who continues to be brilliant. We are behind you every step of the way. Dream big, Ben, and keep reaching for the stars. We love you . . .

ONE

Nina caught the red light only a spit away from the entrance to the boys' school. It was a regular frustration at the beginning of the day and something she tended to see as an omen.

Green light, good day. Red light, bad.

'What's for supper?' Connor asked as he pulled at the seat belt of their Audi and flicked his overly long Bieberesque fringe from his eyes with a well-practised jerk of his head.

'You've only just had breakfast!' Nina smiled at her son, who sat forward with his school bag on his lap. Her youngest, Declan, gave a chuckle from the back seat.

'I know, but I'm planning ahead. I'm always starving after my match.'

'Yes, I'd noticed.' She pictured him in his rugby kit with mud-caked knees, tearing through the kitchen cupboards with locust-like enthusiasm in a desperate search for carbs or sugar, preferably both. 'What have you got on today apart from the big match?'

'Nothing.' Connor extracted his phone from his pocket and began to text with agile thumbs. She decided not to express her concern yet again that all that texting and game playing would lead to arthritis in later life. It didn't stop her from thinking it though.

'Nothing? Is that it? Nothing else to share?' She willed the light to change. It always made her antsy to wait like this, just inches from the school.

'Nothing,' he confirmed.

'That's what you always say.' She pressed the accelerator, letting the engine rev, as if this action might in some way influence the traffic light, encourage it to hurry up.

'Mum,' he began, sounding much like a statesman about to deliver a valuable sound bite, 'it's just my normal schedule, regular classes! I never know what else to tell you.' Connor held his phone in the air and raised the other hand. His gesture reminded Nina so much of his dad it made her smile.

'I know.' She winked at Declan in the rearview mirror. 'I just wish you did.'

There was a beat or two of quiet while she listened to the movement of Connor's fingers as they glided across the screen, punctuated by the odd tut.

'Spaghetti carbonara, by the way,' she said, leaning towards him.

'Huh?'

'For supper, after your match. Spaghetti carbonara. Oh look, there's George.' She raised her hand in a subtle wave.

'What do you think you're doing?' Connor stiffened, eyes blazing.

She stared at him, taken aback. 'I was just waving to George.' She pointed at the boy who was a regular visitor to their house, lumbering along with his sports bag slung across his shoulders.

'God! Don't do that! Don't wave at my friends! That's so embarrassing!' He slid down the upholstery until his chin rested on his chest.

'Really?' She screwed her face up. 'Waving? That's a no-no now?'

'God, yes!' He sighed.

'He . . . he did wave back,' Declan mumbled. His hesitant tone suggested he was torn between wanting to support his mum and not antagonise his big brother. Connor whipped around to glare at his younger sibling.

The traffic light changed from red and amber to green.

Nina pulled away, more than a little embarrassed. The list of things that were forbidden/discouraged/frowned upon where Connor was concerned seemed to be long and ever changing. She found it hard to keep up. She remembered a time not so long ago when this same boy who now seemed to hold her in such contempt ran out of the school gates and straight into her arms, keen to show her whatever he had made that day, while rummaging in her pockets for snacks. Upon discovering a treat, he would reward her with a kiss on the cheek and place his plump little hand inside hers for the walk back to the car. She looked at the tall, muscular boy trying to sink down below the level of the dashboard while texting furiously and felt a flush of sadness; what wouldn't she give to feel those chubby little arms around her neck one more time.

Thankfully, the Internet had proved to be her parenting buddy. The many forums she could dip into – asking the anonymous question '*Why does my teenager hate me?*' – offered reassurance by the bucketload that he didn't hate her, far from it, but was going through a stage of discovery where his love for his mum might at times feel a little . . . repulsive. But it was just a phase. Nina was happy she was not alone. The messages that most gladdened her heart were those that repeated the wisdom: '*I have been through this. He will come back to you. He will open up. You'll see.*' She longed for the day when she'd once again be a person of interest in his life, and not just the inept and profoundly embarrassing cook and chauffeur.

'Have a great day! See you later,' she called out as her boys climbed from the car. Connor strolled confidently ahead, with Declan trotting behind him on the path, happy to follow in his wake.

She shopped for groceries, lobbing smoked salmon and dainty petits fours into her basket. Back home, she tackled two of the never-diminishing dirty clothes mountains that grew in her laundry room and ran the vacuum over the acres of flooring in their large farmhouse. Finn had suggested more than once that she get help with the housework, but this idea rankled. It was her thing, her *job*, for want of a better description, and she enjoyed it. It was early afternoon by the time she pulled back into the boys' school and killed the car engine.

Looking at her reflection in the rearview mirror, she took a deep breath, then exhaled through pursed lips. Steeling herself, she rubbed her palm over the waistband of her jeans, trying to quieten the familiar flutter of nerves as she parked her shiny off-roader among the other sleek models. A car like this was part of the standard requirement when you were a Kings Norton College parent, along with a confident stride, the right accent and a weighty bauble or two glinting on your fingers and dangling from your wrist. She had been gifted the car and the jewellery, but the other two items had proved a little harder to attain. Closing her eyes, she damned the anxiety that left her feeling flustered.

After spritzing her favoured Chanel behind her ears and over her throat, she grabbed her padded jacket from the back seat. The January ground was still hard, and despite the bright blue sky, a chill wind whipped across the playing field. She hesitated at the mini lunch box containing a bottle of water, a ham and cheese sandwich and a bar of chocolate that sat on the passenger seat. She wasn't sure of the etiquette when playing with the A team. This was the first time for Connor and therefore a big deal for her sports-loving boy. Her instinct had been to prepare snacks, but she was wary of doing the wrong thing, like her earlier waving antics. The thought of embarrassing him or herself sent heat to her face.

Smiling now at the absurdity of her concerns, she thought how ridiculous it was that whether to take a snack or not felt like a decision of such mammoth proportions. She left the lunch box where it was; she could always nip back for it. Hitching her handbag onto her shoulder, she trudged from the car park to the rugby field. Glancing at her watch, she saw it was 1.50. Kick-off was at 2 p.m. There was just enough time

4

to go and find a good place to stand, where Finn would be able to see her easily when he arrived. He'd promised Connor last night he would come. She wished he would hurry up. Nina put her phone in her pocket – it was a useful tool for avoiding eye contact with other parents.

The sports field was busy. Clearly the top team was a big draw; she had never seen quite so many spectators. Her stomach bunched; there were groups of people she didn't recognise, parents and supporters from the opposing school all wearing the Coteswell Park colours of burgundy and navy, and already calling out instructions to their boys before the match had even kicked off.

'Come on, Tom!'

'Keep your eye on the ball, Max!'

'Stay with your man, Cameron!'

Slow claps followed these shouts, as if these words and gestures could spur their sons on to great things. Nina blinked and looked at the ground, nervous that some of the attention the parents drew to themselves might float upwards and fall on her shoulders. Over the years, her confidence in social situations had eroded. Her world existed within the four walls of their home, 'The Tynings', an archaic English word derived from the verb meaning 'to enclose with a fence or hedge' – and they had done just that, making a haven for their family. To interact with others exposed the fear that she had nothing of interest to say.

She found it hard to explain to Finn how she felt, knowing he didn't fully understand what it was like to have grown up in humble circumstances, with shabby rooms and a lack of space. She made no secret of the fact that she loved their home and felt an overwhelming sense of pride every time she walked in the front door. It was where she felt safest, happiest. It lifted her spirits to see how far she had come from the grubby corridors and shared bathroom of her childhood in a rundown Southampton suburb. She had never fully realised how poor they had been, until she grew up and met Finn. Not that he had grown up with the wealth that now surrounded him, but at ten years older, he was more self-assured than her and was well on his way towards success when they started dating. By the time they married, his construction firm was beginning to really take off and they had never had to struggle.

Nina waved briefly to the few parents she did recognise on the other side of the pitch, before positioning herself alone on the touchline. It mattered little that her boys had been at the school for over a decade; she watched as other women greeted each other with the loose embrace and wide, comfortable smiles of people who knew each other well and who she imagined chatting over brunch and taking long weekends away together, drinking wine in front of a sinking sun while their respective broods played football on an expanse of grass. Finn often reminded her that rugby was the common bond at these events and that this was a good starting point for conversation between her and the other parents, and what she lacked in enthusiasm for their chosen sport, he and the boys more than made up for.

The invites had come thick and fast when Connor had first started school, the requests as numerous as they were varied: birthday parties, barbecues and even sailing weekends. Her own feelings of awkwardness meant she felt unable to accept, and after so many polite refusals and insincere rain checks, people had stopped asking, saving both parties any further embarrassment. Connor, she knew, wished that she were as sociable as his peers' parents, expressing his admiration for the gregarious nature of George's mum, who after a couple of glasses of Prosecco was the life and soul, but it wasn't that simple. Nina felt bad that she was in some way letting him down, knowing she had got into a rut of isolation, and with every year that passed she felt less capable of climbing out. Finn told her it was nobody's business and as long as they were happy that was all that really mattered. And they were. This placated her, but didn't make Connor's huffs of disapproval any easier to bear.

The match officials checked the pitch, stamping the chilled soil with their heels and walking the perimeter. Nina tucked her chin into her scarf, trying to avoid the wind. She regularly glanced over her shoulder towards the car park, hoping to see Finn loping up the slight incline with his hands in the pockets of his overcoat and his easy smile of apology that always made everything better.

At least fifteen Kings Norton boys had gathered on the pitch. All looked remarkably similar in their navy shorts and navy-and-white-hooped rugby shirts bearing the school crest and motto: *Pertinacia, fortitudo et fides* – determination, courage and faith. The cluster of boys made her think about those dedicated penguins that walked miles in Antarctic blasts to find food for their young and then waddled slowly back, among tens of thousands of identical-looking chicks, to find and feed their own.

'I'd be a rubbish penguin,' she whispered, unable to pick out her son among the troop.

Suddenly there he was, Connor, not five feet away and in the middle of a huddle of boys who were passing rugby balls to each other, catching and spinning them with confidence. He looked taller, older than he had mere hours ago. She was certain that this posturing was as much about intimidating the other team as it was about practising. She caught his eye and remembered not to wave. Instead she raised her eyebrows and smiled.

'Where's Dad?' he mouthed, looking over her shoulder as if this might reveal Finn in the empty space behind her.

She tapped her watch and made a face that was part smile, part groan.

Connor gave a shake of his head and turned his broad back, continuing to throw and catch the ball.

She sighed, angry again. Not only was she going to have to explain or justify Finn's absence for the umpteenth time, but it also gave Connor the opportunity to let her know where she ranked in the favourite stakes. Not that she needed the reminder.

The referee had a word with the captains of both teams in the middle of the pitch and then, with great enthusiasm, blew his whistle.

The game was on.

Connor was good, fast, present, and seemed to be wherever the action was. She enjoyed the flicker of pride that stirred in her as her son held the ball tight against his chest, head bent, and handed off a tackle from an upper sixth form boy and skirted past him with a set expression of sheer determination on his face.

Where on earth are you, Finn? You are missing all this!

'You shouldn't say you'll be at Connor's match tomorrow if you can't be,' she'd told him as they climbed into bed last night. 'I think it's worse for him to be expecting you and be disappointed. Far better if he knows you can't make it and that's just how it is.'

'You make it sound like I deliberately let him down. Work is crazy at the moment.'

Work is always crazy . . . She swallowed the thought, without the courage to say it out loud.

'Hey, Nina!'

Kathy Topps's shout pulled her into the present. Turning towards Kathy, Nina forced a smile as her stomach flipped. The svelte, ponytail-swinging mum stood with her freshly French-manicured nails resting on her bony Lycra-covered hips. Paying no heed to the season, Kathy was always happy to show off her arms and irritatingly flat tummy.

'Glad I've caught you,' Kathy said in her breathy tone. 'Can you believe it, another holiday? I always say the more you pay, the less they seem to be in school, drives me crackers,' she trilled, batting her hand as if to dismiss the topic like a fly. 'Anyhoo, is Declan going to be around for the half-term holiday?'

Nina concentrated on keeping her expression neutral. Declan would probably prefer not to spend time out of school with Henry, who had a tendency to be mean if things weren't going his way – and it seemed things didn't go his way quite a lot.

'I'm not entirely sure.' She coughed. 'We're hoping to grab a last-minute break if Finn can get away.' This would make Finn laugh later in the retelling, the way her fallback was to make him the bad guy. Well, today he deserved it for his tardiness alone.

'Tell me about it. Trying to get these guys to give dates and make a plan is always harder than it should be.' Kathy sulked, damning the whole of the male gender. 'I was thinking that Declan might like to join Henry for his tennis lessons? I think they learn so much better when there's an element of competition in it, don't you?'

Competition? No – I think it's the worst way to teach things. Who needs that added pressure? Rather than voice this, Nina looked down at her tan suede boots and tried to think of how best to explain that unlike his big brother, Declan disliked most sports and would rather be reading in a quiet corner than leaping about on the Toppses' floodlit tennis court with a private tutor firing balls and instructions at him while Henry sneered at his lack of prowess with a racket. 'Can I have a think about it and let you know?'

'Sure you can!' Kathy raised her palms as if this were not an issue, but the set of her jaw suggested the opposite. 'Is Connor playing?' She nodded towards the field.

'Yes.' Nina beamed with maternal pride.

'Wow! He's done well to get a shot – he's got to be the youngest on the team by at least two years.' Kathy turned her mouth down and narrowed her eyes, as if there might be more to it, something underhand or intriguing.

'Come on, Piers! Keep it tight!' Kathy suddenly bellowed so loudly with her hands cupped around her mouth that Nina flinched. 'Going to have to go around the other side and give him some advice. Idiot's getting bloody mauled.' Kathy sighed with disappointment and walked away with a slight wave of her dainty hand.

Connor looked in Nina's direction repeatedly, clearly distracted by his father's absence. Her jaw tightened with tension. 'For God's sake, Finn, hurry up!' she muttered into the clear sky.

Suddenly she sensed his presence and inhaled the distinct scent of him and she felt her resolve weaken, as it always had. There was something about the way he smelled that she found intoxicating. Her breathing slowed and her shoulders slackened in warm relief as she readied to hear one of his many well-practised excuses for his lack of punctuality. But that wasn't of concern right now; all that mattered was that he was here.

Only he wasn't.

The empty field stretched down towards the car park. It was the strangest thing; she was sure he was there, but Finn was nowhere to be seen.

Her phone buzzed in her pocket. She didn't recognise the number, but this wouldn't be the first time he had used some hapless assistant to break the news of his absence.

'Hello?' She failed to keep a note of irritation from her voice.

'Is this Mrs McCarrick?'

'Yes.'

She gave the thumbs-up to Connor who had just executed a rather nifty zigzag run down the blind side.

'My name is Leslie Ranton and I am a doctor at Royal United Hospital in Bath.'

'Oh, right.' Nina thought hard. What appointment had she missed and who with? Declan's optometrist? Her gynaecologist? Had she neglected to put something on the calendar? Her eyes rolled at the inevitable inconvenience of having to reschedule.

'I am calling about your husband, Finn McCarrick?' The woman's voice faltered a little, even though her tone and words suggested the communication was well rehearsed.

'Uh-huh.' She nodded absently, forgetting the woman couldn't see her.

The woman on the end of the line took a breath. 'I am afraid that Mr McCarrick has been involved in an accident.'

Nina's response came out automatic and odd: 'I don't think so.'

'He was brought in an hour ago and I think it would be best if you came to the hospital right away. Is there someone who can drive you?' The woman spoke softly, as if Nina were a child.

'Is he hurt?' Nina held the phone with both hands, waiting for the response, her legs shaking, heart pounding.

The slight pause spoke volumes.

'I am sorry to tell you, Mrs McCarrick, that he was very badly hurt.'

Oh my God . . . No!

She pictured him leaving that morning, grabbing a slice of toast from the plate on the counter-top, reaching for his keys . . . An ordinary farewell on an ordinary day that was now being made so very extraordinary.

'Is he . . . is he going to be okay?' The question slipped past her lips like the sneakiest of poisons, souring her tongue and sucking out any joy that lurked within. She and Dr Ranton were playing a game, with her not wanting to ask if her husband was dying or had died, and Dr Ranton doing her level best to avoid saying anything along those lines.

Again that pause, a silent nothingness that told her more than any words possibly could. How hard was it to say 'No, he's going to be fine'? But she didn't; instead the woman's words were calm and yet insistent. 'I think you should come straight to the hospital, Mrs McCarrick.'

And just like that, Nina *felt* like a child, scared and alone. She pictured the little room in their home in Frederiksberg on that cold day, when the snow lay deep and an icy wind stole warmth from even the cosiest corner. A fire crackled in the open grate, and she, not yet four years old, had watched her dad, Joe, crouch down, resting on his haunches. The stiff leather of his ankle boots creaked with the movement. She sat with her big sister on the red sofa, huddled under a fur throw that absorbed the smell of the fire. She remembered the tears of anguish that snaked down her father's ruddy cheeks.

This felt the same. Her stomach twisted with the knowledge that there was about to be a seismic shift in her world.

She nodded into the phone and stared at her son. He held her gaze from the other side of the pitch and she noted his stance, his incongruous serenity in the midst of the chaotic jumble of limbs on the pitch.

He looked pale as he walked calmly towards her, as if he were strolling across a meadow, unaware of the grunts, shouts and scuffles of mud-covered bodies all around him. Like a ghost leaving the fray.

She would learn later that she had been making a strange sound, part moan, part scream: a single, guttural yell. This was why her son had walked towards her, but at the time, in her altered state of mind, she was unaware.

Four hours later she put the key into the front door and closed it behind her. The house was silent with a stillness that she had never known before. Kathy would be back with the boys any time now.

Standing in the middle of the kitchen, Nina looked around the room; she couldn't decide what to do. Even making a cup of tea felt like a Herculean task, as well as utterly pointless. Ordinarily at this time of night, her fingers would be darting in and out of the wide self-closing drawers, reaching into familiar spaces for glass bowls, her hand whisk, or a deep enamel frying pan in the same pale blue colour as her custom-made five-oven range. She would be humming as she made her way across the smooth oak flooring to the double-fronted, stainless steel, larder-door fridge, pulling out all manner of goodies – a quart of double cream; wax-wrapped slabs of bacon; and fat, fresh organic eggs delivered by the farm shop, as she prepared supper for her boys and her man, due home.

But not tonight.

Placing her hand on the cool granite she let the cold surface suck away the heat of her palm. Her breathing was loud in her ears, as if she were underwater. She swallowed, hoping this might help; it didn't. She pictured bursting through the surface of the swimming pool last summer, having swum the entire length underwater. Finn sat on the diving board with his Tom Collins over ice in a tall glass, as he whooped and cheered, 'You did it! The whole length! Go, Nina!' If the weather perked up over Easter, they would get the pool cleaned and re-create those lovely evenings of messing about in the water. It was her favourite thing to do. Fire up the grill and sit with their legs dangling in the water, admiring the view—

Oh no. The thought stopped the breath in her throat. *That can't happen now. That won't happen again.* There it was: the realisation like a door slamming in her mind. Nina braced her shaking arms on the counter-top, fearing that if she let go, she might tumble to the floor, and if she did, she wasn't sure she would find the energy to stand up. *God, that felt scary, I want to speak to Finn . . .* and bang! There it was again.

And again.

And again.

And again . . .

'Oh my God, Finn!' She spoke aloud. 'I can't imagine a me without you. I can't picture the kids without their dad. I can't imagine a world without you in it.'

She wasn't sure how long she stood leaning on the island in the semi-darkness. Time seemed to be playing tricks on her. She heard the front gate buzz and walked slowly to the entry system and pressed the button, picturing the high metal gate swinging open.

Shuffling into the grand hallway, she stood by the round table, inhaling the scent of flowers from the stunning display, a mixed bouquet ordered weekly, but even this offered no comfort. She expected the boys to run at her, imagined them hurtling through the door, dropping their bags and dashing in, frenzied and loud. She tensed her limbs for just this. It was therefore a shock when instead the door handle slowly twisted and the wide door opened gently, revealing her sons, who seemed to have shrunk in the intervening hours. At the match she had told Connor that Finn had been hurt, nothing more, and given him the instruction to look after his little brother, explaining that Kathy would bring them home. Nina had been too numb to be grateful, too distracted by the task of getting to the hospital and being with Finn.

The boys, in front of her now, were bowed and quiet. Gone was the confident colossus of the rugby pitch and in its place stood a fifteen-year-old boy, his skin pale, his eyes vacant and his mouth tight. Declan whimpered quietly. He was nervous and twitchy, his eyes huge behind his glasses. She could see that the uncertainty, the lack of information, was gnawing at them. Bile rose in her throat at the prospect of what she had to do. She swallowed again and tried to stand tall.

'They didn't want any supper. I did offer.' Kathy spoke over their heads as she loitered in the doorway, her voice quiet, apologetic, as if aware that she shouldn't be breaking the silence, shouldn't be there at all.

'Thank you for . . .' And just like that, Nina couldn't remember what she was thanking her for.

'No worries.'

Nina couldn't recall if she said goodbye or spoke further, but she was aware that Kathy had gone, and she was grateful.

Connor stared at her. 'Is he . . . ?' Nina noticed how he clenched his hands so tightly that his fingers were white. His voice trembled, as if the words were too terrible to voice, the whole idea too horrible to contemplate.

She stared at him, and prepared to engage in the same verbal dance that she and Dr Ranton had perfected earlier. The expression on her boys' faces told her they too were smart enough to realise that, were they available, words of comfort and reassurance would be the first thing she would utter to make everything feel better.

Nina reached out her arms towards Declan, who stepped forward carefully, then stopped within touching distance. She pulled him to her chest, stroking his thick, dark hair. It felt easier to address Connor without having to look into her baby's eyes.

'He died.' She spoke the words that sounded unreal: how could they be true? 'Daddy died.' Declan went limp in her arms, and she held him up until the strength returned to his legs.

She had imagined this exchange on her way home, playing out various reactions from her boys, many violent, some loud and all accompanied by a deafening howl of distress. The silence that enveloped the reduced family was something she could not have predicted. Connor pinched his nose, bowed his head and covered his eyes as his tears ran over his fingers and fell in splats on the wooden floor. The three stood, unified, as their distress seeped from them. She reached out her hand and beckoned her eldest son closer, and with desolation and sadness as their glue, they were all joined, arms around backs, heads touching: a three-headed thing, mourning the equally monstrous event that had befallen them.

TWO

Nina sipped her coffee and stared out of the tall kitchen windows at the crisp blue Wiltshire sky. It was a morning like any other, except that it wasn't. Sunshine streamed through the winter clouds and touched the distant fields and the grounds of The Tynings with its golden fingers.

'They're here, Mum,' Connor called softly from the doorway.

Ignoring the tremor of her hand, Nina emptied the coffee down the sink and walked to the foyer to find her black fitted jacket. She buttoned it up, looping the single string of pearls over the collar. Her fingers rested on the delicate silvery orbs, a gift from Finn. Connor and Declan stared at her from the hallway.

The shiny black car wound its way along the lanes taking a route that was familiar. Sitting between the boys, eaten up by her own grief, she found it hard to offer words of solace or distraction on this peculiar day; instead, she held their hands, grateful for the contact. The car dropped them at the Haycombe Crematorium. As Nina stepped from the quiet cocoon of the car, the first face she saw among the small crowd that had gathered outside was her sister's. Nina broke into a smile, quickly followed by the next wave of tears.

'Tiggy.' Saying the name out loud, she felt a rush of relief.

'Nina.' Her sister said it with the Danish inflection as her mother had intended it to be spoken: 'Neeya-naah.' Tiggy stepped forward confidently, as had always been her way, and placed her arms around her younger sibling, squashing her face into the cool, rough fabric of her denim bomber jacket.

Nina closed her eyes and inhaled the familiar scent, a mixture of cigarettes, chewing gum and cheap floral body spray, and for a second she was a child in their grandparents' home in Portswood, Southampton, with the TV blaring, the clutter of life all around them and her gran screaming instructions from the cramped, narrow kitchen. Her heart seemed to squeeze with longing at the memory of that old life; not for the hardship or the discomfort, but for a time when her mamma's spirit still lingered, when her dad came home from work with a whistle on his lips, before she knew what it felt like to wake with her heart and spirit so broken.

Nina took in the inevitable changes that had occurred in the intervening two years since they had last seen each other, at another funeral. Tiggy, at thirty-eight, was four years older, and Nina noted how she now had faint creases of age at the edge of her mouth and eyes and a sallow tinge to her skin, which the cigarettes surely couldn't help. Nina coughed, a little embarrassed, and wondered how she too had aged in the time since they saw each other. Tiggy had always been tall and slender, but she now looked a little gaunt. Nina, the shorter of the two, was also more rounded, with the curve of a bust and generous bottom that she had always disliked and which her sister used to envy. The closeness they had shared during their childhood had diminished to the point where to make a telephone call felt too difficult, where she couldn't confidently predict her sister's reaction; this woman with whom she used to sleep top to toe on a mattress, sharing thoughts and secrets and dreams.

'Thank you for coming.' Nina nodded with a formality she regretted.

'Of course.' Tiggy shrugged. As if this were a given.

The last time they had been together was to stare at each other across a church aisle, when their diminishing clan had gathered for the funeral of their great-uncle, the last survivor of their gran and her siblings. It was sad, but after losing their mum so young and then their dad in their early twenties, these deaths – of uncles, aunts, grandparents – were never going to have the same impact.

Until now.

'How are you doing?' Tiggy asked.

Nina looked beyond her sister to the memorial garden. 'I don't know really.'

Declan walked around the car and held her hand tightly.

'Hey, Dec.' Tiggy ruffled the top of his head.

'Hey.' He whispered his response, standing close to his mum's side as Connor let his aunt briefly wrap him in a loose hug.

'You've grown.' Tiggy looked at the boys, her nephews. Her tone was reflective.

'It's okay, Dec, it's going to be fine,' Nina offered in the most assured manner that she could muster, trying to shift the fear that sat like a stopper in her throat. He gripped her hand with such ferocity that she felt he was squeezing her bones.

Connor walked ahead in his navy suit, bought last year for school speech day, and one of his dad's ties. *Speech day* . . . She recalled the rare occasion when Finn had kept his word and made it to a school event. They had sat at one of many prettily dressed tables on the school field and had tea and cake, clapping as pupils traipsed up to the temporary stage to gather scrolled, beribboned awards. Parents clapped loudly and crowded their kids with congratulatory hugs and handshakes. Finn had teased Connor for not getting an award, gently punching the top of his arm. 'All that bloody money spent on your education and not one single scroll to show for it!' They had all laughed and then ridden home in the car with the radio turned up loud and Billy Ray Cyrus's 'Achy Breaky Heart' blaring, to which they had sung along . . .

Nina stared at the entrance to the crematorium, a building she had entered a couple of times before to bid farewell to a neighbour and one of Finn's staff, never imagining that she would be here today in this surreal situation. She tried to breathe; it felt like she had been kicked in the chest by something so powerful that it had broken her bones. She glanced over her shoulder and for a second considered bolting, running for the fields with her arms spread wide. If her sons on both sides hadn't anchored her, she just might have.

The crematorium was full. People greeted them with pitying looks and quiet murmurs of condolence as they waited for the service to begin. Person after person filed by and reminded Connor well-meaningly that he was now the man of the house and it was his job to look after things. If time, place and her confidence had allowed, she would have screamed at them all that he was a boy of fifteen who was grieving for his dad and they, as a family, would look after each other. Connor's school friends, Charlie and George, stood close, placing hands on his shoulder, reminding him to be strong. They looked to her so much like little boys playing grown-ups. She hated that this thing had come knocking on their door, singling out her children, making them different.

She recognised Mr Monroe, Finn's accountant, a short, fleshy man, as he made his way over to her, cutting a swathe through the mourners with a fixed stare. She felt a flush of unease. It had been easy to ignore his calls, which she wasn't ready to deal with yet, but here, face to face, interaction was inevitable. 'I am so very sorry for your loss.' His eyes looked pained, as if even talking to her were agony.

'Thank you,' she managed, looking down at her shoes. Her voice sounded small.

He pumped her hand up and down in a vigorous shake. 'I am seriously so very, very sorry – about everything.'

'Thank you,' she mumbled again. She almost had to yank her hand free from his grip.

'I left you a couple of messages and emailed you too,' he pressed, before whipping a business card from his top pocket and sliding it into her hand.

Why did he think this might be appropriate on the day of Finn's funeral? What did he want? An apology for her lack of response? An explanation as to just how grief had placed the answering of emails and the returning of calls a little low on her priorities?

She shoved the card into her narrow shoulder bag. 'I really must . . .'

Mr Monroe reached out and held the top of her arm. 'I don't mean to be so pushy, today of all days, but I really do need to talk to you. You have my number now.' He stared directly into her eyes.

Pulling her arm free, she could only nod. Whatever plans or advice he might have for their money and investments could bloody well wait.

The funeral seemed to pass in a blur. She was aware of Finn's brother Michael crying through his eulogy, and his drinking buddy, one of the old site managers from McCarrick Construction, leaning too close to the microphone, distorting the few words he gave about how much they were all going to miss Finn. She felt the eyes of those in the pews behind her on her back and it made her feel sick. She wished they were there alone, she and the kids, without all these people.

With Declan holding on tightly to her hand, the three of them stared, stony-faced, ahead, their tears tracing familiar tracks over skin that was already wet. Declan's noisy sobs punctured the air. She glanced at the coffin only once. She even positioned her fingers to cover the handsome face of her husband on the Order of Service, because to see these things would make it real, whereas right now she could kid herself that the coffin was just a box, the pamphlet in her hand just paper . . .

When it was over, she said her goodbyes as quickly as she could and climbed awkwardly into the back seat of the fancy car with the boys and Tiggy. All were silent. Tiggy's presence did little to help – not quite a stranger in their midst, but pretty close. Nina's thoughts were muddled; she continually reminded herself to tell Finn snippets about the day, the things she had observed that would make him laugh; his cousin Patch taking a leak in a hedge where he thought no one could see, and Kathy Topps and her husband being accosted by Finn's great-aunt Rita who seemed to have consumed more than a couple of gins.

Her fingers flexed, wanting to take up their natural home of the last decade or so, nestling in his wide, warm palm, an act from which she always gained reassurance and confidence. And bang! There it was again, the door slam in her mind that he was gone. The reality still shocked her senses as much as it had ten days ago when he died.

'Are you okay?' she asked the boys for the fiftieth time that day. Like automatons, they nodded the response they knew she wanted. They were all going through the motions, but the simple truth was that they were all far, far from okay. They were bit-part players doing their utmost to uphold the illusion of normality, for whose benefit she wasn't sure.

Back at The Tynings, stoic-faced caterers darted in between the guests like worker bees, proffering glasses of chilled white Chablis and silver platters laden with canapés, which she had chosen from a flimsy catalogue, without energy or interest. The bellowed exchanges of reunion that echoed in the rooms reverberated painfully in her ears. She rubbed the tops of her arms to try to chase away a chill, but nothing worked. Closing her eyes, she wished everyone would leave.

'Do we have to stay down here, Mum?' Connor's eyes wandered among the groups of adults that stood in clusters with drinks held to their chests.

'No, darling. Do whatever makes you comfortable. Take your friends to the TV room or your bedroom or whatever.'

'Thanks.' He gave a brief smile.

'Have you eaten?'

'I'm not hungry.' He looked away, as if offended by a platter of cheese-laden mini-quiches that whizzed past.

'Me neither.' She placed her hand over his back. 'Dad would have been really proud of you today. He was proud of you every day.'

Connor began to walk away, then paused. 'He crashed on the A46, right?'

'Yes.' As if she could ever forget or stop picturing the bend on which he had swerved off at speed, into the fence, careering down into the field below . . .

'That's nowhere near my school. It's on the other side of town. He was heading out of the city. He wasn't on his way to watch me play rugby, was he?'

She hated the disappointment in his eyes. 'I don't . . . I don't know.' This was not something she had really considered. 'He might have been coming back after a meeting, anything could have happened really, Con. We just don't know.'

He looked her in the eyes. Both felt the blush at how she was still covering for the man she loved.

'Jesus Christ! I'd forgotten the size of this place,' her sister broke in. Connor headed for the stairs. Nina watched Tiggy tip her head back and look up at the high ceiling, casting her eyes over the wide sweep of staircase, the pale wood floor and the huge vase of white lilies on the round table. 'It's like a hotel.' Tiggy shook her head from side to side in awe. 'No hotel I've ever stayed in, though.'

'Can I get you a drink?' Nina spoke to mask her discomfort, wishing her sister would keep her voice down.

'Yes, coffee, thanks.'

She made her way through the modest crowd to the kitchen, with Tiggy following, her big sister's high heels clicking on the floor. 'Holy-fricking-moly! You've redone the kitchen. This is like . . .' She paused, seeming at a loss as to what to compare the room to.

Nina was glad the kids were out of earshot. She grabbed a mug from the cupboard and poured her sister some coffee from the pot on the counter. She wished, not for the first time, that she could slip away and crawl under the duvet.

Tiggy stared at her as if making an appraisal, and appeared to take in the depressed slope to her bones. 'So what happened? He had a car crash?'

She felt her stomach flip at the question, asked so casually. It was a reminder of the life she had stepped away from, a life where poverty and reduced horizons meant bluntness was the most expedient way to get things done, a life where there was no time or room for shying away from the topic in hand, no matter how unpleasant. She had thought of this before; the many topics that were taboo in the world she now lived in: money, politics, religion, anything of an overly personal nature. She had learned to be contained and not break the taboos, but it was hard. In her old neighbourhood, in the world Tiggy still inhabited, people lived cheek by jowl and things were discussed at the bus stop or in the shop, and no one cared who heard. It mattered little; it wasn't as if whoever might overhear was going to be shocked or even care. 'You've got no money till Friday? How are you going to get to work?' or 'He was so drunk, he fell down and knocked out his two front teeth. The dog went over to lick him and I left them to it . . .'

'Yes.' She nodded, praying her sister wouldn't ask for any more detail.

'God, that's terrible.'

She nodded. It was.

'So how *are* you doing?' Tiggy asked in a more deferential tone.

Nina shrugged. '*Numb* is the best way to describe it. One minute I'm fine, the next I'm a mess. It still feels like he might walk through the door any minute.' She looked towards the hallway expectantly. 'I think when I realise that it's not going to happen, that's when it will get very scary for me.'

Tiggy nodded. 'It always seemed like he made you happy.'

'He really did.'

She watched her sister reach into the top pocket of her denim jacket and pull out a packet of cigarettes.

'You'll have to smoke on the terrace.' Nina tried to hide her distaste as she nodded towards the French doors at the back of the kitchen. The idea of having cigarette smoke inside her home was repulsive.

Tiggy did a double take and then smiled. 'Sure.'

As Tiggy moved towards the doors, Declan ambled into the room. 'Your mum died too, didn't she?' he asked Tiggy, his mouth drooping with sadness. The words cut with a sharp reminder not only of her other loss, but of the fact that her baby boy was trying to normalise this terrible occurrence; to be reassured that he wasn't the only one to have suffered like this . . .

'Yes.' Tiggy nodded. 'When I was very small. I was only seven and Nina here was even younger. And that's when our dad moved us back to the UK, where he was from, and we lived with his parents while he went off to find work.'

'Do you think your mum will see Daddy?' he turned to ask Nina.

'I think she might.' She smiled.

'Do you think they are in heaven now?'

Nina swallowed the rage that sat on her tongue, wanting to shout that she didn't know how any just God could take away the man she loved. He had already taken her mother, when she was just a child. Instead, she drew breath and kept calm. 'I do, my love. Do you?'

Declan nodded and played with a rubber band he had wrapped around his fingers. 'Do you think that in heaven, your life is the same as it was when you were on earth?'

'Mmm, that's a good question. I'm not sure. What do you think?'

'I'm not sure either, but I hope that people get to have a rest, either because they are very old and tired or because they were very busy, like Dad.'

'Yes, he was very busy.' She nodded, cursing the next wave of tears that hovered just below the surface.

'I wish I could see him. I miss him so much.' Declan suddenly cried, his little chest heaving.

'Me too.' She held him fast.

Every time Finn was mentioned it was like hearing the news for the first time. It made her heart stall and the pain was only intensified when she saw how her child suffered too.

Tiggy slowly pulled out a chair at the breakfast bar, as if wary of doing the wrong thing, and perched on it.

'I think he's in heaven with your mummy,' Declan said, 'and my other gran, Eunice, who was married to Hampy, my dad's dad and our gun dog, Piper. And Mrs Nicholson's husband Dick, who used to paint the lines on the cricket pitch. He had a heart attack at a barn dance.'

Tiggy stared at him, offering a slight nod of understanding. 'Is that right?' She toyed with the cigarette packet in her hand.

'You shouldn't smoke, you know,' he sniffed. 'It can make you get cancer and it gives you asthma.' And with that, he walked off.

'He's so like you when you were a child. Confident, questioning. I remember Mamma saying you were only allowed five "whys" for every-thing she said, otherwise you would go on for infinity.'

Nina smiled, feeling the familiar flash of envy that Tiggy had been old enough to remember their mother, whereas her recollections were reduced to a scent, a shadow, an idea of the woman, leaving her to fill in the gaps.

'But the main difference is that your kid is posh and you weren't.'

Tiggy's words snapped her to the present. Nina placed the hot mug of coffee in front of her sister and walked to the fridge to fetch the milk, bristling at her crass remark. She still felt that the poverty in which she had been raised marked her in some way, formed a grime that still sat on her skin, clung to her clothes and hung around her in a way that gave off noxious fumes perceptible to the more fortunate.

'God, your fridge is enormous, it would fill the bathroom in my flat! How much does it cost to even fill a space that big? What would Gran say if she could see this place? Apart from finding fault, of course. She wouldn't believe it, would she?'

'Tig, are you going to comment on every aspect of my life? My hallway, my kid, my fridge? Because I don't know if I can handle that right now.' She hid her face inside the door and let her head hang forward.

Tiggy jumped down from the stool and again took her sister in her arms. Nina laid one arm half-heartedly across her sister's back. It was at the same time awkward and familiar.

'I'm sorry. I guess I just don't know what to say. And I'm nervous being in this massive house on this day. And a bit nervous about being around you, if I'm being honest.'

This was a rare admission. Another time, on a different day, and her comment would have invited a response, but Nina didn't have the energy. Not today.

'Then say nothing. Okay?' Nina said.

'Okay.' Her sister sighed.

Nina only felt semi-present during the rest of the wake, smiling and nodding in all the right places, reluctantly accepting hugs, and doing her best to graciously acknowledge the offers of help and support. It felt like an age until the last guests left. Nina did her best to hide her slight irritation at Finn's sisters-in-law, Marjorie and Netta, who stumbled towards their waiting minibus, arms linked, whilst wailing their distress for all to hear. His brothers Michael and Anthony were already sitting with heads lolling, sprawled on the back seats. The relationship between Finn and his brothers was somewhat fractious. Things had deteriorated when their father, Hampy, was diagnosed with Alzheimer's. It had riled Finn that both his big brothers had quickly and readily agreed that the old man move in with him and Nina; after all, they had the space and the cash . . . She understood this, but Finn was angered on his dad's behalf that they didn't put up at least the show of wanting to help more. He thought his dad deserved better, and in this she felt he was right.

She thought about the first time she had been introduced to Hampy, as a shy eighteen-year-old. He had been running the office for Finn at the time and had raised his palms the moment she walked in the door. 'Keep your distance, it's always difficult for Finn when he has to introduce a young lady to his better-looking, funnier dad.'

'I see. And have you been introduced to many?' she'd asked quietly, with her hands folded together and her eyes fixed on the man who would become her father-in-law.

'None like you,' Hampy had replied without any prompting, his expression one of kindness. Finn had simply stared at her with a look that told her this was the truth.

The memory comforted her, and today *she* expected better than the wine- and whisky-quaffing antics that had led to this display from Finn's family. It bothered her that the kids might overhear the caterwauling of their aunts.

'What needs doing next? Give me a job,' her sister instructed as she made her way in from the hallway, wiping her hands on her trousers.

Nina looked up, having quite forgotten that Tiggy was still around.

'Thought I might hang around for a bit, help out, look after the kids, cook or something . . . I don't know.' Tiggy coughed, letting her arms rise and fall to her sides, her kindness tinged with shyness as they peered through the invisible walls that sat between them.

'That's so kind.' Nina meant it. 'Have you got time off work? Are you at the same place?' The last time she knew, Tiggy worked in a local pub, The Bear, pulling pints and serving food, living above it in a small flat.

'Yes, Dean, the owner, is good like that.'

Nina knew so little about her sister's life, she didn't know what to ask. Their estrangement had been gradual, a subtle slowing of contact over the years, until it had become sporadic and was now almost non-existent. It was hard for her to recall exactly how it had started, but certainly the cracks in their kinship were cleaved open when Nina left

Southampton and moved in with Finn; they seemed to lose all they had in common when no longer bound by a common environment.

'The dishwasher is on, I've collected stray glasses from the tables in the lounge and swept the terrace,' Tiggy continued.

'Thank you for that. And thank you for all your help today.'

'No worries, I've cling-wrapped all the leftover food and put it in the fridge.'

Nina shook her head. 'Oh, you shouldn't have bothered, Tig. I'll probably just throw it all away.'

'That's such a waste. So much of it hasn't been touched.'

Nina stared at her. So long as everyone had had enough to eat, what did it really matter?

'Do you want me to stay here tonight? I'm happy to.' Tiggy folded a dishcloth and hovered.

'No, Tig, but thank you for offering. I don't want to keep you.'

Tiggy sniffed and reached for her cigarettes that nestled in the pocket of her jacket. 'Good God, Nina, yes! Whatever happens, please don't keep me from my life!' She chuckled, and shook her head. She made her way out to the terrace.

Nina was tipping the dregs of wine bottles down the sink and rinsing them under the tap, ready for the recycling collection, when Tiggy came back inside.

'I'll get my bag and shoot off then.'

'Okay.'

Tiggy leaned on the island and stared.

'Why are you looking at me like that?' She didn't like the way she was being scrutinised.

'Because you've changed, Nina.'

'What do you mean, I've changed? Of course I have, my husband has just died!'

Tiggy shook her head. 'No, before that . . .'

'What are you *talking* about, Tiggy?' She shook her head in exasperation.

'Today is not the day to talk about it. Next time, maybe.' She gave a tight smile. 'I should get going. You know where I am if you need anything. I am here for you. I want to be the first person you call, always.'

Nina nodded at her sister, too sad and tired to properly consider her comment.

Tiggy left as she had arrived: abruptly and without any great fanfare.

THREE

The boys decided to go back to school the day after the funeral, with only a week to go until the half-term holiday. Nina too thought this was a good idea: anything to get Connor to leave the cave of his bedroom, in which he had huddled himself away since Finn's passing. All her efforts at trying to get him to open up to her had been met with monosyllabic grunts of acknowledgement, but very little else. The sound of his crying filtered under her door in the dead of night and she was torn, unsure whether to leave him to grieve alone or to intervene. If she were being completely honest, it was hard to find the energy required to further engage with him. She figured that second best was getting him to open up to his friends, and if this failed, then at least having him out of the house meant he was no longer staring at the four walls of his room.

Declan, too, was quiet, clingier than usual, approaching her for hugs and nestling close to her on the sofa. Not that this was unexpected. She hoped, however, that the distraction of school could only be a good thing. Nina had faith that the staff would be kind and make allowances, and that the boys' network of friends would be helpful.

After a short, silent drive, she pulled in to the kerb on the grey February morning. 'If either of you want to come home, for any reason at all, just call, drop me a text or tell a member of staff and I will be here within twenty minutes.'

Connor nodded and climbed from the car, slinging his large sports bag over his shoulder.

'See you later, Con.'

'Yep.' He nodded and closed the door behind him. She watched him walk around to the back of the car and wait by Declan's door. 'Come on then.' He lightly thumped the window. Declan didn't need asking twice. He grabbed his rucksack and pushed his glasses up onto his nose, then leaned forward to kiss his mum on the cheek. He clambered from the back seat. Nina watched in the side mirror as they loped along the pavement side by side, united by this terrible thing that had happened to them. It caused a lump to rise in her throat and she felt a swell of pride at how Connor, on this occasion, considered his little brother's feelings.

Pulling into the driveway back home, the phone on the front seat buzzed. It was Kathy Topps.

'Hi, Kathy.' She pinched the bridge of her nose with her thumb and forefinger, as if this could relieve some unseen pressure, and closed her eyes.

'Nina, I've been thinking about you.'

'That's kind.'

'How are things?'

Things are surreal, I am numb, I want to wake up . . .

'As you'd expect, really.' It was all she could manage.

'Well, I wanted to say that I don't know if you are still intending to grab a break somewhere over half-term, but if your plans have changed, which would of course be completely understandable, I still have an opening for tennis lessons if Declan is at a loose end.'

'Thanks, Kathy. I'll let you know.' She ended the call abruptly and leaned her head on the steering wheel. What was wrong with the bloody woman? Her husband had died; tennis lessons were about the furthest thing from her mind. Her phone buzzed again – Mr Monroe, the accountant. Nina silenced it. She wasn't up to speaking to him today.

She looked up at the big house and, for the first time ever, felt a little reluctant to go inside. It was her first day alone, without the boys to care for or a funeral to plan; the first day of 'normal', although she was convinced that, for her, nothing would ever feel 'normal' again, not without the sound of Finn's key in the door at the end of the day.

Keeping the house shipshape had always been her preoccupation, and today she sought comfort in the familiarity of her routine. She lugged the recycling box up the driveway and thought of Tiggy. '*Because you've changed . . .*' What had she meant?

After folding the clean bed linen in the laundry room, Nina made her way along the first-floor landing and stopped outside Finn's study. She touched the handle, as she had several times over the last week or so, and considered whether or not she had the courage to go inside. She wondered if he actually had booked something for them over the half-term break; that was always his way: making things happen, bringing them surprises and joy. She felt a surge of longing, coupled with the now familiar flicker of fear at how she was going to cope without him. She laid her palm against the doorframe, picturing him inside, working at his desk with a determined expression, sleeves rolled up, oblivious of the hour, as his fingers skirted over the computer keyboard, or shouting instructions to his team over the phone. She would knock gently and creep in, and he would wink at her, mid-call, as she leaned across and placed a cup of tea or a mug of coffee on his favourite mosaic coaster that Connor had made him at primary school.

Now she placed the laundry pile on the floor, hesitating before she turned the handle and walked in.

The leather swivel chair still held the indentations of Finn's shape. She inhaled the deep aroma of her husband. It lingered here more strongly than anywhere else in the house, as if his scent, his breath, had been preserved within the fabric, within the walls. She looked at the antique boxes and silver trinkets that littered the bespoke mahogany desk, still fresh with his invisible fingerprints. She noticed strands of hair on the rug, his litter in the waste bin, sheets of paper that had been crumpled up in his warm palms and tossed aside; all of it had now taken on new significance. His everyday possessions: his extra notepads, neatly stacked on the desktop; the pen he favoured when attempting the crossword of a weekend; his china mug with 'World's Best Golfer' written on it, the booby prize when he had come last at a work tournament . . . All of his stuff, now redundant and waiting to either be sorted, binned or made into relics, gathering dust in a cardboard box. Seemingly innocuous items had now become so much more than the sum of their parts. On that first night, she had taken his sweatshirt from the hook on the back of the bathroom door and placed her pillow inside it, taking comfort from the fact that it had touched his skin. She drifted in and out of sleep between fits of sobbing and howling. Nina wondered how long she could keep these items in his office preserved in this way.

She climbed into his chair, tears streaming down her face. She let her hands wander lightly over the desktop, fingering the receipts for materials, letters from council planning departments and a leather penholder with his precious Montblanc pen-and-pencil set inside. She pulled a little yellow Post-it from the edge of the computer screen and read 'Mac 64500'. Probably something to do with his computer.

It was the first time she had properly considered that she needed to get a grip of her situation. There was no Finn to filter the emails and take care of the household administration. The call from their lawyer in the days following the accident had been brief and reassuring: he was in possession of Finn's last will and testament and, as she expected, everything was left to her. They had tentatively agreed to meet more formally after the funeral.

She pulled the shiny desk handle of his colonial-style, mahogany inlaid desk, and eased the drawer along the runner. Her tears turned briefly to laughter at the sight of its contents: a haul of items that were deemed illicit in their house.

'Finn!' she called out. 'You little pig!' There were open packets of sweets, mint humbugs, liquorice wheels, jellybeans and bars of milk chocolate. She thought of the many times she had praised his choice of fruit for pudding and encouraged him with honey in his coffee instead of sugar, and all the while he stockpiled this! She laid her head on her arms and once again gave in to sobs that robbed her of all energy. Her eyes were sore and her throat ached. 'Good for you, darling,' she whispered. 'Good for you, my Finn.'

The phone on the desktop rang, making her jump.

Sitting up straight, she closed the drawer and cleared her throat. 'Hello?' She held the receiver close to her face, knowing that the last cheek it touched was that of her husband.

'Mrs McCarrick?' She didn't recognise the stern voice.

'Yes.'

'It's Mr Paulson, from Kings Norton College.'

'Oh, hello, Mr Paulson.' Her heart jumped at the thought that something might have happened to the kids as she tried to recall whether she'd ever spoken to a Mr Paulson.

'I am sorry to disturb you at this time. And I wouldn't do so if it weren't a matter of importance.'

Nina felt her legs weaken. 'Are the boys okay?' Her breath came in fast, shallow bursts; she was not equipped to deal with any more bad news.

'Yes! Yes, the boys are, as far as I am aware, fine.' He managed an odd little chuckle that to her felt misplaced. 'I am calling from the accounts department.'

'Right.' *Get to the point*, she thought.

'It's about the invoice for the boys this term.'

'Uh-huh.' Placing her palm against her forehead, she tried not to sigh in irritation. Surely anything to do with accounts could easily be conducted via email or a phone call at some later date?

'I think there must have been some oversight,' he said slowly, 'but the account has not been settled for the last term, and indeed we have received no payment for this current term, which is well under way.'

'I'm sorry Mr . . .' The man's name had gone clean out of her head. 'Paulson.'

'Yes, sorry, Mr Paulson, my brain is like scrambled egg,' she confessed. 'I'm afraid I haven't had anything to do with the household accounts. They are handled by my husband's office in Bradford-on-Avon.' It was yet another reminder that her life was changing, that she knew that now she needed to step up to the plate and take control of the things that Finn had overseen. But she didn't quite know where to start, and the weight of pressure sat on her skull, causing a headache to spring instantly. Saying the word 'husband' was all it took for the swell of grief to rise in her throat, threatening to choke her.

She had got used to the situation. When they were first married, Finn's insistence on dealing with all the finances was a pleasant change from having to watch every penny and wondering what the future held. Suddenly there was a capable man who loved her and who took the worry right out of her hands. He was highly organised and took control of everything – broadband suppliers, phone contracts, bank accounts, passport renewals and insurance. Far from feeling the lack of emancipation, she appreciated that it was done with love, easing her path through life, removing all worry.

'Ah, yes.' Mr Paulson sighed. 'I was led to believe the same, and trust me, I have tried, but to no avail. The matter is now becoming' – he paused, before stressing the words – '*quite urgent*. I felt I had no option but to contact you, and trust me, I very much hoped to avoid this conversation at what must be a difficult time.'

Yes, it is, very difficult. 'I don't really understand.' She spoke her thoughts aloud as she gripped the receiver.

'Allow me to clarify.' His voice was now considerably more animated. 'You are behind in the payment for Connor and Declan's education, and unfortunately, if we do not receive settlement in full for the outstanding fees within the next forty-eight hours, we will have no choice other than to ask you to make alternative plans for your sons' schooling, as returning to Kings Norton College after the half-term break will *not* be an option.'

A bubble of nervous laughter escaped from her mouth. It was an instinctive, incongruous reaction. 'Mr Paulson. What a thing to say! My sons have been at Kings Norton since they were three. They are Kings Norton boys. Of course they will be returning next term.' The idea was unthinkable. 'I will call our accountant and have the amount transferred into the school account as soon as I possibly can, hopefully by the close of play today. How much is outstanding, exactly?' She reached for a pen from the silver, glass-bottomed tankard used as a pen pot, and found a discarded envelope on which to scribble.

'That would be . . .' There was a pause, presumably while Mr Paulson either totted up or double-checked the figures. 'Twenty-nine thousand, nine hundred and forty-two pounds and seventy-six pence.'

'Right.' She coughed. 'And that would take us up to the end of next term?'

'That's correct, and would clear the amount outstanding from this term.'

'I shall get on to it immediately, Mr Paulson, and will make sure we have a bank transfer set up to ensure this payment happens automatically in the future.'

'That would make my life a lot easier, Mrs McCarrick, and would avoid the need for these calls.' He gave a weasely laugh, and she ended the call.

Nina sat back in Finn's chair and rested her sweating palms on the arms of his chair, composing herself, then dialled the office. Melanie set up the standing orders and filed the bank statements; she would be able to throw some light on things. Nina tried not to think of the countless times she had dialled the number to speak to Finn: '*When will you be home for supper? Did you want me to pop your suit into the cleaner's? Do you know how much I love you?*

'Yep?' a gruff, unfamiliar voice asked. It took her aback, then angered her that whoever was on the other end of the line was so clearly taking advantage of the fact that Finn was not there to keep order.

'Who is this?' she demanded.

'Matt. Who's this?' he challenged.

'I'm Nina, Finn's wife,' she said, trying to assert herself with whoever this cocky Matt was, 'and I was hoping to speak to Melanie.'

'I'm afraid you've just missed her,' he said sarcastically. 'Melanie left over a month ago. Is there anything else I can help you with today?'

'She did?' Nina managed to ask. How weird that Finn hadn't told her. 'I . . . Is Luke there?'

'Luke the site manager?'

'Yes!'

'Ah, Luke went about two months ago. Look, sorry, love, but I haven't got time to chat to you. I'm with the creditors and we are nearly done here.' He hung up abruptly.

'What the hell?' Nina stared at the phone, her heart racing. She racked her brains. Creditors? Why were creditors in the office? Did they owe money? Surely not. Why had Finn not told her that he had got rid of Melanie and Luke? It made no sense: he trusted Luke, who had been with him for years! She tried to picture who from work had come to the funeral, but it was all a blur. And shock was making it hard for her to join the dots.

Mr Monroe.

Of course, the accountant had been there and had given her his card. She jumped up and ran to the bedroom, opening her bedside table where she had shoved his business card, along with the funeral's Order of Service, which she still found almost impossible to look at. Sitting back on the bed, she lifted her mobile and punched in his telephone number.

'Mr Monroe?' she asked, trying to control the quaver in her voice.

'Mrs McCarrick.' He gave an audible sigh. 'I am very glad to hear from you. Thank you for returning my call. I had all but given up hope and was planning to come out and see you in person. But it might be best if you come here.'

◆　◆　◆

Nina woke early the next morning. She hadn't slept, not properly. She had instead lain in the wide bed, with her head on Finn's sweatshirt, feeling a cloak of unease heavy on her body, watching as the hands of the clock trotted merrily on towards dawn. Finally, she shrugged off the duvet, rising reluctantly to get the day started; this silent brooding did nothing to help her fragile mental state. After hauling her leaden limbs from the bed, she tiptoed past the boys' rooms to the kitchen, where she took solace in her favourite chair. She watched the sunrise over the distant fields, shrouded in a haze of morning mist, and was rewarded by the sight of two deer grazing on the gentle slopes, standing proudly in front of a purple-tinged sky. It always felt like a special gift to be able to observe these majestic creatures, as if they were sharing a secret with her. She felt her face break into one of the first genuine smiles since Finn's passing.

Later she placed a bowl of scrambled eggs, flecked with freshly ground black pepper and chilli flakes, and a plate of toasted bagels on the breakfast bar, with two tall glasses of fresh orange juice. She looked up and imagined Finn rushing into the room. 'Any chance of a coffee, love, I'm running late?' he would ask as he grabbed a bagel and gave her a kiss before rushing off again. His woody scent lingered around her and she closed her eyes and breathed deeply.

'I miss you.'

'Who are you talking to, Mum?' Declan asked, staring at her as he took a seat and spooned scrambled egg onto his plate.

'Dad.' She smiled sheepishly.

'I talk to him too,' he whispered, holding the spoon in mid-air.

Connor strode in and changed the atmosphere, stirring the air with his words and breaking the beat of grief that had held them. His voice when he spoke was quiet; he looked downward, as if unsure of the etiquette, awkward in his own home.

'I . . . I was talking to the coach about next term and I wasn't sure if we have anything planned for the break. But he asked if I could join the squad for training. It's quite a big deal. I didn't know what to say, but I'd quite like to go. I think . . .' His voice trailed off and he looked sheepish, as if it were wrong to express joy or an interest in something.

'You should tell him yes, definitely, Con.' She spoke with a tone of reassurance. 'It'll put you in a good place for the team next year.'

I'll get the fees paid today. Mr Monroe can make the necessary transfer. It'll all be okay . . . Her self-calming mantra helped.

'The first thing I thought when he asked me was that I couldn't wait to tell Dad.' The wobble to his bottom lip when he was trying to be brave was somehow harder to watch than when he gave in to the sadness. It ripped at her heart.

'He would be so pleased for you, honey. You know that.'

He gave a brief nod. 'I should be pleased, too, but without him around, everything feels like' – he shrugged his shoulders – 'like "so what?". Everything is only half as good . . . a bit pointless.'

She drew breath to remind him that she was still here, but changed her mind. This wasn't about her, but was simply her son longing for contact with his daddy.

'It won't always be that way. I promise you. And I understand how it feels, having lost my mum.' She shook her head. 'Not that I remember her too much, but I felt her absence, always. It does get easier, but oh my word, not being able to introduce her to the man I was going to marry, or see her hold you . . .' She looked up and saw the look of horror on Connor's face. She hadn't meant to go on. Pointing out the prospect of living this half-life of disappointment and muted joy forever was clearly more than he could bear.

An idea struck. 'Maybe we should go somewhere for half-term, just the three of us?' Her tone brightened a little as the notion grew in her mind. 'It might do us all good to get away. How about Italy? We could find a nice hotel in Tuscany, eat good food, walk in the sunshine?' She looked at their less than eager faces. 'I know it will be strange without Dad, but there will be a lot of firsts without him and once we have done them, we won't fear them any more. This could be *our* first holiday. What do you think?'

Connor stared at the bagel and egg on his plate, 'If I'm going to make the A team next year, then I need to be around for training and I don't really want to go away, Mum.' He spoke softly, as if to counter her disappointment.

'I don't want to go anywhere without Dad,' Declan confessed.

Nina turned her attention to the making of tea. She didn't want to do *anything* without Finn either, nothing at all. All she did want to do was take to her bed, hide under the duvet and sleep and cry . . . but carrying on was what was required for all those who got left behind. No matter how hard it got. 'That's okay, boys. We shall stay here.'

'I also need to finalise my subject options for next year,' Connor said, as if further justification were needed. 'Dad was going through it all with me and we had a vague plan.'

'I can help you with that if you like,' she offered.

'Sure,' he said unenthusiastically. 'Ms Rabieno says I should take Biology and Chemistry, and I really want to do History too because I love it. But apparently top unis want subjects in matching clusters of topics – nothing too broad. So maybe I should choose Physics, even though I don't really like it.'

'I think to study at the level required for university, and to do it justice, you have to love the subject matter or you won't get the best out of it and it won't get the best out of you.'

'Thanks for that insight,' Connor muttered, and turned his attention to his phone. 'I'll talk to Ms Rabieno.'

It made her feel like her opinion was worthless, but he was probably right. What did she know? She never went to university. She felt her stomach cave with a sinking feeling of inadequacy.

After breakfast the three of them made their way to the car. It was a bitingly cold winter's day. They drove the few minutes to the boys' school in silence.

'Are you okay, Connor?' she asked, looking at his profile.

'Yep. I'll speak to the coach today.'

'I meant more, how are you feeling in general, not just today?'

He took a deep breath. 'In general? I feel sad, Mum. Sadder than I knew was possible.' He stared out the window at the solid pale villas that lined the route to school. 'And I feel angry, at how unfair it is. Some of the guys at school tell me how their dads treat them, hassling them about grades, punishing them even, you know?' He shrugged. 'But Dad was' – he swallowed – 'Dad was the best, and it makes me mad because he's the one that died. I thought I had more time.'

Nina nodded and struggled to find words that might help. 'Me too. I thought we had all the time in the world.'

The heart-wrenching sound of Declan's sobbing filled the car. She reached back and patted his arm. 'Don't cry, my darling.'

'I . . . I can't . . . help it,' he managed. It was a stark reminder that they were always only a heartbeat, a phrase, a mention and a reminder away from this raw distress that they all tried so hard to keep at bay, and it was exhausting. She neared the traffic lights and was greeted by a green light: a good omen for a good day.

Mr Monroe's offices were in the centre of Bath, entered via a small, unobtrusive door next to the rear entrances of the shops, and at the top of a winding staircase, high above Milsom Street. They offered a glorious view over the shoppers and tourists ambling around the Georgian city. That was if you were tall enough to see out of the apex window. The room was cluttered with boxes and files and smelled of old books. The aroma wasn't wholly unpleasant but, rather, evocative of libraries and real fires and winter nights and the escape of stories. This in turn made Nina think of her mamma and those early, early years in Frederiksberg, and the cold winter nights when darkness drew its blind on the day. She didn't remember too much about that time, but the odd memory stood out clear and distinct. She could picture herself with Tiggy huddled under a fur blanket, in the small, slate-floored room, happy and content, with a log fire crackling in the grate, and lamplight casting gentle shadows on the wall, and listening to the rustle of crisp pages turning, with her mum's beautiful, soft voice reading to them the story of Thumbelina.

Her tears pooled; it was as if Finn's death had made her miss her mamma more, too. Nina coughed, doing her best to defeat the nerves that threatened to swamp her.

'Ah, Mrs McCarrick, here you are. Please sit down.' Mr Monroe extended his hand. He was as wide as he was tall and had a certain awkwardness about his manner, as if apologising in advance for his cumbersome demeanour. He pulled a chair away from the desk and awkwardly wedged himself in.

'Thank you. And I'm sorry not to have retuned your calls. I've had my head in the sand a bit.'

'Not at all, it's perfectly understandable, and believe me, I hated disturbing you. But as I mentioned on the phone, I have been *very* keen to talk to you.' Mr Monroe gave a tight smile and held his suit jacket closed over his shirtfront. He was far too big a man to be holed up in such a small office; she was sure that with one deep breath he might take all the air from the room. She placed her handbag on her lap and sat up straight.

'I really don't know what's going on,' she said. 'I had a call from school about fees, and I called the bank to try to see what had happened to the standing order to try to sort the situation, but I could only get through to an automated system that asked for numeric codes and passwords. The trouble is they have all been set up by Finn, and I have no idea what they are.' She shook her head at the absurdity of the situation. 'And when I eventually got through to an *actual* human, they said that as I had failed their security measures, they could only talk to the primary account holder – who is Finn.' She bit her lip, remembering the utter desolation at having to explain to the uninterested call handler that her husband had passed away and being told her best chance of success was to write a letter . . . 'Apparently we are behind on school fees, which I find hard to believe, as Finn has always been such a stickler for paying punctually. I need that sorted today, without question. It's become quite urgent.' She swallowed.

Mr Monroe sat forward and formed his fingers into a pyramid that hovered at his chest. She stared at his thick moustache, thinking it must be strange to have more hair on your face than your head as his bald pate shone under the lights.

'You have had *nothing* to do with your accounts?' he asked.

Nina shook her head, embarrassment heating her neck and chest. 'Not really. Finn always took care of the financial side of things. I haven't worked outside of the home.' She felt the blush on her cheeks, as if she needed to justify her position. She wanted to explain that looking after the big house, and Hampy when he lived with them, nursing him until he died, and childcare, running errands – all of it was work in itself. Not that she needed to explain her life to anyone; it had worked for her and Finn, and that was all that mattered. '*You've had to worry about money your whole life, but not any more. I will take care of you. Take care of us* . . .' Nina bit her lip, remembering how his words had filled her with peace, reassurance. She had felt any worry over her financial future slip from her bones, warmed by the fact her kids would never know what it felt like to try to squeeze their feet into last year's shoes, which she knew from experience made you feel as if you yourself didn't quite fit.

She looked across the desk at Mr Monroe. 'I had a bankcard and a couple of credit cards, and there is always cash in the house.' She felt the weight of the man's stare. 'The money, our money, is all tied up with the business, so it always felt more like Finn's responsibility than mine.' She closed her mouth, aware that she was gabbling, in part to hide her discomfort. His stare made her feel he was judging her. How could she begin to explain that the idea of looking after the accounts had never occurred to her, that it was just how it was?

'And your husband didn't discuss your current financial situation with you? Didn't say anything before he passed away?' He tapped his fingertips together, and she noticed that his fingernails were a little grubby, with half-moons of dirt sitting underneath the tips.

'No.' She shook her head. She felt nauseous and her legs began to shake. She pushed the soles of her boots down against the wooden floor. 'But I did speak to our lawyer, Mr Firth, who told me that Finn had left everything to me. I mean, I already knew. We had discussed what would happen under these circumstances, a long time ago.' She closed her eyes briefly. They had spoken casually over a cup of coffee while reading the Sunday papers together on the couch, sitting top to toe on the sofa in comfy socks, never believing the measures would be needed; they fully intended to live side by side, just as they were, until a ripe old age. It still shocked her that she was having this conversation, shocked her that she was a widow, shocked that the word was hers now. *Widow*. Would it ever get easier?

Mr Monroe sat back. She saw the rise and fall of his Adam's apple as he swallowed. 'I hate having to be the bearer of bad news, Mrs McCarrick, particularly in light of what you have been through.'

She felt the tremor of anxiety shudder through her limbs once more. 'Bad news, how?'

He looked up. 'I am afraid that when it comes to the money situation, things are not good.'

She unglued her tongue from the dry roof of her mouth. 'Not good?' Nina's mind raced to think what he might be referring to. As a couple, they had had many things to worry about over the years, but money had never been one of them.

Mr Monroe gave a wry laugh and looked up to a stain on the ceiling. She could tell that this wasn't easy for him. 'No, not good. In fact, things are about as bad as they can get. I didn't want to burden you with the details at the funeral.'

'Is the business in trouble?' Nina felt her chest tighten, thinking of all the people Finn employed: loyal men and women with mortgages and rent to pay, food to buy, kids and families to support. She felt sick at the idea of some of them losing their livelihoods.

'The business is gone.'

'The business is . . . ?' She must have misheard him.

'Gone. The business is gone.'

Nina stared at him. She felt her jaw open involuntarily and her stomach drop. His words were clear and audible, but they made no sense. Gone? What did that even mean?

'What do you mean, gone?' She laughed nervously after a moment's silence. She pictured Finn's latest project: a low-rise block of ten upscale apartments on a prime spot on the river, with a roof terrace to die for, state-of-the-art appliances, ecotechnology, twenty-four-hour security, the finest-quality materials, and five high-end retail units below, a restaurant, a deli . . . The land alone was worth millions.

'The bank foreclosed on the new development. Finn overstretched on the borrowing to complete the construction, then he ran out of time to complete the sales. Interest rates have been hiked and the bank called in the loan.' He splayed his palms as if it were that simple, that obvious. 'Everything else was mortgaged against the success of the new development, so it all fell apart quickly.'

She continued to stare at him, picturing her husband leaving for work every day with a smile on his face, sipping his coffee, kissing her firmly on the mouth, her strong man who kept all the cogs turning, so confident and assured. The man who provided their wonderful, wonderful life.

'I don't... don't understand.' Her voice was a cracked whisper.

Mr Monroe took a deep breath, and just as she had feared, all the air left the room.

'McCarrick Construction is bankrupt. And Finn's other companies sat under the umbrella of Gerhild Holdings.'

Gerhild was my mum's name. That's where it came from, all those years ago. Finn named it in tribute to her. I remember the day – his gesture made me cry.

'Gerhild Holdings is liable for the debt and there is no money to pay that debt.' He shook his head. 'There is a long list of creditors. Outstanding tax liabilities, land registry fees, wages, consultancy, utilities, advertising, service charges . . .' He shook his head again, and she wished he would stop. 'The list goes on and on.'

'I don't . . .' Nina struggled to get the words out. 'How . . . how much do we owe?' She had begun to run through a list of things she might be able to sell: things of value that might make a dent in the shortfall – anything she might have lying around the house that could help make up the deficit: her jewellery, a spare laptop . . . Her mind darted around the rooms of her home, trying to think of what might be secreted in drawers, anything valuable, and how best to shift it. She vaguely remembered Finn buying some vintage bottles of whisky. Maybe she could find them.

'All in all, close to eight million.'

There was a beat of silence while the figure flew from his mouth, bounced around the room and settled on her shoulders, where it would weigh her down, stroke her face in the early hours, disturb her sleep and irritate her sensibilities.

'Eight million pounds?' she squeaked.

'Yes.' He nodded.

Her limbs turned to concrete.

Eight million pounds, eight million pounds, eight million pounds . . .

The amount tumbled in her head on a never-ending loop. It was a huge, huge sum. The two sat in silence for a minute or two. Mr Monroe's hand hovered near a large box of tissues, as if he were expecting her to cry. She was, however, too numb for that.

When she recovered the power of speech, it was to ask the question that was the most important to her. 'Have I got enough money to pay the boys' school fees?' It seemed impossible, but perhaps somehow, somewhere, there was another account or . . .

The accountant gave a short snort of uncomfortable laughter and ran his hand over his moustache. He shook his head.

'I'm afraid you have no money at all. There is nothing left,' he said. 'Nothing.' He used his straightened hand to chop at the air. His tone was blunt, punchy, as if this were the approach he now considered necessary to make himself understood.

She tried to picture telling Connor, tried to picture her boys leaving the only school they had ever known, at a time when what they needed more than anything was stability and to be able to grieve in a safe, familiar environment.

I'll have to sell the house. Oh my God, our home! She placed a shaking hand over her mouth as the facts began to permeate. *It should sell quite quickly and then I can pay the school. How are we supposed to live until the sale of the house goes through? Will they let me use any of the proceeds? The overheads are huge. I'm sure they'll wait if I explain the situation to them.* Her head swam at the prospect. 'I don't know what to say. I feel sick.' She placed her hand on her stomach and took a deep breath. 'What am I supposed to do? What does that mean, no money? What the hell is going on?'

Mr Monroe smiled kindly. 'I know it's a lot for you to take in.'

'I need to get a job, I need to . . .' She shook her head, trying to think of what job she could get and how.

Mr Monroe spoke again. 'And I hate to think that I am the one who might be shedding light on Finn's untimely death . . .' He paused, as if warned off by the look she fired at him.

What exactly was he suggesting? Finn had died in an accident, and the last thing he would have wanted in the whole wide world was to leave behind the family he loved, especially now. She felt a surge of anger, not only at the man's words, but also at the possibility that what Mr Monroe was suggesting might be true. *You wouldn't do that to me, Finn, would you? You wouldn't create this mess and then leave me . . .*

Nina felt her skin prickle with sweat as she flushed hot, then cold. 'I never thought we'd leave The Tynings, but I know it'll need to be sold.' She nodded her acceptance of this fact. 'I love it, of course, it's our home, but at the end of the day it's only bricks and mortar. The funds it'll raise will give us some breathing space, time to plan what to do for the best, and we can downsize. At least it's fully paid for.' Even the idea of parting with the house she and Finn had built together, the family home where memories of him lurked in every room, was more than she could bear.

Mr Monroe's hand again hovered near the tissue box. 'Mrs McCarrick,' the man said, then paused again. 'I don't think you've fully understood the situation. Let me explain.'

She looked up at him, her mind racing, hoping to hear something positive, a solution.

He squared his shoulders, speaking slowly. 'The Tynings was an asset of the business. As I said, it was massively mortgaged.' And there it was again: that blunt, punchy tone.

Her chest felt tight. 'No. No, that's not right, it can't be.' She sat forward, adamant, leaning on the edge of the desk; it was a mistake, and Finn wasn't here to put him straight; she had to do it, had to take control. 'We paid cash for our house. Because we could!' She remembered

Connor as a toddler running through the rooms as she and Finn walked hand in hand around the vast empty spaces, planning for furniture and accessories. Finn had turned to her, kissed her on the mouth and whispered, 'This is our home, and it will always be our home, and it doesn't matter what happens outside of that front door, in here you will always be safe.'

'Yes . . .' he said. 'But Mr McCarrick took out mortgages on the property – a few over the years. I think it kept the wolf, or more specifically the bank, from the door on more than one occasion.'

How could you, Finn? How could you put our house in danger and not tell me? How could you do that?

'But . . .' She searched for the words. 'But how could that happen if I was living in it? How was I not made aware?' she asked.

'With only Mr McCarrick's name on the deeds, your signature or indeed your approval would not have been necessary. From a legal perspective,' he offered, suggesting that, morally, it was a whole other matter.

Nina slumped in her chair. She felt the strength leave her core as her thoughts tumbled in her brain. *How could I have been so bloody stupid? I trusted him, without question.*

'I can see that you were unaware of this. And again I am sorry to be the one to have to break it to you.'

She met the man's stare, struggling to breathe.

'They have served notice and you are being evicted.' Mr Monroe's stark words felt like a jolt.

Bang! There it was again, that door slam in her mind. Her body shook.

'Evicted?' she repeated, with a nervous twitch playing about her mouth, as if waiting for the punchline. This couldn't be right. She fought for breath.

'Yes. They will evict your family, seize your possessions, change the locks and put the house on the market.'

'Really?' Her voice faltered. 'When will they do that?'

'I can't tell you when exactly, but in my experience it will be sooner rather than later. I am only giving it to you straight like this because I need you to fully understand the events that will unfold and just who we are dealing with.'

She pictured the lock on the front door, for which she had a key nestling in her purse.

'And sadly,' he continued, 'they will probably sell it for a fraction of its value, because it's all about getting *some* money in as quickly as possible.'

'But . . . I . . . I don't . . .' She tried to speak, but instead bent forward, pulling her thick, curly hair from her face and throwing up into the soft-leather chocolate-brown interior of her Mulberry bag.

FOUR

Nina left the accountant's office with the strangest feeling that she was floating. Her feet didn't seem to be touching the ground, but she felt herself move slowly and deliberately towards the car.

We're losing our home! WE ARE LOSING OUR HOME! Oh my God, my God, Finn! I am scared. Eight million pounds. Eight million pounds. Eight million pounds.

She started driving. Suddenly she found herself at the school, with no memory of the minutes that had elapsed.

'Do you have an appointment?' The Headmaster's secretary leaned across the panelled reception desk, peering at Nina through her gold-framed glasses. Gripping her phone and car keys, she folded her arms across her chest, hoping this might stop the shaking. She was embarrassingly aware of the smell of sweat and vomit that lingered about her. She was always neat, always clean: she'd never forgotten the time when soap, scent and bubble bath were in short supply in her life. Right now her slovenly state was the least of her concerns. 'No, I don't have an appointment, and I would normally make one, but this is an emergency.'

The woman pursed her lips. 'Take a seat, Mrs . . . ?'

'McCarrick. I'm Connor and Declan's mum,' she added. She pictured the boys, at that very moment somewhere in this building, heads down and pens poised, without any idea of how their future rested on what might happen in the next few minutes. It made her feel sick all over again. She thought about the bag back in the car, full of vomit, from which she had extracted her wallet, keys, make-up and phone.

'Please take a seat and let me see if the Headmaster can squeeze you in.' She gestured towards a sofa.

Nina sank into the luxurious cream cushions.

What are you going to say to him? How can you pay? Think! I'm losing my home. Our house! Our beautiful house! Where will we go? Her thoughts were so noisy and intrusive, she feared she might have shouted them out loud. She clamped her teeth tightly just in case.

A few minutes later the woman returned. 'The Headmaster will see you now.'

'Thank you.' She breathed gratitude, unsure what her next port of call might have been had he refused. Standing on wobbly legs, she stepped towards the door. Her stomach churned with a familiar fear. It still petrified her, being in this building, having to interact with the educated and wealthy individuals who taught at or attended the school, even after a decade or more of doing just that. She knew it shouldn't; she'd met enough of the upper crust to know that, just because someone had money, it didn't mean they were smart, and just because they were educated, it didn't mean their opinions were any more valid than hers. She remembered George's mum trilling, while waving her bejewelled hands, 'George hates all things green, pacifically Brussels sprouts – it's an ongoing battle!' Nina had fought the desire to shout, 'You mean *specifically*! That's the right word. I know this!' Today the memory did little to bolster her.

The Headmaster's study was designed to reassure you that your hard-earned cash was being well spent, and that every penny you ploughed into this fine establishment was a sound investment in your child's future. The glass-fronted cabinet was bursting with trophies and photographs of the various sports teams holding shields and looking triumphant, and on the cork noticeboard next to it, the most recent good news item cut from a newspaper was strategically pinned.

'Mrs McCarrick, how are you?' He shook her hand, cupping her palm inside both of his.

She breathed out. This was a loaded question. Where to begin? She reminded herself to pace her words; there was a very real danger that she might simply vent the panic swirling inside her. She knew Mr Moor would respond best to a calm, logical discussion without a trace of hysteria.

'It's a very difficult time,' she managed, sitting in the chair in front of his desk, which he indicated as he took his seat.

'Of course. We were all so very sorry to hear about Mr McCarrick. Connor and Declan's tutors were sent a bulletin and have been keeping a close eye on them.' He nodded, his tone respectfully low.

'Thank you,' she offered sincerely; it meant a lot to know someone was looking out for them in her absence. 'They're coping amazingly well.' She stopped; Connor wouldn't have thanked her for being so personal with the Headmaster. She coughed to clear her throat, feeling embarrassed.

'I had a call from Mr Paulson,' she began.

'Yes . . .' He nodded, indicating that of this he was already aware.

'There has been a bit of a mix-up with the fees.'

Again he nodded his neatly coiffed head. 'A mix-up? How so?'

'He told me they haven't been paid in full for this term.' She sucked her cheeks in, trying to summon the spit that might aid her speech.

'That's right, and so far, no monies have been paid for the last term either,' he said steadily.

She felt her pseudo-confident façade all but disappearing.

'The thing is, Mr Moor, I am at the moment sorting my situation with the accountant and would like to ask if it's possible that I could delay payment.' She spoke quickly, deciding not to take a pause and give him the chance to deny her request. 'It won't be for long – just until we have sorted our accounts. I am sure this isn't the first time this has happened.' She tried out a hesitant smile for good measure.

Mr Moor sighed. 'No, not the first time.' He gave a knowing smile. 'And regretfully I must say to you what I say to all who make a similar request.' He drew breath and gave a slow blink in a most reverential manner. 'Everybody would like to eat in Michelin-starred restaurants, but when the pockets are empty, it simply isn't possible. Without the funds, you would be turned away at the door.'

Nina stared at the man, astonished, hating his well-practised, glib response. It felt all the more demeaning in the face of her situation.

'And I'm afraid that even if it were within my hands to action such a deferment, it might not be advisable. I have never in my experience known a financial problem to get less knotty with more time and with more debt accruing. Quite the opposite, in fact.' He smiled, his perfect teeth glinting at her. 'And trust me, the only people who suffer with such a delay are those to whom the monies are owed.'

Nina sat forward in the chair. Placing her fingertips on the edge of his desk and fighting the desire to explode, she implored, 'I don't think you understand, Mr Moor. My boys have lost their father, things are in a state of flux, and I am just about hanging on.' This admission caused tears to prick her eyes. 'The one constant the boys have is their school. All I am asking is for a bit of flexibility.'

'I think the school has already shown a lot of flexibility. The fact that the fees are unpaid in full for this current term should have instantly precluded them from returning after the Christmas break, but we gave Mr McCarrick the benefit of the doubt.'

'You . . . you spoke to him?' This was news to her.

'Yes. He sat where you are now and his speech was pretty much the same as yours, give or take the odd word.'

She pushed her thighs against the seat, feeling the now familiar flash of humiliation at being kept in the dark. She swiped the beads of sweat from her forehead with her palm. 'I didn't know this, Mr Moor, and all I am asking is for a little bit more time.' She had no idea where she could get the money from, but she would find a way.

'And I am trying to tell you that you have already had more time. And that time has, sadly, run out,' he said flatly.

Nina shook her head, feeling the anger rise. 'I don't believe this. Connor is about to enter his exam year. He plays his rugby here, it's where all his friends are, and it's all he has ever known. Declan, too – they are Kings Norton boys!' Her voice was rising uncontrollably.

'And we have given them the very best education during their time here, and we of course wish them every success for the future.' He lifted his chin as if in conclusion.

'We have paid over half a million pounds to this school – more if we consider the donations, prizes, trips, sports events . . .' She shook her head. 'And now, when I am most vulnerable, when I have come to you to ask for help, *this* is how you treat me?'

'I can assure you it's not personal, Mrs McCarrick. We are a business and these are the rules, and if I break the rules for you, I have to break the rules for all, and we wouldn't last very long like that, would we?' His condescension made it sound like he were chastising a child.

'Not personal?' She levelled her gaze at him. 'You make the kids sound like any other commodity, but they are little boys with fragile natures and hearts.' Her voice cracked. 'We paid that huge sum of money to your school because we believed you were going to help make our sons into good people, lovely citizens of the planet, but if this is their example, if this is how you treat people in need . . .'

'We have fourteen pupils with offers for Oxford and Cambridge this year. That's quite something.'

She stared at him. 'What has that got to do with anything? Are they nice people? Are those kids happy?'

'I think we are done here, Mrs McCarrick.' He reached for a sheet of paper and seated his glasses on his nose, as if to show he had other matters to attend to. 'I wish your boys well, but it's just the way it is. Kings Norton is an expensive club, and membership costs.'

Nina stood up and spoke steadily and clearly. 'I feel angry. Not at you – at myself, for ever thinking that this was a club I wanted my boys to belong to.'

The Headmaster looked up at her with narrowed eyes, and adjusted his spectacles. 'Now I am most confused. Only minutes ago you were asking that they be allowed to remain.'

His condescension was the final straw. Nina drew on her life before she had married, before she had been given access to wander within these esteemed walls, before she had been told the right and wrong way of behaving. Leaning on the desk, she spoke levelly. 'Screw you, Mr Moor.'

She swept from the building, hoping that Finn's parting shot had been similar.

Give or take the odd word.

◆ ◆ ◆

Nina drove over to the nearby lay-by, where she sat in her usual spot. Her legs shook. She put the heater on, until she realised her tremors were due to fear and adrenaline and not the temperature.

'Eight million pounds, Finn? I can't believe it. It won't sink into my head!' She spoke to her reflection in the windscreen, alarmed by the expression of naked fear that greeted her.

She used the time waiting for the kids to come out of school to phone their lawyer.

'I am so sorry for your loss. I liked Finn. I liked him very much.' Mr Firth sounded choked.

'He liked you too.' She rubbed her eyes, suddenly exhausted. 'I wanted to ask you about the will?'

'It is pretty much as we discussed before. Finn stated that in the event of his death, everything is left to you, after any and all outstanding debts have been met, yada yada, the usual.' He paused.

'But that's what I am concerned about, Mr Firth. There is so much debt.'

'Yes, I *am* now aware of the situation.' He spoke softly, thankfully sparing her the need to elaborate.

'I suppose my question is, is there anything we can do to keep some money or hide something? I know how that sounds, and I don't mean anything illegal. I'm just trying to find a way to keep my kids' heads above water.'

His response sent a bolt of anxiety through her gut.

'I'm afraid it's a bit late for that kind of planning. If we had known the bankruptcy was looming, or just how bad things were, we might have been able to do something, put stuff in others' names, that kind of thing. But we didn't know. It all came about very quickly. I know Finn tried all he could to get the sales through quicker, but he ran out of time. I'm as shocked as you.'

He ran out of time . . . The phrase spun around her head. *Didn't he just.* Nina tried to imagine his face as the car broke through the barrier and careered down the embankment. *Was he afraid or calm? Shocked or resigned?* Nina shook her head, refusing to believe that her husband's death was anything other than a terrible accident.

She held the phone close to her face, feeling the last of her safety ropes sliced clean by the blade of the lawyer's reasoning.

'There is a life insurance policy.'

'There is?' For the first time since she could remember, she felt a surge of hope ripple through her. It was hard not to give in to a smile of relief.

'Oh, that's great news!' She threw her head back, offering up a silent prayer of thanks.

She heard the lawyer swallow. 'It's not as wonderful as you might think.' His words were a pin that deflated her bubble of happiness. 'It pays about a million pounds, but that money will be considered part of Finn's assets and will be taken to help settle some of the debt. I know the house is being taken, and the creditors will all be trying to grab what they can, knowing they are one of many who are owed, and if they don't pounce first or shout loudest, they might end up with nothing.'

'How much can the bailiffs take?'

He let out a sigh, as if reluctant to answer the question. 'In short, anything of value that isn't a structural fixture or is on your person, so your wedding ring and such is safe, but other than that, pretty much everything, unless an item can be proved to be of educational necessity or a disability aid, that kind of thing.'

'Oh God, I need to go and move stuff. I need to go and hide things! I need to get boxes from the basement, and I need to act fast!'

'Yes,' he confirmed, with what sounded like relief.

Nina cracked the window a little, grateful for the lifting breeze in the small, safe space. She found it hard to concentrate on any one thing as a tsunami of thoughts and ideas tumbled through her mind. She pictured tearing through the house looking for what might be of most value before the bailiffs arrived – and then where would they go? Where on earth would they go? She pictured her boys' faces as she told them they would not be coming back to school. Both ideas were too horrific to contemplate. She thought about their friends, neighbours and acquaintances who had brought casseroles to the house, written heartfelt cards of sympathy and held her tightly but briefly upon leaving. She pictured her brothers-in-law, wondering if they could help. Who did she feel comfortable asking for money from? How many of them could she confidently pick up the phone to and ask if they could all come and stay for a while . . . ? The horrible truth was that she didn't know. She made the decision to hit the phone the moment she got home.

'I'm so sorry, Mrs McCarrick.' She jumped at the sound of his voice; she was so lost in her thoughts she had quite forgotten he was on the end of the line.

'Yes.' Everyone was sorry; it didn't help her one jot.

'I know it's probably of little comfort, but we have a farm out at Saltford. There are empty barns and a lot of space. If you need storage – and you might – please let me send one of the horseboxes down to collect and keep anything you might want for you for as long as you need.'

'Thank you. I will think about what I need to pack and how to get it done.'

'Please do. And I can't stress enough that time is of the essence.'

'Right. Thank you.' She knew she had to go home and start making calls and packing, but wished she could instead run, and keep running.

'It's the least I can do for Finn. He was a good man and often did me a favour. We wanted a stable block converting to holiday lets. McCarrick Construction did a magnificent job and his invoice was very fair. Anyway' – he coughed – 'the offer's there.'

'Thank you.'

Minutes later she heard the glorious, familiar sound of her son's laughter.

She rolled her window down a sliver further, watching Connor and his friends approach through the rearview mirror.

'No way!' Charlie shouted, and shoved George on the arm. 'I think *you* like her and this is your way of distracting us, by ribbing me.'

'I don't!' George protested, 'I like Florence, which is pointless because she thinks I'm a dick.'

'Because you *are* a dick,' Charlie added.

'Thanks for that!' George laughed. 'And as for you, Connor, not only are you a dick, but you are an unpopular dick, and girls like Phoebe only go out with the popular boys. She is way out of your league.'

Connor placed his hand on his heart and feigned being wounded. She could see from his hesitant stance that he was trying to join in, trying for normal, as if he weren't living under the wearying shadow of grief. 'Hey, I know I'm not popular, but playing rugby for the first team can't harm my chances.'

'Mate, it's your *only* chance!' Charlie slapped his friend's back.

The sound of their comical banter and easy laughter made Nina's stomach lurch. She remembered when she had enrolled Connor into the primary school, the pride she felt at being able to drop into conversation that her boy was going to be attending. It had felt wonderful. In her mind, it elevated her, as tangible proof that she had risen above her life of hardship. She was no longer a poor girl from Portswood, Southampton: her son went to Kings Norton College, and that was really something. She wore her wealth like a suit of armour; it offered protection from all that had frightened her growing up. Marrying the newly wealthy Finn meant she didn't have to worry about hunger, discomfort or displacement; their financial position gave her stability. Or so she had believed.

'Smoke and mirrors,' she whispered, 'smoke and mirrors,' as she watched her boy flick his long fringe from his eyes before opening the door to the passenger seat.

'How was your day, love?' she asked, as calmly as she could manage.

'Okay,' he responded as he pulled his phone from his pocket and began texting, likely someone who he had seen in person not a minute before.

'I saw you chatting to George and Charlie. What are they up to?'

Connor shrugged. 'Not much.'

Nina nodded and stared ahead. Today silence was welcome.

Soon Declan appeared – relatively chatty, though a little more subdued than was usual, but that was no less than she expected. She did her best to nod in the right places, but all she could think of was telling the boys of the situation they were in. So many questions spun in her mind. Would it be better to tell them right away and give them a chance to say goodbye to their teachers, their friends? Or to give them one more night of blissful, uninterrupted sleep, and let them enjoy the normality of their routine? If only she could consult with Finn. Nina pictured him again, leaving for work with a smile and a wink, sipping his coffee and kissing her on the cheek.

'I could have helped. You could have trusted me. I would have liked that chance.'

'What?' Connor turned his head towards her.

'Nothing.' She cleared her throat, surprised that she had spoken out loud.

Nina pulled into the driveway and tried to hold the front door key steady in her shaking hand. It was hard not to consider how many more times she would perform this ritual, walking into the only proper home she and her boys had ever known. Her eyes lingered on the decadent vase of blooms and the wide, plush staircase. Suddenly she felt the flush of wonder at the magnificence of it all, just as she had when they had first moved in: when it took an age to sink in that this fine property was actually hers, it was her key that fitted the lock! She had the same feeling she got when a wonderful holiday was coming to an end. The sight of the sea in stunning moonlit iridescence, the sand that felt extra fine under the soles of her tanned feet, the clink of ice in a glass . . . The whole house was suddenly alive with the same awe she felt on the first day she saw it, because she knew that, very soon, she would be leaving it all behind. A little voice in her head spoke calmly: *You didn't really think this was your life, did you, Nina? Didn't really think that someone like you deserved all this?*

She looked at the grain of the front door and committed it to memory. Her heart lurched at the prospect of what might come next. Where might they go? It was as if the problem were too huge to consider, and she could only see the vast sum of money, as if written on a cheque in the air: *Eight million pounds . . .*

'When you're ready.' Connor stood slightly to her right and nodded at the door, irritated by his mum's unhurried pace.

The boys dumped their bags at the foot of the stairs and clambered up to their bedrooms. She stood frozen in the foyer. What had she done with her life, other than marry well? She had sworn when she left Portswood that she would never be poor again, that she would accomplish something, take up nursing – the profession that had called to her during her childhood, perhaps a result of losing her mum and wanting to learn, as best she could, how to fix people. But what had she actually done? Other than becoming a mum and learning how to arrange flowers? Not much. Without Finn and his money, she was helpless.

The reverie broke. Nina walked briskly into the kitchen and flicked the switch. The light reflected the diamond-like sparkle in the black granite counter-tops.

She pictured herself at eight years of age, standing with a chipped plate held to her chest, turning in a circle, looking for a place to sit or stand to eat the stew her gran had made for supper, the thick gravy of which threatened to slop from the shallow sides with every move she made. 'Sit and eat! You're making me dizzy,' Gran had shouted, but that was the trouble: she couldn't find a space. The chairs were piled high with laundry, both clean and dirty, and the drop-leaf table was crowded with all manner of clutter: a stack of newspapers, and seedlings that had taken root in the soil-filled bottoms of old cordial bottles, which had been lopped in half for this very purpose. There was a pair of boots with one sole flapping like a thirsty mouth, awaiting glue, and a fancy padded rainbow-filled box of make-up that belonged to her Aunty June. How she would have loved to stick her little hands inside and dabble in the unknown, plaster her face with the powders and preparations that her aunt was so deft with, applied liberally before she went out on the town in her short, short skirts. But she was too shy to ask.

'For the love of God, sit down and eat your bloody tea!' her gran had barked again. Nina jumped, her daydream of blue sparkly eyeshadow broken, and suddenly the gravy was dripping like a sludgy, dark waterfall over her white school shirt, onto her skirt, and dribbling onto the hairy carpet.

'Sweet Jesus!' her gran had shouted, which meant another jump of fear and the chewy blocks of stewing steak tumbling like tiny meat rocks down her front. The dog ran over, hoovering up the treat and licking at the carpet. Tiggy laughed into her hand, her grandad turned his doughy face away, as if he might be able to distance himself from the whole affair. Nina remembered looking up at her gran, her legs shaking as she waited to feel the full force of her wrath . . .

Nina shook the memory from her mind. She needed to focus. She picked up the phone and called Finn's brother Anthony, rehearsing in her head what she might say. '*Hi, Anthony, I know this is a little out of the blue, but we need somewhere to stay . . .*' *You can't just blurt that!* She tried again. '*Hello Anthony, I was hoping to ask you a favour . . .*' She felt a combination of relief and disappointment when the answering machine eventually kicked in. 'Hi, Anthony, it's Nina, erm . . . if you could give me a shout, that would be great. Thanks.'

Michael answered her call immediately. 'Nina, it's good to hear from you.' She felt uncomfortable at his intonation, as if the lack of contact could be laid squarely on her shoulders, hers the responsibility to call him, and not the other way around. 'How are you?' He kept his tone low.

She closed her eyes, as if the words might flow better if she could hide a little. 'Not so good actually, Michael.'

'I'm sure. That was a daft question, of course you're not good. *I* can't believe he's gone, so God only knows what it's like for you and the kids.'

She felt her muscles unknot a little at his words of empathy. 'The thing is, Michael, we are in a bit of a fix.'

'Oh?'

Nina steadied herself against the counter-top. 'We need to get out of the house, it's being sold, and I was wondering if we might be able to come and stay with you and Marjorie for a bit.'

'Come and stay with us?' His tone made the request sound ridiculous.

'Yes,' she managed.

She heard him swallow. 'For how long?'

'I don't know. I wouldn't ask if we weren't desperate.' She pictured her dad, hands in his pockets, asking at the next shop, 'I need a job. I need it, man. I have two kids, and things are tight . . .' She remembered the stench of desperation that had hung around him and the way he turned to her after each rejection with a big false smile that made her tummy flip. She now knew how he felt. And it killed her.

'Desperate?'

She ignored the humorous inflection to his question.

'Yes. We are bankrupt. Things are pretty bad.'

'Wow. Bankrupt, really? I'm shocked. How come?'

She paused. 'I guess a combination of things outside of our control, one thing too many for us to cope with, and things have folded.'

'I feel terrible, Nina, of course I want to help you out, but we are tight on space. Marjorie's mum lives with us now and so that's the spare room gone.'

'I didn't know that.'

'Yes, ever since her fall . . .' His voice trailed off.

She felt her energy fade. 'Does Anthony have the space?' she pushed.

'He's just sold his house. He and Netta are downsizing to a flat in Bournemouth, but not before going on a three-month cruise. Their stuff is in storage. I don't know what else to suggest.'

'That's okay, Michael,' she lied.

'Look, if you are really stuck, then of course you can all come and crash on the lounge floor for a night or two.'

She noted the way his volume had dropped, as if hiding this offer from Marjorie. It told her all she needed to know.

The call finished with the usual politeness and she stared out of the window, her eyes roving the covered wood store. It gave her an idea.

'Just stepping out for a minute, boys – be right back!' she called up the stairs. She walked out into the dark, making her way along the winding road, using her phone as a torch. Before she lost her nerve, she knocked on Mrs Appleton's door. The neighbour had been one of the first to arrive in the wake of the news of Finn's passing, and had brought a peach cobbler, along with a prayer card. Nina closed her eyes, thinking she might be the answer to her particular prayer.

'Oh, Nina! Hello, dear.' The old woman spoke with clear relief that she recognised the person rapping on the door in the dark, her gnarled hand at her chest.

'Mrs Appleton, I am sorry to disturb you, and this is going to sound like a very odd request.'

The woman's brow wrinkled with curiosity as she remained half hidden behind the door.

'The boys and I need somewhere to stay for a while and I was wondering if you had ever considered having lodgers here, or whether we might stay in your guest lodge in the garden?' The low, flat-roofed building sat at the bottom of her rambling garden.

'A lodger?' The old lady fingered her pearl necklace.

'Yes. I wouldn't ask, only we are a bit stuck.' Nina tried out the false smile that had stood her dad in good stead for all those years. 'We would be no trouble and only clutter up a couple of your bedrooms, or as I mentioned, we could take the guest lodge?'

'It's a trailer!' Mrs Appleton pointed out.

'Yes, it would be fine. We'd be happy out there.'

The woman shook her head. 'It would not be fine. You would not be happy out there. It's out of the question. It has a big hole in the roof. It's waterlogged, ready for knocking down – no one can stay in it.'

'I see.' Nina took a step closer. 'Well, then how would you feel about having lodgers in your home for a while?' It took all her courage to be this pushy, but desperate times called for desperate measures. 'I'd be happy to pay, Mrs Appleton. I have some money and can get more, once Finn's affairs are settled.'

'I don't want your money! Good Lord!' The woman's lip curled in repugnance as she retreated a little further inside. 'And lodging here is out of the question too. Mr Busby hates strangers and noise and children.'

'Mr Busby?'

'My cat.'

'But . . . but we are *people*, and we need help, and I am asking you for that help, and he is a cat! A cat!' She hadn't meant to raise her voice.

The old woman pushed the door until she was speaking through a small crack. 'You can't come here in the dead of night and shout at me!'

'I'm sorry, I didn't mean to shout at you,' Nina stammered. She chose not to point out that it was only teatime.

'And the fact is, Mr Busby is my cat and this is his home.' With that, she closed the door and the light disappeared from inside the hallway.

Nina retreated into the dark, walking along the lane with her heart hammering in her chest. Grinding her teeth, she felt the stirring of anger, even hatred, towards the man she grieved for. He had placed them in this situation and she had been swept along like flotsam on the tide. 'What the fuck am I supposed to do now, Finn?' she shouted into the night air. She whipped her head around to check no one was within hearing distance.

Back in the kitchen she grabbed two fat steaks from the fridge and then got to work on the onion rings and fresh garden peas. Preparing the food helped block out all the upsetting and intrusive thoughts that rattled around inside her skull. After supper she would start to pack.

She called to the boys to come and eat. Eventually both boys loped into the kitchen and took up their regular seats at the table. She hovered, sipping a glass of water. The boys ate quickly, eager to get back to their rooms where they too could drop the act and do as they pleased.

'I need my kit for the holiday training, Mum.' Connor swallowed a chunk of steak. 'Coach says he wants me to bulk up a bit, so more protein, and I'm going to start lifting some weights.'

She gave a small nod. 'Have you ever thought about joining another rugby club outside of school?' She hoped she sounded nonchalant.

Both Connor and Declan let out loud bursts of laughter, as if she had told the funniest joke in the world.

'Another rugby club?' Connor stared at her. 'There *is* no better place to play rugby. We have produced more England players than any other school. We are at the top of the school league for the fifth year in a row. We have pitches that professional teams come and practise on. The squad is trained by an ex-international coach. What other club could top that?'

'I just thought it might be nice to meet other people, broaden your horizons a bit.' Nina busied herself at the sink.

Connor returned to his supper, as if her suggestion were so crazy it didn't even warrant a reply. When his plate was clean, he scooted his chair back from the table. 'Thanks,' he called as he raced up the stairs.

Declan laid his knife and fork on his plate. 'Mum?'

'Yes, darling?' She looked up. 'Oh, Dec, don't cry.' She rushed to him and held him close in a hug.

'When I start laughing, I start to cry. It's like my eyes won't let me feel happy. They remind me that Dad died.' He pulled away so he could see her face. 'And today was horrible. Something keeps . . . keeps happening to me,' he stammered.

'What keeps happening?'

'I was chatting to Harri and I forgot, Mum. I forgot. I forgot about Dad. And I was looking forward to telling him about my Chemistry project and was going to ask him if he had any more ideas about the holidays, and then I remembered he wasn't here any more and I couldn't breathe and I got a pain here' – he touched his fingers to his breastbone – 'and Harri got me a glass of water and told Mrs Dupré.'

'That was kind of Harri.' She smoothed his thick, dark hair. 'One thing I do know is that Daddy wouldn't want you to be sad when you thought about him. He always wanted to make us happy.' She was aware of the slight rush to her words; the phrases felt slightly sour in her mouth. She saw Mrs Appleton closing the front door on her, pictured Mr Monroe as he shifted uncomfortably in his chair, saying, 'Things are not good . . .' She was unsure of what his dad would say or want, unsure of the man she had been married to for all these years, the man who had consigned them all to live in a downward spiral over which she had no control. It was awful to feel the cracks appear in the love she had for him, knowing there was no chance of seeing him, of making it right.

'I can't feel happy, Mum. I miss him so much.'

Her son's tears fell anew and it was all she could do not to sink to her knees and cry with him.

After the boys were tucked up in their beds, Nina crept into Finn's study and switched on the desk lamp and the computer. She let her fingers trail the bookshelves and wondered where to start, unsure of what she was looking for. The computer blinked at her, requesting a password. She went through all of their names, and then tried the places they had visited and loved, all to no avail; Finn had clearly gone for something less obvious. She then entered the same all over again, but added their ages or the dates they had made the trips, anything she could think of, hoping to get lucky.

She didn't.

'You bloody fool, Nina!'

Frustration made her slap the desktop, which only served to sting her palm. She flexed and splayed her fingers, trying to ease the sharp pain. She pulled open the deep bottom drawer of the desk and found a black leather folder. It was empty, but inside the metal rings had pressed into the soft contours of the calf leather, suggesting that it had once been full of weighty documents.

'Why would you empty your folders? How long were you hiding things from me?' she whispered, running her hands through her hair and feeling the anger grow in her gut. 'How could you do this to me, Finn?'

In the middle drawer under a stack of boating magazines was a bundle of letters, only about half of which had been opened, from a company called Mackintosh and Vooght. They had all been addressed to the business premises in Bradford-on-Avon, and each one was branded with ugly red letters 'URGENT' and 'DO NOT IGNORE'. She could only imagine how it must have felt to receive these daily, and again pictured the mask he wore, his jovial tone, kidding her that all was well, letting her pore over swatches of fabric for the new curtains in the spare room – and all the while he was edging backwards, each step taking him closer to the cliff edge . . . His subterfuge hit her again and filled her with rage.

'*Pay now in full or we will have no choice but to commence proceedings to recover,*' she read aloud. '*Each missed payment is incurring an added penalty of five per cent over and above your original debt . . .*' Nina couldn't bear to look at any more. She returned them to the drawer and closed it. As she moved the keyboard of the computer, the desk jotter shifted and she saw something underneath. She picked up the keyboard and found a white envelope underneath.

'*Nina,*' she read in her husband's instantly recognisable hand.

Her heart jumped. He had written to her? Her fingers shook as she balanced the slim envelope on her palm and brought it to her nose, inhaling the faintest scent of his smoky cologne. Slowly, carefully, she turned it over in the lamplight, finding it was open. The letter inside was just three lines long. She knew her husband's script well and could tell instantly that it had been written hurriedly.

Her heart felt like it might leap from her chest as she scanned the words.

> *My Nina,*
> *Things are hard for me – I feel like I am living in a world made of glass & with every day comes a new pressure that is pushing down down down & I don't know what will break first, me or my world . . .*

That was all.

She held the paper to her chest, then looked at it again. She turned it over and scanned it a second time, a third, ridiculously hoping that under closer scrutiny new words or vital information might suddenly appear. She was thankful that she was sitting, fearing she might faint otherwise. She pictured his face on the morning he left the house for the last time. There had been no clue that anything was amiss. She was sure that if he had been in an altered state of mind she would have seen it, sensed it. The little voice echoed in her mind again.

Would you really, Nina? He kept all of this from you! You were clueless, in the dark.

Tears dripped from her chin as she scanned the lines again. She thought of Mr Monroe's words: 'And I hate to think that I am the one who might be shedding light on Finn's untimely death . . .'

Nina began to shake. She reread the note, feeling fairly certain that this was the beginning of her husband's goodbye.

She folded the letter, placed it in her pocket and ran out of the room, across the soft carpet of the landing and down the stairs, grabbing her car keys from the hall table en route. Creeping from the house, she locked the front door and ran to the car.

She carefully, slowly, turned the car around despite her shaking hands, and drove through the gates. When she cleared the gravel drive she put her foot down. Hard. Her heart thumped as she increased her speed, racing through streets slick with the residue of rainfall.

The note seemed to pulse in her pocket. She saw the words vividly imprinted in her mind. Her knuckles twisted against the leather of the steering wheel, gripping it so hard her fingers turned white. Every muscle was coiled, tense, expectant. She screeched around bends, head down, ignoring the speedometer and racing up and down the gears. Let the police try to stop her; she was in the mood for a fight. Suddenly there she was: on the top ridge in Alexandra Park.

She parked under a large tree and cut the engine. She balled her fists and punched the steering wheel as hard as she could, over and over, thumping her head back on the headrest repeatedly.

'What have you done? What have you done to us, Finn? Eight million pounds! Eight million pounds!' she screamed. 'How did you manage that? You have destroyed us! Destroyed our lives and now it seems there is the chance that you took yourself out of the bloody equation, just jumped and left us to cope without you . . . How could you do that to me, to the kids? How could you? Did you do that? Did you leave me on purpose?' Tears of anger, frustration and sadness choked her.

She jumped out of the car and paced back and forth, before kicking the wheel with all her might. 'How could you? You bastard!' she screamed at the top of her voice. An owl hooted its response. Under any other circumstances this might have made her laugh, but not tonight. 'Sod off!' she shouted at the poor creature as it fled.

She slunk back to the car and climbed inside, where she laid her head on the steering wheel, feeling all of her energy seep out of her. She stared over the hills and down the ridge towards the city she loved, then closed her eyes for a moment.

When she tried to open them, they were stuck together with a thick paste of mascara and tears.

'The thing is, if you left me by choice, then I didn't know you, and if you felt you couldn't tell me about our situation, then you didn't know me. And if that is the case then what did we have, Finn? I feel like I have been living a lie and I don't know how much more I can take.'

She stared at the twinkling lights of the city, muted in the haze of rain; they looked like amber-coloured stars. She had come up here with Finn when they first met, both intent on getting the kissing business out of the way, both nervous, shy. In his newly acquired flashy car, they had sat awkwardly until she suggested they best go home. 'My dad'll be waiting for me . . .' she had offered, knowing that even the confident Finn wouldn't want to upset Big Joe.

She felt her face collapse, thinking of everyone she loved who had gone: her mamma, dad, gran, grandad, aunts, uncles and her Finn. She looked up through the window and wondered how many of them were trying to offer comfort and support from a place so out of reach. She pressed her head to the glass and whispered, hoping her words would rise up and reach them, 'You need to try harder. I need more help. I feel like I am falling apart and I don't know how much longer I can hang on.'

Slowly she drove up to the house and cut the engine. Every sound seemed magnified. Once safely inside, she peeped in on the boys; both slept soundly. Padding across the landing, Nina walked straight to the bedroom, where she teetered past her dressing room and bathroom, shunning her usual bedtime routine of make-up removal and teeth cleaning. She threw herself down onto the bed, where she buried her face in her husband's sweatshirt and cried until she ran out of tears. She hated that her memory of him was changing, distorting the last solid foundation on which her life was built. She looked around the bedroom. It made her sad and reflective to be placing her marriage under a microscope in a way that she knew she never would have done had Finn not been killed. This only confused her even more. She felt bereft and lonely and despite her muddle of thoughts would have given anything to feel his arms around her.

Eventually she sat up and held the covered pillow to her chest. She rested against the headboard of their wide bed. A fresh wave of tears found their way to the surface; Nina scooted them away with her sleeve and wished they would stop, beyond exhausted by her sadness. She stared into the darkness of the night. The only light came from the walkway to the terrace where muted beams illuminated the path to the house. She had not changed the bed linen since his death, unable to think that the essence of him would be laundered away, preferring to sleep with his scent on the softened sheets and the feel of him around her, cocooning her in the night, soothing away the nightmares.

Only this wasn't a nightmare, it was her real, waking life and she didn't know how she was going to survive it.

FIVE

After a fitful sleep, Nina awoke before dawn. The boys still safely in bed, she tied her hair up with a square scarf and headed down to the basement to tape together cardboard boxes. She brought them upstairs, slowly filling them with ornaments and lamps from her bedroom as quietly as she could, packing stealthily, without any clue as to where she would next be setting up home.

I need to rent somewhere, anywhere. I've probably got enough cash for a few weeks' rent on something basic, and I need to get a job. But first, you have to pack stuff up, Nina, pack it away and keep it safe . . .

She reached her hand to the back of the drawer in her bedside cabinet and stopped suddenly. She pulled out the fragile gold-coloured matchbox and stared at the words '*Tordenskjold tœndstikker*' still visible on the aged container, along with a faded picture of a rather grand-looking admiral on the lid.

There were only a couple of clear memories that stood out in her mind. In one – she could only have been a young three, making it not long before her mother died – she was standing by a window, and there was snow on the ground outside, the image framed in her mind by the heavy red-and-white-checked curtains. Her mum had placed a marble in the palm of her hand; she heard her voice clearly and could picture the embroidered edge of her smocked blouse. 'This is a little world,

Nina.' Nina had run her fingers over the cool glass, marvelling at the shiny round thing with the blue wispy wave captured in its centre. 'And if ever the real world feels too big or too scary, remember that it is nothing more than a little ball travelling through space and it fits right into the palm of your hand, and the more courage you have, the braver you are when facing it, the easier it is to conquer!'

Nina carefully pushed the little cardboard insert, taking the marble out of the small box, rolling it between her thumb and forefinger before closing her palm around the cool glass.

'Oh, Mum. I don't think the world has ever felt so big or scary to me as it does right now. I'm going to take each day as it comes and not think too far ahead. As for conquering it? I think that might be a little way off.' She kissed the little glass orb and placed it carefully in its cotton wool nest before closing the matchbox and placing it in the soft, navy-coloured handbag she was now using.

She made breakfast for the boys and drove them to school. Every moment she thought it might be appropriate to tell them what was happening, like during the ride that morning, she lost her nerve. She wanted to preserve their happiness for as long as she was physically able.

Back home she spent the day in limbo, packing up the study and starting on the sitting room before retreating to her bed and lying there, stealing minutes of sleep from the thoughts, ideas and fears that crowded her mind. It was like a hundred people were all shouting at her, all at once, each of the belief that the louder they shouted, the more chance they had of being heard. The reality was that no one thought was distinct, and all were part of the wall of noise that blocked anything coherent. She imagined screaming at Finn, and then trying to tell the boys of their situation in a way that would not damage the memory of their dad. It was an impossible position. And one she could barely reconcile. It felt easier, if not vital, to shut down and nap in the grubby bed where her husband's shape lingered. Before she knew it, it was school collection time and once again she was forced from her refuge.

She met Declan, and the two of them walked along Milsom Street alone; George's mum was dropping Connor at home after their rugby match on the outskirts of town. Declan was long overdue for a haircut, and it was important that things like this were not allowed to slip, important that she kept up the standard for her boys. Usually they went to the fancy salon where she had been a regular for years and where her curly blonde locks were kept in tiptop condition from regular trims and treatments. Her visits there were as much a social activity as they were about keeping her unruly tresses in good shape. She had liked to sit anonymously in the leather chair and listen to the hubbub of gossip all around her. She had cash in her purse, but now knew how important it was to keep hold of it. Today she was taking Declan to a barber for the first time, where his cut would be a fraction of the cost.

'So what are we going to do for the holiday, Mum?' Declan asked. Shop windows screamed of discounts, and the stores all seemed to feature soft wool products and warm lighting, trying to draw people in during the lull between Christmas and Easter. One sign read 'Winter's nearly done! Look towards spring!' but she could see no sunshine in sight.

'I don't know yet, darling,' she said as lightly as she could. Forget the holiday, she didn't know where they were going to live! *How* they were going to live! The realisation shattered her thoughts like a pick to the brain. 'It doesn't really matter, does it? We'll have fun no matter what.'

Her phone buzzed in her pocket. Connor. A barrage of screams and shouts instantly sent her heart rate soaring.

'Mum!' he yelled. She heard the panic in his voice and her stomach leapt into her throat, was he hurt? In danger? It was a split second of pure agony until he spoke again. 'There are men in the house! I thought they were burglars, they rushed in behind me and I told them I'd call the police, but they just laughed. Where are you? I don't know what to do! I . . .'

'Connor, take a deep breath! Take a deep breath, darling.' Grabbing Declan's hand, she began to run up the street towards the car park, cursing the fact that she had not been there when he got home. *Oh, God help me. I thought I had longer.* 'Don't go near the men. Go and sit in the garden or the driveway – I'm on my way.'

'They're . . . They're taking our stuff, Mum! What's going on?' His voice was shrill and childlike.

'I'll be there as soon as I can. Just hang on, Con. I'm coming!' she shouted, ignoring the stares of passers-by who started at the woman yelling and dragging her bewildered eleven-year-old by the hand as she ran back up the street she had only just sauntered down.

Nina ran towards the car and after making sure Declan was buckled up, jumped in, slamming the door and trying twice to secure her seat belt before managing to connect the metal end with the slot. Her fingers shook on the steering wheel and she cursed and yelled 'Come on! Come on! Dammit!' at every red light that made the fourteen-minute journey feel like a lifetime. Declan sat in wide-eyed shock on the back seat.

'What's happened, Mummy?' he whispered.

'I think there's a mix-up at home. Don't worry, I'll sort it out.' She tried out a look of reassurance in the rearview mirror.

Nina pulled the car through the gate and came to a screeching halt on the gravel driveway, parking behind a large battered lorry with the tailgate lifted and a ramp lowered to the ground. Connor stood to the left of the front door with his school bag and blazer in a heap by his feet and his fingers in his hair as he paced back and forth with a look of utter anguish on his face. Declan started crying. The fear and misery were infectious.

'Listen to me, Declan. I need you to do exactly as I tell you.' She spoke sharply. 'I need you to be a big boy and stay here quietly in the car, until I come and fetch you. I'll put the radio on and I will be back. Okay?' She tried to hide the desperation from her voice as she pushed the button, filling the space with the tuneful chorus of an upbeat pop song; its incongruence to the situation was maddening.

'Okay,' he managed, pushing his glasses up his nose before wriggling back in his seat and sitting up straight, as if his life depended on it.

Nina jumped from the driver's seat and ran to Connor, placing her arms around his tense form and trying to maintain eye contact. 'Listen to me, Connor, it's okay!' she said, trying to sound convincing.

'What's going on? What's happening, Mum?' He looked and sounded like the little boy he had been only a heartbeat ago, when all manner of things from bumps in the night to shapes in the garden frightened him straight into her arms.

She released her grip and stared at him, knowing that time was of the essence. Panic swam through her veins, but this time there was no daddy around to cushion the blows with a witty retort or the promise of a treat. She had to take control. 'Things are a bit of a mess. Dad had some problems with the business and we have been struggling to pay the bills.' She levelled with him. 'I think this might be connected with that. In fact, I know it is.'

Connor shook his head; she could see that he was in shock and this small explanation made little or no sense.

'I didn't mean to let them in.' He pointed towards the house. 'They were here on the drive when I arrived home,' he gasped, his eyes darting towards the truck. 'And they had this paper, they waved it at me, saying something about court. I didn't know what to do!'

'This is not your fault. It's not your fault.' She tried to reassure him. 'I'll go inside now and talk to the men and get to the bottom of it. You go and wait with Declan in the car and—'

'No. I'm coming in with you. You are not going in there on your own.'

She squeezed her son's arm, torn between the rush of love at the boy showing how grown-up he could be, and angry at the fact that he had to. Nina pushed through the door and headed into the grand hallway. She caught sight of dirty footprints on the marble and felt a strange sensation. These muddy marks of invasion had served to do something that nothing else had managed, not since she and Finn had first walked through the door all those years ago: they made her want to be somewhere else.

'The owner of the property?' A short, fat, balding man in a padded waistcoat strolled from the kitchen and asked the question in a casual, presumptuous manner, as if on a sales call. She stared at him and then looked through to the kitchen, her kitchen, where two very large men with big meaty arms and shaved heads and wearing thick, heavy anoraks seemed to be packing up her small appliances.

They leaned over the counter-tops, reaching up into her cupboards, their unfamiliar fingers delving into the neat, clean, organised spaces. Their eyes darted about, searching among her possessions. She shuddered with revulsion, knowing the room would forever be tainted by the invasion – not that she would be here to remember, and this realisation only heightened her anguish.

One of the men caught her eye and didn't look away, his stare a challenge, with none of the awkwardness she might have expected him to feel. If anything, he looked triumphant, as if he were teaching her a lesson. She felt her skin shiver into goosebumps. The other man unplugged a food processor and placed it in a cardboard box, already full of other appliances.

'Yes,' she finally answered, 'I am the owner of the property.'

The man stepped forward with his clipboard and a stubby pencil held between his grubby fingers on which he wore two very large, weighty gold rings. She smelled the sweat and grime that sat on his skin in a greasy sheen.

'My name is Mr Ludlow and I am here today representing the company Mackintosh and Vooght.'

'Yes.' She pictured the letters in the drawer, saw the red stamp with their words of warning. Connor took a step closer to her and she was grateful. She had always felt better able to cope when someone else was in close proximity: her mum, dad, Tiggy, Finn . . . Mr Ludlow spoke in a monotonous, well-rehearsed, slightly irritated manner, as though this was business as usual, just another job, which of course, for him, it was.

'Mr Finn McCarrick was served with notice to attend the original court hearing on February the fifteenth last year, which he failed to attend. He was then summoned to a second hearing held on March the fifteenth, which he also failed to attend and then finally having failed to turn up to his third and final hearing on April the fifth, the court made the judgement in absentia and appointed my company to act in our capacity as bailiffs to retrieve goods to the value of the full amount owing to Mackintosh and Vooght. We are exercising that duty today and can confirm we did not enter your property with force.'

'He didn't turn up? Not once?' She momentarily forgot Connor was close by.

'Not once. Hence our visit today.' The man placed his palm on his chest and bowed his head obsequiously. She couldn't have hated anyone more.

'I didn't mean to let them in. They walked past me when I put the key in the door,' Connor reminded her. She nodded without taking her eyes off the little man.

He continued. 'We will today be removing goods to cover the cost of the debt, plus the court fees and our services. Is that quite clear?' He breathed through his nose and she heard a faint whistle of a dirty nose.

'Are you allowed to do this?'

He gave a wide smile, revealing coffee-coloured teeth. 'Oh yes, all legal and above board.' Apparently he welcomed questions like this – a chance for him to give the many practised responses he knew by heart, as if this were a game.

'But I live here with my kids! You can't just come in and take things from my kitchen! I demand that you stop!'

'I would take the matter up with Mr McCarrick.'

Connor balled his fingers into a fist. Nina reached for his arm and shook her head. 'It's okay, Connor.' She tried to keep the tremor from her voice and looked again at the men who grabbed rarely used bouquets of silver cutlery from presentation drawers, dropping them like clanking confetti into cardboard boxes.

'I do not want you and these men in my house!' She stood her ground.

'My advice?' Mr Ludlow sniffed. 'Would be to stand back and let the boys get on with their job. That makes it easier for everyone.' He walked towards the front door and shouted back at her, without turning his head, 'I will be cataloguing everything we remove and you will of course be given a receipt.'

'I didn't mean to let them in,' Connor repeated, his breath coming in short bursts.

'Connor, this is not your fault.' She tried again to reassure him. 'I'm going to call the police!' she shouted.

'Yep.' The man lifted his clipboard in a jovial acknowledgement, as if this too were par for the course.

She felt Connor's eyes on her as she spoke to the person on the line, who asked if she had been physically threatened.

'No.'

'Did they force entry into the property?'

'No.'

She ended the call, despondent. It was a court matter and the bailiffs were acting legitimately. She felt utterly powerless and wondered not for the first time why people thought it was okay to treat her this way – first Finn, now these men – as if she weren't worthy of consultation, as if she had no voice.

Connor stared at her with his chest heaving.

'Listen to me, Connor. They are only taking things, stuff. It doesn't matter, not really,' she managed. 'What's important is that we keep things as normal as possible for Declan. We don't want him frightened,' she whispered, and just like that she made her eldest son an ally, an equal. This realisation was quickly followed by a wave of guilt. 'I know this is a terrible, terrible day, but soon it will be tomorrow and we will move on, go forward.'

Connor gave a brief nod, his eyes wide.

One of the burly men walked out the door with a box full of kitchen equipment and put it next to the lorry. Mr Ludlow licked the end of the pencil and jotted a note, cataloguing the items onto a sheet designed for the purpose. Nina walked up to him to try again. 'I understand that you are only doing your job.' she said.

'That's good,' he acknowledged, and carried on scribbling furiously.

She concentrated on keeping the wobble from her voice. Her throat felt as if it was full of razor blades, such was the effort of breathing and not howling. 'But is there anything I can do to stop this? My boys have just lost their dad. He died,' she clarified, 'and I just need a bit of time . . .'

Mr Ludlow smiled and cocked his head to one side. 'All we need is the outstanding amount settled in full and we will return these items and be on our way.'

'How . . . how much do we owe you?' She swallowed.

'Sixty-four thousand, seven hundred and eighty-two pounds and forty-three pence.'

Nina pictured the Post-it note stuck to the side of Finn's computer. 'Mac 64500': not in fact a computer reference – it was 'Mac' short for 'Mackintosh', and the amount, over sixty-four thousand pounds. She had no words. It seemed that everywhere she turned she faced an avalanche of debt that was coming at her quicker than she could take a breath. 'For fuck's sake!' she muttered under her breath, twisting her wedding ring, trying to take comfort from the small band of gold given in love and binding her forever to Finn McCarrick. 'For richer or poorer. You were not supposed to run out on me, Finn! You bastard,' she whispered.

Mr Ludlow had resumed his scribbling. 'Your expensive watch, and the rings on your fingers are exempt because they are on your person, but any other jewellery found in the premises will be taken.'

She pictured the boxes she had already packed up, the jewellery nestled inside along with ornaments and other electronica. With a plan forming, she ran inside and up the stairs, and tucked one of the boxes under her arm. She ran down and past Mr Ludlow, who coughed loudly. Nina stood with her shoulders back, and tried to sound authoritative. 'These things aren't mine. They are things I've been looking after for a friend. So I'm going to put them to one side.'

'I'm afraid it doesn't quite work like that.' Mr Ludlow sucked his teeth. 'You'd be surprised at the things people say to try and hide the good stuff, and trust me, we have heard them all. Not that I am suggesting that you are being anything other than honest.' He smiled. 'Best thing you can do is explain the situation to your friend and if they can produce a legitimate receipt or record or ownership, we can of course return those items to them. This will all be explained in the literature I shall leave with you.'

'But that's ridiculous! I have told you they aren't mine, you can't take them!'

'I'm afraid we can, Mrs McCarrick.'

She became aware of someone touching her arm and looked down to see Declan patting her.

'Declan! I told you to stay in the car!' She shouted louder than she had intended.

'I did stay there, Mum, for a bit, but I got scared and I am worried about you and Connor.' He looked up at her wide-eyed. 'Why are they taking our things?'

'We owe them some money, darling.' She couldn't think of a lie quick enough and as her energy diminished, the truth felt like the best thing. She placed the boxes on the driveway.

'Why don't you just give them the money?'

'Because I don't have it. But everything is going to be okay. I promise.' She wondered how often she could regurgitate this phrase without screaming.

A sudden yell made them both look towards the front door. Connor stumbled from the house. His expression was one she had never seen; he looked bewildered as he tried to hold on to his laptop, tussling with a heavyset man who sneered at the boy who was trying to hang on to this one thing. 'That's mine!' he yelled, his voice hoarse. 'Tell them, Mum! It's got everything on it! Everything, all my photos, everything!'

The sight sent a bolt of anger through her very being. How dare they treat her son this way, especially when he was already grieving?

'For God's sake, let him keep his laptop! What kind of people are you? He needs it and it's got photos of him and his dad on it. Please!' she urged Mr Ludlow.

He looked at the boy and then at her, before letting his eyes sweep over their grand, solid home. 'Here's the thing, Mrs McCarrick. Rules is rules. You and your husband failed to attend the court despite the hearing being scheduled three times, and as I explained, we are now at liberty to enter your home and take goods to the value of the amount owed, unless you can pay the amount in full.'

'You know I can't!' she shouted. 'Take all of my possessions, furniture, anything, but please let the kids keep their laptops and their things. Please!'

'I'm afraid it doesn't quite work like that.' The little man shook his head. 'The time to negotiate is in front of the judge where you failed to turn up. Put it in the lorry.' He nodded at the laptop and then at the big man holding it on one side.

Connor let the slim silver laptop slide through his fingers. He took a deep breath and yelled, 'You can't do this! These are our things! How am I going to do my schoolwork? I've got projects on there that I need to hand in next term!'

'You won't be at that school next term, Connor!' Nina blurted, instantly regretting it. 'We can't afford the fees. You have to leave. I am sorry! I am so sorry!' All her consideration over the last couple of days, and instead it all came out in this rushed, unconsidered outburst that tumbled from her mouth in an unguarded moment. She knew it was as damaging as it was shocking.

There was a beat of silence while the news settled in the boys' minds. Declan began to whimper as Connor sank down onto his knees on the gravel and held his chest, struggling to catch a breath. 'What the fuck is going on?' he screamed. 'What the fuck is happening?'

'Connor!' She walked over to him and laid her hand on his back. 'Listen to me. We will find a way. It'll be fine. We will get through this. It's only things, just stuff . . .'

He looked up at her, his expression tortured. 'How can you keep saying that? Do you think it makes things better? Because it doesn't! It's not going to be fine, is it, Mum? I don't think anything is going to be fine ever again. And it's not "just stuff". They are packing up our life and taking it away, bit by bit.' He placed his hands on his thighs and closed his eyes as he took deep breaths.

'Actually, on reflection, you are right. If you need the laptop for *educational* purposes, then it is exempt,' Mr Ludlow interrupted, before handing Connor back the laptop. The boy stared at him, unable to thank him.

Declan clung to her. She could feel his small body shaking. 'I want my dad,' he whispered. 'I want my dad.'

'Well Dad's not here, is he? You've got me, Declan! That's it, just me!' Nina yelled, then instantly felt aghast at the look of horror on her son's face. He released his grip on her and let his arms fall to his sides, sobbing openly.

Nina sought the words that might offer comfort, remove the harm she'd done. But how could she explain to her kids the struggle to reconcile the man they loved and missed, the man who might be able to get them out of the situation and who always had a plan, with the man who had led them into this mess and left her to pick up the pieces?

She shepherded the boys inside as dusk descended. They sat at the breakfast bar, watching as the men tramped from room to room, over the beautiful oak flooring and onto the pale carpets in their heavy, dirty shoes. The men went upstairs, returning almost immediately with a television set. They made the trip over and over, with tablets in their arms and watches taken from Finn's bedside cabinet. They got into a rhythm, handing the smaller items to Mr Ludlow, who made a note with his pencil, loading the bigger things up onto the van. One of the men smiled at her.

'Don't you smile at me! How dare you? Do you take pleasure from your work? What kind of person comes into a home and takes possessions from children?' she spat. The man continued to smile. Nina felt impotent and exhausted. It was an effort to remain upright. 'Are you hungry?' she whispered to her sons, suddenly aware they hadn't eaten. They both shook their heads. She was relieved, unsure how she would have managed in the kitchen with what remained of their plates and cutlery.

'I didn't know what to do, Mum,' Connor explained. 'They sort of rushed at the door and I only opened it because I wanted to get inside.'

'Connor, you have to stop going over it. I have told you it's not your fault!' she snapped again. 'They would have got in anyway. I'd have let them in. It's not your fault. And over-analysing it will not help anyone.'

He stared at her with his eyes blazing. Two men sidled past the open doorway, carrying a leather chair between them.

Nina closed her eyes, unable to watch the parade of their belongings, things she and Finn had chosen together, worked for and kept in their home, the fabric of their lives being unstitched piece by piece. The trouser press, digital radio, foot spa, the oversized lamps from the sitting room, her dinner service, which had been on display in the dining room, pictures from the walls, the wireless telephone from the study and three of her designer handbags from the front hallway. The garage yielded similar booty, including the family's bikes. Finally one of the men walked into the kitchen and asked for her car keys.

'My car keys? You have to be kidding me,' she said with incredulity. It hadn't occurred to her that they might take the car.

The man nodded and cracked his knuckles.

'I need to empty it.' She exchanged a look with Connor and went out to the front drive, removing the handbag she had forgotten about from the boot and her make-up bag from the console.

'I will be taking the bag.' Mr Ludlow fixed his beady, piggy eyes on the Mulberry badge.

'But it's—' she began.

'I know,' he interrupted her. 'Of great sentimental value, I'm sure, but you already have one handbag on your person and this one has value.' Nina handed over the empty bag. She had been going to say, '*It's full of vomit*,' but he had cut her short. Let him find out the hard way.

She made her way back into the kitchen and sat next to Connor.

'Are you okay?'

He gave a single, brief nod, his mouth set in a thin line. His laptop rested under his palm, as if he were afraid to lose contact with it.

Darkness drew in. 'I know!' She banged the table top. 'Let's play a game.'

'I don't want to play a game,' Connor snapped.

'Well, this is not about what we want, this is about staying focused.' She thought it best to distract the kids from the events going on outside of the kitchen door.

'Okay, I'll start.' She nudged Declan, who looked like he was a million miles away. 'We have to go through the alphabet, taking turns to think of an appropriate lettered answer for our topic. So, let's start with countries. A, America! Your turn Dec.'

'B, Belgium.' His voice was small.

'I don't want to play.' Connor stared at her.

'You just got a strike, two more and you are out!' she yelled. 'Try again. C,' she prompted.

'C, Colombia,' he snarled.

'Bravo! Colombia! My turn. D, Denmark.'

Declan tapped the table, 'E . . .' He wrinkled his nose. 'I can't think of one.'

She and Connor stared at him. 'Okay, here's a clue, Dec. You live there.' She winked.

'Egypt!' he yelled.

Nina's laughter, in spite of the dire circumstances, was genuine. Her tears quickly pooled; she wiped them away with her hand. 'Oh, Dec. I love you so much. Egypt! I wish we did live in bloody Egypt, far away from Mr Ludlow and his horrible helpers.'

Even Connor had a slight smile on his lips. 'Egypt!' he muttered as he shook his head.

◆ ◆ ◆

An hour later she made her way out to the front of the house to check on progress. She heard Mr Ludlow shouting 'Back her up!' as one of the men reversed the lorry to the tuneless beep that accompanied the manoeuvre. He put on the brakes and jumped down from the cab to help his colleagues load the desks and the velvet sofas from the cinema room, along with three or four large mirrors.

Nina pictured strolling through The Lanes in Brighton and coming across the antique shop, pulling a reluctant Finn through the door and leaving with their beautiful mirror, paid for and waiting to be shipped to their stunning new home. She felt like she should cry, but was too numb, too shattered to produce tears.

Mr Ludlow gave her a leaflet, along with some flimsy duplicate yellow sheets – an inventory listing all the items they had removed – before doffing an invisible cap at her and shutting the front door behind him.

She listened as the man driving her car over-revved the engine. It made her wince.

She and the boys sat in silence. They looked around at the opened cupboards and disturbed drawers, the spaces on the floor where the dining chairs had sat and the bare counter-tops, stripped of all the things that made this room the heart of the house.

'I think we should lock the doors and windows and all sleep together in my room, like we used to when you were little, Con, and Dec was a baby and Dad was away.' She tried to make it sound like an adventure. 'What do you think?' she managed, thinking that the warm, safe space was the haven they needed. Connor nodded; with his laptop under his arm, he climbed down from the stool at the breakfast bar, one of two seats deemed either too insignificant in value to take or overlooked by the men who had ransacked their home.

'But first, we are going scavenging! Let's split up and take a room each and gather anything we can find that we can carry, and bring it in here to be packaged up. I'm sure those monsters must have missed some things. Who's up for it?'

The kids, buoyed up at the thought of the activity, ran from the room. Nina leaned on the wall and closed her eyes briefly, trying to steady her pulse. 'Okay,' she called out, 'I'm going to take the dining room!'

Their efforts gathered together a surprising haul: a carriage clock that had been secreted behind a wall of books, a chunky, vintage brass ink well and a silver letter opener, side tables, a large painting from the downstairs cloakroom, and any number of books. Nina ran her fingers over the objects and felt a slight lift to her spirits that these things would be salvaged from the greasy paws of the bailiffs.

They went from room to room together, checking the windows and locking the doors, doing their best to ignore the bare walls, mantels and shelves now devoid of their ornaments, and the wall lights hanging over chunks of bare plaster where paintings had hung only an hour before.

She simply drew the curtains, as if she could keep the world at bay, as if the damage had not already been done.

The devastation upstairs was harder to take. Bedrooms and studies were usually such private domains that to see the drawers emptied, wardrobes opened, beds pulled away from the walls and the dusty squares where computers and radios used to sit was truly awful.

Declan went to his mum's room while Connor went into his room. The sound he made was one that she would never, ever forget. It was part whimper, part sob, and it was the call of the wounded. 'Oh no!' he called out. 'Oh no, no, no!' he cried without restraint. The sight of his refuge, his personal space, so invaded was clearly hard for him to take. Nina rushed to comfort him.

'Connor,' she began, taking a step towards him.

'Don't touch me!' he snarled. His lips narrowed and his arm muscles tensed. 'I hate you! Don't you dare tell me it's going to be okay, don't you dare! I hate you! How could you do this to us? How could Dad do this to us?'

His words hit her like punches. 'Do you know what, Connor? I know you are angry and hurting, but guess what? I am angry and hurting too! None of this is my choice, none of it. And this feels like the time to remind you that I had no idea of the state we were in, none at all! You think this is fun for me? Watching everything we have built over the years be dismantled in hours? It's a living nightmare!' She felt a now familiar flash of anger towards Finn: if only he had told her, given her a chance to make a plan. 'And to be honest, over the last few days, I am wondering who got the roughest deal. At least Dad had the full picture, but it's me left here to deal with all this shit!' She kicked the wall.

'Are you saying you would have preferred to die too?'

Her son's words stopped her in her tracks.

'No. No, of course not.' She stared at her boy, remembering it was her job to try to protect him, and not allow Finn's memory to be tarnished, knowing Connor's own self-esteem in part relied on it. 'I'm sure Dad did all he could to protect us for as long as possible.'

'But he wasn't protecting us, was he? He was lying to us! God, he was even suggesting we go to the Maldives for a holiday – how was he going to pull that off?'

'Maybe he had a plan. I honestly don't know.' She shrugged, her words insipid to her ears.

'Yep, he always had a plan.' Connor squeezed his eyes shut. It killed her to see her son's hero lose his cape. Connor opened his eyes and took a sharp breath. 'Mum?' He swallowed. 'You don't think he . . . ?' He paused.

The two exchanged a knowing look. The unspoken words ricocheted around the walls like stray bullets.

'I think we have to plough on, doing the very best we can for Declan. He's been through enough,' she whispered.

'What about me, Mum? What about what I have been through, what I am still going through?'

'Yes, of course, you too. But don't think you have the monopoly on hurt and disruption around here, because you don't.' It had felt better when thinking of him as an ally, but he wasn't, he was her fifteen-year-old son. 'I am so aware of how this has affected you and I wish with every fibre of my being that you weren't going through it, that none of us were. It's terrible for us all. And honestly, Connor, having those men in our home has felt like losing your dad all over again . . .' She let this trail; there was no value in reminding him of the horror when it was still so raw.

'I feel like I'm going to fall over, I feel like the world is spinning.' Connor exhaled.

'Because it is, Con, it is. And all we can do is hold on tight.' She pictured her precious little marble nestling in the base of her handbag.

Nina crept into her bedroom, restoring drawers that had been pulled wide and shutting the wardrobe doors. She took the blankets and duvets and made a den on the thick carpet in front of the wide window that gave a beautiful view of the full moon that hung overhead. There was plenty of room for the three of them to sleep as they slumped down on the floor.

'It's like a camping trip,' Declan managed, with a hint of enthusiasm that Nina envied.

She kissed his forehead. 'Yep. That's what we are doing tonight, Dec, camping here on the floor, all of us together.'

'I liked it when Dad took us camping in Wales, and that goat came into our tent and Daddy screamed.' All were quiet for a second or so, picturing that day.

'Mummy?'

'Yes, love?' she whispered, her vocal cords taut with fatigue.

'Did you speak to Dad before he died? Did . . . did he say anything to you?' he asked.

She shook her head. 'No, darling. He was already gone by the time I got to the hospital.' She gulped as the images of those moments came rushing back. Nina pictured the sheet-wrapped body on the trolley, remembered the iron smell of his blood that hung pungently in the air. When she lifted the sheet from his face, she saw the spread of purple bruise that swelled under his right eye, across his forehead and over the bridge of his nose. This man didn't look like her husband, not really. He looked like he had been in a fight. A fight that he had lost. She had gripped the clear plastic bag in her hand that contained his watch, wallet, wedding and signet rings. It crinkled loudly as she bent over and touched her lips to his cool cheek.

'I don't want him to be dead, Mum. I want it to be how it was and I want all our things put back where they are supposed to be.' Declan spoke loudly now as his tears raced down his face, his chest heaving.

All she could do was hold him.

'I miss my dad!' Declan sobbed, 'I want him back. I don't like it now, Mum. I want my dad.' He cried as he fell against her.

She looked over at Connor, who stared, dry-eyed, up into the night sky.

SIX

Nina spent much of the night watching the boys sleep. If they woke upset or alarmed, she wanted to be awake to comfort them. At 2 a.m. she thought she heard noises downstairs and her imagination ran wild, picturing the ham-fisted removal men, returned and roaming the rooms, looking for more items by torchlight. The idea caused her pulse to race and a fine film of sweat to break out over her body. She slipped from her bedroom and tiptoed down the stairs to the kitchen where she grabbed a left-behind butcher's knife from the drawer. With her arm raised and teeth bared, she padded quietly from room to room, pulse racing, ready to lunge at whomever she found.

There was no one, no sign of entry. With the knife still in her hand, she made her way back upstairs and opened the linen closet, the largest and most obvious place for someone to hide. Nothing. Lowering her weapon, she placed her hand on a wicker hamper inside. A memory sprang back to her. She remembered Finn giggling after a bottle of wine, telling her he had squirrelled away a thousand pounds, folded into sports socks in the bottom of the hamper. 'For emergencies,' he had whispered, showing her where it was hidden. She had thought him foolish, tutting at the cloak and dagger nature of his hidden treasure as they tumbled into bed. It didn't seem quite so funny now. Lifting the lid, she dug beneath the sheets and found the sports socks, and there, coiled inside, was a roll of cash. Nina snatched it to her chest. Closing her eyes, she offered up silent thanks. 'For emergencies,' she whispered into the night.

Nina slipped back into the bedroom. As dawn broke, it brought some clarity with it. It would only be more damaging to them all if they hung around and waited to be evicted from the house. They had to get out immediately, just pack up and go. But where?

A thought came to her as she splashed her face with cold water and cleaned her teeth. Asking someone to put all three of them up for a while might be too much, but surely the boys' friends wouldn't mind having one of them to stay. She detested the thought of separation from her kids, especially when they were so bruised. The idea of not being able to keep an eye on them horrified her – but if it meant they got to stay in the area, giving her the breathing space to figure out their next move before school started again after the half-term break, then it might be worth it. Whichever school it was they would now attend. There was a lot to do.

She wandered from room to room; the disarray hit her hard, leaving her winded but also determined. *Bastards.* She pictured Mr Ludlow sneering. Nina closed the kitchen door and dialled Kathy Topps's number. She wandered the long, empty room, waiting, swallowing the nerves that filled her up and threatened to make her chicken out and end the call.

'Nina,' Kathy answered, as if she had half been expecting her call.

'Hi, Kathy. I'm not disturbing you, am I?' She closed her eyes, picturing the Topps family seated around a dining table that was paid for, enjoying an organic breakfast whilst chatting about the fun they would have over the holiday.

'Not at all.' Her tone was a little clipped.

'How are you?' Her voice filled the empty airwaves. It perturbed her; Kathy was usually such a chatterbox.

'Good.'

'This is a bit out of the blue, Kathy, but I was wondering if I could ask you a massive favour?' She drew breath and rehearsed what she wanted to say in her mind: '*Could I take you up on the offer of shared tennis lessons with Henry, and could Declan possibly stay with you for a week or two? Just while I put things in place, figure out our next move?*'

Nina opened her mouth to speak, but Kathy broke in. 'I can save us both a lot of trouble, Nina. I can *guess* at the favour you want to ask, and I'm afraid the answer is no. And frankly it's made me feel most uncomfortable that you would even consider asking. It's not the done thing.'

'I . . .' She screwed her face up in confusion.

'Are you going to force me to say it?' Kathy asked.

'Force you to say what?' To Nina it felt like they were having parallel conversations.

'Money, Nina! You are obviously after money.' The woman let the accusation hang in the air.

'No . . . I . . .' She tried to form a response. Her childhood had taught her that to ask for money was shameful; to ask for help, a job, a hand, was one thing, but money quite another. Nina felt her cheeks flame at the suggestion.

Kathy spoke quickly, condescendingly. 'The Kings Norton community is a small one and people talk. Jayne Rutherford's sister-in-law works in the accounts department and, well, let's just say that people are aware of the situation.'

This was her worst nightmare, to be spoken to like this by Kathy and to know that her peers were discussing her, judging her, as not quite good enough, failing, as if she were once again the girl in the shoes that didn't quite fit. Nina found her voice. 'I don't know what people have been saying—' she began, before Kathy interrupted.

'Primarily that you can't pay school fees and the boys are having to leave.' Her diction was sharp, each word like a dagger that cut.

Nina felt anger rising. How could she contain the gossip before it got back, unfiltered, raw and accusatory to Connor and Declan via their friends, before they had a chance to fully process their situation and before she had come up with a strategy? 'I can assure you that is not entirely true and I am absolutely furious that the school thinks it's okay to give out such private information about its pupils. It's unbelievable.'

'You are probably right, but I think the implication is that the boys are now ex-pupils,' Kathy pointed out.

'Do you know what, Kathy? I expected better from you. I was calling to see if Declan was still invited to join Henry for his tennis lessons.'

'Well you can forget that.' Kathy cut her off. 'I was thinking it might be good for the boys to form a friendship for the new term, but there's very little point if Declan isn't going to be there. You know what Kings Norton boys are like. A very close bunch. Outsiders are not their first choice.'

'God, Kathy, what a horrible, horrible thing to say to me. My boys have been at that school since they were three years of age, they are not outsiders!' She felt the blood rushing to her face. 'You brought my boys home on the day their dad died, you came to his bloody funeral, hugging me, offering condolence while drinking his wine! I can't believe this. Do you really think that bankruptcy and tragedy are contagious? Is that what you are worried about?'

As Kathy drew breath, Nina interjected. 'You know what? You can shove your tennis lessons up your arse, Kathy. Declan would rather do anything than play with Henry, the unsporting little shit.' She hung up and stared out over the pool. Her body shook with adrenaline and something close to triumph.

She thought about Joe Marsh-Evans, a little boy in Connor's class who had left school suddenly and without explanation when they were about five. What had she done? Called Joe's mum to see if they were okay? Enquired as to his whereabouts so he and Connor could still be friends? No. She had simply crossed him off the invite list for Connor's birthday party. She thought about Joe, possibly for the first time since he had left, and felt a wave of sickness. It crystallised a thought in her mind: not only how she needed to raise her kids to show kindness to others, but also that no matter what, and no matter where, she and her boys would stick together as outsiders to face what may come.

The boys had come down from their rooms to the kitchen. Nina banged the counter, making them both jump. 'Okay.' She drew their attention and tried to sound assertive. 'Firstly I think you should stay home today and we should use the time to make a plan.' She spoke loudly and positively, hoping *that* might be infectious. She didn't want the boys at the rumour mill of school. 'I have been thinking a lot over the last few days and spent most of last night mulling over our options. And I think we need to leave Bath and go somewhere new. Start over.' She indicated the French doors at the back of the room, as if the future beckoned on the other side of the swimming pool, and in a sense it did.

'Leave Bath?' Declan asked in a tone that suggested she might be crazy.

'Yes, leave Bath. I'm thinking that if you are going to have to go to a new school, then let's find a new place where you can be whoever you want to be and no one knows where you have come from or what has happened. Starting over, it will be like shedding skin.'

Connor let his head hang forward. 'What I *want* to be is the winger for the Kings Norton College first team. That's what I always wanted and I nearly had it. I nearly had it, Mum.' His face seemed to crumple as he rushed from the kitchen and back up the wide staircase.

Declan wrinkled his nose at her, 'I don't mind where we live, Mum, but I don't want to go anywhere really cold, like the North Pole.'

She felt the unfamiliar sensation of laughter bubbling on her lips in the midst of this nightmare. 'Oh, Dec. I love you so much. What would I do without you?'

She watched her youngest run into the garden. With Connor still ensconced in his room, Nina felt suddenly very much alone. The silence of the room taunted her. What wouldn't she give to have the noise of family life, the sounds of extended family, around her right now? Even to have her gran's loud scolds echoing off the walls would be something – proof that she were not in this on her own.

'*I am here for you. I want to be the first person you call, always.*' Her sister's words were loud in her mind. '*You know where I am if you need anything.*' Well, she did need something – a bit of advice, a sounding board. Nina picked up the landline and dialled Tiggy, wary of the reception she might get after how they left things.

'Hey.'

'Hi, Tiggy.'

'It's good to hear from you.' This she knew was an olive branch of sorts for how her visit had ended, a drawing of a line in the sand, keeping communication open. 'How's it going? How are the boys doing?'

Her sister's kind enquiry was enough to summon tears. She sniffed them away; this was no time for crying. It seemed that any turbulence between them had passed.

Nina took a deep breath. 'We are in a bit of trouble.'

'What kind of trouble?' Tiggy spoke quickly, with concern.

Nina braced herself to say the words out loud.

'I found a note from Finn, he said that he felt like his world was made of glass and that he was cracking under the pressure and now that pressure is mine and I don't know what to do next.' She'd let slip more than had been her intention.

'You're not making a whole bunch of sense. What pressure? I don't understand, Nina, but I do know that nothing can be that bad and there is always a solution.'

'Things *are* that bad. We have nowhere to live, Tig. We need to move, start over. And I am broke.' Nina rubbed her face.

'For real?' There was a hint of laughter in her question. Nina understood that this was not because her sister found the facts amusing, but simply that the idea that her wealthy sister in her huge house could even come close to being broke was indeed so unbelievable as to be laughable.

'I need to find somewhere for the kids to sleep and I don't have any money. I'm thinking we might go to Trowbridge or Chippenham or Swindon, somewhere not too far away, but a fresh start.'

There was a moment of silence.

'I don't understand. What's happened? How come you don't have any money?'

Nina felt the grit of irritation between her teeth. It was draining to have to recount the facts. 'Finn lost the business and we are losing the house, losing everything.' She tried not to picture the previous night when her possessions, the things she held dear, had been carted off to auction.

She heard Tiggy take a sharp intake of breath. 'Shit!'

'Yes,' she agreed. 'Shit.'

'Don't you have savings and stuff? Or things you can sell?'

'Our savings have long gone trying to save the business, apparently, and anything I would have to sell wouldn't come close to matching the debt. We owe a little under eight million pounds.'

Nina listened to the stunned silence on the other end of the line. There were no quips, no questions. This figure gave the true scale of her trouble and it was as sobering as it was frightening.

'And you didn't know?' Tiggy asked softly.

She looked out over the gardens. 'No. I didn't know.'

Her sister gave a heavy sigh. 'Shit,' she offered again.

Nina held the phone close to her mouth and felt comforted by the connection.

'Are the boys okay?'

She appreciated Tiggy's concern; she thought of Kathy's cool, mean response from earlier. Not once had she enquired as to any of their welfare.

'They are lost, confused, upset – all as you'd expect.'

'Come here,' Tiggy stated matter-of-factly.

'What?'

'Come here. You know Southampton, and that must make it preferable to Trowbridge or Swindon where you have no support,' Tiggy said sensibly.

'We can't just come there, you don't have the space. But thanks for the offer.'

Nina didn't want to share her thought that, actually, anywhere might be better than the city in which she had grown up. She heard her sister's teeth grinding; Nina had quite forgotten that Tiggy did this when in thought.

'Oh, I know! Aunty Mary's flat is empty. The tenants have just moved out and they are having viewings on it right now. I saw the "To Let" board outside. I could have a word with Cousin Fred?' Tiggy enthused loudly.

Nina pictured the ground-floor flat in a low-rise 1950s block that she had visited countless times in her childhood; it had belonged to her gran's youngest sister, quiet and kind spinster Mary. When they went over Aunt Mary gave them sweets that stuck to the flimsy plastic wrapper, as if they had got warm and then cooled and the wrapper had become enmeshed with the sugar. Nina tried to remember the last time she had been there; it had to be over twenty years ago – more. She felt no enthusiasm for living in her aunt's flat, but this wasn't about enthusiasm, it was about being desperate.

'How much is it?'

'About six hundred and fifty a month, I think. Can you manage that?'

Nina thought of the small amount of cash she had in her purse. This, along with the cash that Finn had left in the hamper, was the sum total of her liquidity. She pictured the grubby notes: just a little over a couple of months of rent, *eight weeks of security*! Her heart jumped with fear.

That was all she had.

And this before she considered food, bills and sundries. She thought of the monthly florist bill that was about half this amount and felt a sickening ball of shame bounce in her gut. 'I can manage for a short while, a couple of months, and I will get a job as soon as I can.' She tried to picture living in Aunty Mary's flat, tried to imagine working; both ideas felt surreal.

'The area has gone downhill a bit, but it's friendly enough,' Tiggy said. Nina felt her throat constrict. Her memory of the place was not favourable, and to think that it might have declined further . . .

How can I take my boys there?

'It's very central, as you know, and it's very cheap.' Tiggy pointed out the obvious. 'Fred still lives in Canada, and I'm sure he'd rather you lived in it than a stranger.'

Nina pictured the people Tiggy referred to with a lump of guilt in her throat. She'd had no communication with Cousin Fred in years, other than the exchange of impersonal Christmas cards each year. She had only been a few years old than Connor when she had settled into a routine with Finn as a newlywed in Bath, and then she had a new baby, and her whole miserable teenagehood faded into the grey shade of another life and another time. There had been no explosive row, no cataclysmic event; their rift had occurred subtly, aided by physical separation. The longer they spent apart, the wider the chasm had become. There was only Tiggy left in Portswood, bar Cousin Fred's occasional visits home with his Canadian wife and two daughters in tow. Right now, however, it was this place, the one she had been so keen to escape from, that was calling her back, providing a potential lifeline.

'And our school is within walking distance,' Nina thought aloud.

'Surely you are not thinking of sending your boys to Cottrell's?'

'I am. I need to get them in somewhere. It's almost halfway through the school year and we need a roof over our heads. It's as simple as that. And it won't be forever, just until I figure out what to do next. I need to get a job, Tig, and quickly.' The thought sent a jolt of nervous energy along her spine.

'How will you . . . ?' Tiggy halted mid-sentence.

Nina again sensed that there were so many things that Tiggy wanted to say, but thought better of it.

'I'll figure things out. I have to,' Nina asserted.

There was another beat of silence.

'Do you want me to have a word with Fred, then? I have his numbers, I can do that today if you like?'

She was overwhelmed by her sister's instant and genuine offer of help.

'That'd be great, thank you, Tiggy.'

'It'll be okay, you know. Nothing is ever as bad as you imagine.'

No wonder Connor had felt frustrated. The meaningless rhetoric made her realise how pointless it was to offer a cure-all without anything more concrete to back it up.

'Who were you talking to?' Connor asked, entering the kitchen, his brother trailing him.

'Tiggy. I'm trying to sort out some accommodation.'

Connor stared at her. 'Is this really happening?'

'Connor . . .' She sighed, hoping she didn't have to find the energy for a fight. 'This has already happened. Look at us!' She raised her palms towards the ceiling. 'Today we need to pack up our things.'

'What's left of them,' Connor quipped.

Nina ignored him.

'What can we take with us?' Declan asked.

'Clothes, books, anything precious to you, but that's all. We won't have that much space.' She listed pretty much all that was left after the bailiffs had made their sweep. 'Anything else we'll box up and put into storage.' She swallowed, thinking about Mr Firth's offer to hold on to their things. Without the fog of grief and shock, he had probably been at least three steps ahead of her thought process; she had only vaguely understood his suggestion for haste. 'So go up to your rooms and make three piles. One of the things you want to take with you – but not too much. As I said, space is limited. Pack like it's a long holiday.'

Connor sneered. She could read his mind: *Some holiday.*

She continued, undeterred. 'Make another pile of everything to be packed and stored, and a third pile of everything you want to give to charity.'

Declan nodded and left the room, his instructions clear.

'And you, Connor.'

'George has invited me to a party next Saturday, but I won't be here, will I?'

'What do you want me to say, Connor?'

She knew that this was about so much more than a party – this was about his whole life that felt as if it were in free fall – but there was nothing else she could say. He seemed to look through her as he walked slowly from the room, and her heart sank at her inability to give him a more satisfactory response.

A few hours later, boxes were packed, sealed and labelled. There were a few other items Mackintosh and Vooght missed that she placed in her bag: an antique silver cigarette case, Finn's Montblanc pen-and-pencil set that had been in her cotton book bag, and three sets of gold cufflinks, each set engraved with the McCarrick family crest. She placed them in the zip pouch inside her bag with Finn's watch and signet and wedding rings.

'When will we go, Mum?' Declan asked as he flicked through an encyclopaedia of insects.

'As soon as we get the word from Tiggy. Hopefully tomorrow.'

'But what if we can't get that flat you told us about?' he asked, pushing his glasses up onto his nose.

'Then we activate Plan B. We get a truck, load up our stuff and go to Swindon or Trowbridge and hit the rental agencies until we find a place,' she asserted, hoping she sounded confident. The enormity of their situation made her want to vomit. But this was not the time for weakness, of any kind. She had to be strong, for all of them.

◆ ◆ ◆

A text arrived from Tiggy late afternoon:

THE FLAT IS YOURS IF YOU WANT IT. I HAVE THE KEYS!!!

Nina looked at the text and wished she felt similarly enthusiastic. For her, the news came with relief, followed by a wave of dread.

It was almost unthinkable to Nina that this was going to be her last night in their family home; ironically, the prospect was made a little easier by the invasion of Mr Ludlow and his henchmen. She felt their echo in every room she entered, felt the weight of their challenging stares. These new images crowded out memories of her family – birthdays and celebrations and milestones – and she hated them for that. She and the boys ate soup and crackers, before tucking straight into large half-eaten tubs of ice cream. They watched TV on Connor's laptop for a while, then they all trudged silently upstairs. The boys went to their rooms. She wished them goodnight, and then she made her way to Finn's study, where she stood for an age, looking out the window over the grounds. Ancient trees edged the lawn, spiky without their leaves and licked by frost, lined up like dark sentinels in the stillness.

'So beautiful,' she breathed, staring out into the darkness of the February night.

And it was.

Nina lay in the centre of their bed, with Finn's sweatshirt on her pillow by her side. She lay back on the mattress and looked up at the ceiling, thinking of the many times she had done so with the skin of the man she loved against hers. Tears trickled down her temples and into her hair. The man she thought she knew inside out and back to front had so many secrets . . .

Nina stirred at the first light that filtered through her bedroom window. Squeezing her eyes shut, she tried to delay the dawn, to pretend this day wasn't actually happening, as if she could cheat time and hang on to the night, deferring what she knew would come to pass.

The touch of Finn's finger against her cheek . . . She nuzzled against his warm skin. Her eyelids fluttered in the first throes of wakefulness, sensing the light and soft chirp of birdsong, providing the most blissful alarm. Smiling, she thought of the unplanned day ahead, with nothing but the hours happily unpunctuated in the calendar – no appointments, nowhere she needed to be. She felt a burst of excitement at what the day might hold. She opened her eyes and saw Finn's face so close it startled her. She giggled, gripping the edge of the crisp white cotton sheet and pulling it over her face, a little shy at his scrutiny. Finn pulled back the cover.

'I've been watching you.'

'Was I drooling or sleep talking again?'

He shook his head and she saw the rare but unmistakable glint of tears in his eyes. 'I used to watch you all the time when we were first married. I couldn't quite believe that I had landed you.'

'Landed me?' She giggled. 'You make me sound like a fish,' she whispered. 'Would I be an ugly old cod or a sweet little goldfish?'

He smiled. 'I woke up an hour ago and saw you sound asleep on the pillow next to me, and I felt this overwhelming sense of peace. This is enough. It's always been enough, you and me, waking up side by side. That's it!' He leaned forward to kiss her face. 'This is my happiness, waking up with you, and no matter how far apart we are, it's the thought of this that gets me through . . .'

Nina inhaled his scent and felt the graze of his lips on hers . . .

A bang on the landing caused her to wake with a start. She sat up in bed, looking at the space Finn had occupied in her dream. She placed her hand on the mattress, longing to return to the sweet oblivion of fantasy.

She lay back, knowing this was the last time she would wake up in the room where she had lain in her husband's arms, where he had laughed as she crawled over the carpet after too much wine; the last time she would lie on the bed that her toddlers had jumped upon on Christmas morning, bouncing up and down, keen to get on with the business of opening presents. She didn't have time for this, not today. She leapt up, pulling the sheet from the bed and inhaling it deeply, before rolling it into a bundle and shoving it with her pillow into a suitcase.

She swept from the room without looking back, knowing it was up to her to encourage the boys to only look forward.

'Have you ever driven a van before, Mum?' Declan asked a little nervously as he eyed the Ford Transit crew van. She had hired it via telephone the previous day. It was delivered that morning, paid for with cash from her precious reserves.

'No,' she answered stiffly, 'but I am used to driving big cars and off-roaders and this is really no different from that.' She hoped she sounded convincing.

Connor quietly stood apart. He seemed to be watching proceedings, but not quite part of them. Nina wanted to hold him tight and kiss his face, but his body language screamed of the need for space. Her heart broke for her boy–man, who was trying to put on a brave face, but was clearly broken inside.

I wish I could wave a magic wand, Con. I wish I could take away your pain and make it all better.

Declan sat in one of the back seats crammed next to cardboard boxes, while Connor rode shotgun. Their bags, cases and a couple of small bits of furniture, the two breakfast bar chairs, two side tables, a laundry hamper, a large art canvas, the kettle and toaster, three small lamps and linens were piled into the cargo space. Both boys had items stashed around their feet and on their laps, rucksacks with their laptops inside, Connor's rugby trophies, boxes of books, photograph albums, some pillows, and the stock of toilet tissue and washing powder from the laundry cupboard.

'Okay, we're all set!' She spoke with an energy that she didn't feel, hoping it might be infectious.

'Okay, Mum!' Declan echoed. 'Off we go!' Nina swallowed the lump in her throat as she listened to her youngest's positive energy on this, the most emotional of mornings.

She was thankful for the obstructed windows at the back of the vehicle, denying her one last look at their home. This didn't stop her picturing it getting smaller and smaller as they drove away. A quick glance at the sat nav told her it was 63.4 miles and would take one hour, thirty-five minutes, to reach their destination. Nina knew this was a lie; she knew that where they were headed was a million miles from where they had started, and that it might take years for them to arrive.

SEVEN

Tiggy pulled the cigarette from her mouth and ground the butt into the kerb with her heel before waving slowly. Nina pulled the van up onto the pavement and cut the engine. It was without any of the imagined nostalgia that she returned to the postcode of her childhood. Instead there was a bitter tinge in her mouth that tasted a lot like failure. She looked across at Connor, who leaned forward, staring up at the dark brick building with an expression of horror.

'This . . . this is where you grew up?' he stuttered.

His disbelieving tone made her feel raw, vulnerable. Letting this boy, whose opinion she valued above all others, see where she had lived stripped her of the carefully constructed façade he had known her by his whole life.

'When we came here from Denmark, yes, after my mum died. We lived just around the corner.' She was painfully aware of the catch to her voice and the way her face flared. It was an admission, a confession almost, that she was not like the other Kings Norton mums, the majority of whom had hopped from the professions into motherhood; her journey had been different. She had caught Finn's eye on a building site while her dad touted for work, and he had scooped her up and she had been happy, living her fairy tale, until Finn had rewritten for her the most unexpected ending.

'This looks like the petrol station at home,' Declan whispered as he took in the rotted wood cladding of the fascia and the small flashes of graffiti on the front porch of the building.

She looked out, seeing the building through the eyes of her boys who had lived in splendour, in a gracious house, attended a beautiful school and had taken their leisure among the pale stone buildings of Bath, an orderly, prosperous city. And all for what? They had ended up back at the beginning, her beginning, and one she had fought to escape. She felt the strength leave her core and wished, not for the first time, for the escape of sleep.

Her eyes fixated on a misshapen ampersand in blue spray paint with two dots in the loop, a symbol that must have meant something to the person who scrawled it there. At this moment, she too felt it symbolised more. It was a stamp, a mark, proof that she had gone backwards, her life running in an endless loop, returning to a place where people thought it was okay to write graffiti on someone's home, in the way others might a dustbin or a derelict wall.

'Do you think it looks like the petrol station at home, Mum?' Declan asked again, quietly.

Nina gave a single nod. 'Yes,' she whispered, wishing her son would do what he did best and only point out the positives, if there were any, as if via a mind trick they could collectively pretend things were not that bad. She had to admit, the two buildings were indeed of a similar design and era. *At home* . . . She erased the image from her head.

'So here we are.' She turned in the seat, trying to maintain eye contact with Declan, who had gone very pale on the back seat. 'Let's get inside and get drinks.'

Tiggy opened the driver's door, leaning in; she wrapped her arms around Nina in a tight, brief squeeze. 'Hey, family! God, it's freezing out here. Welcome home! Nice wheels.' She gave the tyre a playful kick. 'Hi, kids.' She ducked her head and smiled at her nephews.

Declan raised his hand in a wave. Connor didn't answer. Nina and Tiggy exchanged a look.

'The good news, Con, is that you are only a hop, skip and a jump from your new school!' Tiggy was clearly trying to make things better, but only served to heap more tension onto the already fraught situation; the last thing the boys needed was a reminder that in just a week or so's time they would be starting at Cottrell's School, mid-term.

'Do you know what their rugby team is like?'

The note of desperation in her son's voice was almost more than Nina could bear.

''Fraid not,' Tiggy levelled, breathing in through her teeth, 'but I know that one or two of them are spitting champions. I have on more than one occasion had to wipe that lovely gift from the front window of the pub.'

Nina saw the look of abject horror in Connor's eyes. At a loss for words, she climbed out and looked down the street that was to be their temporary home. It was not as she remembered it. Not at all. In her mind, Portswood, as a suburb, was a place of genteel poverty and overcrowding, houses and flats for those who earned their living with their hands. It had been filled with the jovial banter of those who found humour in the face of adversity, who often shared the little they had with those who fell on harder times. Today Nina could see nothing charming about the boarded-up windows, the grime, the noise and the feeling of unease that meant she felt she should constantly be looking over her shoulder. The terraced houses further along the street had a clutch of green and black wheelie bins crammed along the outside wall, each daubed with the house number, written in white paint. Discarded refuse and waste had been dumped on the kerb, and an old mattress and redundant fridge sat in what should have been a parking space. On the couple of occasions she had brought Finn here, he always commented that it felt run-down, but not broken. He had seen a certain charm in the Victorian family terraces, lacy net curtains and shiny front steps, but this was not the case any more. Gone was the feeling of safety that she had associated with the place. With childhood memories dashed, and on this grey, miserable day, all she saw was dirt and decay. The blue ampersand somehow personified this.

Connor clutched his bag to his chest and looked around wide-eyed, mistrusting and afraid. Nina hated that she was going to have to be the translator, felt ashamed that the language of these streets was familiar to her.

'Student housing now most of it, and a couple of hostels,' Tiggy offered, having seen the expression of alarm on her sister's face. She tried to explain the dire state of the properties, where weeds sprouted from cracks in the uneven paving slabs and boxes full of discarded beer cans and empty bottles sat in the narrow doorways. Nina shivered, picturing the kinds of people who might end up in hostel accommodation and who were now her neighbours. A stab of fear followed – knowing that if she didn't get a job, the hostels might well be their next port of call. Her heart skipped a beat at the prospect.

Opposite the flats was a convenience store with 'special offer' stickers and posters advertising junk food, the Lotto and fizzy drinks cluttering up the windows. The kerbs were full of dark soot, accumulated from the constant stream of diesel fumes from the cars that passed by in a slow procession, spewing fumes. She thought of the tarmac lane that ran along the front of their property in Bath, pictured the occasional tractor or Land Rover that trundled along, usually with a Labrador in tow and most of the drivers offering a wave. Even the vehicles here were bashed and rusting, the drivers unfriendly and scowling. Nina still felt a flash of envy towards each and every one of them, the taxi drivers, deliverymen and passengers in the many, many cars, and the fact that they all had a car, and a final destination that wasn't here.

A young woman with pink hair pushing a pram, and with a phone wedged under her chin, looked a little irritated as she was forced to navigate the crowded pavement. A drunken man, in a greatcoat and a furry hat, swayed on the other side of the road as he raised a beer can in his palm and shouted out, 'Good morning!'

Nina avoided eye contact with Connor, knowing it would be that much harder to keep up her calm façade if she noted his expression of abject disappointment. And fearing that she might just lose it if she did. Her stomach felt leaden with the rocks of self-loathing and guilt. *I hate it here, I have always hated it here and yet I have brought my boys here. What was I thinking?*

The odd troupe hovered like a paused conga procession on the icy pavement as Tiggy handed her sister the small bunch of keys with a flimsy yellow plastic fob and stood back. Nina climbed the steps to the communal entrance, opened the spring-loaded front door to the shared front hallway, and swallowed. She tried not to react to the acrid smell of communal cooking, laced with bleach and stale cigarette smoke. She kept her head high and her eyes straight ahead as she turned to the first door on the left, what had been Aunty Mary's warm welcoming home, a pleasant refuge from her gran's cold hearth and sharp tongue. It was only as an adult that Nina recognised the warm cupping of her face inside her aunt's elderly calloused palms, and the issuing of sweets and hugs was her way of saying, 'I know what you go through with that sister of mine, and this is one small way that I can make you feel better.'

And she did.

Nina opened the front door. Tiggy wandered in while she and the boys hovered just inside the door.

The flat had either been remodelled or else she had a false memory of the size and layout. They stood in a dark, long hallway. Directly opposite was the bare bathroom. Peering inside they saw a small frosted glass window let in some light; there was a toilet and an old sink, with a small square of mirror with a chunk missing hanging just above. A white plastic bathtub was well worn; in some spots, the colour was now grey. The rings and loops, the result of a harsh scouring pad on the plastic, reminded her of the ice on the rink at Rockefeller Center in New York, where she and Finn had looped around one Christmas, arm in arm, and it had felt like the most romantic thing in the world. She pushed the memory away; there was no time right now to think about that other life.

Despite her efforts to remain focused and strong, tears gathered, as if the momentum of the day finally caught up with her and the sight of the dismal bathroom was just too much. She was finding that grief was disorganised, random; it struck at the most inopportune moment, could make her legs buckle under her, suck the air from her lungs and leave her deflated, winded and disoriented. She coughed and wiped her eyes on her sleeve, burying the howl of distress that threatened to leave her body, for the sake of her boys.

She scanned the white tiles and the green-and-white linoleum that sat in the strip of space between the side of the bath and the wall. A threadbare green-and-orange-patterned hand towel had been carefully folded in half and hung over the single chrome bar of the towel stand. The thoughtfulness of it made her want to weep all over again.

'It's very cold in here.' Declan shivered.

She nodded. 'I'll put the fire on.'

'It's very small,' Declan noted in a nervous whisper.

'It's big enough.' She gave a tight-lipped smile. 'What more do you need? Other than space to stand in the shower and room to sit on the loo?'

'There isn't a shower.' Declan looked up at her.

'Then a lovely warm bubble bath will do just fine. It'll warm you up too,' she responded as quick as a flash.

They all looked towards the window as the glass rattled in the frame. A train hurtled by, filling the room with a rhythmic, deafening thrum, followed by knocks that echoed down the line.

Connor stared at her.

'Let's look at the bedrooms!' she trilled with false brightness, trying to move everyone's attention from the terrible noise of the train.

Declan ran ahead. With his arms stretched out he could reach both walls of the hallway, showing just how very narrow the space was. It was claustrophobic, tight, tiny. Horrible. She walked behind him, closing her eyes briefly and gathering strength as she approached the two doors. The white gloss paint was chipped and scratched, and splashed with the droplets of tea that an elderly or hurried hand had been unable to contain. She knew this moment would stay etched in her mind, the desperate feeling at being back in the place from which she thought she had escaped forever. Dragging her two sons along with her was almost more than she could bear. Finn had promised her a life free of worry, a good life for her and their children.

Finn had lied.

Declan walked into the room to the left. A set of bunk beds sat in front of the window. 'I'm sharing with you, Connor!' he said. Even in this dire situation, he found it hard to keep the flicker of delight from his voice.

'You are kidding me? I have to share with Declan? In bunk beds?' Connor said, as if this was the worst discovery so far.

'It won't be forever. Just a short while,' Nina whispered, wondering just how long a 'short while' might be. 'I'll get a job and we will move. This is just temporary, and we need to make the best of it until that point.'

He stared at her mistrustfully. It tore at her heart.

Tiggy followed them into the room. 'How we all doing?'

'Just awesome!' Connor offered sarcastically, giving her a double thumbs-up.

'Great!' Tiggy responded in a matching tone. 'In that case, Connor, I nominate you to start unloading the van and find the kettle.' She gave him double thumbs-up right back.

'We can all do it, that will be quickest.' Nina squeezed past her sons and sister, keen to get back outside and shake off the feeling of claustrophobia. She looked back at her family squished together forlornly in the dark, narrow space, all staring at her expectantly. Finn's words came to her: '*I feel like I am living in a world made of glass & with every day comes a new pressure that is pushing down down down . . .*'

And did you think this was best, Finn? To put me in your world made of glass? Because you have! That's what you have done! A bubble of laughter burst from her mouth. 'Sorry,' she managed, stifling her laughter into her hand.

It was that or scream.

After she and Tiggy had returned the rental van, Nina dipped into her meagre funds for a fish-and-chip supper, carefully peeling off notes and rubbing them between her thumb and forefinger to make sure none were stuck together. The idea of giving money away or losing it was terrifying. They now walked along the pavement, back towards the boys waiting at the flat, with the hot supper sweating in a plastic bag.

'How are you for money?' Tiggy asked. Nina flinched, remembering Finn's mantra that it was one of three things they weren't to discuss.

'I've got a little bit of cash, enough for a couple of months' rent, and I have some things to sell. Could you help me with that?' She didn't know where to start.

'Sure. And then what?' her sister pushed.

'Things are tight. I need to get a job.' She nodded, trying to sound more confident than she felt. 'And fast.'

'What do you fancy doing?' Tiggy asked, as though Nina were at liberty to choose.

'I don't know, anything that fits in with school hours. I know that sounds pathetic. I'm in my mid-thirties, I should have more of an idea, shouldn't I?' She bit her lip to stop it from trembling. 'I've been so cosseted. It never occurred to me that I would need a career plan. I'm scared,' she whispered, wondering how she would juggle all that she needed to. How could she help the boys settle into a new school, and be the sole provider at the same time? The prospect of *not* going out to work and earning money was even more scary.

'You always wanted to be a nurse,' Tiggy reminded her.

'I did, but I think most little girls do, don't they, at some point?'

Tiggy shook her head. 'Not me. I wanted to be an astronaut.'

'How's that working out for ya?'

They both laughed. Tiggy held her sister's gaze. 'I decided to give it a miss. I prefer the pub. Better working hours and a much sexier uniform.'

'Oh, Tig, I can laugh, but I am really in the shit.'

'Yep, but the good news is, you are *only* in your mid-thirties, you have decades of good work left in you. That's valuable to an employer.' Tiggy lit up a cigarette.

'I guess so.' She tried to take comfort from this positive, but these mind tricks were harder to pull off than she thought. However, she loved her sister for trying.

'You'll get back in the saddle and you'll be fine. You'll see. You used to love going to work!'

Nina nodded. 'I did.' She remembered her first Saturday job in the florist's, and then later working in the restaurant at the cruise ship terminal down by the docks. 'It's not that I don't want to work. I'll do whatever it takes. I'm just worried about how much I can realistically earn and that no one will want me.'

'They will. You have a lot to offer.' She paused. 'I have hated to see your confidence so eroded over the years.'

The comment jarred her.

'I can't help it. I feel so anxious. I don't want to be.'

'I know,' Tiggy said, her intonation suggesting that the fault lay with something or someone else. 'And I know everything must be hard right now. It must make every step feel as if you are jumping into quicksand.'

'It does.' Nina's voice was small. She chose not to pick up her sister's thread. She didn't have an ounce of spare energy for analysis of her situation. 'I've had a good life, a life I wouldn't change. But right now

I can't see my future. Can't see the kids' future, and that's the scariest thing. I love them so much.'

'I know you do, and you should. They are great boys, of course. You were not much more than Connor's age when you left here,' Tiggy reminded her.

Nina pictured herself at seventeen, naive, trusting, malleable. 'God, I was so young.'

She thought again about the last time she had worked, running around for twelve-hour shifts at her waitressing job, with aching limbs and throbbing feet, sustained by the camaraderie of her colleagues as they dealt with the drunk, the absurd and the ridiculous: people who drank and ate with a gluttonous holiday mentality even though they were yet to leave port. She did love the interaction with the different people from all walks of life, imagining the many places they would visit on the vast shiny ships that left her behind on the grey shores of Southampton. And she recalled the sense of pride when she got her pay cheque at the end of the working week.

One night after passing out with exhaustion, she awoke when her dad had crept into her room, pulled the duvet up over her back and smoothed the curls from her cheek, like she was still a small child. Bending low, he kissed her gently on the face and whispered, '*There is no sleep as sweet as the sleep taken after a hard day's work, Nina . . .*' She had never forgotten it.

Her plan had been to find a job in Bath, once her dad had secured a role, and then on that fateful day, Big Joe chatted to the man in charge, the young, flashy Finn McCarrick, construction company owner, he had noticed her, and her life changed instantly. She'd sat in the front of the van shyly eyeing the young man in his sharp suit, who happened to be looking over her dad's shoulder and straight into her eyes, nodding distractedly as if, while giving Big Joe's request only the smallest of considerations, he had his mind on a bigger prize. She smiled at him, and just like that, all her plans went out of the window and she began to walk a different path.

It was hard to believe that was so long ago. Her dad had thought it wonderful that a man in Finn McCarrick's position was interested in his daughter. Gran, however, had offered stark words of warning that were still imprinted in her mind: 'You'll be better off sticking to your own kind.'

'I want to find a career,' she'd enthused to Finn after only a few weeks of dating. 'I think I might try to get into nursing, I've always fancied that.'

'You won't have time for a career!' Finn had chuckled dismissively. 'You'll have the wedding to plan and the renovations of the house to oversee and then who knows' – he had run his fingers over her stomach – 'maybe a baby to look after?'

Her face had blushed at the prospect. And she'd felt a mixture of guilt and sheer joy knowing the kind of life she could have with a man like Finn.

'You are more valuable to me at home.' He had kissed her firmly on the cheek.

What about what was more valuable to me, Finn? Again she shook her head, thinking of how quickly, with the implicit trust of youth and in the first throes of love, she had capitulated, believing that a man like Finn McCarrick, an older man, a successful man, must know best.

The four of them ate fish and chips out of the paper with their fingers. Nina tried to enjoy her food, but she was painfully aware that she'd spent twenty precious pounds on it. Connor left half of his fish and she found herself calculating in her mind just how much that waste had cost her. She made a resolution to shop first thing and buy smartly, avoiding spur-of-the-moment takeaways in the future that had cost so dear. An image of the jam-packed freezer in The Tynings floated into her mind.

I need to get a job, tomorrow. I need a job . . .

After dinner, Nina paced between the cold rooms that carried the scents and echoes of the previous tenants. She pulled their bed linen from the suitcases and made the beds. She put the laundry hamper under the sink in the bathroom, and the two bar stools against the narrow counter-top in the kitchen. She arranged her toiletries on the pale wood bookshelves in the corner of the main bedroom and put the boys' suitcases and boxes in their room, awaiting their attention.

'I know this is not what you planned, but it's nice to have you back,' Tiggy offered as she prepared to leave. Nina bit her lip to stop herself from ruining the moment with the fact that she wasn't staying; that this was temporary.

Nina closed the door behind her sister and walked down to the bedroom. Her eyes roamed over the saggy double bed that had been her great-aunt's. She plugged in her bedside lamp and put her clothes in the walnut-veneered wardrobe, placing two more boxes of her possessions in the corner of the room. She would sort them another time. Nina couldn't remember coming into this bedroom as a child, but clearly recalled her aunt leaving the cold sitting room to come and delve into a cupboard in here, returning with a vivid patchwork quilt to throw over Nina's chilly legs, snuggling her to bring warmth. It had felt lovely. Aunty Mary told her that the different fabrics had belonged to members of her dad's family, an aunt's favourite apron and a cousin's bridesmaid dress, amongst other things. It was the first time she remembered being aware that half of her blood was from her dad's family here in Southampton. Prior to this, she could only see herself as Danish, where her mamma had come from. Funny, that.

Fatigue now pawed at her senses; she was sorely tempted to submit to it, but wanted to check on the boys before climbing into the lopsided bed.

Hovering on the landing outside the boys' room, she spied through the small opening and listened to Declan's chatter. 'I think I saw a sign for a zoo on the way here. We could go and visit it, couldn't we?'

Nina saw Connor on the top bunk, facing towards the window and ignoring his brother. Declan persevered with another topic. 'I liked the fish and chips. It reminded me of going to the seaside with Daddy and eating them in the car and that time he threw chips out of the window and the seagulls swooped down and caught them before they hit the ground, do you remember? I thought they were going to come in the car. I was really scared.'

Nina pushed open the door and smiled at her son, '*I* remember that, Dec, and Daddy said their squawks were gull-speak for "Too much salt! Too much salt!"' She did her best gull-speak.

She heard Connor's sigh of irritation.

The bedroom was long and narrow with no furniture other than the bunk beds that, sadly, were too long to fit widthways in the room, which would have given the whole place a more spacious feel.

Declan pulled out his jeans, hoodies and sports kit from his bag and looked around at the bare walls. 'Where can I hang my clothes?'

'You can't. There's no wardrobe.' Connor growled his irritation from the top bunk, keen to point out yet another shortcoming.

Nina closed her eyes briefly; every disgruntled, negative observation caused the knot of stress in her gut to tighten. She thought back to when she had shared a room with Tiggy in circumstances not dissimilar to this. 'I can show you a neat trick.' She went into the sitting room to fetch a bunch of clothes hangers. She came back and popped Declan's hoodie on a hanger and then hung it from the base of Connor's bed so it hung down over the end of Declan's. 'Look, if we put all your clothes along here like this, when you climb in, it's like having a cosy curtain that hides you and keeps you snug.'

Declan smiled and proceeded to hang up his clothes. 'This is a bit like when you built me a wigwam out of clothes in the garden in the south of France, isn't it, Mum? And Connor found a toad in his wash bag.'

'Yes, my darling, it's a bit like that.' Nina took a crumb of hope from the fact that no matter what happened, her boys had had a short lifetime of wonderful experiences, enough to stave off the darker moments of want, something that she knew would have made her own childhood easier to bear, had she been able to dip into a pocketful of glorious memories. She wished she had more memories like this of her own mum, wished that she hadn't been so young when she'd lost her; at three, she was too young to properly know how to store a lot of memories and was far too busy learning about the world. Curiously, she recalled the feel of her mother holding her, wrapping her in love, but couldn't remember the exact colour of her hair. She could remember the deep earthy scent of the wood smoke that filled their little home in Frederiksberg, but wouldn't have been able to pinpoint it easily on a map. In her mind, it made her mum a shadowy figure, a presence rather than a real person.

'Are you going to be okay tonight?' she asked.

'Yes,' Declan responded.

Her heart flexed with love for her baby, who was showing maturity beyond his years. 'Well, I'm next door if you need me. Just the other side of the wall.' She looked up towards the top bunk. 'Night-night, Connor.' She reached up and patted his back.

He ignored her. She could feel the tension coming off him in waves.

Nina stood at the sitting-room door, taking a second to reacquaint herself with the shape and layout of the room. It was rectangular with a defunct brown-glazed tiled fireplace in the centre of the main wall, and alcoves either side of it. Tall metal-framed doors opened out onto a Juliet balcony that she vaguely remembered being open in the summers of her youth. They were now covered with old-fashioned lacy net curtains that were very worn, stained in places and frayed in others. The carpet was yellow, red and brown, a hideous pattern of swirls and loops that reminded her of the ketchup and mustard mess that was left on plates after a crowded hot-dog supper. It felt sticky underfoot and was so full of nylon that her hair stood up with static. The wallpaper was smooth and could best be described as oatmeal in colour with a slight sheen to it. Two bare light bulbs hung at either end of the room, casting noose-like shadows on the walls.

Sadly, the kitchen was just as she had remembered: a chunk of the sitting room that had been commandeered decades ago for the purpose, with a stud wall separating a six-foot square space that housed a cooker, fridge, a sink and a couple of loose-doored cupboards, all of which had seen better days, but were nonetheless functional. The red linoleum floor was also the original, and she pictured her little feet standing on it, waiting for the treat of a boiled sweet to be placed in her hand, a little gift of sugar that meant so much in a world of deprivation. Closing the door, she made her way along the dark hallway and into the bedroom, where she stood at the window, squashed between the wall and the bed. Her sobs came in great gulping bursts. She felt like she was drowning. 'What's happened to us? I'm here with the kids in this cold, miserable place and it's happened so fast I can't think straight.' She sniffed and wiped her eyes on her sleeve. 'I have been so bloody stupid. In the early days I let you bulldoze me, never questioned anything because I wanted to believe you, wanted the life you promised. But that set a pattern, didn't it? And that suggests I wasn't smart enough to see it happening. And I don't want to be that person,' she whispered, taking a breath and lifting her head to look out at the street beyond the window. 'I don't.'

Her eyes took in the neon sign outside the window that flashed the word 'OPEN' as cars and delivery motorbikes whizzed by. The pink-haired woman, now baby-less, hurried along the pavement with a holdall under her arm. The thrum and squeak of engines and brakes drifted in, along with music from stereos and shouts from further down the street. After the silence and peace of The Tynings, she found the noise deafening and knew the boys must too. The thought fuelled her next bout of tears.

Nina let the thin, dusty lace curtain fall over the glass and stared ahead, exhausted at the end of the long and trying day. She shivered in the cold, but knew that with her brain whirring and filled with distress, sleep was not going to come easy.

EIGHT

Despite her exhaustion, Nina slept fitfully. The misshapen mattress, the cold and damp air, the bus that stopped outside their window, all interrupted the rest she desperately needed. The bus's air brakes screeched at each approaching stop, making collections and drop-offs of drunken revellers, paying no heed to the fact that others might be sleeping in the middle of the night.

'Joshy! Joshy! You dropped your scarf!'

She jumped up from the mattress at an ungodly hour to see a blond boy holding up a burgundy knitted scarf and his tall, dark-haired friend – Joshy she assumed – walking back to retrieve it with a lilt to his gait that suggested drunkenness.

'Cheers, Liam!' Joshy shouted. 'See you later!' As if it were mid-afternoon. If she thought there wasn't the risk of waking her kids, she would have found the courage and yelled at Joshy and Liam to be quiet.

Giving up on any more sleep, she stretched her aching back and put on her slippers, not only to stave off the cold but also because she was wary of going barefoot in this strange environment, where unfamiliar bare feet had also ventured. Softly she trod the narrow strip of carpet in the hallway. Pulling the light switch in the bathroom, she sighed. For some reason this room bothered her the most. She tried not to picture her luxurious mirrored bathroom at The Tynings; tried not to remember the joy at stripping off her clothes and stepping into the cavernously deep bubble bath, the room lit low, with scented candles glowing, and the promise of her fluffy, luxurious bathrobe afterwards. One of her greatest pleasures had been soaking in a bath and then climbing into bed, with its expensive, pretty white bed linen and goose-down pillows.

Nina winced as she pulled the creaky door, her fingers flinching on the icy-cold doorknob. She ran a bath, hoping and praying that there would be hot water and recoiling as her skin touched the scratchy plastic base of the bath. Bath time here would be functional, a means of getting clean, all joy and luxury removed. She sank into the tub and tried to relax, but it was no use. She scrubbed, and pulled the plug. The moment she climbed from the warm water, her skin was instantly peppered in goosebumps. She couldn't pull her underwear, jeans, shirt and jersey on quick enough, cursing the cold.

After two strong coffees, from a tin of her favourite brand, brought from home and one she knew would be replaced by something cheaper when she ran out, Nina paced the kitchen, placing items on freshly wiped shelves, driven by a nervous energy. Declan woke early, and was washed, dressed, fed and sitting on the sofa, playing on his laptop with his sweatshirt pulled over his hands by 7.30. When Connor eventually appeared, he carried two dark circles under his listless eyes.

'Good morning, Con.' She tried to sound upbeat, to hide her very distress at the sight of him.

He stared at her. 'There is absolutely nothing *good* about it.'

'How did you sleep?'

'On and off. Better once I'd got up and put my cricket jersey on and a pair of thick socks.'

She nodded. There was no denying it was cold. She pointed towards the gas fire that pumped out heat in a limited circle. He went and stood close to it.

'Can I get you a cup of tea, a glass of juice?'

He shook his head. 'What are we supposed to do here?' He looked at the sofa where his brother sat.

'How do you mean?'

'I mean, how are we supposed to spend our days in this tiny space, without a TV or room to move or a car to get around or any friends to call on? What exactly are we supposed to do?' His voice had a wobble to it.

She wanted to remind him that she, like lots of people, had grown up without a car, but knew the timing wasn't right for this life lesson.

'Well, for a start you can have a bath and then unpack your bits and bobs and then you can walk up to the supermarket with me and we can get the groceries we need. Or you can go for a walk, explore the area.'

'Go for a walk? Have you seen it out there? There's homeless guys and junkies and traffic and shit everywhere!' he spat.

'Please don't use that word in front of your brother, or in fact in front of anyone.' Still she plumbed for a neutral, appeasing tone, wanting to keep things as pleasant as possible for Declan and knowing that this was far from easy for her boys. 'And I think you might be confusing Portswood with a war zone. You are quite safe, Connor.' She hoped this was true.

'And I think you might be confusing Portswood with somewhere that I might actually want to spend a second of my time in! I hate it here!' Connor shouted, and fled the room.

Unable to think of a helpful response, Nina continued to unpack, piling crockery in the cupboard and putting the cutlery into the drawer. She silently hated having to place their lovely items into the worn units where strangers' hands had scrabbled around for years.

'What *are* we going to do today, Mum?' Declan chewed his bottom lip.

'We are going to unpack and I am going to start looking for a job!' She placed her hands on her hips, trying to make it sound as much like an adventure as possible.

'Why don't you become a teacher? I think you'd be really good. You could teach at my new school and then I would get to see you during the day.'

Nina walked over and sat on the sofa with her boy in her arms, quashing the feelings of inadequacy and shame that washed over her. 'I wish I could be your teacher and I would like nothing more than to see you every day, all day. My sweet boy.' She kissed his head. 'But I think being a teacher is a bit beyond me.' *I am sorry, Dec. Sorry I didn't pursue my dreams of nursing, didn't push harder, didn't have the courage. Things would be a lot different for us now if I had . . .*

By late morning, wrapped in jackets and scarves, the boys set off to explore the high street. She gave them strict instructions to stick together, not to talk to any strangers and to stay on the one road that was busy. Connor gave her a stern look that suggested her lecture was being added to the list of things he hated about her and his life. And frankly she was at a loss how to respond.

She set open Declan's laptop on the counter, and took a seat, looking around at job websites. It was discouraging, to say the least. The sites burst with roles that she had no hope of attaining: Senior Brand Manager – minimum four years in similar role or recent Marketing graduate. She swallowed and moved her finger down the screen. Pharmacy Assistant: Qualified Pharmacist wanted for busy hospital dispensary. Nina felt her stomach shrink: these were all so far out of her league. The job titles continued to come at her thick and fast and she only had the vaguest idea of what some of them meant.

Switching sites, she trawled the local online paper. This looked a bit more promising. She got to work, firing off applications for every kind of job from estate agent to traffic warden, and one about which she was most optimistic she read aloud with enthusiasm: '*Data Entry Clerk wanted for busy hotel chain in their centralised booking office.*' If there was one thing she knew about, it was staying in hotels. Her heart and spirit lifted, and as her eyes scanned the details – '*twelve pounds an hour, flexible hours to suit*' – she felt her face break into a smile. And then the line that deflated her hopes instantly: '*Second language a must – Spanish/ French/German/ Dutch/Portuguese/Polish. Contact us today!*'

Nina felt her spirits sink as a response popped into her email account. '*Dear Sir or Madam . . .*' The impersonal, automated response told her all she needed to know. She clicked on an advert for 'Incredible Telesales Opportunities' but noticed this was a rolling advert with no start or end date, and the job was paid in commission only. She needed something more concrete than possible commission. Another advert caught her eye, a Senior Housekeeper position at a country house hotel on the outskirts of town.

Nina scanned the article, and picked up her phone before she lost her nerve; she was grateful that the boys were out and that she didn't have an audience. It wasn't what she had hoped for, housekeeping, not what she would have chosen at all, washing sheets and emptying bins, but she now knew the old adage wasn't wrong: beggars could not be choosers. If it meant regular money, then so be it; a housekeeper she would be. Nina placed her hand on her stomach to try to calm her butterflies. *You can do this!* She spoke the words of encouragement in her mind, taking a deep breath.

'Good morning, Winterton's. How can I help you?'

'Morning,' she ventured, working to keep the anxiety from her voice. 'I am calling about the job advertisement?'

'Do you have a reference number? We have several vacancies.' She heard the sigh in the man's tone.

'Erm . . .' She ran her finger over the advert and gave him the long number, hoping she had got it right. There was a silence on the other end of the line.

'Hello?' she prompted.

'Yes, madam, one minute please. I am trying to find it on my computer.' He sounded irritated. She wondered if she should offer to call back at a more convenient time.

'Senior Housekeeper, got it. And if I may ask, where are you currently employed?'

'Oh! I'm not.' She swallowed.

'So if you could give me your last position in this or a similar role and tell me a little of your experience?'

'I . . . I don't have any experience, but I have kept my own large house and looked after my sons for the last few years, and I think I can manage as a housekeeper.'

'You *think* you can manage?' This time he made no effort to hide his irritation. 'Do you have any relevant experience as a commercial housekeeper?'

'Other than looking after my own house?'

'Yes. Other than that. Have you for example managed a team of housekeepers? Worked to a budget? Organised rotas? Dealt with commercial suppliers? Handled contracts for industrial linens . . . Any of the like?'

'I . . . I haven't, but, I did have a large house and . . .' She cursed her tears that threatened, thickening in her throat. She tried not to picture her lovely life in her beautiful home that she missed. 'The thing is, I need a job.'

'Well, we all *need* a job. The difference is, some of us are qualified to do a job and others are trying to wing it without the relevant experience. Was there anything else I can help you with today?'

Nina hung up, then sat at the counter-top with her face in her hands and cried.

'Don't cry, Mum.' Declan's small voice from the doorway threw her; she hadn't heard them return. And she was so used to spending time alone in the kitchen at The Tynings with the boys off elsewhere. She spun around to face him. Connor walked straight into the bedroom without any greeting. She didn't challenge him, thinking it best he was warm, and hoping he might calm a little before their next heated interaction; every exchange felt like they were in a long drawn-out boxing match. *Ding, ding.*

'Oh, darling!' she sniffed at Declan. 'Just feeling a bit sorry for myself. I thought a job as a housekeeper would be a doddle for me. Turns out I'm not even qualified to do that. I think there might be more to it than I realised. If only they'd give me a shot, I'm sure I could learn.'

Declan walked forward and placed his little hand on her back. 'When I grow up and have my own business, I'll give you a job, Mum.'

Her heart swelled. 'Well, I appreciate that. What business do you think you might have?'

'I am going to have a sweet factory or a farm.'

'Both of those sound good.' She winked at her boy, hiding the naked fear that if she didn't find a job soon, they were going to be in real trouble. Nina then turned her attention back to the computer. Regaining her composure, she continued to scan the screen, rereading adverts for jobs she had first rejected, hoping to find something within the ad that she had missed.

'We had a bit of an explore. But it was so cold, we came back.' Declan unwound his scarf from his neck.

'Did you? That's good. What did you see?' She spoke over her shoulder, wishing she could work in silence.

'I collected these.'

She looked down to see the clutch of cards in her son's hand. He held up an array of scantily clad women with names like Crystal, Emerald and Candy, all offering heavily discounted services, emblazoned with a premium rate telephone number.

'Oh good Lord!' she called out. 'Where did you get those?'

'I found them. They are everywhere – the telephone boxes, the lamp posts. I'm going to collect them,' he stated matter-of-factly.

Nina leapt from the stool and took them from her child. 'Actually, I think it's against the law to take these, Dec.' She fell back on the old staple that had served her well in the past, knowing that her boy, like most kids, had a fear of falling foul of the legal system. 'It's something to do with advertising and they have to be left alone.'

'Oh.' Declan shrugged. 'Okay.'

She pulled him by the arm. 'Come on, let's go and give our hands a good old scrub!' She shoved the cards in her jeans pocket, considering how and where to dispose of them as she marched her youngest off towards the bathroom.

The next few days were some of the hardest days of Nina's life, and the nights some of the darkest. The weather was brutal. Ice formed on the inside of the windows, which she scraped at with her thumbnail, gently rubbing the crystals away. She kept the fire burning when the boys were in the room, but other than that, she wore an extra jersey and thick socks to save money. The feeling of being depressed by her environment had been so constant in her childhood, yet she had almost forgotten it. She hated how often she suggested they all take to their beds during the day, knowing they would at least be snug under their duvets and extra blankets. It was as if the weather dealt them this one final blow to crush any bud of happiness that might form on their miserable family tree.

Every day she trawled the job sites, looking for new openings, applying for anything and everything, sipping hot water that warmed her bones and laughing to herself at how particular she had been when first searching. Now, some days later, she sent off applications to anyone who was hiring, from janitor to rat catcher, to legal assistant, her theory being that if she fired enough bullets with this scattergun approach, surely one had to hit a target. Only they didn't, and with every rejection her spirits sank a little lower, taking all her efforts not to give in to the blind panic that threatened. What would she do when they ran out of money?

The few replies she did receive, standard letters and emails explaining that she wasn't qualified or that the position had been filled, were more often than not for roles that she had forgotten she had applied for. She even eagerly called about the 'Incredible Telesales Opportunity' that she had been so dismissive of – commission only it may be, but it would be better than nothing. She spoke energetically to the young woman on the end of the line, trying to sell herself, hoping her sunny nature might make her a more attractive prospect. The woman quickly yet politely informed her that her lack of keyboard skills and sales experience precluded her from applying.

It was a new low point.

Every day that ended with a lack of success meant she felt the black cloak of despair throw itself over her little family, and it took all of her strength to cast it off and encourage them to look towards the light. She started handwriting letters of introduction, asking about any employment opportunities, and posting them through all the letter boxes of businesses up and down the streets, thinking this personal, local touch might make a difference. With the shake of nerves, she handed one over the counter to the pink-haired girl who she discovered worked in the convenience store opposite.

The girl was very pretty at close quarters; she took the envelope with a smile. 'I shall give it to my boss.' It was the most hopeful encounter she had had, and Nina felt guilty for how she might have judged the girl.

'I'm Nina, by the way. I only moved in a little while ago. With my sons.' She turned and pointed towards the flats over the road.

'I'm Lucia.'

'Hi, Lucia.'

'We are neighbours actually, I live four doors down from you.'

'Well hello, neighbour,' Nina said with a smile.

'Welcome to Portswood! And I will pass your letter on as soon as I see him.'

'Thank you.' Nina meant it. She liked the way the girl spoke clearly and firmly; she liked her manner very much and envied her youthful confidence.

'I do a night shift, cleaning at the hospital. It's a bit crap, but the money's good. I could have an ask for you there as well if you'd like?'

'That's so kind of you, thank you. Yes, that would be great.' Nina walked away, praying something else would come along before she was forced to leave the boys alone every night, although good money was exactly what she needed.

It was mid-morning by the time Nina let herself back into the flat. Connor was quiet, surly, but now with a new air of melancholy that she hadn't seen before. It placed her worry for him on a whole new level.

'You can always talk to me you know, Con,' she offered as she turned on the kettle.

'About what?' he fired.

'About anything.'

He shook his head and ground his teeth, leaving the room to once again seek out the isolation of his bed.

She sipped at hot tea that warmed her throat and gave an instant feeling of relief, which was welcome, no matter how short lived. In this environment, living this reduced life, she had discovered that it was the small lifts that brought her tiny bursts of joy. 'Mummy . . .' Declan's voice was barely more than a whisper.

'Yes, darling?' She turned and saw him cowering by the doorframe. She wondered what Connor had done or said to cause such a reaction, and her anger flared.

'Can we go to the launderette?' he asked, looking at his feet.

Nina smiled. 'Well now, that's not a request I get every day.' She expected him to laugh, join in, but instead he shrank further against the wall and bowed his head. 'Oh Dec, what's the matter?' She knelt in front of him and tilted his chin so she could better see his face.

'Nothing,' he squeaked.

'Well it sure looks like something,' she coaxed, smoothing his hair from his forehead, 'but I do know that nothing is worth looking this worried about. Plus, if you don't tell me what's bothering you, then I can't fix it, can I?' She kissed his nose.

'You mustn't tell anyone!' he implored.

'Okay.' She nodded her oath.

'I . . . I did a wee in my bed.'

'Oh, darling.' Nina held him close to her chest. It took all her strength not to weep with him. 'That doesn't matter, we can fix that right away.'

'I did it before as well and hid the sheet under my bed.' He sobbed, pulling away from her clutches. 'Please don't tell Connor!' He held her gaze, his eyes begging.

'I won't tell a soul.' She kissed his teary cheeks. 'But you know everyone has wet the bed, even Connor,' she whispered. 'Now, let's go and get those sheets, and you and I shall take a trip to the launderette and we might even stop for sweets. How does that sound?'

Declan sniffed as his tears abated. 'Sounds good.'

'Right, you go and wash your face and we'll set off in a bit.' She ruffled his hair and watched as he loped off. She kept her smile of reassurance fixed in place until he had disappeared. Poor kid must be going through so much inside, contrary to the outward displays of happiness at which he was so deft. *My baby boy, I am so sorry . . .*

Opening the boys' bedroom door, she was hit by the smell. It was evident that Connor couldn't help but know what had happened: the smell was overpowering in the small room. They exchanged a knowing look. Nina felt overwhelmed with gratitude for his pretend ignorance. After stripping Declan's bed and reaching underneath to retrieve the other sheet, she looked up at Connor's back. He had turned, hunched over in his favoured position, facing the window.

'I know you probably don't want to hear this, Con. But I really love you and I love the way you are kind to Dec. It means the world right now. He's lucky to have you. We all are.'

A slight shift in his position told her that he had heard.

After bundling the sheets, she and Declan walked towards the launderette in a matter-of-fact manner, both trying to pretend it was any other jaunt. Nina was torn between ignoring the event, hoping to minimise his embarrassment, and wanting to fire a thousand questions at him about how he was feeling and how she might help. Obviously he was shell-shocked by their move, by losing his father, by trying to adjust to their new life.

'I'm sorry, Mum.'

'You have nothing to feel sorry for. I know how hard things feel at the moment. But it will get easier.'

Declan blinked and looked up at her. 'I was very busy when we were at home, but here I'm not so busy and I notice that Daddy isn't here even more.'

Nina understood this perfectly. Without the distraction of life in their lovely house, the funeral and the rest of term to distract them, they were able to fully focus on their loss, and no wonder it hit them hard. She bit her bottom lip, trying to ignore the fact that for her it felt like the exact opposite. Living in this cold, dark, sullen place made her grieve for Finn a little less and dislike him a little more. Not that she would ever disclose this to her kids, knowing they would never understand. In fact it was hard for *her* to understand, but the nagging thought that pawed at her senses was that he was the one who had dropped them into this living hell, and he had done so without giving her fair warning, without giving her any choice or time to act, and that was unforgivable.

She and Dec pushed open the door to the launderette and were met by the grey-haired lady who managed the place, who had previously introduced herself as 'Toothless Vera'. One gummy smile and Nina had no need to ask why. Vera was quite a character; she had more of a cackle than a laugh, and gave out the change for the coin slots and made cups of tea in the back room, which she then served in Styrofoam cups.

Without a washing machine in the flat, Nina had become a little more comfortable using the launderette along the road. The first time she had used it, the idea of putting her family's clothes into a communal machine that had washed strangers' soiled items had made her shudder with revulsion. In her spacious laundry room at home, the washing machine and two tumble dryers had run almost constantly. She used to think nothing of popping a tablecloth, some sports kit or a favoured pair of jeans in if they were asked for. Now, after a couple of trips, trotting up the street with dirty clothes was becoming normal. Sometimes Toothless Vera would unload the machine in her absence and fold the clothes into a cardboard box. Nina had to admit it was nice to have someone assist her in this odious chore. The place was warmed by the constant whirr of the industrial dryers and on a cold, damp day like today, she realised that it wasn't wholly unpleasant. Nina felt her shoulder muscles loosen in the heat.

'Oi, oi! What we got here then?' Vera called in greeting and Declan laughed, a genuine laugh at the funny lady who was so different from anyone he had ever met.

◆ ◆ ◆

As she and Declan made their way home a little while later, Nina spied Tiggy strolling along the pavement towards them.

'Hey, you!' she called out. It was still a thrilling novelty for Nina to see her sister so casually without pre-planning or arrangement. Today, the sight provided a much-needed lift to her spirits.

'Where you heading?' Nina called.

'Coming to find you, actually. Connor said you might be at the launderette. Fancy a cup of tea?'

'Yes, lovely.'

Tiggy did an about-turn and the three made their way along the pavement. Declan skipped ahead and then walked backwards, facing them as he spoke.

'We didn't *need* to go and wash anything, we just wanted to. There was nothing that we *had* to wash, Mum and I just went with my sheets because we wanted to,' he was keen to explain.

'Okay then!' Tiggy gave her sister a quizzical look and Nina reminded herself to have a chat with her youngest about how much information it was necessary to give away when trying to keep a secret. Nina winked at her sister.

It was as if for now the two had papered over the cracks formed during their years of estrangement, and for this Nina was grateful, knowing that to bring the topic to a head, to go over the reasons why, and who was to blame, was more than she was able to cope with right now. Nina woke each day with a feeling of dread, living with the windows permanently shut, hoping for a respite in the cold, cold weather and praying for the sun's warmth in the small, fusty rooms. In her lower moments, in between job hunting and cleaning the flat, Nina often sat and stared out the French windows, watching the world go by on the pavement three feet below. She often saw Lucia, rushing off to work, sometimes with the baby in tow and sometimes alone, but always in a hurry. It took all of her resolve not to bombard the girl with questions as to whether her boss had seen her application and if there were any vacancies at the hospital. She was wary of slowing her down, and figured that if Lucia had news, she would share it. She caught her eye once through the nets and smiled; she was rewarded with a little wave and a mouthed 'Hi, Nina!' It had made her day, this show of friendship.

'God, it's cold!' Nina rubbed her hands together and stamped her feet as they made their way inside the flat. Declan ran to her room and dived under her duvet.

'Yep.' Tiggy removed her hat and ran her fingers through her wavy hair. 'You look awful, by the way.'

'Why thank you!' she said sarcastically. This she knew.

'So, how's things?'

'Same.' Nina pulled a face. 'Still no job, though not from lack of trying. Connor is barely talking to me and Declan is trying to look at it as an adventure, but I think he does it for my sake. He is in turmoil more than he is letting on. I must admit, even though I know he isn't being that open about what's worrying him, in some ways I'm quite grateful. It feels like one less thing to have to cope with, and I kind of pretend with him. Does that make me a bad mum?'

'I'd say so, yes. It sounds like a cop-out.' Tiggy stared at her.

Nina felt her mouth move as her brain sought the words of gentle rebuttal that would also press home that there was no way her sister could know what she was going through. Grief, loss, betrayal – it was more than most people could cope with in one hit. 'It's not easy, Tig. We are all squashed in here together, and it feels like there's no room to stretch, to relax. Not that I'm not grateful to Cousin Fred. I really am. I know having me here is a risk. If I don't find a job soon . . .' She let this trail.

Tiggy gave a small nod, but chose not to comment. 'Where's Connor?'

Her sister's sudden coolness made Nina uneasy.

'On his bed, at a guess. That's where he usually is when he's not out roaming the high street, avoiding the armed gangs and pushers.'

'Good God, it's not that bad!' Tiggy scoffed.

'I know, but try telling him that.' She rolled her eyes. 'I can joke with you about it, but I'm tired, Tig, and I keep thinking that it will be good to get home. I picture my lovely bed – and it's like a jolt to my system when I realise that our home is gone.' She bit her lip. 'Anyway, enough of my moaning.'

'Yes, let's have tea. I'm just passing and thought I'd pop in. Do you need anything? Are you okay for money?'

Nina looked at her big sister, who was there for her when the chips were down, offering practical help when it was most needed. She stepped forward and placed her head on her sister's shoulder.

'I'm sorry, Tiggy.'

There was a silent moment while both considered what the apology meant. In Nina's mind it was clear. She knew that Tiggy did not have money to spare and was making this generous offer. How many times had Nina done a similar thing when money had been plentiful? The answer was rarely, as it hadn't occurred to her, and the shame of that suddenly hit her.

Tiggy held her close and cooed into her hair, '*Jeg har dig, Nina*. It'll all come good. You'll see.'

Nina closed her eyes and inhaled the scent of her sister, and in an instant she was back in the little cottage in Frederiksberg on the day her mamma died.

'Your mamma has gone to sleep and she is at peace now,' her dad whispered. 'In fact she is having the loveliest sleep you can imagine, and she'll dream of you forever and ever.' Tiggy, at seven years of age, knew better, and began to cry.

'I don't want her to dream about me, I don't want her to be asleep! I want her to be here with me!' Nina yelled with her fists clenched.

'I know, I know, and we will miss her, but you don't have to worry. I am not going anywhere and even though it hurts now, we will be fine. We just have to keep looking forward.' She recalled the way he had let his head fall to his chest, as if the strength had left every part of him.

'*Jeg har dig, Nina*.' I've got you, Nina . . . Tiggy had taken Nina's hand and pulled her close, and this was how they sat, while their father silently wept. 'That's it, my girls,' he managed. 'You need to look after each other, always.'

But they hadn't looked after each other; Nina had let down her side of the bargain. 'I am so sorry.' Nina spoke again, hoping that repetition might reinforce just how horrible she felt.

After Tiggy left, Nina splashed her face with cold water and left the flat for the supermarket. She gripped her purse tightly. Hers was now a world of cash, and previously, if that cash fell from her pocket or was spent, the hole in the wall would simply provide more and, God forbid, if that failed, she could then call her husband . . . There would simply be more to fill its place. Things were so different; the small amount of money she had now was all that kept her and her boys from sliding into the abyss.

Making her way up and down the aisles, Nina cast an envious eye over women who shopped at great speed, tossing items into their cart with abandon as they worked down a long list of family favourites and reached for anything that caught their eye.

That used to be me . . .

She shopped slowly, careful to buy only what they really needed, comparing prices with precision. They now ate foods that she knew would fill them cheaply and warmly. Hovering at the pasta section, she ran her fingers over labels, looking for the biggest pack at the cheapest price, no longer concerned about the shape, design or even taste of a meal; these aspects were all secondary. It was about bulk in the healthiest, cheapest way possible. She selected a weighty pack of penne and laid it in the basket before moving on to potatoes and rice. Her own meals consisted of what was left on the boys' plates and one bowl of porridge in the mornings. She had lost weight quickly and re-remembered the gnaw of hunger in her belly from childhood, when she would retire to bed with the feeling that the sides of her tummy were touching each other, her body coiled against the damp feel of the bed sheets.

She added up the cost so far, nervous of going over her allocated amount. It was a funny thing, how she was adapting to life in these circumstances. Memories came back to her, thrifty little tips and hints that hadn't occurred to her for years, habits of her gran – like keeping roasting tins in the stove so as not to clutter up precious, limited cupboard space; stacking bowls within bowls within bowls; rinsing cordial bottles with water to get every last drop; and placing a glug of vinegar in a half-bottle of ketchup and giving it a good shake, to make it last longer. And now as she wandered the aisles, she visualised the meals she would make and shopped accordingly, no longer frivolous or cavalier in her choices. Instead, she chose value brand everything, along with the mauled and dented tins that were reduced, figuring that canned soup was canned soup whether it came in pristine packaging or not. She made her way to the front, paid, and packed her bag, stopping to look at the community noticeboard on her way out.

There were several leaflets advertising yoga, Pilates, playgroups and book circles, as well as handwritten cards where gardeners, handymen and babysitters touted their skills. Her eyes fell upon a typed card and the words 'COOK WANTED'. Nina reached up and ran her finger over the print. It was for a place called Celandine Court. *I can do that. I can cook. I know I can!*

'It's only just gone up, that one.' A girl in supermarket uniform nodded towards the board.

'Right, thanks.' She gave a small smile. This information felt like currency, a head start. Her heart raced. If she went there now, straight away, it not only showed eagerness, but also gave her an advantage over anyone else. Making a note of the address, Nina hurried from the store. With her bag of groceries over her arm, she half ran, half walked the length of Portswood Road, turning right and then left until, fifteen minutes later, she found herself outside Celandine Court, home for senior citizens. She walked up the block-paved driveway with a sense of trepidation. Suddenly she felt sick to her stomach and hurried to hide behind a bush. 'I can't do this. I can't!' she whispered.

The bag of value brand pasta caught her eye in the shopping bag and reality hit: her funds were running out and in a matter of weeks they would be absolutely desperate. She pictured her boys going to school with empty stomachs and having to move to a hostel. Closing her eyes, she took deep breaths. 'Okay.' She pulled back her shoulders, wishing she wasn't carrying her shopping and that she had dressed a little more appropriately. She looked down at her jeans and padded coat that hid a raglan T-shirt.

It would have to do.

The 1970s red-brick building was a little uninspiring but two ornamental shrubs at either side of the door had been lovingly shaped and the sight of them lifted her spirits. She cast her eye over the pristine paintwork and clean windows and tried to picture the inside. *It will be cold and institutional, but I don't need to like it, I just need a job.*

She pressed the buzzer for access into the sparse, square foyer.

'Can I help you?' the male voice was loud, but pleasant.

'My name is Mrs McCarrick, I don't have an appointment but I am here about the position of cook that you are advertising?'

There was a pause on the other end of the entryphone.

'One moment please.'

Nina looked back at the path and considered running off, before remembering she had already given her name. *Come on, Nina, courage! You can conquer the world! It's just that tiny ball in the palm of your hand!* She pictured her little marble in its matchbox and felt a rush of confidence. She put her shoulders back and stood tall.

The woman who opened the door was wearing a smart burgundy suit, a cream silk blouse, a string of pearls and neat square heels that matched the thin tortoiseshell headband that held back her dark, shiny hair. Nina's scruffy jeans seemed even worse for wear. She ran her fingers through her hair, as if this might make the difference.

'Can I help you? I'm Fiona. I manage Celandine Court.' She stuck out her hand, which Nina shook.

'Hello. I'm Nina.' The woman was dazzling; it didn't help her nerves an ounce.

'Nina, I think there might have been a bit of a mix-up, for which I must apologise. My assistant Daisy is scheduling interviews and she's off for a few days and hadn't told me you were coming.' She placed her hand on her chest in a heartfelt gesture. 'So firstly, I am so sorry if we seem a bit unprepared, but that's because we are!' She laughed. Nina liked her honesty and felt the urge to match it.

'Fiona, the fault is mine.'

'Oh?' Fiona studied her face.

'I didn't organise an interview with Daisy or anyone else. I just saw the card in the supermarket and came on the off chance. I figured I might be able to beat the competition and get here first!'

'I did think it was unlike her.' Fiona looked her up and down, as if checking her out, making a judgement call. 'Well, as you're here, I may as well show you around. Sign in, and I shall go over the basics and we can go from there. How does that sound? You can leave your bag here while we walk.'

'That sounds great. Thank you.' Nina breathed with relief; this was the furthest she had got in her quest to find work.

Fiona punched a code into the internal door and Nina found herself in a vast reception that felt part hospital, part hotel. She looked at the grand display of white hydrangeas, the bushy heads of lilacs and the delicate stems of white tulips, and smiled. Flowers she knew, and they would always be the thing she loved. She looked up at the high cathedral-like glass roof, and was struck by the vast proportions. The place was light and bright. There was nothing cold or institutional about it.

'This is lovely.'

'It is, isn't it?' the woman spoke with obvious pride. 'Can I ask you to sign in? Name, time of arrival and telephone number.'

Nina gripped the pen, leaned over the visitor book and scribbled down her details.

'I always like to start with a tour, so you can get a feel for the place and our residents.' The woman clapped her hands together, as if this was the cue to get the tour under way. 'This area is known as the atrium. It's the heart of the building, where residents can greet visitors or just hang out for a cup of something.' Fiona pointed to fancy coffee machines, shiny white cups and saucers, and plates of biscuits sitting alongside. Smart sofas were positioned in squares around low coffee tables. Residents and guests sat on the wide comfy seats, some sipping coffee, some chatting; at least one was fast asleep, with his hands clasped across his chest and his head thrown back. Nina thought of Hampy, her father-in-law, whom she had dearly loved.

A few young toddlers played with toys in a corner where a shelf overflowed with books and a big red plastic chest was stuffed with toys, puzzles and other items. 'We encourage whole families to come and spend time here. It's important for our residents that they can receive their friends and family, just as if they were in their own home, only with someone else doing the washing-up!' She smiled. 'There is no set visiting time. If people want to come here at three in the morning or ten o'clock at night, they are more than welcome. We are also able to put guest beds in the residents' rooms for overnight stays. It means the kitchen is always busy, providing three balanced meals a day and catering for varied, special diets. You are just as likely to get a request for fish fingers or a plate of sandwiches for guests. We need that flexibility.'

'Well, luckily I am flexible and fish fingers and sandwiches I can manage!' Nina felt a surge of optimism. This was going well.

Fiona returned her smile and the tour continued. The staff members wore bright pink polo shirts so they were easily identifiable and name badges pinned to their shirts. They reminded her of holiday reps whose responsibility it was to ensure that everyone had a good time. There was the faint tang in the air of decay, of urine, of rotting teeth and of breath laden with the chemical residue of pills, that no amount of bleach or room scent could mask. This she knew was the reality of old age behind the shiny veneer.

That aside, it was all very inspiring, she had to admit; the bright dining room was clean and comfortable with a beautiful view of the gardens, and the treatment rooms were well kept. There was even a hair salon and chiropodist. Nina managed to keep a lid on her excitement, smiling and nodding with enthusiasm in all the right places with half her mind on the time, thinking how the boys might be wondering what had happened to her.

Fiona took her up to the residents' floor above. They stopped outside a room. Nina looked at a shallow memory box on the wall. Inside were a few family pictures, what looked to be a striped regimental tie, and an image of a plane cut from a magazine. There were other boxes like it lining the wall.

'What's this?' she asked.

'We find that a lot of our residents don't respond to a number or a colour, but will know their room because they recognise the things that mean something to them – a photograph of a loved one or, as in Mr Sandler's case, a plane. He used to be a pilot.' She nodded. The door opened and a middle-aged man came out.

'I couldn't help but overhear. Do come in and have a look. Feel free, Dad loves a visitor.'

'Oh, no, I really don't want to impose!' Nina felt awkward, embarrassed.

'Not at all, in you come!' the man urged.

Nina walked in slowly. 'I heard, Mr Sandler that you used to be a pilot. I can't think of anything more amazing than flying above the clouds.' She smiled at him, as though they were engaged in conversation, though Mr Sandler was staring out blankly into space with his head on his chest.

'I think it's lovely here,' Nina said, smiling at the son.

He answered on his dad's behalf. 'It really is. Dad is calm, safe, well-fed and settled.'

'Ah yes, and well-fed is where Nina's interest lies.' Fiona gave her a knowing look and Nina pictured herself working here, preparing fish fingers for people like Mr Sandler . . .

'Right, let's make our way to the kitchen. I'm sure you're keen to see it.'

Nina followed along the corridor. 'Food, as I am sure you know, becomes the focus of the day for residents and visitors alike. It punctuates the time and is very much looked forward to. We hold afternoon tea dances with lovely cakes and themed evenings, Italian and so forth, so the catering is varied. Would that suit you?'

'Yes.' Nina nodded, thinking how she might make fancy cakes and trying to remember sponges and fancies she had whipped up for the boys on occasion.

'We have a lot of parties.' Fiona smiled.

'Don't listen to her! This place is a prison!'

Nina turned to look at a diminutive elderly lady with short-cropped grey hair, steel blue eyes and a wraparound cardigan encasing her tiny frame. 'I had a date with Humphrey Bogart and they wouldn't let me go. He was pressing that buzzer all night and they wouldn't let him in.'

'This is Eliza.' Fiona smiled.

'I tell you what, Eliza. My husband had to ask me out three times before I agreed to go. I think you've done the right thing, making Mr Bogart wait. He'll only be keener when you *do* go for that date,' Nina whispered.

Eliza seemed to consider this. 'Where's your husband now?' she shouted.

'He died,' she managed. It didn't get any easier saying it out loud and was no less confusing for her, still torn between missing him and cursing him.

'So did mine.' Eliza held her gaze for a second, 'It's terrible, isn't it?'

'Yes.' She nodded. 'It really is.'

Eliza patted her bent fingers against her arm, before shuffling off along the corridor. 'Come and talk to me any time.'

'Thank you.' Nina felt quite overcome by the gesture.

Fiona gave her a knowing smile and they made their way to the kitchen. There were two older women in hairnets and tabards, one mixing bread dough and the other peeling vegetables. Nina smiled meekly at them.

'So, it's a fairly standard industrial kitchen,' Fiona said with a wave. Nina stared at the vast multi-rack ovens, the large, shiny chrome mixing machine and a huge griddle, all unfamiliar. The counter-tops were shiny stainless steel and a packed fire blanket and extinguisher sat within reach on the walls. She felt her enthusiasm sink, her smile fade and her nerves bite once again.

'Where are you working at the moment?' Fiona asked, her tone a little altered as if picking up on her unease.

'I . . . I'm not. I am new to the area and job hunting.' She hoped this practised response would suffice.

'So, tell me about your last role.' Fiona folded her arms across her chest.

'I've been a homemaker for the last few years,' she said, the heat rising to her cheeks and neck. 'But I am a passionate cook and a quick learner.'

The two women stood in silence for a beat or two, until Fiona asked the direct question.

'Forgive me, Nina, but what culinary qualifications do you have?'

'I . . .' She faltered, remembering the man on the phone who had been so sharp: '*We all* need *a job. The difference is, some of us are qualified*

to do a job and others are trying to wing it without the relevant experience.'
She felt her confidence crumble; her eyes darted towards the exit.

Fiona again prompted. 'Tell me about your experience in mass catering. Any culinary qualifications? Anything?'

Nina shook her head. 'I am sorry to have wasted your time. I just need a job. I really need a job.' She faltered again. 'I didn't think it through. I can cook and I hoped that might be enough.' She turned to leave and looked back at the woman and the two kitchen assistants who all stared at her. 'I do think it's lovely here, and can you please tell Eliza that I hope our paths cross again. I would have liked to talk to her.' With her head held high, she walked back to the atrium to collect her bag, and then left the building.

Nina felt the sting of tears at the back of her throat.

'Are you okay, love?' called a man in fingerless gloves and a grubby fur hat. He swapped his beer can to the other hand and reached out as if to hold her arm.

'I'm fine, thank you.' She smiled at the kindness of the stranger.

'Then why are you crying?' He pointed at her face.

Running her palm over her cheeks, she looked at him. 'I didn't realise I was.'

'Would you like a drink?' He held out his can of beer towards her.

'No, but thank you, that's really kind.' She squeezed his arm as she left, making her way back along Portswood Road.

She heard Declan run towards the front door at the sound of her key in the door, and watched his smile disappear, replaced by fear as he took in her distress.

'What's happened, Mum?' His chest heaved and his brow furrowed. She hated that she was making him worry, recalling their recent trip with his bed linen bundled into a bin bag.

'Nothing to worry about. Not really.' She tried to stifle the sobs, but she couldn't stop. 'I'm sorry, I can't seem to stop crying. I just feel a bit stupid and a bit sad. I . . . I went to try to get a job, but I couldn't do the job and I'm angry with myself for thinking that I could.' Her tears sprang in a fresh wave.

'Shall I . . .' The little boy looked around, as if trying to figure out what needed to be done that might make things better. 'Shall I get you a glass of juice?'

Nina reached out and stroked his hair, her face wet with tears and mucus. 'No, thank you, my sweet boy, but I tell you what,' she sniffed. She mustered a fake smile. 'You can . . . you can put the groceries away while I have a little nap. I think I am just very tired.'

Connor came out of the bathroom. 'What's happened? Are you okay?' He too looked worried. She knew he would have heard some of their conversation.

She nodded. 'I'm feeling sorry for myself and I'm going to have a little nap.'

'I'll help Dec.' She was grateful for his conciliatory gesture, not sure how much more she could have coped with today, and left the two of them in the kitchen. Closing the bedroom door behind her, she fell onto the mattress without removing her shoes and closed her eyes. 'Do you know, Finn, I used to think I was capable of lots of things. I should have insisted. I should have worked. I should have done a lot of things . . .' She closed her eyes, and the sobs came again.

As her eyes flickered open, she was for a second surprised to find herself fully clothed on the bed and was unsure of how long she had slept. Her sadness was a little diluted, but the swell of embarrassment would take a little longer to dissipate. She sat up on the bed. Her eyes felt as if they were full of sand and her throat was dry. Stretching up towards the ceiling she took a deep breath and reluctantly climbed from the bed where she knew, without the boys to tend to, she would happily have stayed for eternity.

Declan sat on the sofa under his duvet with a book, mouthing the words he read silently. He looked up. 'Are you feeling better?'

'I am.' She nodded. 'The wonderful restorative powers of sleep.' She heard Connor in the kitchen. Turning her head, the first thing she saw was the pickle jar on the counter-top, half-filled with water and stuffed with snowdrops she'd seen growing on the verge. She walked slowly towards them.

'I thought they might cheer you up a bit,' Connor said, shifting from one foot to the other, as if he might be regretting the gesture.

Nina ran her fingers over the relief pattern on the edge of the glass and then the little sticky area where glue stubbornly held on to a sliver of the label, before picking up the jar and cradling it to her chest. She thought again about the grand display of blooms that used to grace the round table in the hallway at The Tynings.

So much money. I wasted so much money . . .

This pickle jar filled with simple flowers was the most beautiful expression of love, the most precious gift of flowers, that she had ever received.

'Thank you. Thank you, Connor.' She stared at her boy.

'Oh no, are you crying again? They were supposed to *stop* you crying,' he pointed out, sighing.

'Happy tears, darling,' she explained. 'These are happy tears.'

NINE

The three of them sat together on the green velour sofa, empty break-fast bowls nestling on their laps. Surprisingly, with this the only seating option, it was rare that the three sat like this, in a line, staring at the wall. Usually one of the kids took his breakfast cereal to the bedroom, or hung around the fridge in case a milk top-up was required. But it was cold out and sitting this way provided some measure of warmth. Nina sipped her first tea of the day and felt a little cleansed after yesterday's bout of exhaustive crying. Both boys seemed to be in better moods, and the atmosphere was as pleasant as it had been in a while. There was a hint of spring to the sunny February morning; it felt like a fresh start. Just a few days before the next challenge: the boys starting at a new school.

'I have to say that I know things are far from perfect, but right now I feel quite peaceful,' she told the boys honestly.

A bus wheezed to a halt outside the window and the noise of ran-dom shouts filtered in.

'Oh yes, because it's so peaceful here, you weirdo,' Connor joked.

Declan twisted on the sofa and placed his bare toes on her leg for added warmth.

'Do you think it's odd, Mum, that our house is empty, and there's all that space with no one in it, and yet we are here squashed in like sardines in this little flat?'

She placed her free arm around his shoulders, unable to remember the last time the three had been happy to sit closely like this without one of them rushing off. It was nice. 'I guess it is odd, darling, but there's lots of things that are odd about our lives at the moment.'

Connor tipped his head back and stretched his legs out in front of him as he spoke to the ceiling. 'I've had loads of messages from George and Charlie . . .'

She tried not to think of what would happen when the boys' phone contracts, with all-you-could-eat data, expired.

'. . . and I don't reply because I don't know what to say, don't know what to tell them. I don't want them to know how rubbish it is.' He let his eyes sweep the room. 'In some ways I wish they wouldn't get in contact because I don't want to know what they are up to and what they've got planned. It makes me feel like crap.'

'I understand.' She felt the same when she pictured their home with a new family roaming the empty rooms, discussing paint colours and deciding what furniture might suit the space. 'But they are your friends, Connor, and you should keep in touch, even if it's just the odd word or message, and when things are less raw, it will be easier to hear from them.'

He shrugged, as if he only half believed her. 'Maybe. They keep talking about the rugby training because they know that's my thing.'

'They probably think they are being kind, keeping you informed.'

Connor nodded. 'I guess, but I wish they wouldn't.'

She squeezed his arm.

'And I wish I'd used the swimming pool more. I keep thinking about it. I thought it would always be there, and I couldn't be bothered to go outside a lot of the time. God, I wish I'd had parties!'

'You didn't have enough friends to invite to a party,' Declan quipped.

'Thanks, Dec. You're probably right though.'

Both boys laughed at the truth.

It was Declan's turn. 'I wish I'd rolled down the hill in the paddock from the top to the bottom. I wanted to put myself in a carpet and roll down it, but I never did.'

'You are such a weirdo!' Connor laughed.

'Well, that's both of us who have been labelled weirdos in the last few minutes,' Nina protested mockingly.

'Maybe he takes after you!' Connor fired back.

'Maybe he does.' She kissed Declan's head. 'That wouldn't be such a bad thing, would it, Dec?'

'I'd rather take after Daddy. He could run really fast and he knew all the flags of the world,' he whispered.

And just like that, the sledgehammer of grief shattered the chat, the joy, the normality, as Declan gulped on a sob. She rubbed his toes and noted that Connor looked skyward and blinked repeatedly, trying to will away the tears. Her heart flexed with love for her sons, and not for the first time she wished she could make it all go away. It was a stark reminder of what lurked so close to the surface. Nina knew that they, like her, not only wished that they could turn the clock back and use the swimming pool or roll down a hill, but that they could have one more night with the man they all missed, living that easy life.

She would like more than one night back; she would like years back, years when she would stand tall, recalibrate their relationship, get involved in the business, lose some of her fear and ask more questions, make her mark. Maybe then they would all be in a very different situation.

◆ ◆ ◆

Later that afternoon Nina and Tiggy jumped off the bus and made their way into the centre of town. The boys had been sent to the launderette. Not only did Nina think it was good for them to be involved in chores, but it was good to get them out of the house. It also meant she could turn off the fire and save money.

She and Tiggy walked side by side in silence. They stopped outside the shop, recognisable by the three brass orbs hanging above the door. It was the first time Nina had visited a pawnbroker and she already felt humiliated. Even walking inside and facing the bearded man through the safety grille behind which he sat sent a wave of embarrassment over her. She looked from side to side before closing the door behind her, but no one on the busy street gave her a second glance.

The chances of running into Kathy Topps or any of her peers here was next to nothing. She recalled how she had judged the hopeless and hapless people that she had spied trudging into a similar establishment in Bath. Maybe some of them had been far from hopeless and hapless; maybe they were just individuals who were a little down on their luck, whose lives had been thrown into disarray by events over which they had little or no control.

People like her.

'Hello. How can I help you?' The man sat forward on his stool.

At some level she had anticipated rolls of grubby banknotes, fat cigars, smoky corners and a set of knuckle-dusters sitting within his reach. This place was nothing like that; it was part bank, part junk shop, part jeweller's, and his matter-of-fact approach and polite demeanour made things easier.

'My sister would like to sell some items.' Tiggy tapped the grille and nodded at him sternly. It made her smile, the fact that her big sister was looking out for her.

Nina stepped forward and gingerly removed the antique silver cigarette case from her handbag, along with Finn's gold cufflink sets. She placed them on the wooden surface, along with his Montblanc pen-and-pencil set. She swallowed the wave of emotion at seeing these items from their home, things her husband had used in everyday life. But that was the nature of hardship, she reminded herself; it left no room for sentiment. She pushed them into the metal chute in front of him and watched them slide towards his outstretched fingers.

The man placed an eyeglass into his eye socket to appraise the markings on the antique silver cigarette case and weighed the items on his official-looking scale.

'I have antique dealer friends who will take some of this from me, but not all of it.' He removed his eyeglass and gave her a brief smile. 'Some items are more commercial than the rest.' He fingered the three sets of gold cufflinks and weighed them. 'The price of gold is down slightly, there's been a ten per cent drop in the last two months. They will, however, fetch less if sold as scrap, so I would keep them in the window.' To hear him talk of market values again bolstered her faith in him and took away some of her discomfort. He then scrutinised the Montblanc pen-and-pencil set, before twisting his head from side to side, as if adding up numbers in his head.

'I can give you four hundred and forty for the lot.'

Nina blew out, feeling crushed to see Finn's possessions reduced to nothing more than a number, and not a very big number at that.

'Is that all?' She did her best to keep her voice steady and remove the emotion, her fingers drumming lightly on the counter-top. 'I don't want to be rude, but it doesn't seem like much. I know what we paid for them and it was more than double that.' She did her best to keep the images from her mind, tried not to think of the items of value that Mackintosh and Vooght had spirited away into the depths of that dirty lorry. She placed her hand on her waistband to try to soothe her anxious stomach.

'I'm sorry.' He gave a small, sincere smile and raised his palms. 'I hear this every day, and believe me, I understand, but it's the same as buying a brand new car. The moment you drive it off the forecourt it goes down by at least twenty per cent – that's without a mile on the clock.' He shrugged his shoulders. 'I can only give you a percentage of the resale value, plus a small amount of commission on top and that figure, in my opinion, is the market value.'

Nina nodded and fixed her eyes on the cufflinks that had sat next to her husband's skin in a shirt he wore to go to work, when their life was very different, when she had been in the dark . . .

'I'll tell you what I can do.' He sat back on his stool. 'I can increase that by thirty – four hundred and seventy. That's my final offer, and that is only because I am soft hearted and you seem like a very nice lady.'

Nina matched his smile. 'Thank you. Thank you very much.' She watched as he counted the notes, licking his thumb. She left with the roll of cash in her pocket, an amount that wouldn't have paid her monthly food bill at The Tynings, but right now it was a lifeline.

'You okay?' Tiggy asked as they walked away. It felt like they had conducted something illicit, the way her sister looked at her sideways. Nina nodded. To have cash in her pocket that would top up her meagre funds gave her a feeling of instant relief. She thought about her dad on a Friday night, walking through the door with a wider smile than usual and a playfulness to his demeanour. He must have felt the same, happy to know that he could provide whatever might be needed, with his wages in his wallet; a brief moment when worry evaporated – a feeling that she could now relate to. She then pictured her dad's ashen face on a Monday morning and knew that this moment of relief would be short lived . . . *I need a job.*

They rode the bus home in silence, as if each considering how very much Nina's life had altered in the space of a few weeks. They sat with thighs touching.

Something caught her eye in the charity shop, a little way along the road.

'How do you put a window blind up? Is it hard?' she asked Tiggy.

'No. It's easy. No more than a couple of screws into a wooden baton.'

Nina smiled at her sister as she rang the bell to call for a stop.

◆ ◆ ◆

They returned to a note from Connor to say the boys had taken a rugby ball up to the common.

'It's funny. I used to long for them to spend more time together, to be closer. Yet right now I'm wishing they had their own friends. That would mean they were settled.' She folded the note.

'It'll come.'

Nina ran a damp cloth over the glass of the French windows, removing the residue of dust and dirt. She unhooked the net curtains and folded them neatly, in case Cousin Fred wanted them back. Tiggy unpacked the tool bag she had grabbed from the pub and charged up her drill. The white venetian blind was a little bent, a little grubby, but it had cost pence and Nina knew it would let in more light when open than the curtains, not only brightening the room, but when shut would also hopefully help keep out noise and draughts. It would surely be better than the drab, dated, discoloured nets.

'How come you've got a drill?' Nina asked. 'Was it your boyfriend's?' She didn't know the name of Tiggy's last beau, but all the men she had known her date were curiously interchangeable: quiet, moody drinkers with little drive and a penchant for a gamble. She had always hated to see and hear about the men who traipsed through her sister's life, knowing she could do so much better.

Tiggy slowly turned to face her sister with her drill in her hand. 'Did you really just say that? Are you living in the 1950s? You are *aware* that you don't need a penis to operate a power tool? And I hear that if you are *really* modern, women can actually go out to work too and earn their own money! Some of them even drive! But only if your husband agrees it's a good idea, of course.'

'Very funny. You know what I mean.' Nina unscrewed the light bulbs and hung the new paper ball lampshades she had also bought at the charity shop, instantly cosying up the space. There was something about bare bulbs that to her felt like a constant reminder of their deprivation. This was much better.

'Actually, I don't know what you mean. You sound like one of those women with tiny waists who advertise products with a grin and have a set role as a housewife. Imagine – all the chores in the house divided up by gender, with the little lady cooking and the man of the house going out to bring home the bacon – *and that's just how it is*!' she offered sarcastically.

'I guess that *is* kind of how it is, or how it *was*,' she quietly acknowledged, a little shamefully.

She felt her sister's stare bore into her. Tiggy drew breath. 'Well, I'm not judging you, Nina. The only right way is the way that works for you. And you obviously feel that you and Finn worked.'

'We did. In some ways.' It was a small admission that maybe things hadn't been perfect. There was a moment of silence.

'I used to worry . . .' Tiggy trailed off mid-sentence.

'Used to worry about what?' Nina stroked the ceramic white owl that she had grabbed as she left the house, a birthday gift last year from the kids. She had found it in the depths of a cardboard box that she had only just got round to unpacking.

'About you.' She paused, as if she wanted to say more. 'But right now I'm worried about how we get this room looking fabulous!' Tiggy clapped in an exaggerated fashion. Her sudden change of tone was an obvious diversion.

The two worked diligently, unwrapping a large, modern, abstract canvas that had sat in the downstairs cloakroom of The Tynings and had travelled along the motorway propped between the seats.

'How come Mr Nasty and his cronies didn't take this?' Tiggy nodded at the piece.

'Firstly it's not valuable, just a print, but also I don't think they spent much time in the little loo. It was wedged behind the cistern. Truth be told, I never liked it that much, it was a space filler, but I grabbed it when I had the chance, as if I knew we might need a splash of colour in our lives. And funnily enough, now I *really* like it.'

They placed it on the mantelpiece and it did indeed lift the whole space, adding a welcome brightness, as well as a focal point.

'That looks great.' Tiggy stood back and admired it.

'I wish I had some bookshelves.'

'You could move the ones from the bedroom?'

'That's a great idea! I can find a smaller unit eventually for all my bits and bobs.'

They hauled the shelf along the narrow corridor and into the sitting room, where they manoeuvred it into position in the corner alcove to the right of the fireplace. Nina unpacked her favourite books, including the ancient copy of *The Complete Fairy Tales of Hans Christian Andersen.* Tiggy ran her fingers over the weathered spine. 'Ah, Nina!'

'Yep. I treasure it.'

'God! I always get really choked when I touch something Mamma has touched.' She lifted the book to her nose and inhaled the scent of it.

'Me too.' Nina smiled.

'I used to nag her to read to me all the time and she'd be busy cooking or sewing, and eventually she'd get so sick of me asking, she'd smile and nod and I'd go and jump up onto the sofa, as though that was the only place she could read to me, and you'd nestle in by my side, like a little magnet. Mamma would throw that old fur rug over our legs.'

'I remember that. I remember the way it felt and smelled – like bonfires!'

'Yes.' Tiggy nodded. 'It did smell like bonfires. Exactly!'

'And that smell always makes me think of Mamma.' She had only ever shared this with Finn.

'Do you remember her getting sick?' Nina lowered her tone, folding the duster in her hand.

Tiggy shook her head. 'I didn't know she was sick. But I do remember her being very tired and Dad doing all the chores when he got home from work, so I guess that was probably the start of it.'

'I remember the day she died, Dad coming home to tell us.' Nina lowered her voice.

'I remember that too. You were very brave.' Tiggy looked away.

'I don't think I was that brave, I think I just didn't really know what was going on, not properly. And even though I was little, I wondered if there was anything I could have done to help make her better.'

Tiggy closed her eyes, clearly touched. 'Oh bless you, honey.'

Nina recalled the way her dad had crouched in front of them, hitching his dark, corduroy trousers up his thighs, and giving a crooked smile that offered little by way of reassurance, before breaking the news that she had gone . . .

The ripples of that one event changed everything. Losing her mamma reversed her daddy's life plan, sending him back to the bleak city in which he had grown up, where his parents would take a far greater role in her upbringing than anyone would have wanted.

She coughed to clear the sadness that gathered in her throat. 'I feel sad that we didn't get the life she probably wanted for us. And I hate that she missed so much,' Nina said. The words made her think of Finn, the old Finn, and all that he would miss.

'You just have to keep moving forward. What's the alternative?' Tiggy shook her head and pushed the book onto the shelf.

'I've still got my little marble in its matchbox. I can hardly stand to touch it, especially now, when I have never felt less like I can conquer the world.'

'Oh, your marble! I had forgotten about that. I remember her giving it to you and feeling quite jealous. Especially after she'd died, you used to get it out all the time. I thought it might have magical powers that let you talk to her.'

Nina looked up at her sister. 'I guess it did in a way. I think Mamma might have known me well enough to know that I would need a talisman like that, something to focus on.'

'Uh-uh.' Tiggy shook her head. 'I think she knew you well enough to know that one day you could conquer the world.'

Nina bit her lip.

'You're doing better than you think,' Tiggy asserted as she made tiny crosses on the wall above the window where she was going to drill.

'Well that's good because sometimes I feel like I'm falling through the cracks,' Nina admitted. 'I just want a job. I can't think of much else. And I know that once I have one, it'll be like having a safety net beneath us that means I can let go of the ledge.' She hooked her fingers and raised her hands, demonstrating the metaphorical cliff face on to which she clung. 'I've fired another thirty applications off this week, and I haven't had a single reply – not one. Declan is getting fed up at how I keep hogging his laptop. He stands over me, asking if I've nearly finished. And after the debacle at Celandine Court I've lost my confidence to go and knock on doors.' She rubbed her face with her palms.

'Something will turn up, you'll see.'

'I wish I shared your optimism.' Nina sighed. 'I am so worried about money, especially with the boys about to start their new school. I can hardly think about it. I dread them coming home and saying we need this and that.' She shook her head, thinking of the piles of clothes, stationery, new bags, all of the things that came along with the start of each new term in their old life. The indulgence now made her feel sick. 'I can only cope if I don't think too far ahead. I literally live one hour at a time. And each one that ticks by without disaster feels like a small win.' She closed her eyes briefly.

'The boys are going to be fine,' Tiggy said.

'I hope so.'

'Come on, we've still got work to do.'

Nina carefully unwrapped family photos of Finn and the boys in Chinatown in New York, and another of them in Italy, eating spaghetti alle vongole al fresco, white china on a red-and-white-checked tablecloth, the masts of the boats in the little fishing harbour in the background.

'Happy days.' Tiggy nodded at the pictures.

'Yes. God, I loved it when they were little. I mean, I love them now, of course, but when they were cuddly and sweet, it was bliss.'

'I bet.' Tiggy blew onto the drill tip to clear the dust.

'Did you ever think about having kids? I think you'd be a great mum.'

'I did.' Tiggy paused, blushing a little at the compliment. 'But I think that ship has sailed.'

'Not necessarily,' she pushed.

'Maybe, but without the right man in my life, and living over the pub, it's hardly ideal.'

'You could always get a different job?' she suggested.

They smiled wryly at the fact that it was her *job* Nina focused on and not the lack of man.

'I like working there. I'm happy enough. I think I'm stuck in my routine, and it's not so bad that I want to change anything.' Tiggy looked up. 'It's a job. You know, not great, but not terrible. And the longer I work there, the less I can imagine working anywhere else, if that makes sense.'

Nina thought of how, when she got a job, she'd keep working to get them out of Portswood and on to something better, somewhere better, as soon as she was able. 'It does, but I hate to think you might have dreams on hold. Don't you ever want more?'

Tiggy stared at her, and there was a beat of consideration before she answered. 'All the time, Nina. All the time.'

Nina nodded at her sister, understanding, possibly for the first time in years, that Tiggy had been trapped by circumstance. 'I could come and see you at work – is that allowed?'

'Yes! It's allowed!'

The way Tiggy beamed her response spoke volumes, and Nina felt a new spike of guilt for not taking more of an interest in her sister's life. 'That's what I'll do then.'

'This looks really nice. You've got the knack,' Tiggy said.

'It does look much, much better,' Nina conceded as her sister finished putting up the venetian blind. She let it drop to the floor, but angled the slats to allow the light to filter in. 'Thank you, Tig, that looks fantastic! Privacy at last, without those horrible net curtains. I would love to paint it. The whole place.' She ran her hand over the oatmeal-coloured walls. 'I might ask Cousin Fred if he'd mind. Not now, of course, but when I am more on my feet.'

'He'd probably be glad you were updating it.'

'Yes, probably. I mean, I don't want to do anything grand – I don't exactly have the funds – and all in good time. But just a coat of paint. And I would love to get rid of this kitchen wall. It's only flimsy. Reckon I could push it down, it wouldn't take much, and that would make the place feel more spacious, instead of two quite poky rooms.' Nina knocked on the wall, listening to the echoey sound; being married to the owner of McCarrick Construction, she had picked up a few tips. 'It's definitely hollow and not supporting anything, and the stove and sink are along the back wall. It should be easy.'

Tiggy strode forward, before placing the long drill bit on the flimsy surface and drilling a hole straight through the two sheets of plasterboard and coming out the other side.

'What you are doing?' Nina yelled, with her hands in her hair, as if horrified, but her tone gave a different message: one of excitement.

'Chain drilling,' Tiggy replied as she inserted the drill bit again and again.

'Can I have a go?' Nina wiped her hands on her jeans.

'Sure.' Tiggy handed her the drill and watched as Nina copied her actions, continuing to drill until she had finished the square pattern of holes through which the light passed through. 'Very good!' Tiggy gave a nod of approval.

Declan and Connor, arriving home, ran in to see the source of the noise.

'What's going on?' Declan asked excitedly as Connor stared at his mother wielding the power tool.

'I'm drilling!' Nina flashed a smile in their direction and pulled the trigger for effect.

'We are knocking down the wall!' Tiggy laughed.

'We are?' Nina threw her head back and laughed loudly. 'Holy shit, we are knocking down the wall! I think Fred would prefer it was done professionally?'

'Awesome!' Declan rubbed his hands together, joining his aunt and ignoring his mother's concerns.

'Nina, I have done this a million times before. I am practically a professional.' She rolled her eyes indignantly.

'Won't the ceiling fall down or something?' Connor asked with mild concern, arms folded.

'I have no idea, but that's the fun part, right? Waiting to find out!' Tiggy wrapped a dishcloth around her fist and punched where they had drilled. The two squares of dust-covered dry wall toppled to the floor, leaving her fist pushed through to the other side. Declan stood on the other side and shook her hand through the gap 'How do you do?' He chuckled.

'Hang on!' Connor came back with his phone and snapped a picture of his brother shaking hands with the disembodied fingers poking through.

'Right, Con, Dec, come in here,' Tiggy ordered. 'We are going to barge the wall down!'

'Oh God, Tiggy, are you sure that's a good idea?' Nina swallowed.

'No, but there is only one way to find out if this is going to work. Come on, boys!'

They came over eagerly. 'Okay, on the count of three we barge it with our shoulders as hard as we can, and see if it shifts.'

'Tiggy, I'm not sure if this is a good . . .'

Her sister's counting cut her short: 'One! Two! Three!'

The boys both yelled as they barged into the wall with all their might. They punched against the surface and bounced back. Declan clutched his shoulder.

'Look! It's moved at the top. I can see where it shifted,' Connor said excitedly.

Nina screamed, then laughed. 'Oh my God! The wall is going to fall down!' she yelled with a mixture of fear and excitement.

'I think you'll find that's the whole point,' Tiggy said as she high-fived her chuckling nephews. 'Right, we need you, Nina. More shoulder power is required. Come on, get over here!'

'I'm not sure . . .'

'Come on, Mum!' Declan grabbed her and pulled her over.

Spurred on by her boys' energy and caught up in the moment, Nina stood in line and braced her shoulders like the others. 'Okay, and again!' Tiggy shouted. 'One! Two! Three!'

The four of them charged the wall, which seemed to slip a little further from its creaky wooden anchors with ease.

Tiggy surveyed the wall; Connor did the same on the other side. 'I reckon one more go,' he said, a glint of excitement in his eyes. Nina wanted to cry with happiness, but this was not the time for tears, happy or otherwise; instead, she got behind the project with gusto. 'All right then, one more go. Come on, folks!'

They resumed their positions. 'One! Two! Three!' They ran forward, letting out loud yells as their bodies met with the surface.

There was a cracking sound and a thick plume of dust filled the room, whooshing up their noses and into their mouths. Nina prayed there were no injuries and tried to figure out exactly what had happened.

'We did it!' Declan yelled, jumping up and down on the spot. They looked as if they had walked through flour, with the fine dust and grime of over sixty years clinging to their hair and eyelashes. Each coughed and spat the grit that crunched between their teeth, and they all laughed at the sight of how ridiculous they looked.

'That was absolutely brilliant!' Declan raced around, climbing over the shattered chunks of plasterboard that now lay in a shallow heap on the sitting-room floor.

'It's huge!' Nina turned in a circle with her arms spread wide and took in the big open space that they had created.

There was the unmistakable sound of banging on the ceiling from the flat above. 'What the bloody hell is going on down there?' a voice yelled from above.

'That's Mr Broom Handle,' Tiggy whispered, giggling. She stood on her tiptoes and, with a piece of wood in her hand, knocked back. It made Nina cringe and laugh at the same time.

'Shall we do another wall?' Connor asked, half-jokingly.

'No!' she and Tiggy yelled in unison.

'Spoilsports.' He walked forward and opened the French doors, watching as a cloud of dust escaped and rose up to float high above Portswood Road. 'What's going on in there?' Toothless Vera called from the pavement, on her way to the launderette.

'We've just knocked down a wall, Vera!' Nina called out with a wave. 'But don't worry. We as good as have the owner's permission – he's our cousin! And my sister is practically a professional.'

'I am?' Tiggy looked at her sister with her eyebrows raised.

'You said you were!' she gasped, blinking powder from her eyes. 'You said you'd done it loads of times!'

'God, you believe anything!' Tiggy laughed and pulled out a packet of cigarettes. 'Want one?' she held the pack out towards her sister.

'No, I do not. I can't believe I just let you talk me into that!' She chuckled, watching as her sister lit up, blowing the acrid smoke out the door. 'I love you, Tiggy,' she said.

Her sister turned to face her. 'Well you can cut that out for a start.' She tutted and took a deep drag on her cigarette.

TEN

Nina lay for a while staring at the door of the bedroom, picturing a particular morning about a month before Finn died. He had peeled off notes from a wad in his wallet and laid them on the counter-top with a wink, as if tipping her: a fifties housewife being given her allowance. Now it made her blood run cold. *I never for one second felt tricked or uncertain, but now? I'm not sure of anything, and that makes me sadder than I can say.*

Sitting up, she rubbed her face, ran her fingers through her wild hair and rose slowly to face this momentous day: the day her boys started their new school. It was also the day she would redouble her efforts in looking for a job, cast the net even wider and be prepared to travel even further. The prospect of both petrified her.

With a mug of tea in her hand and ignoring the growl of hunger in her stomach, she raised the blind. The cold snap had thankfully passed and the winter sun sent a blue swathe over the rooftops. It was still chilly, but without the bone-numbing cold and damp that had made life in the flat so very unpleasant. Portswood Road was coming to life. A slight man jumped from a poorly parked white van and dropped a bundle of newspapers on the pavement outside the convenience store, before roaring off to his next delivery point. Early dog walkers were out in force, nodding knowingly to each other as the sun rose on this fresh

February day. The idea jolted in her mind that a paper round or dog walking would be a good way to bring in a little bit of money. A young couple in coordinating Lycra and matching gloves jogged side by side along the kerb, looking stern and matching each other stride for stride. The idea of her and Finn doing that made her smile. Their health and fitness measures were mainly saying no to more cheese and stopping after one glass of wine. She pictured sitting with her feet resting on his lap on the sofa, eating cheese and crackers and sipping wine, laughing. Happy times.

She looked up over the chimney pots, wondering what was going on inside the numerous homes all squished together in this little corner of the city. She knew that in many of them, parents just like her would be waking children for their first day of school after the half-term break and, just like her, they would be sitting with nerves shredded, torn between wanting to get the day started and wishing she could delay it.

A bus pulled up and Lucia got off, wearing her striped overall over a tracksuit. Nina could see she was tired, and remembered Lucia had a night job, cleaning. She waved her hand in greeting and Lucia managed a smile, then a yawn, followed by the universally recognised sign for sleep, her two hands in prayer, laid against her tilted head.

Nina gestured for her to come inside, remembering her dad coming home from night shifts, the joy he took in easing off his cumbersome work boots and flexing his feet inside the thick socks, and the look of bliss on his face as he sipped hot tea that seemed to offer momentary restoration.

Lucia came over to the door, which Nina opened. 'Can't I get you a cup of tea?'

'I can't. Babysitting duties.' She pulled a face. 'My baby sister, Jemima.'

Nina had thought the baby was hers. 'Oh how lovely, your lucky mum!' She meant it.

'Yes, lucky. I'm one of six and she just keeps getting lucky!'

One of six? Nina bit her lip, not wanting to blurt out what she was thinking: that having six children could do nothing to help when your life was a struggle financially. It was another wake-up to just how much her life with Finn had shielded her from the harsh reality of what she had left behind.

'Are you the oldest?'

'No, I have two older brothers, both moved away, one at college, and then the three little ones are at home with Mum and me.'

'Hard work, I bet.'

'Yes, hard work, and the reason *I* can't go away to college for my art, my painting. There's just not the money – a student loan would barely cover it and I don't know how Mum would cope without me.'

'That's such a shame.' Nina didn't want to judge or pry, but she wished she could tell her that it was important she live her life too, follow her dreams. 'I bet you are talented.'

'I love painting. I'm really good.' Lucia held her gaze and Nina envied her confidence in her ability.

'You shouldn't let it go to waste.'

The girl shrugged, as if the sentiment, no matter how well intended, were irrelevant. 'Anyway, better get home. A quick nap, then the kids are up for school.'

'Your mum's certainly lucky to have you.'

Lucia blushed. 'I'll take you up on that cup of tea another time.'

'You bet.' Nina hoped she would. Here, in this community, alone, she felt comfortable in reaching out the neighbourly hand of friendship, wanting to engage. Yet at The Tynings, where she had had enough room to house the entire neighbourhood, and an abundance of beverages to offer, the thought didn't occur to her. An image of Mrs Appleton flashed into her mind and she cringed, remembering the damp, dark evening she had practically begged the woman, who was little more than a stranger, for shelter.

She heard the boys' bedroom door open and the sound of Connor running a bath. The bathroom was harder to spruce up. The addition of lime green towels and bath mats from home had certainly brought a welcome splash of colour. These additions, however, counted for little when her skin met with the scratched base of the plastic bath and the icy wall tiles when climbing in and out.

She hadn't told the boys, thinking it might unsettle them, but only the day before she had taken a call from Mr Firth. He had told her softly, kindly, that the liquidators had been inside and taken any bits of large furniture that were left, the gates had been padlocked, the locks changed, and a 'For Sale' sign put up. It was hard for her not to picture the numerous times she had driven through those gates, pulling up in her fancy car with groceries, shopping or kids in tow . . . She couldn't imagine being locked out of the home they had created. Mr Firth was a good man and she was thankful that he had thought to ring. She flashed back to Connor's distressed call and the battered lorry on the driveway. Even the thought of it left her feeling a little queasy. Nina tried not to imagine the house now, preferring to think of it in its pristine state, even managing to erase the image of two sets of dirty footprints left by Mr Ludlow's associates on her hallway floor.

She shivered and took a glug of her tea. There simply wasn't enough headspace available for her to go over that day again. Not with everything else to occupy her thoughts.

'Mum?' Declan stood in the doorway, clutching his stomach, 'I've got an upset tummy.' He grimaced.

'That'll just be nerves, darling. It's okay, once you get settled and your day is under way you'll be right as rain, you'll see.' She winked at him, trying to lighten the mood, fighting her desire to scoop him into her arms and hold him close. She thought of the bedwetting incident, the stress that Declan hid, and that pained her so.

Declan screwed up his face, 'It's not that, Mum. I need the bathroom. I need it badly, but Connor is in there.'

'Oh, oh God.' She put her tea down and rushed along the hallway, knocking gently on the door, 'Con, sorry to disturb you, but Declan needs to use the bathroom and he needs it now!'

'I'll be five minutes!' he snapped.

'I don't think we've got five minutes!' she yelled, whilst smiling reassuringly at her youngest.

'Oh for God's sake!'

She heard a loud splash and then the stamp of her son's feet on the linoleum floor. The door flung open and Connor stood dripping wet with a towel wrapped around his waist.

Declan rushed in and slammed the door, then banged the toilet seat against the bowl.

'Thank you, Connor.'

He ignored her, shaking his head and twisting his jaw in frustration before he started banging on the door with his fist. 'Hurry up, Declan!'

'Please don't take it out on him, he can't help it, he needs the loo!'

'And I need a bath and here we are stuck in this shitty flat on this shitty day!'

'You need to pipe down, Connor. You can't talk to me like that. I am aware that our situation is far from perfect—'

'You think?' he snorted, interrupting her.

'Losing your temper is not going to help anything.'

He huffed and stared at his feet.

Nina felt the first throb of a headache. This was not the start she had hoped for.

The boys ate their breakfast of cereal in the narrow kitchen. The lack of space meant they stood side by side, leaning against the cupboards.

'You both look lovely,' she tried.

Connor tugged at the thin polo shirt collar that sat under his sweatshirt and turned up his nose, as if both the material and school logo offended him.

'This is, like, something you might wear for PE!' He shook his head. She had to admit it was a world away from his old uniform of a stiff-collared white shirt, navy sweater and pure wool blazer with the school crest and motto emblazoned on the chest. Nina felt a spike of disgust when she recalled just how much she had enjoyed traipsing around the city with her boys in tow, quietly acknowledging the knowing looks from other residents who knew what it took to be a Kings Norton College boy.

'And the good news is, you finish at four fifteen. That's a whole hour earlier than you are used to. You'll have more free time of an evening.'

'You are right, Mum, this whole move is a *great* idea because rather than carry on with the education I was getting and being able to play my rugby, I now get to spend an extra hour sitting on my bunk bed trying to block out the noise of the road we live on and Declan's non-stop talking!'

Declan shrank at his brother's comments.

'I know you are anxious about today and I understand that. It sucks that we are in this situation, it sucks that you have had to change schools and it sucks that we live here with one bathroom and that Declan needs a shit while you need a bath. I get it.'

Both boys looked up at her. Declan sucked in his cheeks, whether to stifle any potential laughter at her language, or whether to stem his embarrassment, she wasn't sure.

'I wish I could wave a magic wand and make it all better, but I can't. I can't.' She paused. 'And the one thing I do know is that you are a great kid, Connor. You both are.' She smiled at Declan. 'You know how to make the best of a situation – you learned that on the rugby field, right? Looking for the opportunity! Adapting quickly to whatever might come

172

your way! Thinking fast! That's you, Con, and these are your skills! And that is what will get you through this.'

Connor stood up straighter. Declan continued to look at the floor. 'And you, Declan, have nothing to worry about. There is nobody on the planet that has ever met you and not wanted to be your friend. Plus, your big brother is only ever going to be a corridor away.' She brushed his cheek and thought again of Tiggy and how comforting it was to have a sibling looking out for you.

Connor turned and walked back into the bedroom, closing the door behind him loudly. Nina felt the apartment shudder, quickly followed by a banging on the ceiling above and a shout of 'Don't slam the doors!'

'It was hardly a slam, was it?' she whispered to Declan, and they both looked upwards towards where Mr Broom Handle's yell had come from. 'You and Connor have a right to be angry with me and angry at the world. You have had more to deal with than most adults ever have to. But everything will settle, you'll see.'

Declan looked up at her hopefully.

Nina waved the boys off with a false smile masking a feeling of dread. The three of them had rehearsed the walk to school twice, and both times it had taken a little less than twenty minutes. They had robustly rebuffed her offer to walk with them on their first day. Knowing they would take their lead from her, she smiled and bade them farewell, wishing them luck and promising a nice celebratory supper when they returned.

She went over to the French windows to wave at Declan, who glanced briefly over his shoulder. A loud wheeze of bus brakes on the road opposite made her jump. It was a physical reminder that her old life was gone, and in this life what she needed to do was not stand and lament what she had lost, but find a job.

Closing the French doors, she sat on the sofa and opened Declan's laptop, typing the familiar search for 'JOB VACANCIES SOUTHAMPTON', which took her straight to her favoured local paper site. She stared, yet again at the job titles on offer, reading aloud: 'Gardening Apprentice, School Cleaner, Office Manager, Money Coach.' She gave a snort of laughter. 'Money Coach? That'd be a quick interview.' She clicked on the school cleaner advertisement and read the details, figuring it sounded like her best bet. If there was one thing she could do, it was clean. 'From 4 p.m. to 9 p.m.' She read the opening line and her spirits sank. She didn't have the luxury of choosing suitable hours. As heartbreaking as it may be, she might not be there to greet the boys from school, as she always had been, and they might have to forage for their own supper. She couldn't sit back and watch their money dwindle to nothing. Amending her saved letter of application, she filled out the online form. The template was now so familiar to her she could almost do it instinctively. She looked at the time – 8.45 – and wondered how the boys were faring. Were they lonely? Nervous? Afraid?

'You can do this, kids!' she called towards the window.

An unexpected wave of sadness rose in her. She sank back into the sofa and took a deep breath, feeling slightly woozy. Recent experience had taught her that if she ate in the late morning and then again in the late afternoon, this would get her through the day on two meals. If she ate early she was hungry again by midday and then again in the evening. This way, she saved money and lessened the effect of too little food on her day.

I just want a job, any job. How come all these people outside my window, running for the bus and walking along the pavement, can manage it and I can't? I feel like nothing. I feel like I am on the outside of the world looking in, peeping out from behind my tree, hiding . . . 'And I think I have been for quite a while,' she said out loud to the walls. She decided to get moving. An idea had been forming for a while and this, she knew, was the day to put it into action.

Nina fixed up the flat for three hours, folding bed linen, hanging clothes, hefting furniture and shifting heavy boxes until her arms shuddered. The muddle she created caused her to doubt her idea, worrying that she was making things worse rather than better. By the time she had finished, however, with the place dusted, aired and vacuumed, and with sweat on her brow, she was able to stand back and admire her efforts.

The boys' bedroom had been somewhat transformed. She had cleverly bisected the space by dismantling the bunk beds and pushing Connor's to the opposite side and moving his clothes rail to the top of his bed to form a barrier of sorts. Declan's clothes rail mirrored this on the other side of the room. Two side tables she had brought from The Tynings sat at the heads of the boys' beds with a little lamp on each, so they could now at least read, or have their own light, and not have to rely on the communal overhead bulb that had sat uncomfortably close to Connor in the top bunk. Not only did the new arrangement instantly let light from the previously blocked window flood in, but it meant that each boy now had a modicum of privacy. She stood back with her hands on her waist feeling a rare sense of achievement. She had worked her way through the whole house.

Looking up at the clock, it was nearly time. She placed the cut slices of shop-bought cookie dough in the oven and waited. The boys would be home soon. Her stomach was in knots. She closed her eyes, and prayed silently that their first day had gone well, knowing it could set the tone for the coming months. Her heart leapt when the front doorbell rang and she ran to answer it. 'Hey, boys, there you are! How did it go?'

Declan wrinkled his nose and gave a little shrug. 'It was okay.' The child who always managed to find a silver lining damned the experience with his faint praise. She ran her hand over his head.

'Hello, darling,' she said to Connor. 'How was it?'

Connor gave her a dark look and remained silent. He rushed past her and into the bedroom, saying nothing about the changes. Instead, he climbed into his bed, pulling the quilt up over his head and curling himself into a ball. Nina felt awash with disappointment. She had hoped that the thoughtfulness with which he had gathered her flowers, and the openness of their recent communication, might have continued, but as was the way with disgruntled, complicated teens, his mood and treatment of her continued to ebb and flow. One step forward and two steps back.

'I think we should leave him,' Declan said. Even he sensed her desire to run after Connor and quiz him on how best she could fix things.

She smiled. 'Maybe for a bit, then he might want to talk to his mum.'

Declan wrinkled his nose, as if he found this idea most unlikely.

The two of them sat on the sofa and nibbled the warm oatmeal and raisin biscuits; an indulgence, and a celebration.

'So come on, how was your day?' She nudged him.

'Different,' he managed, through a mouthful of crumbs. 'Very different.'

'In what way?'

'Every way, Mum!'

'Are your teachers nice?'

'My form tutor, Miss Butler is nice, but . . .'

'But what?'

'Some of the girls in my class ignored her. She was telling us what to expect on our first day and she asked me to stand up so that she could introduce me, and all the time she was talking, these three girls at the back of the class were chatting and laughing, really loudly, as if she wasn't there!' He looked at his mum with an expression of incredulity.

This behaviour would have been unthinkable at Kings Norton, where kids were respectful of the teaching staff and equally as fearful of the punishments.

'Maybe Miss Butler was just letting everyone get settled in and she might be very strict tomorrow?' *Please God* . . .

'Yep, maybe,' he conceded.

'I'll go and check on Connor.' She hoped that the half an hour she had given him to calm down and gather his thoughts might have done the trick. She knocked on the door and gingerly approached his bed. Thankfully he had emerged from under the duvet. He still looked miserable as he banged away on his laptop.

'How are you doing, my love?'

He shrugged. She laid a hand on his shoulder and gently squeezed. It was the closest thing to a hug that he would allow.

'Do you want a biscuit? I baked some. Actually it might be pointless offering you one – I think Declan is working his way through them.'

'I'm okay, thanks.'

'You don't seem okay, Con. You seem agitated, upset, and that is understandable, of course. Today was a huge day. And at the risk of sounding like a broken record, I can only help if you tell me what's on your mind.'

She stood in silence for a second or two, giving him a chance to change his mind and speak. He didn't.

'I changed the room around.' She stated the obvious for want of something to say. 'It's better, isn't it? More space, and a little bit of privacy.'

He briefly caught her eye as if to acknowledge her efforts.

'I'll make you a nice supper in a little while.'

'I'm not hungry.'

'Please talk to me, Con!' she implored, sitting on the edge of his bed. 'I'm not going anywhere.'

He looked at her. Nina smiled at how she had won him over with the reasoning that the sooner he spoke, the sooner she would leave.

'It wasn't great,' he mumbled.

'What wasn't great?' She was grateful for the insight and grabbed it like a hook.

'All of it,' he fired back.

'Connor, put your laptop away and *talk* to me properly, please. Tell me how it went and how you are feeling.'

He gave a short laugh and sucked his teeth. 'What is it you want to know?' He closed his laptop as instructed, and rubbed his eyes.

'Everything!' She held out her hands.

Connor sat up in the bed and rested his back against the shallow headboard.

'They follow a different order for sciences so I am about a year behind, but they are confident I can catch up, which is easy for them to say, it's not them that's going to have to do the extra work. Everyone, literally everyone, either told me I was posh or took the piss out of my accent. No one told me that they don't stand up when a tutor comes into the room, and so in the first lesson the master came in and I jumped up with my arms by my sides and waited to be told to sit, and the whole class doubled up laughing. The teacher shouted at me, asking if I thought I was being funny.' He shook his head. 'I felt like such an idiot.'

Nina silently berated herself. This hadn't occurred to her. Her son continued.

'I am used to a system where pupils are only allowed to walk in twos along the right-hand corridor wall, which means everything flows, but at this school' – he shook his head – 'it's like a free-for-all, crowds getting bottlenecked and everyone yelling, all of the time. It's chaos, so noisy. I have a headache. And apparently I am only allowed to take one language, so I have to drop German or French because "That's how the timetable works if I want to do three sciences".' He drew invisible speech marks in the air. 'Have you ever heard anything so ridiculous? And the very best thing?' His words dripped with sarcasm. 'I already have a nickname – can you believe it? One day in, and my new name is Snow.' He looked up and bit his lip.

'Why Snow?' She struggled to figure it out.

'Oh, don't try and guess, you never could,' he spat. 'There was already a guy called Connor in my class whose dad keeps horses in the New Forest. He is known as Connor Ponies, obviously.'

'Obviously.' She nodded.

'So this kid, Brandon I think his name is, started calling me "Connor's Got No Ponies", shortened to "'S'no Ponies", and by the end of the day they had dropped the pony idea all together and I am now "Snow", apparently.'

'Maybe it's a term of endearment?'

He looked at her with daggers in his eyes. 'They're dickheads! All of them, especially Brandon, who I hate! Snow? I mean is that the best they could come up with? Jesus, it's not even clever! They are pathetic. And they had never heard of Kings Norton.'

'Well, why would they have? It's a long way from here.'

Her son's comments were just another reminder of how he felt the whole wide world revolved around his school. She thought again of little Joe Marsh-Evans, who had had to leave school, and her pulse raced. It tore at her heart to think of her lovely boys being similarly forgotten so quickly.

Connor looked desperate. 'I'm telling you now, Mum, if they don't let me play rugby, I won't stay there – how can I?' His eyes brimmed with tears.

'Did they *say* you couldn't play rugby?'

'No, but they made it clear that they have a stable team and there is only about five months for me to get a place and make my mark. It's all

I want to do, and if I can't train and can't go to a professional club later and say that I played throughout my school, it'll be pointless!'

She watched the anxious rise and fall of his chest, knowing just how much this would mean to him.

'I am confident that as soon as they see you play you will get a spot on the team. Don't forget you won your place in the A team at Kings Norton, it wasn't gifted to you. There were several boys after your spot, but you fought hard and the coach picked you. You got it on talent, and that talent is still there, waiting to be seen. You can dazzle them when you get the opportunity.'

'You don't know anything, Mum! How can you be confident about anything? You just don't get it! The rugby training has started at Kings Norton and it was all I could think about, picturing the boys on the field, wearing the kit that I was so proud to put on. And I was stuck in that horrible place, with everyone asking me to repeat words and laughing at my voice, wearing this . . .' He pulled roughly at the logo on the sweatshirt. 'And I didn't ask for any of it! And I don't understand what's happened to my life!'

She felt a wave of anxiety at the thought that not only was her son deeply unhappy, but that it was her fault. Finn's fault.

'I understand, Connor, and you have every right to be angry, but I meant what I said to you this morning. You are an amazing boy, and you have the strength and resilience to come through this. I don't think it will always be easy, not at all, but I do have faith that things will get better.' She hoped her words might act as a balm in some way, or if nothing else as a distraction.

She smoothed his hair and laid her hand on his arm. 'I know everything feels tough right now, but you need to give it a chance. You are only one day in, and who knows what will happen tomorrow?'

'I think I can have a good guess at what will happen tomorrow.' He ground his teeth. 'More of the same. I hate it here. I hate it. I want to go home.'

Nina pictured the padlocked gate of The Tynings and the empty shell of the house. It broke her heart that her boy had been forced to take this onto his shoulders, to face these challenges at his tender years.

'I know. And I miss it too. I miss everything. This couldn't be more different, could it? But this is home for now. No matter how grim, or cold, or' – she borrowed his word – 'shitty. I can't make promises, Connor, I can only tell you what I believe: the Kings Norton motto – determination, courage and faith – and those attributes will get you through.'

He looked up. 'George and Charlie FaceTimed me today during my break – they were hanging out on the pitch.' The expression on Connor's face was enough to make her weep.

'That must have been tough to see.'

'It was.' He nodded. 'I felt like running away.'

'Don't do that. I shall only run after you, and my running isn't what it used to be. I have my gran's dodgy knees, sadly.' She tried out a smile, which he failed to return. 'They can always come here to see you, or you can go back and see them, if you want to,' she suggested softly.

Connor shook his head. 'I don't want them to come here and I definitely don't want to go to Bath and have to hear all about who got my place on the team.' He gulped and pushed his hair from his forehead.

'I get that. And it probably feels like little reward now, but at least when you go through bad times, like this, you really appreciate the good. I pray for you that they are just around the corner.'

His distress flared again. 'Well, you keep praying, because I can't wait, Mum. Feeling like this sucks. It really does!'

It was going to take a bit more than a few changes to the bedroom and a well-placed side table to make everything feel better. She felt her bubble of joy from earlier well and truly lanced.

Connor kicked off the duvet and jumped up, standing in the gap by the side of his bed; he narrowly avoided tripping over her feet. His breathing got faster and shallower. He looked perilously close to tears and she hated how quickly his sadness turned to anger.

'If I have to live here, I need to study. Where am I supposed to do that? Sitting on my bed? Or on the crappy sofa?' He blinked quickly.

'We can pick up a little desk, eventually, and put it where you are standing,' she answered quietly, trying to keep her calm.

'Yes that will make it perfect!' he sneered. 'And talking of studying, I got the piss taken out of me for calling it "prep" because they say "homework", and I have some crappy assignment to do that needs to be in tomorrow.' He jumped over her legs with an athletic leap and made his way into the sitting room. She got the feeling he wanted to be anywhere she wasn't.

Sitting on her son's bed for a second or two, she closed her eyes and tried to picture her mum's hand on her shoulder. Times like this, all she wanted was to feel her mother's arms around her and to hear her words of advice.

'Mum!' Declan yelled from the other room.

She opened her eyes. 'Yes, love?' she managed.

'Are there any more biscuits?'

She walked into the sitting room and stared at the crumb-filled plate on her boy's lap.

'Connor said he didn't want any,' Declan offered in his defence.

'Not like I had any choice! You'd eaten them all!' Connor spat. 'Pretty much sums up my life.'

'Oh, sweet Jesus, Con!' She rubbed her temples. 'Do you know what, love? You need to cut it out!'

He leapt up, shifting again to the bedroom, any place where she was not, and ran back towards the bedroom. She thought of Finn and considered for a second how lovely it might be to simply run away . . .

The boys had been at school for a whole week, and there had been little change. It took all her resolve to remain upbeat and to keep momentum going on her job search. She spent hours with her face inches from the laptop screen, firing off letters and applications to companies she thought might be hiring in the future. The money had dwindled to two grubby twenty-pound notes and a handful of coins. To think about the situation caused her to nearly choke and made sleep damn near impossible. As she waved across the street to Lucia one morning and considered the girl's love of art and the advice she had given her, Nina had a light-bulb moment. And there was only one person she wanted to share her realisation with.

She climbed into her jeans and boots and pulled a sweatshirt over her pyjama top before locking the door and tramping the pavements, heading towards The Bear. She covered the two miles with a small seed of hope growing in her gut. After ringing the doorbell, she stood back, looking up at the lattice windows of the flat above that showed no sign of life.

'You're a bit early, love!' a man called from the passenger seat of a white van that drove past. She nodded a small smile in his direction. When she turned again to the front door, Tiggy was there in her pyjamas and dressing gown. Her hair was mussed and her cheek held a faint line of a pillowslip crease.

'Have I woken you up?'

Tiggy looked at her, with one eye still clamped shut, and nodded. 'Tell me this is a matter of great urgency.'

'Not really, but it's quite important to me.' She put her hands in her pockets.

'It had better not be about a cushion you've found in a charity shop.'

'No! I'm sorry. I forgot that you have very late nights.'

'Is everything okay with the boys?' Tiggy now had both eyes open.

'Yes! Well, I think so. They haven't been expelled yet, so that's something. Mind you' – she glanced at her watch – 'there's still plenty of hours left in the day for that. Can I come in?'

'Sure.' Tiggy stood back. Nina walked past her, watching as her sister secured the bolts and relocked the door. Her eyes roamed the spacious bar. It was as she remembered it from her last visit two years ago, with its wooden floor, clusters of tables and red-velvet-backed chairs, all looking rather forlorn and abandoned in the early hours of the day. Large lanterns hung down near a vast, brick-built inglenook fireplace. The scent of stale beer and floor wax hung in the air; blindfolded, no one would be in any doubt that they were in a typical, slightly rundown English boozer.

'So how *are* the boys doing? I've been thinking about them. How much did they love knocking down that wall?'

'A lot!' Nina smiled. 'They're still a little edgy, nervous. Dec had an upset tum on his first day, poor little thing, and Connor perpetually looks like he wants to kill me, but they are definitely calmer than they were. Slowly, slowly, and all that . . .' She looked skywards and crossed her fingers.

'Would you like a drink?'

'God, no! Are you kidding?' Nina waved her hand. 'It's way too early for me.'

'Jesus, Nina, I meant coffee!'

'Oh, coffee would be great, I thought you meant . . .'

'It's nice to see you here.' Tiggy stated as she reached up onto the shelf for two white china cups.

Nina looked around. 'I like this pub.'

'Thanks. I like it too.'

'And actually, taking control and getting back on my feet is what I wanted to talk to you about.' She bit her bottom lip excitedly.

'Go on.' The welcome smell of coffee brewing filled the air.

'I was talking to Lucia – pink-hair Lucia?'

'Oh, right, yup. I know who you mean,' Tiggy said.

'I wanted to tell her it was important to live her life and follow her dreams, but that advice feels very easy to give out and not always that easy to follow.'

Tiggy grimaced. 'It is hard, otherwise I'd be working on the Space Station right about now.'

'So I *am* going to follow my dreams. I am going to go back to school. Not now, but eventually, part-time evening and weekends, or whenever I can fit it in. I am going to sit my exams and I am going to become a nurse.'

'Oh my word, that's big news!'

'I think so. It might take ten years, longer even, but I am going to do it. And just making the decision feels like a big step towards my future. I am going to have a career so that I can take better care of me and the kids.'

'You always used to want to be a nurse. I remember when you were little, turning the couch into a hospital with your teddies and dolls lying in rows, with tissues stuck to their limbs as bandages,' Tiggy said.

'I remember that too. I lost my way with that, stepped off the path, but it's not too late for me. For us. You are right, Tig, I have decades of work left in me yet.'

'Wow.' Tiggy looked at her squarely.

'Is that good wow, or you-must-be-crazy wow?' She cowered a little, awaiting her sister's response.

'It's . . .' Tiggy was clearly searching for the right words. 'My-little-sister-just-might-have-walked-back-into-the-room wow!'

'Really?'

'Yes, really.'

Her chest swelled at the compliment; it was good to know her big sister thought this.

'I think about when you were young and first left school. You were bursting with energy for life and . . .'

'And what?' Nina wondered which words now faltered in Tiggy's throat.

'I don't know . . . A drive, I guess, that made you seem invincible. That was when you went with Dad to Bath. I couldn't believe you opted to go with him. But nothing fazed you.'

'As I recall, you didn't want to come. You were in love with what's-his-name,' Nina said.

'Dad was relieved, I think.'

'Oh for goodness' sake, you were twenty-odd, Tiggy. And Dad adored you, did everything he could for us. For you . . .'

Her sister sighed. 'Really?' She folded her arms over her chest.

'Yes, really! I went with Dad to Bath so he wouldn't be alone. I knew he'd spent lonely periods of his life wandering the UK after he lost Mamma, working wherever the next dead-end job took him, and I could see he wasn't well. I didn't *want* to leave you here, and you could have come, but you were keen on Ross Baker at the time and didn't want to.' The boy's name sprang into her head. 'I remember it clearly. You chose Ross-bloody-Baker over us!'

'Yep, and look where that has got me! I didn't get the life we had always dreamed of, the fairy tale, I got to stay here in bloody Portswood, sitting with Gran and Pop and scrabbling enough cash together to go out and snog boys like Ross Baker outside Jesters. And then after they died, it was just me.'

'I hate to think of you unhappy here on your own,' Nina said.

'I wasn't really on my own. I have always had mates, and a job, people around, you know?'

Nina nodded, wishing Tiggy didn't always feel the need to be so brave. 'But it would have been better to have me here, though, right?'

Tiggy ran her tongue over her bottom lip, as if deciding whether to speak frankly again. 'Yes. Yes, it would.'

'Thank you.' Nina felt a little overcome. 'Thank you, Tig, for saying that. It makes me happy.'

The two sipped their coffee and Nina followed her sister up the narrow, winding staircase to Tiggy's room. It was spacious, and well fitted with a bed at one end and a sofa and TV at the other, but it was still just a room. The bathroom she shared with the landlord was down the hall. Nina realised that the flat she and the boys lived in, that she had bemoaned on countless occasions to her sister, was spacious in comparison, and she felt a pang of guilt. She took a seat on the unmade bed.

Her mobile phone rang. She fumbled for it in her pocket, racing to answer it, fearing it might be from the boys' new school. She squinted at the screen – she didn't know the number.

'Nina?'

'Yes, hello?' She vaguely recognised the voice on the other end of the line but couldn't quite place it.

'It's Fiona Walters, from Celandine Court.'

'Oh, Fiona!' Nina gripped the phone and waited, trying to imagine why she would call. Maybe Nina had inadvertently broken the law in turning up unannounced. Her mind raced at all the unlikely possibilities.

'I hope you don't mind me calling, but I wanted to talk to you about something.'

'Yes, I . . . I quite understand, and I am so sorry for turning up like I did. I'm more than a little embarrassed,' she stuttered, nerves filling her stomach with butterflies. 'I . . . I didn't think it through.' She closed her eyes and faced the bedroom wall, as if this might give her a bit of privacy from Tiggy, who stood only feet away.

'No, no need to apologise, and please don't feel embarrassed. But safe to say you aren't the cook we are looking for.'

'That much I know.'

'But I do think I have a role that might suit you, if you are interested.'

Nina felt her heart race. 'Oh my God! Really?'

'Yes, really. You were wonderful around the residents. Very relaxed and tactful. A natural. It's a real gift you have, and I would like to talk to you about an opportunity that I have been thinking about for a while.'

'Oh my! I really am interested!' She couldn't disguise her shock or delight.

'Come in and see me this afternoon – shall we say about two? – and we can chat some more. How does that sound?'

'That sounds great!' She felt the prick of the second batch of happy tears in recent weeks.

'I'll see you then, Nina.'

'See you then, and . . . Fiona?'

'Yes?'

'Thank you! Thank you so much.'

Nina put the phone back in her pocket and turned to her sister. 'Looks like I might have got myself a job!' She jumped from the bed. Tiggy came to join her and they leapt up and down on the worn carpet, laughing and whooping.

'What job is it?' Tiggy paused to ask.

'I have no idea!' She giggled. 'But right now, I will literally take anything.'

◆　◆　◆

Nina couldn't wait for the boys to come home from school so she could share her news. The second she heard them on the path outside, she ran to the front door, greeting them with a wide smile.

'Guess what? I got a job!' She clapped her hands, rushing forward, giving them the answer to her question before they had a chance to respond, and sweeping them both into a hug from which they struggled to escape.

'Really?' Declan asked, not hiding his incredulity.

'Yes! Really!'

'What job is it?' Connor asked, dumping his school bag on the floor in the kitchen. He leaned against the fridge, long legs crossed at the ankles.

'You are looking at the new Resident Liaison Contact for Celandine Court!' She held her arms out like a showman.

'Is that the old people's home where you said you could cook, and then ran away?' Declan asked.

'Yes!' She laughed. 'The very same.'

'It's an impressive title, but what does it actually mean?' Connor queried.

Fiona had leaned across the desk. 'You would be showing prospective families around, giving them the tour and answering any questions they might have.'

'I could do that!' she enthused.

'Yes, you could, once we have got you up to speed on how the place works.'

She smiled at her boys, still not quite able to believe it. 'I'll be overseeing the orientation programme for new residents, and when I am not doing that, I will be spending a few hours each day checking everyone is happy, chatting to visiting families, sorting any on-the-spot queries. And most importantly, I will be on the lookout for loneliness, and those who might be feeling anxious or excluded, kind of like a daily happiness health check. That way my boss, Fiona, can spend more time in the office dealing with the paperwork mountain that she never quite defeats,' she quoted.

'Are there *that* many vacancies, then? How often will you show people around?'

'Weekly. There is always a waiting list. And yes, Con, there *are* that many vacancies.' She paused. 'The residents are old and often ill.' She let this hang.

'Oh!' She could see the realisation dawning on him as to why there was such a high turnover.

'It has a great atmosphere. I felt it again today when I went to chat with Fiona – that's my boss.' Nina looked at her boys. 'My boss! Oh my God, it feels so good to be able to say that! You have no idea!'

'You sound happy, Mum,' Declan observed.

'I am, darling. And if all goes well, I have decided to study, too. I want to go into nursing, eventually. It's something that has always appealed to me, but I thought the chance had passed me by.'

'That's great, Mum,' Connor offered sincerely.

Nina felt her face split into a broad smile once again. She felt she was able to breathe again. 'And it's the ideal location. I can walk there or jump on the bus if the weather is bad.' She beamed with joy at the fact that, not only would she be earning money, but also someone thought she had 'a gift', no less!

'Are you going to earn a lot of money?' Declan got straight down to practicalities.

'You know what? As I said to Tig earlier, I have been earning no money, and so any money is an improvement. It will be enough for our rent and food and other little bits and pieces we might need. I shall still have to budget, but that's fine. We will have all we need. We will have enough.'

'That's great,' Declan said.

'I am so excited,' Nina continued. 'But also overwhelmed. What if I'm rubbish and they sack me?' She looked at Connor with a flutter of self-doubt.

Connor stared at her. 'Dad always said you shouldn't let yourself be limited by what you think you can or can't do. You should believe that you can do anything you set your mind to.'

Nina laid her hand on her son's arm, happy that her boy could mention his dad without the flicker of sadness in his pupils. This was progress. 'That sounds like good advice.'

Connor looked at her squarely. 'I am pleased for you. Pleased for us. Congratulations.'

'Thank you.'

He smiled at her with an expression that looked a lot like pride.

ELEVEN

Seven days later, Nina headed for her first day at work. She was nervous all the way there, but felt much better once she donned her hot pink polo shirt and was told the gentle agenda for the day: to shadow Fiona and a couple of the other girls.

By 1 p.m., when they stopped for lunch, she took her seat in the break room with three other staff members, tucking into a delicious tuna and mayo sandwich, courtesy of the kitchen in which she was never destined to work. The break felt like a treat and she was more than grateful for the food. A big woman with a disarming laugh and a cap of bright red hair waved from across the narrow break room.

'So how's your first day going?' the woman asked. 'I'm Gilly, by the way.'

'There's a lot to take in, but so far so good. And I'm Nina.'

'Well, we are a friendly bunch. You only have to shout if you're unsure about anything. Or if you get really desperate, just pull one of them red emergency cords. That usually gets us running!'

'Oh, really? I didn't know that.'

'No! Nina! Not really! Dear God, *don't* do that other than in an emergency. I was joking.' Gilly laughed.

Nina bit her lip. 'I'm too nervous to joke right now. Give me a couple of weeks!' She smiled.

'Got it.' Gilly nodded. 'Do you have children?'

'Yes, two boys. A teenager and an eleven-year-old.'

'Oh, a teenager. Isn't it fun?' She winked. 'I have told my husband that I'll take the shift from nought to thirteen, and he can do thirteen to eighteen, and then it's back to me for any grandchildren that might come along. It's working out pretty good so far. He's now the one that ferries them around, does the dashes to the emergency room, and has the birds and the bees chat, that kind of thing.' She chuckled.

I don't have a husband any more . . . I don't know what I'd do in an emergency. I need to speak to Tiggy, I need to rewrite my will, ask her if she'd be the kids' guardian . . . These thoughts took the fun out of their jovial chat.

Nina changed tack. 'Mine have just started their new school, so we are just trying to get settled and into a routine.'

'Where do they go?'

'Cottrell's.'

'Ah, mine too. A girl and a boy, fourteen and seventeen.'

'Do they like it there?' she asked hopefully.

'As much as they are going to like any school. But you know how it is. Just got to find a way to keep them out of trouble and hope they come out the other side as nice people.' The woman rolled her eyes and crossed her fingers. Her words struck a chord. *Nice people*: it was a revelation. A montage of all the Kings Norton College mums played in her head:

'We are getting him a work placement with the BBC. He wants to be a journalist.'

'She's off to Paris. Her uncle is a diplomat, and it'll be a good use of her languages!'

'He's got an internship with his dad's law firm. Expect he'll be making the tea, but every barrister has to start somewhere!'

It was another world, a world full of pressure and expectation. Only now that she was on the outside was she able to question whether she even wanted that for her boys.

'Seriously, Nina . . .' Gilly stood, downing the last of her coffee. 'If you have any questions or need anything, then just holler,' she offered, tapping the doorframe with her wedding ring.

Nina was grateful. 'Thank you. And just to clarify, was that *do* pull the red cord or *do not*? I can't remember!' Her face broke into a smile.

Gilly smiled at her. 'You are going to fit in just fine.'

At the end of the day, having learned more than she knew she was capable of and looking forward to the next day, Nina felt like a kid, walking with a spring in her step and a feeling of achievement.

'Hello, darling! Well, here I am. Day One, and I made it!' She beamed at Declan.

'How did it go?' he asked, sounding so much like a grown-up it made her heart swell.

'Well, I missed you guys of course. . . Where's Con?' she asked as she eased off her shoes.

'In the bedroom.' He indicated with a bow of his head.

'One of the resident nursing staff, Gilly, has children at your school.' She paused, looking at her boy to witness the familiar wince at the topic. It had, she noted, lessened, but was still present nonetheless. 'I'm tired, but all in all it was a good day, and I get to go and do it all again tomorrow!'

'Can I make you a cup of tea, Mum?'

She turned to face Connor, who had come in from the bedroom. 'Me?' Nina asked.

'Of course you,' Connor let his lip hitch in the way it often did when he addressed her.

'Really? It's just that making me a cup of tea is a nice thing to do and I just wondered if you were doing so by mistake. First you pick me flowers and now you offer me tea. Where is my son and what have you done with him?' She narrowed her eyes at him.

'Very funny.' He smiled, despite his attempts to the contrary. He pulled a mug from the shelf in the kitchen and put in a tea bag. 'So how's your job?' he asked.

Nina took a deep breath as she leaned against the counter-top in the tiny kitchen area. 'I was just telling Dec. It was good. I was nervous to start with – I thought I was going to be sick. I shadowed Fiona, and learned a bit more about how the place runs, and I met some of the other staff, and I visited Harry – Mr Sandler, one of the residents, who used to be a pilot. He has dementia, but seems happy.'

'I guess it's hard not to be happy when you don't know what's going on,' he said thoughtfully.

She stared at her son as he made her tea and offered this mature insight. *Is that what Finn did? Kept the problems from me so I could be happy? Just like when I wanted to give the boys one more night of normality, one more peaceful sleep . . . ? I get it, Finn, but I am a grown-up. Your wife! I would have wanted to know.*

'You look miles away,' Connor observed.

'I'm just thinking about what you said. I think most people would assume it was the other way around – that it was hard to *be* happy if you didn't know what was going on, but I think you might be right.'

'I mean, we assume that people like Harry are sad or confused, but what if he is in the best dream imaginable that lasts forever? What if he is happy because in his mind he is in the bar with his flying buddies, reliving the days when he took to the skies and could run and jump?'

A smile spread over her face. 'I love that, Connor. You might be right.'

'Harry won't be upset or worried about the things that bother other people and that must be nice . . .' He paused.

'Yes, it must.'

'And he probably doesn't feel afraid because he doesn't know that there is anything in his future to feel afraid of.'

'Are you afraid?' she asked tentatively, hoping Connor might open up to her.

'No! God, what a stupid thing to say. What would I would afraid of? Jesus, Mum!' he spat, reaching behind her for the milk.

And just like that, her teenage boy was back in the room. 'It's okay to feel afraid, you know. I have spent every day since Dad died feeling frightened. I would understand if you were. It would be the most normal reaction to the huge upheaval we've gone through, the uncertainty.'

Connor handed her her mug of tea. 'Actually, Mum, I think uncertainty would be a little easier to cope with than the thought that this is as good as it gets.' He waved at the flat. 'At least with uncertainty there's the chance that this really is only temporary, a staging post, and that would be something.'

She sipped her tea and listened, unsure of how to respond. But at least they were talking – and that *really* was something.

The novelty hadn't worn off in the month since she'd been working, but she found that by the time she got back to the flat each evening she was exhausted. Sticking to the rigid timetable of her shifts was new to her. It felt alien, having to plan everything around her working day. She was used to her time being her own, punctuated only by the drop-off and collection of the boys at school. It bothered her that along with the new routine, when she worked a late shift, Connor and Declan were left to their own devices far more than she was comfortable with. It was a small price to pay for gainful employment, but it was a huge change in her life to which she had to grow accustomed. And the simple fact was she missed them. She felt so proud to arrive home and see the dishes washed, the rubbish taken out, the counter-tops wiped down and crumb free. It was tempered by a sadness that they had to do these things at all. She had liked being the mum who looked after her boys – spoiled them, even – leaving them free to be kids for as long as possible.

Today was her day off, and the security of a job meant that the knot of worry that lived at the base of her skull had loosened, allowing her to sleep a little more soundly and making space in her head so she could focus on the many little chores that she had been postponing. The first thing she did was venture outside with a bucketful of soapy water and a metal scourer. She scrubbed with determination at the blue ampersand until her fingers cramped, reducing the tag to nothing more than a faded smudge. Standing back to look at her efforts, she smiled. It felt like a win.

She and Tiggy had made plans to raid the charity shops in the area. It was the one good thing about her sister working nights in the pub: it meant her days were largely free. Nina had only ever dropped off donations at such a shop; the idea of having anything in her home that was another person's rubbish would have been unthinkable. Now, however, she thought about the items she had once given: the boys' barely used trainers, unwanted clothes, still with the tags on, and any book she had finished reading. She hoped it had all been useful to someone. And now here she was, admiring hand-knitted blankets and checking the price of a cushion or two, knowing that with the addition of colour, she could continue to transform their little space into something much brighter.

'What do you think?' Nina called across the crowded shop as she sucked in her cheeks and posed in a garish orange floppy hat.

'Very you!' Tiggy called out. She put on a large, lacy wedding veil, complete with bunches of dried red roses stuck in a clump to the top, just above her forehead.

'Very *Big Fat Greek Wedding*!'

'Charming! And seeing as we are Danish, not Greek, I should probably be looking for a wedding crown.' Tiggy laughed as she pulled off the scrap of lace. They turned their attention to the kitsch ornaments that lined the shelves, doubling up with laughter at the sight of a china clown figurine with, of all things, a working clock where his stomach should be. It was hideous – and the kind of thing their gran would have favoured, and placed in a crowded, dusty display cabinet.

'Oh no! That's too horrible! It would give me nightmares.' Nina pulled a face.

'Who would want this in their home?' Tiggy questioned.

A matronly lady with an ample bosom broke in. 'I should have you know that I have only just brought that in, and it has sat on my mantelpiece for years! It has always been much admired!'

The sisters managed to mumble their apologies before shuffling from the shop and collapsing onto each other on the pavement, giggling like kids.

Still tittering at the memory as they sat on the bus, Nina thought of the furniture and bits and bobs that were in storage with Mr Firth. Everything had happened in such a rush that she hadn't made the best job of deciding what to take, what to leave and what to discard. She thought of the slender desk table that Connor could use. There were also a couple of lampshades she would like, more towels, some bed linen and even their summer clothes.

The two tramped home with a bright wool-knit throw and two matching cushions. Nina looked at the items lying in a heap on the sitting-room floor and marvelled at just how much these little touches meant.

Removing the sofa seat cushions, she plumped them and vacuumed the crumbs and dust from underneath. She then folded the new throw over one of the arms and arranged the new cushions against the back. When Nina stood back to admire her handiwork, she had to admit that the green velour sofa now seemed more vintage chic than secondhand skip-worthy. It made her smile.

'You're finding your stride, Nina,' Tiggy remarked.

'I think maybe I am.' It was still hard for her to think further than a day ahead. And whilst there were high points, her thoughts were still a tangle. She still felt alone, and more than a little afraid for the future. Her job was great, but they weren't out of the woods.

'I had a thought on how we could make three bedrooms here,' Tiggy said. Nina followed her along the hallway which, interestingly, she no longer thought of as claustrophobic, as if her mind had shifted its expectations to fit the space she now inhabited. Her bedroom was a decent size, with two windows that looked out over the street.

'I was thinking about it last night. All we have to do is put a wall up!' Tiggy smiled. 'With a clever bit of shifting around, and the addition of a stud wall, we could turn this space into two bedrooms, giving all of you a decent place to sleep. I know it would all depend on the cost, and permission of course from Fred. But I think it's possible.'

Nina remembered her old life, when all she had to do to get a spot of remodelling done was pick up the phone to McCarrick Construction and, like magic, workmen would appear who were all highly motivated to do the very best job. She thought about the number she had last dialled all those weeks ago and the surly man that had then answered the phone.

'Are you okay?' Tiggy grabbed her arm. 'You look like you're about to fall over!'

'I'm fine.' She forced a smile. 'It's a good idea, but there'd be no point, as I doubt we'll be staying here that long.'

'Where is it you are going?' her sister asked flatly.

'I . . . I don't know, but I will save from my job and try to get a bigger flat with a bit more space for us all. There's no storage here, and the boys are crammed in . . .'

'And then what? An even bigger place? A swimming pool? Two swimming pools?'

'No! Of course not.' She chafed at Tiggy's judgemental tone. 'I only want enough.'

'And when will you know when you have enough? When will you sit back and look up at the sky and feel satisfied?' Tiggy cocked her head to one side.

Nina pictured her sister's homely room above the pub, and blinked with the familiar feelings of guilt and uncertainty. 'I don't know,' came her truthful reply. 'I just have it set in my head: work hard, save, move on.'

'But don't you get it?' Tiggy asked. 'That's what everybody wants, what everyone thinks and plans, but look' – she pointed out of the window – 'we are all still here!'

'I hadn't . . .'

'Hadn't what?' Tiggy pushed.

'Hadn't considered that this might be our final destination.'

'No, because you are hoping for better,' Tiggy accurately assessed. 'But here's the thing, Nina. I think happiness lies in being content now – right now! Every day! That's not to say you can't plan and work for change, but if you are constantly waiting for happiness to start, waiting for the change that will make it happen, then you just might miss some really good days along the way.'

Tiggy's words hit her hard. 'You make me sound ungrateful and I'm not. I only want to make life as nice as I can for the boys. I keep wondering why the previous tenants didn't fix this place up a bit.'

'It's called poverty, Nina,' Tiggy spat.

Nina gave her a sharp look. 'I know that. You think I don't? I'm in a crappy rented flat on a main road that is so noisy I can hardly think! You think I don't know about hardship?' Her voice cracked.

'Nina.' Tiggy stood tall. 'You have been living here for a matter of weeks. You have had a life of charm and luxury up until this point. And you and the kids aren't starving, and you are not homeless. You really need to keep things in perspective.'

It was alarming to both how quickly their exchange had escalated, especially after such a pleasant afternoon, as if the cork had been shifted accidentally and the genie had come flying out of the bottle quicker than anyone could contain.

'*I* need to keep things in perspective?' She gave an ironic laugh. 'Jesus Christ, my whole life has been turned upside down! I have lost my husband, my home, my security, and I am trying to keep everything together.'

'I know, but I have to say, Nina, that the girl who grew up here, who had so much energy, so much confidence . . .' She shook her head. 'She would be horrified to see how you now struggle.'

'You think I *want* to struggle? I don't have much money! I can't do the things that—'

'No.' Tiggy cut her short. 'You misunderstand me. I don't mean struggle *financially*, I mean struggle *with life*, the way everything feels like a hurdle. She wouldn't recognise you!'

'*I* don't recognise me!' Nina felt the threat of tears.

'This is exactly what I mean about how you have changed. Tears never used to be your default setting.'

'That is so unfair!' Nina cursed the tears that gathered, not wanting to prove her sister's point.

'Is it? I know things are rough for you right now and I am sorry for that, but you have to stop playing the part of Mrs Finn McCarrick and find the old Nina!'

'What on earth do you mean by that?'

'I used to worry, when you first met Finn . . .' Tiggy halted mid-sentence.

'Worry about what? Come on, say it!' She put her hands on her hips.

'I used to worry that you weren't always yourself when you were with him.'

'Not myself?' Nina felt her pulse quicken.

Tiggy turned to face her sister. 'It was like you were playing a part, figuring out how to be the person you thought he wanted, wary of your actions, your words. As if Nina from Portswood just wasn't good enough.'

'That's not true!'

'It is. It is true,' Tiggy retorted. 'I watched you, Nina, I watched you shrinking, getting smaller and smaller until you could barely be heard. And it was tough to witness the essence of you eroded with every year you spent with him.'

'What are you talking about, "eroded"?' she spat.

'I'm talking about the fact that you hint that things between you and Finn weren't perfect, and I want to yell "No shit!" He lied to you, kept you in the dark, never treated you like an equal. And he left you in this mess that he created. He was never satisfied. Didn't know when he had enough.'

Nina felt as if she had been punched in the stomach, but Tiggy wasn't done.

'He had a nice life, a great life! With all that you could ever need, and more, but Finn pushed on and on, bigger and better, until you were stretched so thin, things shattered! And he kept it from you, all of it! Why would he do that?'

As hurt as she was shocked by the words, Nina sat down on the sofa. It was as if Tiggy had gone inside her head and pulled out her innermost secrets. It made her feel exposed, raw and embarrassed.

Tiggy folded her arms across her chest. 'You want to know why I stopped visiting? You want to know why it was a relief when you didn't bother calling me and why I found it impossible to pick up the phone to you?'

Nina gave a single nod, petrified and curious.

'I wasn't jealous of your swanky kitchen or your swimming pool, not even a little bit. I was mad that you allowed yourself to be shrunk in that way, that you lost your fight, forgot our life. Forgot every aspect of what things were like for me. You used to send me postcards from weekends in Europe, or pop thirty quid into my birthday card with the message "Have a lovely treat for your birthday". I used to love getting those cards – and I'd grab it from the envelope and pay it straight to the electricity company. That was a real treat.' Tiggy paced the room. 'And I knew you'd picture me getting a manicure or buying some flowers, like you had no idea how I lived, none at all. And I was pissed off at how quickly you forgot that life, how quickly you slipped into being Mrs Finn McCarrick in her grand house, and all that came with that.'

'I . . .' Nina tried to find the words of rebuttal, but struggled. Her chest heaved as she pictured Tiggy in her slippers, trotting up to the bank with her birthday money in her fist to pay a bill. It twisted her heart.

'I was so mad at you that I couldn't risk seeing you,' Tiggy continued, 'knowing I might totally lose it!'

'Because you felt I was thoughtless, or because I couldn't stand up to Finn?'

'Mad because you let me down! You let him isolate you, cut me out and reduce you to someone, something, I didn't recognise. You were like his housemaid, who was grateful and subservient and afraid of her own shadow. It was like you viewed the world from behind a tree trunk, hiding and fearful in case you were seen. I hated what he did to you!'

'He did love me. I have to believe that. And we were equals, we were married—'

'Yes, you were married,' her sister interrupted her, 'and I don't doubt he loved you, but do you honestly believe that you were equals? A partnership? When you had no idea even that you were *bankrupt*?' She snorted. 'Didn't know that you were in deep shit? Christ, you told me you couldn't even log into the computer or access your bank details because Finn hadn't given you the passwords! What was that all about? It's like you were an untrustworthy employee, and the saddest thing is that I just wasn't surprised. I saw the way you glowed in his compliments, fussed over him, fetched his suits from the dry cleaner's, cooked for him and the boys, and then stood by the table listening to them talk sport, on hand in case they needed a drink or more potatoes! Like he was every-thing – and he *was* everything. I saw how he made it so, because without him you couldn't bloody function. Why didn't you have any friends?'

'Of course we had friends! We did, we . . .' She felt sick at the picture her sister was painting, recognising some elements of truth, but trying with every fibre of her body to push against it, prove it wrong, because if she accepted it as the truth, she knew that her history with the man she loved, the story they had written, might dissolve to nothing . . .

'No, you didn't. Not really.' Tiggy calmed, her tone softened. 'I remember you saying Finn preferred it just being the two of you. He controlled you, Nina, and he was so good at it that you didn't even realise. You used to love company. When I think of you as a teenager or a kid, you were always laughing loudly and you were always in a little crowd of mates,' Tiggy continued. 'He built you a beautiful, million-pound gilded cage and gave you the money so you could fill it with lovely, lovely things, and flowers, and you sat and looked out through the bars, over the ter-race and the pool beyond. And it broke my heart. It absolutely broke my heart.' Tiggy's voice cracked in a rare show of emotion.

'I . . . he . . .' Nina struggled to find the words. Her chest felt tight and her frustration grew. 'He loved me! And I loved him!'

'I think he did, in his way, and I know you loved him, baby.' Tiggy took a deep breath and cocked her head to one side. 'But maybe he didn't know how to handle that love, and I believe that he took advan-tage of your past by promising you a different future. You were so young and he was so smart. He patronised you and gave you pocket money. No wonder Connor thinks it's okay to treat you like a doormat – he has watched his dad do it for all these years. I am sorry for your loss, sorry he died, truly, and I hate to see you hurting, but this is your chance to start to live. To reclaim your life.'

'You have no idea what it's like to lose the father of your children. You think I can just dust myself off, move on?' Nina shook her head, her anger rising. 'I want you to leave, I want you to leave now!' she yelled and pointed towards the door with a trembling finger. Her sister's words cut her deep; to hear Connor's bad treatment of her confirmed was galling and embarrassing, and more than she could handle.

'It's okay. I'm going,' Tiggy muttered as she headed for the door. Nina could only glean the odd word as she followed her. 'Waste . . . idiot . . . money . . .' Tiggy paused, and looked back at her sister. 'I have loved you my whole life, Nina. I tried to look after you when Mamma died *and* when we came to England, even though I was only little myself. I had your back. I tried my best. I brushed your hair and told you stories . . .' Tiggy cleared her throat. 'But to see you in recent years, anyone would think that your life started when you arrived in Bath. But it didn't. It started in a cramped cottage in Frederiksberg and you were then shaped by our life here in Portswood. Like it or not.'

'I know where I come from!' she yelled. 'Saying my life started when I moved away makes it sound like I erased my childhood, and that's a terrible suggestion. I love you! You are my connection to Mamma, as if I'd want to forget that!' Nina cursed the tears that gathered in her throat, thickening her speech.

'I just find it hard to believe sometimes how easily Finn usurped me.' Tiggy held her ground. 'You let him shut you away. You didn't fight for me in the way that I would have fought for you.'

And there it was.

Nina felt a wave of shame, recognising the truth to her sister's claim. She'd done her best to counter it, but Tiggy was right: sending off her birthday money, Nina had pictured Tiggy arranging a bunch of yellow roses, her favourites. She felt foolish and sick, and more than a little ashamed at the truth. It was a horrible thought – that she *had* forgotten her old life. She stared at her sister and noticed the shadows of fatigue under her eyes and the lines around her pretty mouth.

There was a long, silent pause while both considered their exchange.

Finally Nina broke the silence. 'I don't know what to say to make it better, Tiggy. I can't think straight. I can't.' She rubbed her temples.

Tiggy looked at her little sister. 'I know, and I didn't intend for us to speak like this. Not today. I don't want to argue with you. But there are things that need to be said, Nina. The very moment I heard about Finn, I came all the way over to Bath to help you, and I was glad to, and I would do that over and over whenever you need me, just like I promised Dad. I am here for you. I want to be the first person you call, always. But my God, Nina, when I reached for my cigarettes in your house you looked like I had shat on the floor! Like I was rubbish. I felt so small, embarrassed, and yet it was *you* who used to hang out of Gran's bathroom window with Parker and Graham, in your sequinned boob tube, blowing smoke out onto the street.'

Nina shuddered. *That was another time. Another person . . .*

Tiggy continued. 'I also noticed I was the only one there helping. None of your posh friends were running around with a mop or making tea, only me, and yet . . .' She paused. 'You didn't seem very grateful, as if it was my job to do those things. I don't blame you. I think Finn wanted to shape you, and you allowed yourself to be shaped, and you became something different – more polished, yes, with all the bells and whistles. But you lost something, too. Lost a bit of you.'

Nina felt weighed down by Tiggy's words. Even if it was the truth, it was still far from easy to hear.

Tiggy opened the sitting room door and it was only then they saw Declan and Connor standing in the hallway by the front door. Nina glanced at them, wondering how long they had stood there and how much they had heard. Her heart raced; the last thing she wanted was for them to be further unsettled by her and Tiggy arguing, and worse still was the idea that they too might have heard some of the criticism of their father, and of her, or recognise some truth in their exchange. She wanted to maintain the illusion that she was just like any other Kings Norton mum, that she was good enough. She knitted her fingers across her stomach, trying to look authoritative, unshaken.

'It looks nice in here.' Declan walked forward calmly and ran his fingers over the new throw and cushions on the sofa.

Tiggy smiled briefly at the small boy whose words diluted the emotion that clung to the walls. Nina watched as she hitched her bag onto her shoulder.

'See you all soon.' With that, Tiggy swept from the room.

The boys kept their eyes fixed on their mum. 'I'll get supper going in a sec,' she said over her shoulder before locking herself in the bathroom, the only place with a lockable door where she could find solitude in the little flat.

Nina sank down with her back against the door. Her sister's words had sparked something inside. The gloss had indeed dulled on her shiny marriage, the one thing she had always held up as a perfect example.

I am thinking about the old me, Finn, the me before you – and you know there was a lot about me I didn't like, but there was a lot that I did like. I used to have the confidence to be funny, to make jokes. Tig is right, I lived as though I were hiding behind a tree, fearful . . .

She pictured the many meals she had served to her family as they sat at the table, with her hovering by the island in case they wanted drinks or more food, while they talked and laughed together. She remembered the man who had answered the phone call that day, and had laughed at her when she was unaware that the business was no more. She thought about her gilded cage, filled with lovely, lovely things . . . and her sister, her protector for as long as she could remember, the girl who brushed her hair when there was no mum to undertake the task, and whom she had abandoned in favour of a new shiny life.

'I'm sorry,' she whispered, hoping her words would float out across the cold sky and land on Tiggy's shoulders as she made her way along Portswood Road.

Nina spent all night lying in bed, replaying the words of their fight. Not only was she saddened that their reconnection had suffered, but their argument had reinforced the fact that, apart from the boys, she only had Tiggy.

Looking out onto the grey, rain-filled street, she remembered days like this from her childhood. Tiggy would always tell her that 'Christmas is right around the corner!' even when it wasn't – it was enough to fuel her happiness for a while. The fact that Christmas was always disappointing as far as presents went, and that good cheer was in fairly short supply in her family, didn't matter; Tiggy had the knack of creating the possibility of magic, and that, in Nina's less than perfect life, was the greatest gift her sister could have given her. Thankful for her afternoon shift at work that day, Nina took advantage of her free morning, pulled on her jacket and boots and walked to the pub.

It was mid-morning, an hour before opening. Nina pushed on the door and, finding it open, she walked in. Tiggy was dusting the table-tops. Nina gave her a tenuous smile. Tiggy looked at her sister, and then immediately away; the embarrassment of their exchange lingered. The two then shared a small, awkward laugh and it broke the ice. They looked at each other with the slow, creeping smiles of an understanding bound by blood, love and shared history.

'I keep thinking about all the things you said to me, and I know that it's the truth,' Nina said. 'I just didn't want to hear it. It was more than I thought I could cope with. I don't want to think of myself as someone who was hoodwinked, fooled. It makes me sound stupid.'

'No, that's not it!' her sister answered strongly. 'That's not what I meant to imply at all. I don't think you are stupid, far from it, but I do think you have had your head in the sand.'

'Or behind a tree.'

'Yep, or behind a tree.' Tiggy held her gaze.

'I know that I hurt you. And I'm sorry.'

Tiggy sighed and nodded as she placed the cloth on a table. 'I didn't intend to speak as I did . . .'

'Well, you know, it's done, and it's good.' Nina shrugged. 'We have big gaps to fill, you and I, and that's going to take time, isn't it?'

'Yep.' Tiggy made her way to the bar and flicked on the coffee machine. 'But I shouldn't have been so blunt.'

'You've always been that way, all or nothing, and I guess I got it all.' Nina tried out another smile, which her sister returned.

'You did, but it was unfair of me. I forgot that you are fragile . . . that you have lost someone you loved, and I am sorry. I stand by what I said, but I should have dished it out in bite-sized chunks.'

Nina rubbed her forehead. 'Finn dying has been the worst thing I could imagine, and then the bankruptcy . . . Losing The Tynings has deprived me of so much more than my home. It has taken away my future. I thought I would grow old there, welcome the boys' partners around the dining table . . . I even saw my grandchildren running over the lawns and splashing in the pool. But worse than that is that the situation has made the past a lie, and it has robbed me of the chance to grieve for the man I loved, made me question whether I knew him at all.'

'I know, and I didn't want to throw you any more off course. No matter what has happened over the last few years, regardless of where the faults lie, I know you can get back on your feet and find balance, take control. I have faith in you.'

Nina flooded with relief. She still hadn't fully dealt with all the points Tiggy had raised, but one thing was for sure: the love she had for her sister was bigger than any row, any difference of opinion.

'I was going to come over to you today anyway, albeit a little bit later,' Tiggy said as she sliced lemons and topped up the ice bucket for her lunchtime shift.

'You were?'

'Yes. I didn't like the idea of us not talking. I've already got used to having you around.'

Nina felt tears rising. 'Me too. I am very wary of crying, even with happiness. I don't want you to think that's my default setting!'

Tiggy let out a roar of laughter. 'You are so dramatic. You know that old phrase, "Laugh and the world laughs with you, weep and you weep alone"?'

Nina gave a brief nod.

'Well, I always think it should be followed by the line, "And the reason is because no one really gives a shit about your woes when they have their own to deal with".'

'In my mind, when I think back to my childhood, you were much kinder,' Nina said, chuckling.

'No, I was always this horrible. I saw it as my job to toughen you up. To help you survive, subtly training you to pick out the liars, stand up for yourself, make good choices – getting you ready to go out into the wild!'

'Did it work?'

Tiggy turned and chased her with the hot teaspoon she had just extracted from her coffee cup, cornering her against the wall. She touched the spoon to the top of her sister's hand. Nina yelped.

Tiggy smiled. 'I'm going to say no. Otherwise you would have learned to disarm the spoon, and you would definitely own your own drill.'

TWELVE

April brought new life, promising green shoots erupting all around them. Daffodils sprouted on the verges and the trees burst with buds. It had been chilly last Easter at home when they had the pool to swim in and the gardens to wander; yet now, in this cramped little box with no outside space, the weather was glorious.

Nina took a little joy in flinging open the French windows every morning to let the day in. She found herself waking naturally a little before her alarm. She made sure the boys had pizza in the fridge or a casserole in the oven if she was going to be home late. They managed. If anything, the responsibility was good for them.

Declan remained a little tight-lipped about his school days, still slightly unnerved by the unruly antics of his peers, but in his usual inimitable fashion, he made the best of it. Connor veered between vociferously informing her how much he hated his school, his home, his life, and going very quiet. It was hard to say which she preferred. All she could do was try to be accessible.

Her confidence was growing daily. The later shift would be a test for her – she was doing a practice run acting as manager, to see if she could handle the role in case Fiona ever had an emergency absence. It was a big day for Connor, too: his official rugby trial. He had been training hard; this was his big shot. Nina, however, had to push her home life from her mind and concentrate.

◆　◆　◆

An elderly lady in a wheelchair approached, pushed by a man. 'I'm Jacob and this is my mum, Miss Molly,' he said as they made their way into the impressive atrium. She knew in advance that Miss Molly had been convalescing in hospital and that this was her first trip out in weeks. She bent low to greet the elderly woman.

'Welcome to Celandine Court. I'm Nina, and I will be showing you around today and helping you settle in. This must feel a bit daunting, but don't worry, Miss Molly. I think you are going to love it here.' She hoped she sounded convincing.

Molly's head hung forward, her expression blank. Slowly the woman's eyes flickered upwards towards the glass roof.

'It's quite something, isn't it?' Nina followed her eyeline up to the sky that was darkening. 'Most people like to sit out here in the sun, but I can let you in to a little secret.' She bent closer. 'The best time to sit here is when it's raining. There is nothing like watching the raindrops hit the roof. That's much more interesting, don't you think?'

Nina walked alongside Molly's chair as Jacob wheeled her from room to room, pointing out the positives in the pretty décor and spacious layout, and trying to distract her from the shouts of some of the residents or the loud television. Not that Molly seemed to notice. Her son, however, seemed to jump at every new noise. Nina smiled reassuringly at the man. He appeared to be in his mid-forties, with short dark hair. He had a fat, bulky watch on his tanned arm, and carried an iPad and a phone in his hand, which rested against the handle of his mother's wheelchair. It reminded her of the kids, who couldn't bear to be separated from their phones, and of Finn, who always needed to be connected to work.

'Oi!' Eliza, who sat alone at a table in the middle of the games room, called out to her.

'Excuse me a moment, Miss Molly.' She laid her hand on the old lady's shoulder.

She walked over to the table and watched as the woman sorted through a packet of large cards that she laid face down. 'Hi, Eliza.'

Eliza looked her up and down, as she always did, as if this were the first time they had met, and maybe for her it was. 'D'you play cards then?' she shouted.

'I do, but very badly.'

'All right then. I'll play with you.' Eliza tutted loudly, as though the very idea were an imposition to her.

'That sounds great. Let me get Miss Molly settled, and I shall come down and join you – how about that?'

Eliza huffed. 'Well, I won't wait all night! I've got places I need to be, you know!'

At the end of their tour, Nina introduced Jacob and his mum to Alma, one of the senior care workers who came from the Philippines, as bossy as she was kind. Then Nina said her goodbyes and returned to find Eliza.

When Nina's shift came to an end, she made her way up to the first floor to check on Miss Molly one last time. The door to the room was ajar, but she hesitated before going in, spying Jacob sitting in the glow of lamplight, holding his mother's hand. The curtains were drawn and the room had an air of serenity.

'You are going to be happy here, I can tell. And I will be in every single day to see you, I promise,' he whispered.

She watched as Miss Molly closed her eyes and Jacob lifted the sheet up to her chin. Her bowed, bulbous knuckles remained peeping over the edge of the bed linen and her fingers lightly touched the cotton; she seemed to take comfort from the soft edge. Nina felt the same maternal pull for this old lady that she did when watching babies fall asleep, their vulnerability similar. She was moved by the tender moment between mother and son. She thought of Connor.

'Night-night, Miss Molly,' Jacob whispered. 'Sweet dreams, and I shall see you tomorrow.'

Nina made her way to the reception desk to sign out, smiling at Roy, the night guard, on the desk. Jacob appeared from the lift. He looked emotional.

'She usually sleeps straight through, but if she doesn't . . .' He hesitated, as if not sure what he wanted to ask.

'Is it her first night?' Roy asked knowingly.

'Yes, it's ridiculous really, she's been sleeping in a hospital for weeks, but that was okay for me because it was temporary. This feels a bit more permanent,' he confessed.

'Have you seen these?' Nina leaned on the reception desk and pointed to a bank of televisions behind Roy's desk. Jacob leaned over and peered at the screens. She watched him squint at monitors, where residents, some with carers, made their way along corridors or into the dining room, in another a resident had stopped for a sit-down in a chair by the lift on the first floor.

'We have every square inch of communal area monitored, and Roy watches all night. There are also sensors in the halls that detect movement, as a double precaution. And if Roy isn't watching, if he has a break or whatever, another member of staff sits here and monitors. We have two nurses who make rounds. The first is at ten thirty and they do so every three hours, checking in. I promise you, Miss Molly will be fine. And I guarantee she will sleep better than you.'

'I feel a bit like I am abandoning her.' He gave a false laugh, as if to balance the display of sentiment.

'I think a lot of people feel like that, and the residents that have someone to care about them in that way are very lucky.' She thought of Eliza, who Nina had never seen to have a visitor.

'She's right,' Roy agreed.

Jacob looked down at his feet. 'I'd best be off, but thank you. I do feel a bit reassured and I shall no doubt see you tomorrow.' Nina waved goodbye to Roy and left the building just after Jacob. She stepped out in the cold, watching as he climbed into a shiny off-road pickup. The diamond-lustre paintwork and smart leather upholstery reminded her of when she too had a flashy car to hop in and out of at will. Jacob called out to her. 'Do you need a lift anywhere?'

'No! I'm only a short walk away. But thank you, that's very kind.' She put her hands in her jacket pockets. 'And try not to worry. They are a great team at Celandine Court and they will let you know exactly how your mum is faring. If they think she's unhappy or needs a change to her care plan, they will let you know. You're not doing this alone.'

Jacob fastened his seat belt. 'Thank you for that. I suppose it'll get easier, leaving her.'

'It will.' She nodded.

'Do you live nearby?' he asked through the open car door.

'Yes, just in Portswood. How about you?'

'On the marina, so a little drive, but to be honest it clears my head. Anyway, have a good evening.'

'You too.' She walked on ahead and heard the roar of the engine as he drove past. She didn't look up. The sound made her think again of Finn and the noise that heralded his arrival, the gunmetal grey Mercedes E-Class that he so loved, the car in which he had died.

'Hello, hello!' Nina called out as she put her key in the door of the flat. Kicking off her shoes in the hallway, she listened carefully, wondering if she might be mistaken, but no, there it was: the unfamiliar sound of Connor's laughter.

'It's true! I am telling you, Connor, you *can* see the Great Wall of China from space. I read it in my magazine,' Declan insisted.

'But's it *not* true! And just because so many people say it is, doesn't make it a fact. It's just one of those things that is said so often that people believe it, like the misconception that all bats are blind. They are not. They all have eyes and are capable of sight.'

'You are *so* wrong, Connor.'

'I am not!' the older brother shouted playfully. 'And when you are ready to admit you're wrong, I will accept your apology, but you need to do it in a public place for maximum impact.'

'How public?'

'Very public, and full of people we know,' Connor fired back.

'Hey, you two!' she called, overjoyed to hear their interaction.

'We've had supper,' Declan announced, as if this in itself were an achievement. The scent of baked potatoes and ham still lingered in the flat.

'How was it?' she asked as she walked down the hall and sank into the sofa.

'Good!' Declan said.

'And how was your try-out, Connor?' She studied the smile that played about his mouth.

'Great.' He nodded.

'Is that all I am going to get? "Great"? I've been on tenterhooks all day! Give me the details!' she yelled.

He brushed the hair from his forehead and met her gaze. 'It was more than great, actually. The team is good, like, really good.' He sat forward. 'I've only ever thought that the Kings Norton boys could play. That's kind of what the coach told us – that we had a certain way of playing that others didn't get – and I believed him.'

'A bit like the fact that the Great Wall of China can be seen from space?' she quipped.

'Yeah, I guess so. But I *did* believe it, Mum, I wanted to believe it. It felt great to be part of something that I thought was the best, and because of that I've been dreading playing anywhere else. But Cottrell's has a good squad.'

'What position were you?'

'Winger.'

'And do you think they'll give you a game?' she asked.

'I do. I've got to keep turning up for practice and working hard, but I reckon I'll make the team. The boys are nearly all two years older than me, but that means even if I only get on the bench, I've got two years to earn a place and keep it,' he said excitedly.

'I'm really proud of you.' She reached out and grabbed his arm, pulling him towards her in a rare hug. To her delight, he didn't push her away.

'Is it okay if I go out tonight?'

'Go out?'

'Yes, with some of the guys from the team?'

His request caught her a little off guard. Her concerns about not being out too late on a school night and whether he had any homework were far outweighed by her sheer delight to think that her eldest boy might have made a friend.

'Yes, of course!' She concentrated on not sounding over-eager.

'Brandon's coming over soon. We're going to the Westquay shopping centre and then to Sprinkles for a milkshake.'

'Brandon, as in Brandon who you hate?' she asked.

Connor laughed loudly. 'He's hilarious, Mum.'

It was the first time in ages she had heard him speak normally and openly, without barbs. It was wonderful.

'So is that okay?'

'It's more than okay,' she said, smiling.

'Just you and me tonight, Mum.' Declan beamed. 'Shall we watch a film on my laptop?'

All she really wanted was a hot bath and her pyjamas.

'I'd love that. Let me just grab a cup of coffee and I am all yours.' She ruffled his hair and made her way to the kitchen. Caffeine would help.

Nina felt warm at the fact that Connor was going out with friends – *friends! How wonderful!* It occurred to her then that, in that moment, with something to celebrate, her first thought had not been to tell Finn. There was no mental door slam of realisation that he was gone, no jarring bolt of grief; instead, she felt a kind of peace, knowing she was doing okay.

◆　◆　◆

She stirred sometime later, after they'd watched the movie and Declan had gone to bed, at the sound of a key in the door.

It was Connor arriving home a little before nine o'clock. She sat up and he lowered himself onto the sofa next to her.

'Declan asleep?'

'Yes, we had a lovely evening. We watched *Avengers Assemble*. Again. I think he spoke every line along with the film.'

'Dad used to go to sleep and wake up just before the end, and then say how much he'd enjoyed it.'

Nina gave a small laugh. 'He worked hard for us, your dad, and when he stopped, and sat down, he couldn't help but nod off. It was like he had one of those power-saving buttons.'

'Do you think . . . ?' Connor paused.

'Do I think what?'

'Do you think that Dad crashed because he had so much on his mind, worrying about the money and everything?'

Connor's words sounded rehearsed, she suspected, diluted and censored after much thought since the night Mackintosh and Vooght had ransacked their home. She recalled the way he had looked at her, a similar expression to the one he now bore, sad and unsure of what answer he sought: '*Mum? You don't think he . . . ?*' She thought she had put the question out of his mind; turns out she had merely tamped it down, where the idea had continued to smoulder.

She looked at him, sensing that he was seeking reassurance as much as truth. 'I think it's possible that he was distracted, yes. But the truth is, we will never know, not for sure, and so for me, and I am sure for you too, it feels gentler, easier, to accept that it was an accident on a horrible bend that is notoriously dangerous, and Dad was going too fast, just like the police report said.'

Connor nodded. Her response was enough, for now.

'I miss him,' he confessed.

'I know, and I think you always will, but we can still go on to have full, happy lives. Because life doesn't end just because someone is no longer with you.'

There was a moment or two of reflective silence.

'Did you have a good time tonight?' she asked.

'Yep.' He picked at the hem of his shirt, smiling. 'We just hung out at the mall.'

'Funny to think it wasn't built when I lived here,' she said.

'Did they even have roads here then?' he queried.

'Just about. We needed them to get our horse and cart around.' She nudged him.

'We had a laugh. It's different, you know, from what I used to do with George and Charlie.'

She nodded, thinking of the hours they had spent in the home cinema or playing tennis or roaming the grounds on the quad bikes. Yes, it was. Very different.

'Have you heard from those guys much?' She was wary of disturbing their newfound peace.

'Not so much, but I know they are busy . . .' He blinked.

'How do you feel about that? Would you like more contact with them?'

'It's funny, last week I would have said yes, but now' – he looked up at her – 'I think it's probably easier to move on if we leave things as they are. If I see them, great, I'd love it, but . . .' He paused. 'It helps when I'm out with the guys from school if I'm not thinking about my old mates. You know?'

'Yep, I do know. Living in the now. It's getting late, Con, and you need to get your prep done, if you have any?'

'My *homework*, you mean? Only a bit of reading. Think I'll do it in bed.'

'Sure. Goodnight, love.' She watched him walk from the room. He looked taller. She knew the questions about Finn's death would arise again and she hoped that, from a more stable foundation, she would be able to work it through with him.

Her chest tightened when she pictured Finn's note, scrawled in haste and left unfinished: '*With every day comes a new pressure that is pushing down down down & I don't know what will break first, me or my world . . .*' The sadness she felt at his isolated distress did not, however, lessen. She wondered if it ever would, and now it was layered with the doubts about her marriage. To try to pick through the mess was mentally exhausting.

Nina reached for Declan's dinner plate and his leftover baked potato. She picked up a chunk and popped in her mouth. She closed her eyes and saw Finn coming in late from work. He had stopped at the kitchen island, under the dazzling spotlights, and she watched as he forked a mouthful of cold cauliflower cheese into his mouth.

'Mmm, delicious!'

'Darling, you don't have to eat it cold, and you don't have to eat off my plate. I can serve you up a fresh bowlful, if you like?' She had run her hand across his broad back, feeling the muscles underneath. 'I knew you'd be in late. There's plenty in the fridge. The boys had it with crispy bacon and a salad – want me to make that for you?'

'No, thanks.' He shook his head, going in for a second forkful. 'Here's the thing.' He waved the long-tined fork in her direction. 'Have you ever noticed that food eaten from someone else's plate or bowl always tastes a thousand times better than it does from your own? It's a similar thing with toast. Toast is simply toast, dry bread made brown, until someone else makes it for you, and then it is transformed into a mouth-watering, delicious feast of Michelin-star proportions.'

'I think you need to come home late more often if this is the mood you arrive in.' She kissed his cheek as she walked past, on her way back to the soft chair with a view over the pool and terrace, where a glass of wine waited for her.

'I love you, Mrs McCarrick,' he had called out.

She looked back at him over her shoulder, heart swelling with joy at her lucky, lucky life. 'And I love you.'

'There was good in our marriage, Finn,' she whispered now as she made her way along the corridor towards her bedroom. 'So much good.'

THIRTEEN

Even though it was now May, the flat was still a little cold in the mornings. With windows only along one side of the building, most of their living space was in shadow. Nina was loath to put on the heaters, picturing the warm air carrying five-pound notes upwards, disintegrating and disappearing through the cracks in the yellowed ceiling; five-pound notes that she didn't have to spare, and which Mr Broom Handle above would gleefully gather up. As the sun rose, it hit the large picture windows and pulled the chill from the place. There was a pleasant hour or so before midday, before the flat quickly became a little stifling, but right now, at this hour, it was cool and unpleasant and still a little damp. It reminded her of Gran's flat, where the air felt icy against her lips, and if she blew out, her breath misted like smoke. Sometimes she'd raise two fingers and make out she was smoking a cigarette, like the grown-ups. She smiled at the thought.

Once the boys were off to school, Nina fastened her hair into a loose knot and stepped into her trainers – the best footwear, she found, for being on her feet all day. A knock on the window made her jump. She tilted the blinds to see Tiggy standing on her tippy-toes, with her nose squashed against the glass.

'Oh, for goodness' sake!' She laughed at her sister's childish antics.

'Thought I'd walk you to work,' Tiggy shouted.

'Thank you.' She looked down at her sister. 'Are you coming in?'

'Yep. Don't bother coming around. Open the window, I'll climb up.'

'You can't climb up!' Nina raised her voice, but opened the window nonetheless. Her sister gripped the window ledge and levered herself up, like climbing out of a swimming pool. She arrived in the sitting room with a thud.

'Are you a burglar?' Toothless Vera shouted as she shuffled past, a cigarette dangling from her mouth.

'No, Vera. Trust me, there is absolutely nothing in here worth taking!' Tiggy yelled back.

Nina heard the woman cackle in response.

'How lovely. And to what do I owe this pleasure?'

'I was up early and thought, as I hadn't seen you for a few days . . .'

Nina smiled. 'That's nice.'

Nina cleaned her teeth and locked up, and the two fell into step along Portswood Road.

The roar of a powerful car engine approached. Nina looked and saw Jacob, sitting in his shiny truck.

'Hi, Nina! Need a lift?' he said, smiling.

'No! No, thanks, Jacob, I'm good!' She waved, feeling her cheeks colour as the vehicle sped off.

'Who was that?' Tiggy asked.

'His mum is one of our residents. Lovely Miss Molly.'

As she and Tiggy rounded the path and approached the front door of Celandine Court, Jacob was digging in a cardboard box in the back of his truck.

'Thanks for walking me in. I'll see you soon.' Nina hoped Tiggy would be on her way; she was wary that she might come out with an inappropriate joke or a blunt observation.

'It's turning into a lovely day!' Jacob called to them.

'Yes.' Nina turned, sensing that Tiggy was in no mood to rush off. 'I spent time with Miss Molly yesterday.'

'She's really settling in,' he said.

'That's so good to hear.' She felt the blush of embarrassment spread over her face and chest, under the weight of Tiggy's stare.

'I mean, it's early days, but yes, so far so good.' Jacob sounded relieved.

Tiggy coughed.

'Oh, this is my sister Albertina.'

'Why have you told him my name is Albertina?' Tiggy raised her hands. As she squawked, Nina felt her blush worsen.

'Because that's your name,' she mumbled through gritted teeth, eyeing her sister awkwardly, silently pleading with her not to squabble.

Tiggy stepped forward and offered her hand. 'My name is Tiggy. Unless I am in deep trouble, or you have a matter of life-changing importance that needs urgent discussion, then you get to call me Albertina. But only then.'

'Got it. Tiggy it is,' he answered, laughing.

'Anyway, Tig,' said Nina, 'I expect you need to get going, and I must certainly get inside for work.' She pulled a face at her as Jacob disappeared inside the building.

'What?' Tiggy shrugged. 'Why didn't you tell me you had a new gentleman friend with a big truck?'

'He is not my gentleman friend!' Nina fired back. 'Don't say that.'

'Oh, I'm sorry.' Tiggy smacked her forehead. 'I could have sworn he was a gentleman, and you seem to be friends?'

'You know that's not what you meant, and it's not funny. Imagine if the boys heard that?'

'Point taken. How old is he?'

'I don't know, Tiggy!'

'Is he married?'

Nina faced her sister. 'I know nothing about him, other than his name, that his mum's called Molly, and she's been living here for a couple of weeks, and that he's got a place up by the marina and an iPad and a big pickup. That's it! Happy now?'

'Happier,' Tiggy said with a smile. 'Can I say one more thing about him?'

'No!' Nina sighed. Tiggy continued anyway.

'You seem to know quite a lot about him, considering he's not your friend.'

'You are such an idiot.' She tutted at her sister as the two went their separate ways.

'Takes one to know one!' Tiggy called out. Nina tried to ignore her, but laughed to herself.

◆　◆　◆

Connor dumped his breakfast bowl in the sink and ran to get his kit together. 'Come and watch, Mum. It's only on the school field. And you may as well, as you aren't working.'

'Really? I wasn't sure of the etiquette at your new school. Especially for your first game.' Nina busied herself wiping down the counter-tops and washing up her coffee cup and the boys' breakfast bowls. She avoided her son's gaze, in case he could read her thoughts about the last game she went to – the time his dad hadn't shown up because of the accident. 'It's been a while since you played a match. I can't wait to see you there,' she said carefully.

'I think some parents go and some don't. Whatever – you don't have to, but I'd like you to.' Connor stuffed his gumshield into the front pocket of his rucksack.

'Thanks, Con. I'd like that too.'

'Cool. Kick-off is at three fifteen, but we are practising before and Coach is giving us a team talk.'

'I'll go grocery shopping and drop the laundry off with Vera and then come along, so I might be a little late, but I'll be there. Are you nervous?' she asked.

Connor paused with his hand on the doorframe. 'No, Mum. It's when I'm happiest.'

'Then go and enjoy every minute, and good luck!' she called after him as he raced out the door.

'Good luck, Con!' Declan called out. 'Mum? Erm, I spoke to my friend Arek,' he said quickly, holding the phone, 'and he says I can go to his house for a sleepover but his mum wants to talk to you!'

'You're not making calls, are you?' She was wary of the contract on his phone running out, but she wanted the boys to have a way to contact her in an emergency.

'No, I promise we talk on WhatsApp. It's free.' She was surprised he would be aware of this. 'Arek's mum said I can go and stay, so can you call her?' he pressed.

'Do you want to go?'

'Yes,' he stated firmly.

'Are you sure?' She instantly regretted the words, aware that she only pushed because *she* wasn't sure she wanted him away from her for a whole night. It would be his first night away since Finn died.

'Yes. I'm sure.' He nodded, but his tone suggested otherwise.

'Well, I'm sure you'll have a lovely time. You had some great sleepovers at The Tynings, didn't you?'

Declan's smile suddenly broke. He laughed as the tears came. Nina understood this reaction: she, too, had often found herself happy to be reminded of something wonderful whilst at the same time reeling from the grief that caught her off guard.

'I'd be happy to talk to Arek's mum.' She ruffled his hair, delighted that he had formed a friendship.

'Don't tell her that I've been crying,' he sniffed.

'You know what, Dec? Your daddy died, and it's still all very new. It's okay to cry. It's okay to feel sad. It would be more odd if you didn't. And I am sure that Arek's mum would understand that.'

'I suppose.' Declan shrugged. 'But don't tell her anyway.'

Arek's mum was sweet and enthusiastic about hosting Declan, and upon hearing they had no car, had even driven over to collect him. Nina saw the flash of sympathy in the woman's eyes as she surveyed their humble surroundings. She saw the way she eyed the smudge of blue spray, all that remained of the painted graffiti on the porch. Indignation flared in Nina's stomach: did it really matter if they had five bathrooms or one? Not to Declan and Arek, certainly, who were pleased to see each other, giggling and nattering like old pals.

Nina waved them off from the window, noting Declan's excitement at being in a car and the prospect of spending the afternoon and evening in a house with a garden. She forced herself to remember the many, many times that both boys had chosen to spend time cloistered in their bedrooms, rather than go outside to roam and enjoy the grounds. But it felt different when there was no choice.

Toothless Vera promised to swap the laundry to the dryer when it finished its cycle; Nina was appreciative of the help. She was nervous about the rugby match. She had visited the school only once since being back in Portswood, on the day after they had moved, when she rushed into the building for her meeting with the admissions secretary with head bowed, her tears constantly hovering close to the surface. She did, however, notice that the place was grey and run-down, the same way she felt at the time.

Today, however, she found herself pleasantly surprised. The school of her childhood, surrounded by jagged, rusting fences, had grey metal-framed windows of opaque safety glass that kept the light out and the gloom in. The building now in front of her had enjoyed a grand facelift.

A vast addition to the left side of the main building faced the wooded area where she and her friends used to hide and smoke. She smiled at the thought. The modern wing looked futuristic, like a contemporary gallery or library. She peered in at the walls as she walked past, where students' artistic canvases were displayed. Clever tropical plantings made use of the heat and light, and created green spaces around informal seating. It was quite something.

She made her way round to the back of the building and would barely have recognised the playing fields. There were now two pitches, both well cared for and lying at the back of the plot of land. Rugby posts stood tall on the left-hand pitch and there was a set of low stands along one side. Another new low-rise building sat to the right, a clubhouse perhaps.

Nina could see the boys, all wearing the Cottrell's rugby kit of red-and-black-hooped shirts with black shorts. The opposing team were in gold and green. Gingerly she made her way to the edge of the pitch and tried to ignore the fluttery nerves in her stomach and the desire to look back over her shoulder to see if Finn had arrived.

As the parent spectators yelled support and whooped and clapped, she shoved her hands into her jeans pockets and drew up her shoulders, feeling as out of place now as she always had. She fought the desire to turn and leave, lest someone might try to engage her in conversation and her fear might come to fruition: that she had absolutely nothing of interest to say. She had thought that the reason she felt so shy at Kings Norton was because she was out of her league, but as she looked at the women and men all around her, who lived in her postcode, whose kids went to Cottrell's School with hers, she realised her insecurity was something deeper than a concern over her lack of pedigree.

I never thought I was good enough, Finn. I let you shape me and I did lose a bit of myself, my confidence, my sparkle. I was so nervous of portraying the wrong thing, I became a cardboard-cutout wife, safe, vanilla, two-dimensional . . . It was a hard thing to process.

She squinted and saw Connor in the thick of it, grappling with a bigger boy on the opposing team for the ball. She winced as another lad came at him from behind and swept his legs from under him. There was a bone-crunching thud as he hit the deck. Her heart raced until he stood, spat heartily and dusted himself off, glaring at his opponent.

He was rewarded by several slaps on his back from his teammates. She caught his eye and gripped the inside of her pockets with her fingers, trying to quell her reflex to wave. Instead she smiled broadly and he gave a small, almost imperceptible nod that flooded her with happiness.

'Hello, you!' An eager voice came from over her shoulder. Nina turned to see a familiar face: Gilly, the big woman from work with the feathered red hair.

'Gilly!' Her relief was genuine. 'I didn't expect to see you here!'

'Likewise. I didn't know your boy played?' She nodded towards the pitch.

'Yes! Connor. He's the tall one . . . I was going to say in red and black, but that doesn't narrow it down much.'

'It doesn't, sweetie!' Gilly laughed. 'Come and sit with us.'

'Oh, I don't . . .' She struggled to think of a reason to decline fast enough.

'Come on!' Gilly insisted. 'It's good to see you.' Gilly tucked Nina's arm inside hers and pulled her along. 'Are you a rugby fan?' she quizzed.

'Erm, not really,' Nina confessed. 'I don't really understand the rules exactly, but Connor's mad about it, so . . .'

'I thought so. You need to come and sit with my friends and me. We are, like you, reluctant supporters and we're up here on the benches.'

'Is that okay?' She looked at the woman with concern, wary of barging in.

'Of course!'

Nina followed her up to the stands. Two women sat on the end of a bench facing the field, chatting and holding china mugs. They looked like any regular mums, in jeans, jackets, boots and scarves, with phones resting on their laps. Gilly pointed to each woman in turn, 'Moira, Lou, this is Nina!'

They both waved and smiled broadly.

'Hi, Nina!'

'Hello!'

'Nina and I are colleagues.' The simple phrase uttered by Gilly sent a bolt of joy through Nina's core. She had a job, she had a place. Nina felt emboldened. She took a seat next to Lou.

'We're not that keen on rugby,' Lou whispered. 'But we need to support the boys, so we sit here and drink this.' Moira handed her a white china mug that was half full of white wine.

Nina nodded, worried about saying something and sounding like a prude.

'We chat about anything other than what's going on on the field, we bring snacks and we take turns doing this.' Gilly nodded at her friend. 'It's you, Lou. Your turn,' she instructed.

The slightly chubby woman with a blonde bob looked at her. 'Are you sure it's me?'

'Yes!'

'Go, girl!' they heckled.

'All right then.' Lou coughed, stood and placed her hands either side of her mouth. 'Come on, Cottrell's! Go, Jack!' The others cheered and Nina joined in, clapping softly and hoping no one paid her any attention.

'We call out every ten minutes or so and we all shout out if they score.'

'But other than that, we talk about the kids, our partners, our diets, our lives, money, TV, anything!'

'I think I can handle that!' Nina laughed and sipped her wine. 'Apart from the shouting out. I couldn't do that. No way!' She balked at the prospect.

'Well that's okay, shouting is optional. There are only two rules here, Nina,' Moira informed her, flicking her long dark plait over her shoulder.

'What?'

'We keep it a secret that there is anything other than coffee in these sacred mugs.'

'Okay.' She nodded, sipping again.

'And secondly we never tell anyone that we couldn't give a damn about rugby.'

'Got it,' she whispered.

They all clinked mugs and laughed loudly.

Nina laughed, marvelling at how happy she felt. She had known these women for a little under five minutes, and what a difference they were making to her today, of all days, keeping the memories at bay, creating new ones. It was so very different to Kings Norton College.

'*I wonder what I missed?*'

She heard her husband's words. '*We like it being just the two of us, don't we?*' Finn had always asserted, and she had readily agreed. Only now was she beginning to wonder how different her life might have been if she had said yes to the odd invitation, set different boundaries at the very beginning.

'Okay, Nina, but it's your turn to call support, in approximately' – Moira looked at her watch – 'four minutes.'

'Oh God, no! I really wasn't joking. There is no way I could do that.' She swallowed like a schoolgirl in the face of a dare, felt her mouth go dry and her cheeks burn crimson.

Gilly placed a hand on her shoulder. 'It's okay. I'll take your go.'

Nina nodded with instant relief, and smiled broadly at Gilly and her new friends.

FOURTEEN

Gilly, Moira and Lou invited her to their WhatsApp group and her phone pulsed daily with messages. It felt exciting to be included. They talked about everything, from baking disasters, shared for the comedy value (mainly from Gilly), to requests for lifts (mainly from Lou) and those round robin messages of support that you were instructed to send to women you admired and loved (largely from Moira).

In the handful of times they had met up since the match, both at rugby training and in the Trago Lounge for the treat of shop-bought coffee, they had included Nina in the loveliest of ways.

'So, my daughter is getting married, and I'm supposed to be dieting, but the more I worry about it and think about it, the more I eat!' Lou reached for a sugar cube for her coffee and the others exchanged knowing smiles. 'The wedding is six months away, and I have too much to do.'

'How can we help?' Moira sipped the foam of her cappuccino.

'Urgh, you can't, honey.' Lou batted away the offer. 'Apart from all the other things, I have to plan and arrange twenty floral centrepieces and two large displays for the top table. And I haven't got a clue!'

'Oh, well, I can help you with that. Flower arranging for my home used to be a big part of my life,' Nina said.

She startled at the loud laughter that followed. Gilly patted her arm. Nina broke into a smile. She guessed that, for these working women, it was laughable: a preoccupation with the indulgence of flowers. A blush of embarrassment rose to her face.

'What? It did!' She chuckled.

The laughter calmed.

'Nina, that would be lovely, thank you.'

And just like that she was able to help. Feeling useful was the best. She knew the old Nina would have found a thousand reasons not to get involved.

The women listened with interest and empathy to how her life had been turned upside down by the death of her husband. She never realised how good it felt to have girlfriends to talk to, and who could offer a range of viewpoints that helped her to figure out how she felt. It was the first time she had confided her situation to anyone other than Tiggy, and whilst it felt odd to be sharing so much with relative strangers, she also felt a little unburdened. It left her with a feeling of belonging that she hadn't felt for some years, in fact not since she last lived in Portswood. She told them how she had lived and what she had lost, keen to stress that what mattered most was not the house or the things, but that she had lost her love and was now alone with her kids, trying to hold everything together. They had squeezed her fingers, sighed, hugged her, and then immediately started to list all the men they knew who might be able to fix her lonely heart.

'No, no! Absolutely not. Thank you, but no.' She shook her head, a little unnerved by the suggestion. She was focused on the boys and on the slow and sometimes painful process of moving on. The last thing she wanted to do was throw more change and challenges into the mix. 'I couldn't imagine being with anyone else, wouldn't want to. I really wouldn't. I'm still trying to reclaim my life. I went from my dad's arms into Finn's, and I think I need to get better at being on my own.' With this admission she put a lid on the well-meaning banter.

Moira spoke up. 'You'll know when you are ready. Maybe you never will be, like you say, and that's all right too, but the morning you wake and your husband is not the first thing that fills your head, then you'll know that your grief has shifted, made space for something or someone else.'

The girls had all clucked their approval at Moira's words. But Nina knew her grief had already shifted, that it wasn't just the loss of her husband she mourned. She was still trying to figure out what had been the true foundation of her marriage whilst coming to terms with her loss.

She considered this now as she stood by the French windows of the sitting room, watching the kids abandoning their bikes on the pavement and traipsing in and out of the shop opposite, leaving with sweets sticking out of their mouths or sipping on fizzy drinks.

It made her think of Halloween the previous year.

She and Finn had gone to fetch Declan from his school party; all his classmates were caked in face paint, trying for spooky. Some had blood dripping from the sides of their mouths, others black-ringed eyes and ill-fitting white plastic Dracula fangs. Nearly all held plastic cauldrons or pumpkins in which to gather their booty. Connor had gone to a house party, with strict instructions to be home before eleven.

She and Finn had pulled into the car park; the air was thick with the damp, earthy tang of autumn. The sky was clear, a beautiful shade of indigo with a blanket of stars. She glanced up and marvelled at the infinite celestial display; it felt like anything was possible.

'Is that Dec?' Finn had nodded towards a side door from where a group of little ghouls and a Frankenstein emerged. She squinted into the darkness, and there was Declan, clutching a fistful of sweets. Nina waved at him and he responded with a happy smile.

'Sweet mother of Betsy!' Finn had gasped. 'What on earth is that boy wearing?' Declan ambled up the path in a pale pink rubbery costume with a tail at the back, and a rounded top for a hat.

'Nina! Your son is dressed as a sperm!'

'He is not!' Nina laughed. 'And might I remind you that he is your son too.'

'Not dressed like that he isn't!' Finn howled.

They tried to contain their laughter as he drew closer to the car. Finn lowered the window.

'Hey, buddy! What are you dressed up as, Dec?' he shouted across the grass.

'I'm an amoeba!'

'See, he's an amoeba,' Nina said, giggling.

'Nina, I swear to God, he may think he's an amoeba, but the kid is dressed as a sperm!' Her husband guffawed. Nina elbowed Finn hard in the ribs, knowing they had precisely three seconds to gain control and present a composed face to Declan.

She gave a little chuckle now, thinking how long she had avoided Finn's gaze for fear of reigniting the laughter that hovered.

'You look like you're miles away.' Tiggy came from the bathroom and filled the space next to her at the window.

'I was.'

'So, tell me again,' Tiggy said, tucking her hair behind her ear. 'You are taking a trip back to Bath?'

'Not Bath, exactly, but I've decided to rent a van and drive out to Saltford, to Mr Firth's place. I got a deal on the van, so I can do it when I get paid at the end of July.' She had worked out that if she economised on food and the bus fare to work in the following weeks, she could just about afford it. It would be cheaper and easier to make the trip, rather than try to buy the desk Connor needed and replace their summer clothes.

'I'll come with you.'

'Thanks, Tiggy, but it's a long way and it'll rob you of a day.' She smiled at her sister and thought of how she had turned up at Finn's funeral, offering help and love, asking nothing in return despite the expense of making the trip, and having taken time off work. Nina had taken that act for granted and knew that if she could go back in time, she would run towards Tiggy, throw her arms around her and hold her close.

'Of course.' Tiggy shrugged, as if it were a fait accompli.

'Mr Firth is a good man. Finn trusted him and he has said if I need anything in the future then just to shout. He's already been really kind. Finn did him a favour, sorted out some building work for him, and in return he has let us store our stuff at his farm.'

'Gosh, that sounds like Finn might have been thinking ahead, if you ask me.'

Nina didn't have time to speak before her body folded, as if punched in the gut. It still caught her off guard sometimes, how raw the emotions still were, this time brought on by the simple statement, a suggestion from the mouth of someone whose opinion she trusted, that Finn might have taken his own life.

'God! I'm sorry!' Tiggy reached for her. 'I didn't mean to upset you, I just spoke without thinking. Shit, I'm sorry, Nina. Are you okay?'

'I find it so hard to think about. The fact that he might be dead because he *wanted* to die. . .' She paused. 'Just the idea that he not only chose not to be with us, but that he did so, leaving us in this mess . . .' She ran her hands over her face. The thought did not get any easier to contend with, no matter how often she wrangled with it.

'I wasn't suggesting that. I . . .' Tiggy floundered.

Nina straightened and tried to catch her breath. 'I know, Tiggy, I know. But it still feels sometimes like I'm running up an escalator that's heading down and I can't get anywhere. I am tired. And yes, the fact that he might have been thinking ahead, making decisions or, God forbid, planning, makes the possibility that he left us by choice seem more likely. And it seems the sole effort of that pre-planning that I can detect was to set up some storage, when we have been reduced to the bones of our arse, and that makes me so angry!' She clenched her fists.

Tiggy stood back at the rare outburst. 'You let it out, girl!'

'I mean it, Tig, I am furious. How did he let things come to this?' Nina ran her hands through her hair and remembered the smirk on Mr Ludlow's face. 'I hate that he was suffering, but I will never forget what it felt like to see my boys walk through the front door and having to tell them that their dad had died. And then the bailiffs pitching up and invading our home . . .' She paused and took a deep breath, her teeth clenched. 'Connor has broached the topic of how Finn died and I can't stand that it's another level of shit for him to deal with! I hate it.' Nina stared at her sister, as if hoping for consolation or a solution. She offered neither. 'And I don't know what I'll say to Connor if he asks again, and the thought of Dec thinking similar makes my heart sink, because they may have lost his dad, but their hero is intact, despite everything. I have insisted that it was an accident because I want to protect them. What would it do to their self-esteem if they suspected their dad didn't even think they were worth hanging round for?'

'It's more complex than that. It always is, honey,' Tiggy offered.

'I know that. But if they believed that their dad had . . .'

They were silent for a beat or two. 'With hindsight, do you think he was coming close to telling you the truth about your situation? Had he given you any hints, mentioned anything?' Tiggy asked.

Nina pictured Finn swilling the red wine around his glass before swallowing it. '*Why don't we go to the Maldives for Easter?*'

'No.' Nina shook off the memory and exchanged a look with her sister. 'No, he didn't show any signs that anything was amiss. The way he spoke and acted, you would have thought that we were on top of the world. And that kills me too.'

'I think, Nina, that not only did Finn not know how to handle his love for you, thinking that keeping you cloistered away was the way to hold you dear, he also didn't know how to dismantle the life he had constructed, the illusion he had created. I don't agree with what he did, but I feel for him, I do, because of how it ended.'

Her sister's words acted like a blanket; they not only comforted her, but also partly smothered the flames of anger that had flared inside her, bringing some measure of calm.

'But you know,' Tiggy continued, 'there is no point mulling over things that you can't change.'

'I guess so.'

'I know so,' Tiggy asserted. 'What would it change if you had it confirmed that his death wasn't accidental?'

'What would it change?'

'Yes. I mean, the end result would be the same. How would it feel different?'

'I think it would change everything! The fact that he left me to face this shit storm alone, the fact that he *chose* to leave us, but *mainly*,' Nina cried, 'mainly the fact that he didn't know me well enough to know that he could talk to me about anything and trust that I would have helped in any way I could.'

Nina felt Tiggy's arm around her waist, pulling her close.

'I think Finn wanted everything to be perfect for you – him included.'

'I can't stand to think that he didn't know the *one* thing about me that mattered the most, the most important thing for him to know. That no matter what, I had his back, I was there for him . . .'

A moment of silence passed before Tiggy spoke. 'I spent years missing Mum so much that I could barely function. With just Dad and us in the house in Frederiksberg, it was quiet, awkward. She was our glue.'

Nina remembered her quiet, brooding sister.

'But then Dad said something to me that made a difference, and it might make a difference to you.'

'What was it?'

'He said that he believed people are on the earth for as long as they need to be. Some for a long, long time, contributing a little bit every day to the world, and others are only here for a shorter time, so they have to do really incredible things in the time they are given. He said that Mum was only on the planet for thirty years, but in that time, she married him and made two beautiful children.' Tiggy looked up and smiled. 'He said she filled us up with all we would need to know, even though she didn't get to stay and see us grow up. I believed him and it made me confident.'

'That's lovely.'

'It is lovely, and maybe Finn did the same. He filled you all up, you, Connor and Declan. He gave you everything you would need to go on, with or without him. Maybe he never had any doubt that you would cope, no matter what, maybe him not planning is a compliment. He saw that determination that lurked inside you, hidden, admittedly for a while, but still there nonetheless.'

Nina exhaled. 'Thank you.'

'See, that's what sisters are for. Sisters put things right, because they *know* you. Much better than any crappy new rugby-mum friends.'

'Are you jealous of my friends now?' Nina laughed, glad to diffuse the heavy atmosphere. 'Jeez, you are so childish!'

'As if I'd be jealous of them! They are boring! Want one?' Tiggy shook a cigarette from the packet and lit up.

'No, I don't!'

'God, your tone! You honestly sound like Gran.'

Tiggy looked like a rocker chick in her skinny jeans and denim jacket, cigarette held aloft. 'That is quite possibly the very worst thing you could ever say to me,' Nina huffed.

'I disagree.' Tiggy took a long drag on her cigarette and blew the smoke out the open window. 'I think the very worst thing would be if I said that you *looked* like Gran!'

Nina turned to face her sister. 'Oh my God! Do I?'

Tiggy studied her face. 'A little bit, yes.'

'I really hate you,' Nina whispered.

'I really hate you too,' Tiggy replied, and took a deep drag.

'Go on then, give me one.'

'What?'

'A cigarette!'

'For real?' Tiggy laughed.

Placing the cigarette between her lips, Nina bent forward for Tiggy to light it. Taking a deep drag, Nina blew the smoke out between pursed lips, fighting the desire to cough.

Today was a big day for Nina: June the twenty-sixth. Connor's sixteenth birthday. The first birthday they had celebrated without Finn. Nina woke to the sound of the alarm clock, and lay back on the pillow with her hand on her stomach, thinking about the day her first child had been born. She pictured Finn standing in the maternity ward, crying with his hands in his hair, 'I'm a dad! I'm a dad! To a boy! I got a boy! A son! I can't believe it!' Nina had watched from her bed as the nurses patted his back, chuckled to each other and offered him tissues. She had the newborn Connor in her arms and, despite the deep ache to her bones, she wondered if she would ever be able to wipe the smile of joy from her face.

Oh, Finn. She sighed before she rose, then washed her face, and fastened her unruly hair with a headband. She heated a croissant, a special treat purchased in secret, and poured glasses of orange juice, trying not to think of the previous year when she had piled the breakfast table with lavishly wrapped gifts. Connor had peeled the paper with little enthusiasm. She and his dad had teased him about getting old, whilst sipping espresso from their fancy built-in machine and recalling how Finn had run around the ward fifteen years ago, crying like he had won the jackpot . . . This was the Finn she wanted to remember, the wonderful dad.

Connor came into the sitting room dressed for school.

'Happy birthday, darling.'

'Thanks, Mum.'

He opened his card from Tiggy and found a crisp ten-pound note. He beamed.

Nina had deliberated long and hard over his birthday gift. For the first time, she wasn't able to buy an array of presents and simply hope that he liked one. And in fact, the thought that she did this in the past left her feeling a little sickened. The solution came to her one evening as she cleaned her bedroom, going through her things.

Nina now placed the small black box in Connor's palm. He looked at her quizzically, before carefully, slowly, lifting the lid of the box. She watched him tuck in his lips and bite down as his eyes misted at the sight of his dad's signet ring.

'He would want you to have this, Connor, and he would want me to tell you happy birthday from your dad, and that he loves you and is so very proud of you. As am I. You have been through far more than I would ever have wished for you at this age, and you are coming through the other side as a wonderful man. A wonderful man.'

She watched the tremble of his mouth as tears escaped down his flushed cheeks. He walked forward and placed his arms around her and she held her son to her while he cried, feeling closer to him than any time in recent memory.

Connor stepped back and pulled his father's ring from the box. Finn had told them all many a time of how he had bought the thick, crested band with some of his first profits. He explained how the rich boys he mixed with sported college rings that screamed of an education he could only dream of. This little chunk of gold represented success to him, and he wore it every day of his life, with pride. She had planned on pawning it last, letting it stay in her possession for as long as possible. And now with a job and an income, she felt able to give it to Connor. A reminder of all his dad had achieved.

Connor placed it on his little finger, before splaying his hand and admiring the gold that glinted in the light. It looked strange on his long fingers, shining in the dimness of their run-down flat, but the look on Connor's face told her it gave him a connection to his dad that was more precious than the item itself.

'It fits me,' he said with measured pride, as if having the same-sized finger as the man he worshipped was a thing of note. 'I shall look after it, Mum.'

'I know you will.'

'I won't wear it to school, only for special occasions.'

'I hope one day you wear it every day and get pleasure from it like your dad did.'

Connor nodded.

'Sixteen, eh?' She smiled. 'Where did those years go?'

Declan walked in and handed his brother a card. 'When I'm sixteen, I am going to fly a glider. Arek told me that you only have to be sixteen do to that.' Declan peered through his glasses.

'Well you've got that to look forward to,' Nina said with a smile. She turned back to Connor. 'You could invite some of your friends over this evening if you'd like.'

'Actually, Mum, if it's okay with you . . .' He hesitated. 'I made plans to go out with Anna. She's . . . she's in my class.'

Nina noted the bloom to his cheek when he spoke her name. Connor had been a little less antsy of late, as keen as ever to engage with his phone when he thought he could get away with it. She watched him of an evening from the end of the sofa, noting the smile of relief flood his face when there was a text waiting for him. He was like a different boy from the one she lived with at The Tynings; gone was the exasperation, the tension, that bookended her every encounter with him, and although she was uncertain if he would admit it or had even fully realised it, he was happy at Cottrell's. What's more, she very much liked the person he was becoming. This situation, which she would never have chosen, was shaping him in a positive way. Hardship eroded his sense of entitlement and in its place a nicer, humbler boy was emerging.

'Oooh, Connor's got a girlfriend!' Declan called out and ran in a circle, trying to avoid his brother's grip. 'Connor and Anna sitting in a tree . . .' Declan ran down the hall as Connor tumbled after him, laughing.

◆ ◆ ◆

After a long day at work with the now familiar ache in her back and her calves from being on her feet all day, Nina was keen to get home and see her boy on his special day. As soon as she walked in the door she could hear Declan splashing about in the bath. It was always a relief that the boys had in fact come home from school safe and sound. She knocked on the bathroom door. 'Hey, darling, I'm home!'

'Hi, Mum!' he called, before continuing to splash.

'Try to keep the water in the bath, okay?' She pictured water pooling on the dodgy floorboards and gave thanks that they were on the ground floor.

Connor was in the bedroom, rifling through his clothes.

'Hey, birthday boy!'

'Hi. I'm wearing my ring tonight.' He lifted his hand to show her. She had to say, it suited him well.

'Perfect.'

While Declan languished in his bath and Connor got dressed, she heated up some leftover pasta and tomato sauce and sat down to eat.

'Are you sure you don't want anything to eat?' she asked Connor as he wafted into the room in a cloud of sweet-smelling body spray.

'I'm sure. We are going to Sprinkles to get a milkshake.'

'You look lovely.' She winked at him.

Nina reached into her handbag, unzipped her wallet, and pulled out three pound coins. 'Here. For your milkshake.' She didn't want him breaking into his birthday ten-pound note. It choked her to recall the bundles of cash that used to lie dormant around the house, and others she would remove from Finn's pockets when laundering his clothes. She would peel off notes and fling them in her son's direction every time he stepped out of the front door.

'Are you sure?' He looked from the coins in her palm to her face.

'Yes! I want you to have fun.'

'Thank you, Mum.' The real thanks was the way he looked at her.

When the buzzer rang, Declan ran out of the bathroom and raced down the hall half dressed. 'I'll get it!'

'No you won't!' Connor practically grabbed his little brother and tossed him into the sitting room. All that rugby training was clearly paying off. Nina rushed over to Declan and whispered, 'We have to be on our best behaviour. This is important to Con, okay?'

''Kay.' Declan sulked on the sofa with his chin on his chest.

Nina heard nervous laughter from the hallway and was surprised to find she, too, was nervous.

Connor stood by the door and held out his arm, encouraging Anna to walk in. Anna looked at Connor admiringly, and Nina knew that she was right to feel the flip of nerves; from the way the two of them looked at each other, this relationship seemed already more than an insignificant crush. 'Mum, this is Anna.'

Nina stood up and smiled at the slight girl, whose thick, dark hair hung about her shoulders in a delicate wave. She was wearing a close-fitting navy dress that had an uneven hem and was of a shiny material that squeaked a little when she moved. Her heeled shoes were a little too big for her, borrowed, Nina suspected, for the occasion. She wore little make-up; the natural prettiness of her heart-shaped face was obvious. Nina remembered the clusters of girls that hung in packs in and around Kings Norton College, the glossy, blonde, tanned girls with designer togs, expensive watches, tiny sporty cars of their own and heads full of their next and last adventures abroad. Anna was different. She carried

243

an air of poverty that Nina recognised and in truth loved her all the more for it. She pictured herself at sixteen, remembering how hard it was to look and smell nice without money; the way she watched other girls, wishing she too could wander into the high street shops and walk out with bags fit to bursting with the latest trends, convinced that if she could, then she would feel less self-conscious. Only a year later, and life with Finn had meant she could do just that, and yet still her lack of confidence persisted, despite trying so hard.

'Hello, Anna,' she offered warmly, giving a small wave, thinking a handshake might be too formal and a hug the exact opposite.

'Hi.' Anna smiled to reveal slightly crooked teeth.

'I'm Declan,' he called from the sofa, without standing or lifting his eyes from his phone.

'I've heard all about you, Declan.' At this, Declan looked up and broke into a wide grin, obviously pleased his big brother had spoken about him.

'We'd better . . .' Connor indicated with a nod towards the door.

'Yep.' Nina smiled, wishing for more of an exchange, but knowing the right thing to do was wish them a nice time and not embarrass her son.

'Have a lovely evening! And don't forget, be back by 10.30,' she managed. Anna gave a wave as Connor placed his hand on her lower back, in a gesture that was so grown-up, so confident, Nina knew it would stay in her memory.

As the door closed, she sat next to Declan. 'Well, Anna seems nice, doesn't she?'

Declan shrugged before turning his attention back to his game.

Nina had often imagined Connor going to prom. She pictured him walking down the wide staircase of their house in a tuxedo, holding a delicate fresh corsage in a box for a lovely girl. She would have taken great joy in ferrying him and his date in Finn's flash car to their grand dance . . . Now she didn't even have a car to go and fetch groceries in, and barely the money to pay for them.

'It's a funny old world,' she said.

'Why is it?' Declan looked up from his game.

She pulled him closer to her. 'I was just thinking about our old life. What do you miss most, Declan, about living at The Tynings, about going to Kings Norton? Is there one thing you would like more than any other? Is it a car?'

'You mean apart from Daddy?'

Her heart swelled at his sweet response. 'Yes, my darling, apart from Daddy.'

Declan sighed and looked towards the window where the neon sign blinked through the blinds. 'I miss my bed.'

'Your bed?' This was unexpected.

'Yep.' He nodded. 'I loved my big bed. I used to be able to spread out and I liked to sleep with my feet hanging off the end, but I can't do that here. The bunk beds are much smaller and they have that board at the bottom that stops me dangling my feet.'

'Oh, Dec!' she put her arm around him and cuddled him to her. 'How can we fix this?'

'Get bigger beds?' he asked hopefully.

Connor arrived home at 10.30 on the dot, as if not to waste a second.

'Did you have a nice evening?' Nina asked from the sofa.

He smiled and nodded, as if he had a happy secret. She hoped so. 'Well, it goes without saying that you can bring anyone here whenever you want to.'

'Thanks.' He nodded, no longer rebuffing the idea as stupid or embarrassing.

He opened his palm and let the three pound coins clatter onto the work surface. 'We didn't go for a milkshake after all. Just hung out, walked around.'

His sweet gesture, not pocketing the money for himself as he so easily could have done, made her want to howl with love for him.

'I'm off to bed,' he said with a yawn.

'Happy birthday, my darling,' she called after him.

FIFTEEN

Nina felt a little unsteady with hunger by the time lunch arrived. She relished the tuna sandwich and fruit salad that had been laid out for her.

'Did Connor have a nice birthday?' Gilly asked as she poured hot water into a mug.

'I think he did. I'm relieved, really. I didn't know what the first one without his dad was going to be like, but it was okay.'

'Well, that can only be a good thing.'

'Yup.' Nina nodded.

'Have you got your tickets for the rugby end-of-season dinner? I've assumed you will be at our table?'

'I don't know anything about it.'

Gilly looked a little shocked. 'Girl, it's the event of the year! After the last game, we have a swanky dinner in the school hall with dancing and awards for the players. It's lovely. The boys all go for free and our ticket price covers the cost of the evening.'

'Oh yes, count me in!' She wondered immediately about the cost.

'Does Tiggy want to come?' Gilly asked. 'It would be good to meet her. You speak so highly of her.'

'I'll ask her!' Nina felt the spread of excitement along her limbs. She loved the idea of connecting the people in her life.

After lunch she had found Harry and Eliza sitting side by side in the atrium sweetly holding hands; he nodded in silence while she rattled out her interior monologue. 'I've got him! Don't you worry!' Eliza yelled in her inimitable way.

As she walked home after work, Nina tried to remember what lurked in the freezer box for supper. She looked forward to an hour to herself, of blissful silence. Declan had asked to go over to Arek's for tea and Connor had plans with friends. She put the key in the door and pushed it open.

'Oh!' Nina yelled.

'Agh!' Anna screamed, and Connor scooted so far away from the girl that Nina thought he might fall through the French windows.

'I didn't realise anyone was in. You guys scared me.' She made her way over to the fridge and opened the freezer compartment, hoping to hide her shock.

'How are you, Anna?' She spoke into the freezer, giving the girl a chance for her blush to subside and her own pulse to settle.

'Good, thank you. In fact I'm just going, I have a lot of homework to do,' she said hurriedly.

'Okay, love, you know you are more than welcome to stay for supper. We are having . . .' Nina looked down at the packets in her hands. 'We are having ice cubes and frozen peas, apparently!' She held up the packet, and all three of them laughed. 'I'm sorry, kids.' She chuckled. 'We need a bigger house.'

'Or we could just tie a bell around your neck like a cat, then we'd hear you coming in,' Connor said.

'I shall make more noise in future.' She smiled at them.

'Actually, I think I will stay for supper, Mrs McCarrick. I can't resist – ice cubes and frozen peas is one of my favourites.'

'Call me Nina, and I am glad you are staying.' She beamed at the girl with the lovely sense of humour. The three eventually enjoyed a meal of pasta with a rich tomato sauce, mopped up with fresh bread.

Nina loved watching the two interact; it felt like a privilege to have a part in this budding relationship.

Later on, Connor walked Anna home and returned just as Nina was finishing off the dishes. 'Expert timing!' she noted as she reached up to put the last of the plates in the cupboard.

'Where's Dec?'

'In the bath.'

'So, what do you think of Anna?' he asked with a wide smile.

She loved that he cared about her opinion.

'I think she seems lovely.' She paused with the dishcloth in her hand. 'But you know, Con, I have no choice but to leave you alone sometimes. But you guys are very young and it's important that you don't ever take advantage of those circumstances, or of her.' She hoped her look was stern enough.

'I know that, Mum, and you don't have to worry. We won't do anything stupid.'

'I'm happy to hear that. You like her, don't you?'

'What's not to like?' He avoided her gaze.

'I mean, you *really* like her.'

'I do.' He looked up at her now, meeting her eyes.

'And she feels the same way?'

Connor nodded. 'Yes, she loves me too.'

And there it was. Her boy was in love.

'You are just starting out, and half of me wants to tell you not to get too involved, to go out there and live! Because you never know what's around the corner. And the other half of me wants to tell you to enjoy your loving commitment, because you never know what's around the corner. So I guess that's not very useful.' She put the dishcloth in the sink and put her hands on her waist. 'I always thought Dad would be by my side to have this chat, to give good advice, but I know that he would say to you: go slow, and remember she is someone's precious daughter.' She hoped this was enough.

'I know that, Mum!' He rolled his eyes in a gesture that had been missing of late. 'Anna is so smart. She won't let anything get in the way of her plan. She's a maths wizard. That's what she wants to do at uni.'

This boded very well. 'And we already know what *you* want to study – anything to do with sport!' She laughed.

'Actually, Mum . . .' He paused. 'I don't think I will do a sporty degree. I'm thinking of doing something like Psychology. I'm rethinking my A levels. I still want to do one science subject, but am thinking of maybe Psychology and Sociology.'

'Oh! Well there's a turn-up for the books.' She was a little taken aback. To play rugby and concentrate on Physical Education had been his plan for as long as she could remember. 'And what do you think you might like to do with that degree?'

He flicked his hair from his eyes. 'I want to help people, work in therapy, something along those lines.'

'I think that sounds wonderful,' she said truthfully. 'Why the sudden change?'

'I've been thinking about a lot of stuff and I want to do something that makes a difference. I have had experiences that most people haven't and I can use them.'

'How do you mean?' She wrapped her arms around her trunk and gave her eldest her full attention. Connor leaned on the wall and looked her in the eye, and just like that, there they were, chatting like equals. The conversation shot a bolt of pride through her very being. Her child was turning into an adult.

Connor took a deep breath. 'It was like a double blow, not only losing Dad, losing the house, losing everything. But it was the speed at which it all happened. That for me has been the hardest thing – no notice, no opportunity to get my head around it. Literally one minute I'm playing rugby and in the next instant my dad had died. And when George's mum dropped me off that day, and I walked through the gates at The Tynings and saw that lorry and those men and the way they looked at me, I won't ever forget it. They sneered at me, they hated me, and I hadn't done anything wrong, it wasn't my fault, they just hated what I stood for, but no matter how much I told myself this, it hurt.'

'I can't imagine what this has been like for you and Dec,' Nina said. 'I think you are right, it's the timing of everything, one horrible moment tumbling into the next like you are caught in a wave, and just when it feels like your head is above water, you take a breath, and bam! Along came the next wave to suck you under again.'

'That's exactly what is has felt like, Mum.' He looked at her with something like relief, happy that she got it.

'And as for those men,' she continued, 'they were only doing their job, a horrible job, but their job nonetheless. I think they probably experience abuse and threats every time they enter a property, and my God I understand why! But they weren't thinking of you personally, it was just another job, and it's probably a case of attack being the best form of defence. Can you see that?'

'I guess so.' Connor nodded. 'But I won't forget it.'

'I hope that the wounding of it lessens in time. I think it might.' Nina took a breath. 'I do have to take some responsibility for that day. I knew a day or two before that it was going to happen soon. I could have given you more warning. I should have probably told you sooner about the finances, but to be honest, Connor, not only was I trying to get it straight in my head, but also I wanted to give you one more day of normality. I thought building a shield around you for as long as I could was the right thing to do.'

Connor gave a wry laugh. 'Like Dad.'

'Like Dad how?' She cocked her head to one side.

'Not wanting to shatter the illusion. Hiding how much trouble we were in. I've been reading a lot about people who are depressed. People who live with extreme stress and those who only see one way out . . .'

She felt her hands shake.

'They often fall into two camps. Those who fall apart externally, seek help, battle it publicly, and then there are those who don't, can't. It's this group of people who interest me most. They are skilled in the art of hiding. I think that my dad must have been like that.'

Nina stared at him, his words so insightful, so mature, that it quite knocked the breath from her. She felt unsure of how to respond, fascinated and frightened in equal measure by his insight.

'I think you might be right.'

Despite the June sunshine of the morning, by the time Nina's shift was over the day had turned foul and dark. Strong winds rattled leaves and debris around the car park. Nina pulled her jacket collar closed as she stepped out into the gloom of the early evening. She couldn't wait to get home, take off her shoes and have a large mug of tea.

She became aware of a car idling.

'Need a lift?' Jacob called to her across the car park. Nina looked up at the black clouds, and with tiredness spreading through her limbs, the warm, comfortable car looked like a much better option than arriving home soaking wet and blown about in the squall.

'Are you sure?' she asked, a little nervous of being in such close proximity to the man who was, after all, still a stranger.

'Yes, of course! Jump in.' He leaned over the central console and pushed the door wide.

Nina slid into the comfortable interior and was instantly and powerfully taken aback by the memory of her old life, when she got into a car not dissimilar to this one, every single day, to nip to the shops, to drop and collect the kids from their fancy school. It felt like a lifetime ago.

'Are you okay?' Jacob asked as she stared at the illuminated dials of the dashboard.

She nodded. 'I forget sometimes about the life I've left. Our circumstances have changed quite a bit and I'm so busy living every day, but just now I climbed into your car, and I realised that it's been a while since I sat in anything this comfortable. I took my beautiful car for granted, took a lot of things for granted.' She pictured her freezer stuffed full of food, the cupboards bursting with expensive crockery, her beautiful, beautiful flowers, delivered weekly, not to mention the spacious beds where her youngest could sprawl with his feet dangling off the end . . .

'And it's not that I miss the things, the stuff, even the house. Strangely, what I miss most is the freedom that being comfortable gave me. I had choices because I could afford to have choices.' She stopped abruptly. 'God, Jacob! You offer me a lift and here I am gabbling on. I am sorry. Ignore me.'

The car pulled ahead slowly in the traffic.

'Don't be sorry, not at all. I understand. And I don't want to make you uncomfortable in any way, but if you ever need anything . . .'

'Oh God! I hope you don't think I was . . .'

'No! No, I really don't.' He held up his hand. 'But I just wanted to put that out there, that if you need help, you know where I am and it would be my pleasure to help you.'

Nina shifted to face him. 'That is very kind of you.'

'There is something I wanted to say to you too, actually . . . but I'm a bit out of practice.' He gave a crooked, nervous smile and tapped the leather steering wheel with his thumbs.

'Oh?' She swallowed, feeling sick at the prospect that he might be about to ask her out. He rested his arms on the steering wheel and leaned forward, avoiding her gaze, and for this slightly removed stance she was grateful. 'I wanted to ask you—'

'You are a lovely man, Jacob,' she interrupted him.

'Thank you.'

She took a deep breath. 'And I am flattered by your attention, but I have a lot going on and I am still finding my feet, really . . .'

Jacob let out a sigh. 'Oh damn, well this is really awkward.'

'No, no.' She placed her hand on his arm. 'Please don't say that. It doesn't have to be. You and I get on so well and we are going to see each other every time you visit Miss Molly. But the thing is . . .'

'No, Nina.' He held up his hand. 'You misunderstand me.'

'I do?' She faltered.

'When I say this is awkward, I don't mean you stating the obvious. I mean I knew you had only recently lost your husband. And I don't think of you as anything other than a friend. A good friend.'

'Oh, okay then.' She smiled, placing her hands in her lap, a little confused and more than a little embarrassed. 'So what's so awkward? What did you want to say to me?'

Jacob let out a deep breath. 'I . . . I was going to ask you for Tiggy's number. I'd like to ask her out.'

Nina let out a squawk of laughter. 'Are you kidding me? Tiggy?' She laughed.

Jacob chuckled, leaning forward on the steering wheel again. 'Yes! I fancy your sister! I've been trying to pluck up the nerve to ask you since I met her in the car park. I thought she seemed brilliant, and I figured the nicer I was to you, the more you'd recommend me to her.'

'Oh my God, I am so embarrassed.' She covered her face with her palm while laughing.

'Nina, don't be.'

'You fancy Tiggy!' She spoke with relief.

'I think she's great. Feisty.' He smiled at her like a schoolboy.

'You'd be right.' She laughed. 'I would be happy to give you her number, once I've okayed it with her first of course.'

'Of course.' He smiled. 'I'd treat her like a lady.'

'Oh well, she would find that very disappointing.'

They both roared with laughter again.

Nina couldn't wait to get in, and texted her sister rather than interrupt her at work. Tiggy called back almost immediately.

'Are you winding me up?'

'No, he asked me for your number, said he'd like to ask you out. He said he thought you were great!' Nina squealed her excitement.

'You're sure he wants to go out with me?'

'Yes, with you! God!'

'But why? He only met me that once.' Tiggy seemed genuinely perplexed.

'And that was enough. He saw that you are gorgeous, and sexy, and funny, and kind, and sweet.'

'Ah, thanks, Nina, but I already know that. Just a sec . . .' Tiggy pulled the phone away from her mouth and bellowed, 'Give me one second. I know you need beer, but I am on the phone to my sister! Sweet Jesus!'

'And you have the lovely dulcet tones of an angel,' Nina added, before they ended the call. She immediately sent Jacob her sister's number and signed the text 'Cupid'.

The next morning, Tiggy appeared at the flat bright and early, bouncing nervously. 'So, I'm going out for dinner with him.'

Nina tried to make sense of her sister's blank expression. 'When?'

'This Thursday. I've taken the night off work.' She huffed. 'Dean was miffed, it's quiz night and it gets busy.'

'Forgive me, Tig, but I can't tell if you are happy or angry about the situation.'

'Both.'

'Would you like to talk about it over a cup of coffee? I've got an hour or so before I have to leave.'

'I'd like that. It's good to talk to you.'

'For me too.'

Tiggy followed her in.

'So, lovely Jacob wants to pick you up and whisk you off for a fancy meal. What's not to like?' Nina asked.

'I don't go out with people like Jacob Sutherland. I go out with guys who are *not* like Jacob Sutherland. I go out with guys who hang around the pub, who ask to borrow a fiver the day before payday and who might, if I'm lucky, split a kebab with me on the way home, but who never, ever take me out to dinner! He seems stable and grown-up and normal. And that scares me.'

'Oh now I get it. Yes, definitely do *not* go out with him. All that stability, grown-upness and normality can be most off-putting,' Nina said.

'You can joke, but I don't think we are going to have anything in common,' Tiggy responded.

'Well, you won't know until you spend time with him, and no one's saying it has to be a regular thing. Go out with him once and see how you get on. What have you got to lose?'

'Erm, my reputation! Imagine if one of the regulars at the pub saw me getting in and out of a fancy pickup. I'd never live it down.'

Nina handed her a cup of coffee. 'Get him to drop you around the back if you are worried.' She tutted. 'Look, I just want you to have a nice time, a good evening, and I think you just might.'

'What am I supposed to wear?' Tiggy pulled at her denim jacket.

'It pains to me say this, but you would look fantastic in anything. Don't stress it. Jeans and a nice shirt, whatever you are comfortable in. It's important you are relaxed and you are yourself, but not too much of yourself.'

Tiggy snorted.

'I mean it, Tig, he already likes you for you. Just go and be you.'

'Supposing it's awful and we sit in silence with nothing to say?'

'Then you go to the loo and text me – and I will give it ten minutes and give you the call, saying I need you here right away! And you can make your excuses and leave.'

'Okay. That's good to know.'

'You could at least try to look a bit happier about the whole event,' Nina said.

Tiggy grinned at her with a fake Cheshire cat smile. 'Can I ask you something?'

'Sure.' Nina shrugged.

Tiggy's expression was sincere. 'If you had your time again with Finn, and this was your first date, what would you do differently?'

I wouldn't jump so quickly. I would make him wait. I wouldn't give up so much of me. I would slow everything right down. I would look beyond the gloss of money . . .

'God, you mean what would I do differently on our first date or for our whole life? Because for our first date I would definitely wear flat shoes – my feet were killing me, as I recall.' She tried to diffuse the very real question that her sister was asking. 'I guess . . .' She paused. 'I guess I would be a lot more open about all the things that frightened me and not be afraid of exposing my faults – I'd try and trust him to love me in spite of those things,' she went on. 'And I guess if he couldn't love me with all my faults then I'd have walked away in the opposite direction.'

'And how could he have not?' Tiggy kissed her sister on the cheek.

Nina sighed. 'But the truth is, I would probably do everything exactly as I did, because I would have been the same girl with the same mind and the same experiences and naivety. It was hard not to be impressed by what was on offer, and swept along.'

'I get that.'

Nina looked at her sister. 'One minute Dad and I were breaking Jaffa Cakes in half to give ourselves a little sugar top-up, but not want-ing to waste a whole one, and the next I am in a restaurant with Finn, with white linen tablecloths and shiny glasses and baskets of fresh-baked bread, which I slathered with butter.' She smiled at the memory. 'I loved it and I wanted more of that life!' She took a breath. 'Even Finn's car . . . The passenger seat was the nicest thing I had ever sat in, and he smelled' – she inhaled, recalling the exact scent that had intoxicated her – 'he smelled *rich*. My clothes were never dried properly and always had a faint tinge of damp wafting from them, I never had fancy shampoo and certainly not scent, but Finn – he was pristine! Every aspect of him shone, from the paintwork of his Porsche to his teeth. And I wanted to shine like that!'

Tiggy took Nina's hand into hers. Her words when they came were heartfelt, considered. 'But that's the thing, Nina. You already did!'

Connor and Anna were on the sofa sharing a set of headphones while studying. She loved that Anna was so at ease in their home and how she pushed Connor: he was keen to study harder, not wanting to fall below Anna's exacting academic standards. Declan and Arek were on the floor constructing a robot out of aluminium foil tubes, fabric-softener lids, ice-cream cartons and even an old calculator. 'Where did you get all that stuff from?' Nina asked.

'Toothless Vera lets us get it out of her recycling.'

'Right.' Nina tried not to picture her youngest child dumpster diving. An image of him in his finest Kings Norton College togs flashed into her mind.

She prepared macaroni cheese and ladled steaming portions into bowls that she handed out; it was now the norm, and not a treat, to eat from the bowl in your hand while sitting on the sofa or the floor. Setting the table in the kitchen or dining room with a view of the grounds was a dim and distant memory. It had always felt like the *right* thing to do, trying to erase the memory of searching for a space to sit in her gran's cluttered parlour. Yet now the whole experience was much more intimate. Gone were the cold looks over the wide tabletop, the clunking sound of serving spoons against the best china and the forced conversation. Here they ate, laughed, chatted and reached across each other in closer proximity, and as a family. Much closer.

'Thank you, this looks lovely!' Anna was her usual sweet, polite self.

'Surely not better than my ice cubes and peas?' Nina feigned a hurt look.

'No! Nothing could beat that. It will always be your signature dish.'

Connor had left to walk Anna back to her house, Arek's mum had come to take him home, and Declan was in bed, with his large robot made of rubbish propped up in the corner. Nina finally had five minutes to catch her breath on the sofa . . .

A little after eleven there was a knock on the French doors. She must have dozed off, as it gave her quite a start. She looked through the blind. Tiggy stood on tiptoes, waving and indicating for her to open up. No sooner had she slid the handle, than Tiggy climbed up the balcony and hoisted her body over the railings.

'I wish you wouldn't do that. Why can't you walk through the door like a normal human?'

'Because I am not a normal human.'

Nina looked up and down the street to see if anyone was watching. Not that anyone cared; at this time of night people were more interested in not spilling their can of beer while eating noodles straight from a foil container or chomping on kebabs. She saw the unmistakable tinge of Lucia's pink hair behind the till in the store.

She works so hard, little love.

'What time is it?' Nina had lost all track.

'Not that late, just after eleven.' Tiggy shrugged. 'I've finished early.'

'One sec. I didn't hear Connor come in. I just need to check he's home.' Her heart pounded as she crept into the bedroom. Her relief was sweet and instant as she saw two sleeping heads sunk deep into the soft pillows. She smiled and retreated quietly, grateful that Connor must have seen her sleeping and chosen not to disturb her. She closed the door silently.

Nina flopped back down on the sofa. 'Okay, I am all ears.' She patted the space next to her. Tiggy sat.

'What are we going to wear to this rugby dinner thing at Cottrell's?'

'Tiggy! You woke me up for that?'

'I'm nervous! I don't know what to wear and I don't want to look out of place.'

'You could wear a bin bag and still look fantastic.'

Tiggy ignored her. 'Plus, I'm thinking of inviting Jacob.'

'You are?' She looked at her sister. 'Well, no surprise after your fabulous date!' she teased.

'Yep, I like him, he's . . .' Nina watched as Tiggy's mouth moved, searching for the words. 'He's not like anyone I have ever met before. I can't stop thinking about him.'

'Wow.'

'Yes, wow! Completely wow! And I can't wait till tomorrow, because that's when I am seeing him again.' Tiggy bit at her fingernails.

'Tomorrow?'

'I know, right?'

'I really hoped you would have a good time with him, but this is off the scale!' Nina sat back on the sofa and giggled.

'I think there is a chance that we might be good together. I mean, early days and all that, but I'm excited!'

Nina hadn't heard Tiggy like this, so excited and happy.

'I am pleased for you, Tig, I really am, pleased for you both. But promise me you will take it slowly. Remember what we spoke about.' She smiled to herself that she had only recently had this conversation with Connor. 'I mean, we like what we know of him, but we don't really know anything about him, do we? And I would hate to see you get hurt.'

Tiggy leaned forward and hugged her sister. 'Me too. But you know what? I've had good advice. I will tell him all the things I am frightened of and let him see my faults. And then if he's still interested . . .'

'He will be, sis. He will be. Because you are lovely.' She closed her eyes and could smell the vaguest hint of bonfires.

SIXTEEN

The mid-July air was warm and full of summer promise. Nina spied the boy Joshy, with the burgundy knitted scarf, sober now and being collected by an over-fussy mother and a patient dad as they loaded his trunk and TV into the back of a family car. Portswood Road was quieter, as if it could take a breather from the constant hum of life that filled it day and night as the throngs of students had dissipated for the summer. Toothless Vera was glad that without the students, her work-load was halved, which meant more time for Styrofoam cups of tea in exchange for a good old gossip. Lucia told Nina she had decided to try to study at home, focusing on her art between cleaning jobs, working in the store and looking after her siblings. Nina told her she should be proud of herself. The smile of thanks she gave her was like a gift. She couldn't wait to be in a similar position and start her nursing course. It was exciting.

She and her boys enjoyed breakfast with the French doors thrown open as they chatted about Connor's final game of the term.

'How are you feeling, Connor? Nervous?'

'A bit, yes, but not because of the match, that'll be fine. But Anna's going to be there, and I want to be really good.'

'Do you know what, love? I have seen the way she looks at you, on and off the pitch, and I have a sneaking suspicion that even if you never touched the ball and rolled around on the touchline, she'd think you were absolutely brilliant.' She watched his face brighten at the compliment. 'And you've packed your clean shirt and tie for the dinner?'

'Yep.' He nodded, sipping his juice.

'I'm glad I'm not going to your stupid dinner. I'd rather have a sleepover at Arek's anyway!' Declan pouted, his expression suggesting the exact opposite.

She couldn't help the laugh that escaped her. 'I think you'll have a lovely time, darling.' She reached over and kissed her baby. 'Arek's mum told me she is making your favourite pierogi.'

Later that morning, searching for hairgrips in her bedside drawer, Nina's hand touched upon the little matchbox. She opened it and placed the marble in the palm of her hand. Closing her eyes, she heard her mother's words: 'This is a little world, Nina. And if ever the real world feels too big or too scary, remember that it is nothing more than a little ball travelling through space and it fits right into the palm of your hand and the more courage you have, the braver you are when facing it, the easier it is to conquer!'

'I hear you, Mamma,' she whispered. And for the first time ever, she knew what she meant.

It had already been a busy day by the time Nina arrived in the stands, with the match about to start. Connor stood tall, mid-pitch, looking determinedly at the opposition, allowing himself the odd glance in Anna's direction.

Lou patted the bench next to her. Moira handed her a mug.

'To friendship.' Gilly made a toast as they clunked their mugs and took a sip.

The whistle blew and the game began. It was instantly fast and ferocious. She watched as the pitch churned under the frantic activity of studded boots, and winced as bodies collided mid-tackle with sickening thuds.

'Okay,' Moira called. 'You are up, Nina – go and call your support.'

Gilly and Lou looked at her. She could tell by their expressions they expected her to protest and decline.

'You don't have to do it,' Gilly whispered. 'I'll take your turn if you like.'

Nina rested her mug on the bench and coughed to clear her throat. 'You know what, Gilly? I do have to do it.'

Courage and bravery, Nina . . . she repeated in her head. Placing her hands either side of her mouth, she felt the rush of empowerment. She was excited, happy, to be here in the place where she lived with her friends. Her son was playing the game he loved and the sun was out.

'Come on, Cottrell's! Go, Connor!' she yelled at the top of her lungs.

Her voice was loud and cut through the activity of the pitch and the chatter all around. She felt as if every pair of eyes in the place swivelled in her direction, including Connor's. He shook his head, a smile of amusement on his face.

Anna clapped from where she stood with her pals on the touchline. 'Go, Nina! Woohoo!' She shouted her support.

The women high-fived each other and chuckled. Moira handed her back her mug of wine. 'Well done, mate. Well done.'

She sat down and pictured Kathy Topps, who had shown her true colours at a time when a kind word would have made all the difference. She pictured The Tynings, the once beautiful place where she and Finn had raised two fine boys and where she had often sat alone, longing for company, as she waited for her husband to come home. Now here she was, and the message was clear. Her happiness was never going to be found in things; it was waiting for her, right here, in people.

◆ ◆ ◆

Gilly wolf-whistled as Nina stepped from the cubicle in the girls' bathroom in her long black skirt and white silk blouse. She had last worn this outfit for a Kings Norton function, where she had spent the evening clinging to Finn's arm and counting down the hours until she could return to the safety of The Tynings. She smoothed the skirt with her hand. Tonight was the first time she would be attending an evening social event without Finn. Having Gilly, Tiggy and Jacob in tow certainly helped.

'You look lovely too.' She nodded at Gilly's ample bust, fitted into a diamanté-laced bodice.

'I know.' Gilly wiggled her hips and giggled.

She met Tiggy and Jacob in the foyer. 'You look fabulous,' Tiggy said.

'I feel a bit self-conscious,' Nina replied. They both knew this was a huge leap forward from her previous anxiety.

'If it makes you feel better, I was wearing a tight shirt the other day and Toothless Vera asked me if I was pregnant.'

'She didn't!' Nina laughed.

'She did! And I have to confess it left me feeling a little confused,' Tiggy said.

'In what way?'

'I didn't know whether to be delighted that she thought I was young enough to have eggs that were still ripe enough for harvesting, or upset that I looked fat enough to be considered pregnant.'

'Would that be such a bad thing?' Jacob interjected.

Tiggy smiled. There was no quip or barb in reply. Instead she let her arm fall through his as they all made their way into the school hall.

The place looked beautiful. Banners hung from the ceiling congratulating the team on their season, and the round tables sparkled with shiny glassware, white china and pretty bowls of white and purple flowers – sweet peas, one of Nina's favourites. Once everyone was seated, the lights dimmed and the rugby team made their grand entrance. Everyone stood and clapped. Nina was struck by the sight of her son and his beautiful girl striding through the hall confidently.

They enjoyed a glorious meal, accompanied by laughter and the sipping of wine. Nina noted the way Tiggy gazed at Jacob and felt a wave of love for her sister. She hoped for the very best for her.

As the pudding was served, the coach stood up and tapped his wine glass with a fork.

'What a team!' he began. He was met with whoops and hollers that took a good few minutes to calm. The atmosphere was electric. 'And now can I ask for your attention while we give out tonight's awards.' A hush fell, punctuated with laughter as boys went up to retrieve trophies, those for 'Highest Scorer' and 'Try of the Season', interspersed with 'Worst Haircut' and another for the 'Most Injuries'. All the boys spoke a few mumbled words of thanks, some more eloquently than others.

Nina loved the fact that the ceremony was inclusive and fun, and again she pictured the dislikeable Mr Moor and his arrogant dismissal of her request.

'And now, the award for most outstanding contribution goes to . . .' There was a beat of silence. 'Connor "Snow" McCarrick.'

Without thinking or hesitation, Nina jumped to her feet and beamed at her boy, who walked slowly up to the claps and shouts of everyone in the room.

'Oh my word!' she managed, looking at Tiggy with tears in her eyes. *Finn! Look at our boy! Look at him!*

She took her seat and smiled at her sister and friends, who all offered their congratulations.

Connor shook hands with the coach. She saw his nerves as he looked out over the sea of faces, all staring at him expectedly.

'My dad died,' he began, 'and I didn't want to come here to play rugby. Didn't want to come here at all.'

Nina swallowed tears. The room was silent. 'But now I am glad I did.' He held up his trophy and a ripple of laughter made its way around the room. 'I've been lucky to have a strong figure in my life who I have always looked up to, who taught me everything that is worth knowing, and the true meaning of determination, courage and faith. I dedicate my award to that person.'

Nina looked down, not wanting the tears to spill, grateful her son still looked up to Finn, mentioned in this way. It meant that, despite the manner of his death hanging over them like a sharp question mark around which they skirted, her son could see beyond that. But Connor's next words knocked her off balance.

Connor continued. 'It's my brilliant mum, Nina.'

As the room erupted with claps and cheers, she knew she would carry this moment of pure joy with her always. She looked up at Connor, her wonderful boy, who had indeed come back to her. His words were the most beautiful expression of love she had ever heard. *You are what we did right, Connor, you and Declan!*

With the speeches finished, the lights dimmed as the DJ set up on the dance floor.

Tiggy shifted along, until she was sitting next to her at the table.

'You've done good, you know,' Tiggy whispered.

'Thank you, yes. It's been a lovely day.' Nina smiled.

She shook her head. 'I don't mean today, Nina. I mean these last few months. You took those posh kids of yours and you swept them up and kept them safe and kept them sane. You are a good mum.'

'Good Lord, what has come over you? How many glasses of wine have you had?'

'I mean it.'

'Thank you, Tig.' She reached over and squeezed her sister's hand. 'I think I like the new you. Being part of a couple suits you.'

'I really like him.'

'I know, Tig.' The two sisters leaned in together, laughing conspiratorially.

Connor strode over with his arm outstretched. 'Come on, Mum.'

'What? You don't want to dance with me!' She tutted.

'Actually I do.' He took her hand and walked her to the dance floor. She felt Finn's signet ring against her fingers. Ed Sheeran's 'Thinking Out Loud' started to play, and she held her son's hand, with his other on her waist.

'I wish Dad could see me,' he said, without anguish.

'Dad is you. He's half of you. He knows you, darling, and he is proud of you. Always was and always will be.'

'And I'm half you.'

'Yep.'

Connor stopped dancing and looked her in the eye. 'I was so scared when we came here, Mum.'

'Me too,' she confessed.

'For my whole life I had never seen you do anything apart from buy things for the house, cook us food and drop us at school. And when I stepped from the van that day, I couldn't begin to imagine how we were going to live. I was petrified. I thought it was going to be down to me to keep everything together and I didn't know how! And you could only say everything was going to be okay, but I could see you didn't have a plan.'

Nina felt the familiar slip of tears down her cheeks. 'I'm sorry . . .' she managed.

'No. Don't be sorry, Mum. It wasn't your fault. You were as ill equipped as I was, as I am, but you did it. We did it.'

'Yes, we did.' She rested her head on his shoulder.

Nina parked the van at the kerb and beeped the horn. She laughed, thinking of all the people she might be disturbing on this Saturday morning and was only saddened that Joshy had gone home – she would have liked to wake him up at this ungodly hour. She had saved the cash for this trip to Saltford and that in itself felt like an achievement. It represented the plain, home-made birthday cake that Connor had been given, hair-washing without shampoo, and countless rumbly tummies for which she had to apologise while she waited to eat her free lunch. Tiggy came out of the building with the boys and jumped into the front seat next to her sister. Despite being up so early, Connor was still high on his award and Declan had jumped at the chance of the trip, of a day out in a van. Nina hoped good might come from it, maybe an open discussion that would help carry them forward, despite their destination.

It was odd driving along the winding A46, the city of Bath looming in the distance. They had been away for nearly six months, but it could have been a lifetime. It was a grey, rainy morning – entirely appropriate as they headed towards the city that held a mishmash of memories, most recently ones of sorrow.

'Are you okay, boys?' She glanced at the back seat. They both gave stiff nods. Connor kept his eyes on the window, unlike Declan clearly aware of the road on which they travelled and the fact that a mile or so further along was the place where his daddy had died.

'I bet it's strange heading back to Bath, is it?' Tiggy asked.

'I keep thinking we are going home and that makes me feel a bit sad, and I think that maybe Dad is at home and that makes me even sadder.' Declan spoke so candidly. Nina's confidence in the decision to bring the boys wavered.

She reached back between the front seats and patted his leg. They drove along in silence until they reached Hollydown Farm, parking in front of the rather grand Georgian farmhouse. It reminded her of a miniature doll's house, but in life size. Mr Firth, his wife and one of their children, a blonde girl in her mid-teens, came out of the front door to greet them. They were well dressed and groomed, and as they stood in front of their duck-egg blue front door with its brass lion-head knocker, Nina felt a wave of déjà vu for a life that had passed.

Beautiful house, check. Expensive clothes and hairdo, check. Happy, smiley child, check. Successful husband, check. And yet, rather than look at the trio with envy, she felt something closer to unease, knowing that her own perfect life had been built on a foundation of shifting sand. And when it shifted, it happened quicker than she could ever have imagined.

'Welcome, Nina! It's good to see you.' Mr Firth was his usual, kind, welcoming self. 'And boys, hello!'

She watched with a measure of pride as first Connor and then Declan stepped forward to shake the man's hand. She introduced Tiggy, and the group declined the offer of tea from his charming wife, who looked at Nina with an expression that was a combination of pity and kindness. She fought the temptation to explain that she now had a job and was planning to study, and that her boys were happier than she had hoped for. Instead, she smiled politely, realising that it didn't matter what Mrs Firth or anyone else thought. It was what *she* thought that counted.

The troupe made their way to a steel-constructed barn, one of a number of outbuildings. Mr Firth undid the giant padlock and hefted the wide door open. Inside sat a ride-on mower and various bikes mounted on wall brackets. Their boxes lined the wall, marked in a hurried scrawl 'Garden Stuff', 'Picnic', 'Christmas Lights'. Just recently the contents had seemed so important, causing her sleepless nights of concern as she planned what and how to pack. She ran her fingers over a box and wondered how the things inside would now fit into her smaller life, where space was at a premium, leisure time was limited and the immediate needs of her family were the primary concern rather than festive holiday lighting. These frivolous trappings contrasted with how close she had grown to her sons *and* her sister, in the face of hardship and struggle, far closer than at any time of affluence.

'Is this the desk? I don't think I've seen it before.'

Connor lifted a paint-spattered dustsheet to reveal a narrow console table. In its former life, it had sat in a spare bedroom with an ornate lamp on either end. Connor had rarely entered the room where it once sat, and months later, their life had been reduced to one sofa, three beds and a couple of odds and ends.

We had too much. Greedy, really. Needless, all that stuff, all that expense . . .
'Yes, that's it.'

Mr Firth helped remove the desk from its hiding place and lift it into the back of the van. They moved on to the boxes loaded with spare blankets, linens, towels and summer clothes. The boys sorted through their belongings and selected a couple of books, school files and one or two frivolous items that made her smile. 'Of course you can't live without that, Dec!' They all laughed as he gripped a plastic Thor Hammer that lit up when whacked.

'And don't worry, Nina, there is no rush. As you can see, we have the space and can keep your things here for as long as you need,' Mr Firth said.

She felt tempted to ask him to consign the lot to charity, but knew enough not to make a rash decision. Strangely, for the first time, she didn't think about the place she might live next; instead, she pictured the flat and knew the last thing they needed was clutter.

'Thank you for being so kind,' she offered sincerely, looking at the man her husband had trusted.

'You look well.' He smiled.

'Getting there,' she replied. 'And thank you once again.'

'Nina.' Mr Firth called her back into the barn as the family piled back into the van. She went to him, bracing herself for some kind of bad news he could only tell her in private. 'You have two fine boys there,' he said.

She smiled at him. Yes, she did.

Nina walked back to the van.

'Okay, wagons roll! My turn!' Tiggy called as she pulled out of Hollydown Farm. 'He seems nice,' she offered.

'He is. And can I just say thank you for coming with us all this way and for being so great?'

'My pleasure, sis. That's what family's for.'

They drove along the lane in silence for a minute or two.

'Can we go and look at our old house?' Declan asked.

Nina had half expected the request. 'I don't know if that's a good idea.' She hesitated.

'Please, Mum!' Declan begged.

She looked at Connor. 'I don't mind.' He gave a shrug of indifference.

'I'm more than happy to take you if you'd like,' Tiggy said.

Nina nodded tightly. 'Okay then.' Maybe it would help them all find closure.

Connor sat forward in his seat, proudly issuing directions and showing off his local knowledge to his aunt. Nina felt strange, sick, as the van drew into the lane. She felt the swirl of nerves in her stomach, a feeling that had been missing of late.

As they approached, she saw the gates were closed with a heavy padlock and chain, as she had pictured. A sign nailed to the front gave the number for a security company to call in the case of emergency. Two back-to-back 'For Sale' signs hung from a post in the driveway.

Tiggy slowed the van and before Nina had a chance to make a plan or say anything, Connor jumped out. 'Connor!' she called, but he didn't move from where he had his nose pressed up to the gate. Then Declan made a break for it and ran up to his brother. Reluctantly she unclipped her seat belt and climbed down.

She had quite forgotten the sound of the gravel crunching underfoot. It was the first jolt to her senses. Her eyes strayed through the bars to the large turning circle, and the many criss-crossed dual lines of tyre marks that had churned up the stones, and of course there was no willing gardener with a wide rake to restore them twice weekly, making sure they looked perfect. She tried to remember the person she had been when this kind of thing felt important. It reminded her of the dirty footprints that Mr Ludlow's men had left in the hallway on that terrible, terrible day. The memory of Connor's horrified face when she found him at the house made her shiver: '. . . *only doing their job, a horrible job, but their job nonetheless.*'

'Let's go in!' Declan jumped up and down.

'We can't, darling. They have changed all the locks, and even if I did still have a key, it doesn't belong to us any more. It would be trespassing,' she explained.

'We could go through the gap in the side hedge and have a look, but not *actually* go inside,' Connor suggested.

Tiggy now stood behind the trio. 'Come on then, Con. If we are going to do this, let's do it quickly!'

Her sister's tone made it sound like some kind of adventure, and without further discussion, Nina found herself being ushered to the side hedge, where Connor and Declan rummaged along the tall, bushy leylandii until they found the gap they were looking for.

'Here it is!' Before she had a chance to remonstrate, Connor had disappeared into the hedge, quickly followed by Declan. Tiggy was next. Nina felt she had little choice but to follow. She crouched low and scrabbled on her knees through the gap. When she emerged, the sight was enough to take her breath away.

She placed her hand over her mouth. She hadn't realised, or rather had forgotten, quite how grand the house was. The pale stone building stood proudly in the sunlight, the many, many windows glinting, hiding a labyrinth of rooms behind.

'Wow!' Tiggy exclaimed. Nina looked towards her with a nod. It was, indeed, wow! Although now, strangely, she felt quite removed from this opulent setting. And the house and grounds looked different from her memory. The grass was longer than she had ever seen it and the border plants had grown wildly without the patient hand and secateurs of the gardener. The apple trees had dropped their fruit, which now lay brown, spoiling and riddled with maggot holes. 'Such a waste,' Nina said, thinking not only of the cost of apples, but of the shortcrust apple pies, the crumbles, chutneys, purées and puddings that she had made year after year, gifting them to people along the lane, piling them up in the freezer or lining jars up in the larder.

The boys ran around the garden, up on to the terrace and around the pool. Declan had his arms spread wide like an aeroplane, appreciating the open space. Connor stood by the edge of the pool and pushed down onto the dirty cover with one foot. She watched him stare at the mosaic edge and wondered if he, like her, saw a memory of larking around with his dad, sending a cascade of droplets high into the air as they splashed and wrangled in the warm water, jumping on and off the inflatable animals that littered the surface, before coming up to the terrace to wrap themselves in plush towels and to sip on a cool drink straight from the iced pitcher.

Another life . . .

Tiggy hung back as Nina trod the meandering path up to the house. The windows were desperate for a clean. She pressed her nose to the glass to take a look at her favourite place in the whole house, where she liked to rest, sitting on her comfortable chair with the incredible view.

She imagined she saw the four of them, sitting around the breakfast table. The image was so real, she leaned in even closer, with her hands splayed on the glass. Her heart raced and her breath came quickly. Finn reading the newspaper, the boys with their heads bowed, devouring cereal. Nina saw herself jump up suddenly to grab the cafetière for a refill of coffee. Her twitchy manner was telling; she looked more like an attentive waitress than a member of the family. It looked like a school morning. She was struck by the opulence of their surroundings, the acres of shining surfaces and the myriad lights, all burning brightly and wastefully for no other reason than aesthetics. She was also shocked by the silence that enveloped them and the sullen expressions on their faces. Nina from Portswood would have thought that to have all this could only mean that you were permanently happy! She leaned closer, watching as Connor bounced his leg, as if he were edgy, wanting to be elsewhere. Declan's shoulders were slumped over; he looked tired. And Finn . . . Finn's brief smile faded the moment she turned her back to go and grab his coffee refill, and in that second she saw the worry etched on his brow. He looked like he had the weight of the world on his shoulders, and that weight was worth approximately eight million pounds.

One of Finn's stock phrases loomed large in her memory: 'You don't have to worry your head about anything. Worrying is my job . . .'

'That was it, Finn, wasn't it?' she whispered into the aether. 'It wasn't that you deliberately lied to me, deceived me. You just wanted to keep the worry from my door, wanted me to glide through life because you loved me . . . and I loved you. I did.'

Pressing her fingers to the window, she saw the imperfections of life in the glass bubble of their home, and in that instant she knew that she would not swap the life she had now for all the money in the world. Her only regret was that Finn, her handsome, flawed husband, had not got to experience this too.

'Goodbye, my darling,' she whispered.

'Don't remember it like this.' Tiggy's voice startled her. With her sister's words the image was gone, and she found herself staring at a vast space that was almost unrecognisable. The kitchen and adjoining breakfast room had been stripped bare. The light fittings were missing; bare wires now hung down forlornly, as if grasping for the stunning glass chandeliers they once held. The stove had been hauled from its casing and where the hob had once sat was now a neatly cut rectangular hole. The walk-in fridge-freezer was gone, revealing an empty alcove, and the furniture, mirrors and granite surfaces had also been removed. The cool, pale floor was covered in a thick layer of what looked like fine sawdust and debris, peppered with dirty footprints and the black marks of wheels that had been carelessly dragged along.

'It's not our home any more, is it, Mum?' The boys were right behind their aunt. Declan looked up at her, and she realised that he, like her, had probably held an image in his head that was a mirage, where a vivid display of flowers lit up the hallway and dinner bubbled on the stove.

'No, my love. It's not our home any more.'

Nina was finally able to make the statement, ending any hankering for the fantasy bricks and mortar of a place that no longer existed – not in any guise that they might recognise. Connor took her into his arms and Declan held her around the waist and she held them fast.

The three stood locked together in the shadow of the grand house, united as a family, with determination and resolution to make a better future.

'I still miss Dad, of course I do, every day, and I wish it hadn't all happened.' Connor spoke. 'But you have a job, we have a home, and things are . . .' He hesitated. 'Things are okay. More than okay.'

Nina nodded in agreement. She closed her eyes and took a deep breath. It felt as if finally the world had stopped spinning, and the path beneath her feet was solid. She knew now she could carry this little family, and was capable of becoming the person she had always wanted to be; someone who could conquer the world.

'Yes, they are, darling.' She smiled at Connor, knowing that from tomorrow onwards, she would look at the sky and feel, not only satisfied, but also optimistic about their future. 'Things are more than okay.'

BOOK CLUB QUESTIONS

1. Did Nina's story alter your view of whether money will guarantee happiness? If so, how?
2. Which member of the McCarrick family did you most sympathise with, and why?
3. Has *The Art of Hiding* changed you or broadened your perspective? If so, how?
4. What, for you, was the book's main message?
5. In a movie, who would play the part of Nina, her eldest son, Connor, his younger brother, Declan and Nina's sister, Tiggy?
6. There were a number of difficult choices that Nina made – what did you think of those choices? Did you agree/disagree with them?
7. Did any parts of the book make you feel uncomfortable? If so, which parts, and why?
8. What will be the overriding memory from *The Art of Hiding*, the one incident or paragraph that will stay with you?

ABOUT THE AUTHOR

Amanda Prowse likens her own life story to those she writes about in her books. After self-publishing her debut novel, *Poppy Day*, in 2011, she has gone on to author sixteen novels and six novellas. Her books have been translated into a dozen languages and she regularly tops bestseller charts all over the world.

Remaining true to her ethos, Amanda writes stories of ordinary women and their families who find their strength, courage and love tested in ways they never imagined. The most prolific female contemporary fiction writer in the UK, with a legion of loyal readers, she goes from strength to strength. Being crowned 'queen of domestic drama' by the *Daily Mail* was one of her finest moments.

Amanda is a regular contributor on TV and radio but her first love is and will always be writing.

You can find her online at www.amandaprowse.com, on Twitter @MrsAmandaProwse, and on Facebook at www.facebook.com/amandaprowsenogreaterlove.